MW00622929

A SERPENT'S TOOTH

AN ANN KINNEAR SUSPENSE NOVEL

MATTY DALRYMPLE

WILLIAM KINGSFIELD PUBLISHERS

For Wade Walton and Mary Dalrymple, for whom I'm deeply thankful.

How sharper than a serpent's tooth it is
    To have a thankless child!

William Shakespeare
    King Lear

1

Del Berendt followed the red Mazda Miata off I-95 and up the gradual incline of Industrial Highway. The tank farms, warehouses, and weed-choked stretches of pavement that flanked the road were just visible in the waning evening light. He passed the spidery structure of a rusting refinery and a few smokestacks standing like giant cacti in a concrete desert. The skyscrapers that defined the Philadelphia skyline hovered like a mirage in the distance.

The Miata turned left. Billboards advertising casinos, Powerball, and personal injury lawyers gave way to apartment buildings and duplexes, plywood-covered windows like black eyes in the buildings' facades.

Where could she be going?

Gradually the buildings became a bit less decrepit, the lawns a bit less trash-strewn. The Miata made a few more turns, and Del found himself in more reassuring surroundings. Modest two-story brick row houses, including one stretch painted in cheerful reds, blues, and yellows, were interspersed with convenience stores, hoagie shops, and churches. On one block, children ran through the spray from an open fire hydrant. Their shrieks reached him only faintly through the windows of his Ford Escape, its air conditioning chugging valiantly against the heavy heat of the August evening.

The traffic thinned, and Del dropped back, trying to avoid notice by the other car's driver.

As he continued to follow the Miata through West Philadelphia, the homes became more well-tended, the vehicles parked along the tree-shaded streets less dented and rusty. Chain-link fences gave way to pocked wrought iron surrounding tiny lawns. Residents sat on porches or strolled the sidewalks with dogs or children.

Del realized with a start that he was seeing houses he had passed a few minutes earlier. Had he been spotted? His hands tightened on the wheel as he debated whether to drop back even further and risk missing one of the Miata's seemingly random turns, or to close the gap and risk a confrontation.

The Miata continued straight for several blocks on Larch Street, then turned left. When Del reached the intersection, he could see no traffic in either direction. He also turned left, uncertain whether to drive slowly so as not to miss the car if it had pulled into a parking space, or to drive quickly to catch it on one of the cross streets. Then he caught a glimpse of taillights in the alley paralleling Larch.

A glance in the rearview mirror showed no traffic behind him. He turned off his headlights, put the Escape in reverse, and rolled backwards until he could see up the alley. The Miata was pulling into a parking spot behind one of the Larch Street houses, next to some kind of sedan and a small white van. Putting the Escape back in drive, he made three rights, putting him on Larch again, but headed in the opposite direction.

The homes on this block were grander than in the blocks he had just passed through: semi-detached and singles, with brick staircases leading to pillared porches, decorative mullions visible in curving second-floor windows, third and even fourth floors extended with elaborately decorated dormers. Most of the houses were dark and only a few of the streetlights worked. The few pools of light they cast showed the sidewalks to be cracked, slabs heaved up by the roots of the trees whose branches arched over the street. Although there were a few cars along the one side of the street where parking was allowed, he could see no people. Maybe they were relaxing in air-conditioned coolness. Or maybe they were hunkered down behind locked doors and drawn curtains, blockaded against the threats posed by a formerly genteel neighborhood slipping into disrepute, or a formerly disreputable neighborhood striving for gentility.

Del rolled slowly down the street, trying to determine which of the houses the Miata had parked behind. Then a figure appeared from around the corner. Even in the darkness, he recognized it as the Miata's driver, her shape and movements as she hurried in his direction familiar. She was staying in the street, no doubt to avoid the hazards of the broken sidewalk. Why hadn't she gone from her car to the back door of the house?

He snapped off his headlights and pulled into a parking space under one of the non-functioning streetlights.

The woman paused, looking toward the Escape. One hand drifted protectively to the bulge under her maternity dress, the other tightened its grip on the strap of the straw purse slung over her shoulder.

He was tempted to slump down in his seat, but a car that stopped but didn't then disgorge a passenger would be suspicious. Reaching up to switch the dome light off automatic, he climbed out of the Escape, his heart hammering. Remembering at the last second not to hit the lock button on the key fob—she would surely recognize the chirp—he turned and ambled off in the opposite direction. He had another moment of panic as he approached the pool of light cast by one of the streetlights bracketing the darkness that engulfed the car. However, before he reached it, he saw a walkway that led from the sidewalk to a "grocer's alley" that passed at ground level between two attached houses. He turned onto the walk, grateful that the tunnel wasn't blocked by a security gate, and stepped into the passageway.

He pressed his back against the wall, although it was a ridiculous move. If she came this way, she would see the Escape long before she saw him. He listened for approaching footsteps. Instead, he heard what sounded like the squeak of rusty hinges. He risked a glance out the tunnel's entrance.

She had stepped through a low metal gate that separated the sidewalk from the tiny front garden of one of the darkened houses—he thought it was the house she had parked behind. She climbed the stairs to the porch, then got her phone out of her purse. She glanced at it, then crossed her arms and turned her gaze back to the deserted street. A minute later, she checked her phone again.

Del checked his own phone: 7:58. Was she waiting until the top of the hour for something? She had taken a somewhat indirect route to Larch Street. Had she been killing time?

Sure enough, just as Del's phone showed 8:00, she dropped her phone back into her purse and knocked lightly on the door. After a few moments, a dim light illuminated a row of small panes at the top of the door. The light brightened, then the door opened.

Inside stood a tall, bearded man carrying what looked like an oil lamp. He wore oddly old-fashioned clothing: a frock coat, an ascot, a vest stretched over an ample belly. He dipped his head to the woman, then stepped back to allow her to enter. She cast one quick glance toward where Del stood in the darkness of the tunnel, then disappeared into the house. The man closed the door behind her and the light in the door's panes gradually dimmed until the house was once again dark. It looked no more inhabited than most of the other houses on the block.

Del hurried back to the Escape, started it up, and coasted down the street. The house she had entered, number 46, was one of the singles.

He turned right at the cross street and then right again into the alley.

The white van and the Miata were still there, but the sedan Del had seen earlier was gone. He continued around the block and pulled into the same shadowed space. With parking allowed only on the side of the street opposite the house, he had an unobstructed view.

He drummed his fingers on the steering wheel, pondering what he had seen. The man who had answered the door was older than Del would have expected, which could be a good thing or a bad thing. But why in the world was he dressed in what looked like Victorian clothes?

Del briefly entertained an image of himself going to the house, banging on the door, demanding an explanation. But no. Despite every impulse to the contrary, he had held his tongue this long. He'd wait a little longer and see how this played out.

Minutes ticked by. He could hear a dog barking a few streets away, could see cars passing periodically on the cross street, but Larch Street remained as quiet as it had been when he arrived. No one emerged from the darkened houses, no intrepid dog-walkers braved the broken sidewalks.

An hour passed. Del had almost decided to check the parking area behind the house again when two people appeared around the same corner from which the woman had appeared. When they passed under one of the streetlights, Del could see it was a well-dressed couple in their late twenties. He heard the woman say something to the man, her tone urgent. Del buzzed down the window of the Escape.

"We're already a couple of minutes late," said the woman, who was a few steps ahead of the man. "Hurry up!"

The man picked up his pace and caught up with her just as her arms flew up and she let out a surprised, "Oh!"

He grabbed her arm, saving her from a tumble. "Won't do us any good to hurry if you break a leg on the way."

The woman's hand now hooked under the man's arm, they stepped through the creaking metal gate and hurried up the steps. At their knock, a dim light once again illuminated the door's glass panes, and the same man opened the door. He tilted them the small bow, stepped back from the door, and ushered them in. After a moment, the light faded out.

Del checked the time: 9:04.

This was the first night Del had followed the Miata, but not the first night its driver had surprised him with an evening outing. He had almost expected her to lead him to an apartment or home in some comfortable Philadelphia suburb, or even to a hotel. That would have been awful but comprehensible—although, he had to admit, less comprehensible now than it might have been nine months earlier. But this? He couldn't imagine what was going on.

He buzzed up the window of the Escape, got out, and started down the street. He would check the alley and see if the Miata was still there.

He had almost reached the corner when a personalized ringtone chimed into the deserted street. His heart hammering, he pulled his phone out of his pocket.

"Rowan?" he answered, unable to keep his voice steady.

He heard her familiar laugh, along with background noise that suggested that she was in a car with the windows down. "Did I catch you by surprise?"

He glanced toward the door through which she had disappeared an hour earlier and managed a weak laugh in return. "Sort of."

"I'm on my way home from Aunt Nola's and I'm going to stop at the Wegman's. I got a craving for some fudge ripple ice cream. At least it's a normal craving to have, right? Not like the cheesesteak craving. Want me to pick anything up for you?"

"Not that I can think of, but thanks." After a moment, he added, "If you want chocolate sprinkles with the ice cream, I think we're out."

She laughed again. "Ah, Del, how well you know me. Thanks for the heads up."

They ended the call, and Del returned to the car. He unlocked it with the key fob. He didn't need to worry any longer about his wife recognizing the chirp.

It took him two tries to get the key in the ignition.

As he rolled past number 46, he took a last look at the darkened windows.

How well he knew her?

Obviously not well enough.

2

A cheerful buzz of conversation greeted Ann Kinnear as she stepped under the sign reading *Welcome to The Cellar Fíona* and entered the tasting room of Kennett Square's Lynch and Son Winery. Her brother Mike held the door for his husband, Scott Pate, and for Ann's date, Corey Duff.

After the oppressive heat of the August afternoon, the room's air-conditioned chill was a welcome relief. Small groups occupied several of the tables. A distinguished-looking gentleman at a corner table held his glass of wine up to the light, peering at it over the top of his wire-framed spectacles. A server, his dreadlocked hair caught back in an elastic band, regaled a group of young women with information about the provenance of their wine flights.

"Table or bar?" Mike asked.

"The bar's the most fun," said Scott, slipping off his chunky black glasses and dropping them into his shirt pocket. "Plus, we'll get to find out about the wines from the winemaker himself."

The man behind the bar was hanging clean glasses on a rack above his head. Ann guessed him to be in his early thirties.

When he saw their group, a smile broke over his face and Ann could imagine that wine might not be the only attraction of the Lynch winery tasting room for some of its customers.

"Hey, Del, how are you doing?" Scott asked as they took four stools at the otherwise unoccupied bar.

"Doing good. It's great to see you guys."

After Mike did the introductions, Del said to Ann. "I have to say I wouldn't have guessed you and Mike were related."

"Yup, I've heard that before," she said. She was fair-haired and slim, while Mike, only slightly taller, was stockier and dark-haired. Ann actually looked more like the tall, blond Scott.

"Del and I go way back," said Mike. "He was one of my first financial planning clients."

"Back before I had much in the way of finances that needed planning," said Del.

"Start small and let math and compounding do the rest," replied Mike.

"Yeah, that's the idea," Del said ruefully.

Mike frowned. "Having problems with the guy I recommended?"

"No, no," said Del hastily. "I just wish the math was compounding a little faster." He shrugged. "But then I'm sure that's what all clients tell their financial planner."

"I understand you're planning for an addition to the Berendt-and-Lynch household," said Scott.

Del smiled. "Yeah. Rowan and I have a little one coming along in about a month."

"That's wonderful," said Scott. "How is Rowan doing?"

"She's doing fine now, but you should have seen her early on —I've never seen someone throw up as much as she did."

Mike grimaced. "Too much information."

Del laughed. "You're right—sorry about that." He pulled four menus from behind the bar.

Scott held up a hand. "I don't even have to look."

"Flight of the reds?" asked Del.

"Absolutely."

Del turned to Ann and Corey. "The reds—specifically the Cabernet Sauvignon and the Cab Franc—are what we're known for. In fact, Niall Lynch, the owner, named his kids Rowan and Harkin, which mean 'little red one' and 'red' in Gaelic. Rowan is the vineyard manager."

"I didn't realize Rowan had a brother," said Scott.

"Yes. He's back here for a family meeting, but he lives in Hawaii. Not really involved in the business." He turned to Mike. "Flight of reds for you as well?"

"Yup. Plus a cheese and charcuterie board for four."

Del offered a menu to Ann.

"I'll have what they're having," she said.

"Me, too," said Corey.

"Very good." The menus disappeared behind the bar. "Flights and boards coming up."

Del retreated a few steps down the bar and began assembling the order.

Ann turned on her stool and looked across the room. Large windows provided an expansive view of the Lynch property. Just outside was a small pond with a short dock on which stood two Adirondack chairs. To the left of the pond, a smaller building sat at a picturesque angle. To the right were tidy rows of vines. Lightly wooded ground rose from the pond to a building just visible through the trees.

"What a great place," she said.

"Lynch is our favorite winery in Chester County," said Scott. "We're so happy both of you could join us, and that Corey is staying with us."

"What's the point of having a guest room if you don't have guests?" added Mike.

Ann thought back to that morning at Mike and Scott's town-house: tripping over Corey's duffle bag, which seemed always to migrate from the luggage rack to the floor of the guest room where she was staying; the four of them dodging each other in a kitchen that was comfortable for two and just manageable for three; Corey accidentally walking in on Mike when Mike failed to latch the bathroom door. Her double bed was too small for two restless sleepers, although she had declined Scott's offer to outfit the room with a queen. It felt too much like a step toward permanence for a living situation she intended to be temporary.

"I really need to stop mooching off you guys," she said. "It's pretty pathetic for a thirty-something woman to be living with her brother and brother-in-law. I need to look around for a place of my own."

"What kind of place would you be looking for?" asked Corey.

"Something small. Probably a rental until I know what my plans will be."

"Plans?"

"Back to the Adirondacks? Settle down here for a while? Philly is more centrally located for where my engagements usually take place."

"Maybe not for long," said Mike. "Someone from Brazil contacted me the other day about an engagement."

Mike was the business manager of Ann Kinnear Sensing, a business whose roots went back to a seven-year-old Ann telling her parents and younger brother about her conversations with a girl who had died decades earlier in the family's home. Later, as teenagers, Mike had encouraged Ann to help in the search for a friend who had disappeared while caving—a friend Ann could find only after the girl died from her injuries. Later still, Mike had offered to punch out Ann's boyfriend Dan, who had recom-mended therapy when he learned that she believed she could communicate with the dead. Mike had been Ann's champion and defender throughout her life, whether others wanted to debunk her ability or to exploit it.

"Brazil?"asked Ann, turning on the stool toward Mike. "That's cool. When is that?"

"I told them now might not be the best time. I recommended that woman in New Mexico."

"Not the best time? Why?"

He glanced from Ann to Corey and back to Ann. "I thought ... you know ..."

"No, Mike," she said with a frown, "I don't know."

"I figured with you and Corey seeing each other, and with him being about to go back to Los Angeles ..."

Ann had been dating Corey for the last several months, ever since the focus of his documentary had shifted from her own spirit-sensing abilities to an investigation into a series of deaths on Mount Desert Island, Maine.

"You passed up an engagement for me in Brazil so that Corey and I wouldn't have to be apart for a week? Less? For heaven's sake—we're already commuting between Pennsylvania and Maine."

She looked toward Corey, expecting him to back her, but he didn't look as affronted by Mike's actions as she expected. "Were you in on this?"

He raised his hands to contradict the accusation. "Nope, I didn't know anything about it. But I can't say I'm entirely disappointed that you won't be jetting off to Brazil—at least right now."

"Corey," she almost wailed, "Brazil! You could have come along!"

"Crap, I should have thought of that myself," said Mike. "Maybe the New Mexico senser will strike out and they'll get in touch with us again," he added hopefully.

"They won't get in touch again," said Ann. "You already

turned them down. They'll go somewhere else. In fact, they'll probably contact Garrick next."

She knew that the dig at Mike—that he might have indirectly sent business to her sometimes-colleague, sometimes-competitor Garrick Masser—would be a measure of payback for the missed trip.

Mike rewarded her with a scowl. "I'll call them back—"

She waved an impatient hand. "No, let it go. But don't be turning down business without consulting me first."

"Okay, okay," said Mike peevishly. "I was just trying to look out for you."

"Maybe I don't need to get a place of my own," she muttered. "Maybe I need to stay at the townhouse to keep an eye on you. Or maybe you need to get a hobby other than my business."

Del's arrival with the charcuterie board prevented any rejoinder from Mike. As Del arranged the wine flights in front of them, he said, "I couldn't help overhear you talking about lodgings. We have a guest house by the pond that's going to be available soon."

"A guest house at the winery?" exclaimed Scott. "I might move in myself!"

"Hey!" said Mike.

Scott patted his hand. "Of course, it would have to accommodate two."

"Might be a little snug, but I'm sure a couple could make it work," said Del.

"I didn't realize you had a guest house here," said Mike. "You can't have much trouble renting it out. Although, I'd think you'd make more money renting it to tourists than to a tenant."

Scott swatted Mike's arm. "You already ruined the Brazil trip. Don't talk Del into withdrawing the offer to rent it to Annie."

Del laughed. "No danger of that. We've tried offering it as a vacation rental, but it's a pain in the ass. People make the reservation but don't show up, or they do show up but have parties and leave it a mess. We're looking for someone who comes with a personal recommendation and who wants to stay a while."

"Is there someone in there now?" asked Mike.

"Actually, Niall Lynch's sister Nola has been staying there." Del's expression became somber. "Niall has been ill—heart problems—and Nola moved into the guest house to be close by to take care of him. But he recently took a turn for the worse and she's moving into the big house with him."

"'The big house'?" asked Corey.

"It's how the Lynches refer to the family home at the top of the hill."

"We're so sorry to hear about your father-in-law," said Scott.

"Yeah, Del," said Mike. "Really sorry. That sucks."

Del nodded. "It's going to be tough. Especially for Rowan." He turned to Ann. "If you're interested, I think Nola will have her things out in the next day or two and you're welcome to take a look at it then."

"Thanks, I'd love to check it out." She gave Del her number. "Just give me a call when there's a time that works for you. I'm flexible." She shot Mike a look. "And evidently I'll be around."

Mike threw up his hands. "I said I was sorry! I promise to look for more South American engagements for you."

The guy with the dreads came to the bar with a wine order for a new group of visitors, and Del left them to fill the order.

Ann picked up the first glass in her flight and turned toward the large window.

Brazil. She had always wanted to see the Christ the Redeemer statue towering, arms outstretched, over Rio de Janeiro. Even the Copacabana would be worth a look ... as long as it wasn't during Carnaval. But she realized that she had to bear some responsibility for Mike overstepping his role as her business manager. She had relied on Mike to take care of everything except the actual sensing for most of her career.

As the men discussed the aroma and mouth feel of the wines, she took a sip of hers and admired the view across the property. A young woman was walking down the path from the parking lot to the pond. She wore a loose T-shirt, jeans, and a broad-brimmed straw hat, and carried a small paper bag. It was no doubt Rowan Lynch, her pregnancy doubly apparent because of her otherwise slight frame. As she stepped onto the short dock that extended over the pond, a group of ducks paddled toward her from the opposite side, their excited quacks audible in the tasting room. She reached into the bag and tossed out a few handfuls of what looked like torn up pieces of bread.

Scott asked Corey, "Things are coming along well with the documentary?"

"So far, so good. I just have a few more interviews to do, need to get a little more B-roll, then I can really focus on the editing."

"Will you do the editing in Maine?"

"I could, but doing it on my laptop is a bit of a challenge. I have a nicer set-up at home in L.A."

"When will you be going back there?"

Ann sensed Corey glancing toward her. "In a couple of weeks."

"So soon?" said Scott. "It's been nice having you on the East Coast."

"Well, California isn't Brazil, but maybe Ann will luck into some West Coast gigs."

She turned back to the bar. "I'll work with my scheduler on that," she said, cocking a meaningful eyebrow at Mike.

Mike raised his glass in a mock salute. "I'm on it, boss."

3

N iall Lynch gazed out the car window as his sister Nola guided his venerable Range Rover down the curving drive. Lynch and Son Winery spread out below them in the waning evening light: the building that housed the fermentation tanks, the barrel room, and the bottling equipment; the Cellar Fíona, where customers came for tastings or to purchase bottles or cases of wine; the small guest house next to the pond; and, beyond the pond, the vineyard. The big house was barely a hundred yards from the Cellar via the footpath through the woods, but Nola had insisted they take the car. She blamed the temperature, which was still steamy even at this hour, but both of them knew the real reason. Niall was unlikely to be able to make the walk in his current condition.

Nola pulled into the small parking area behind the Cellar. During the day, it was where the Lynch staff parked. Now the only vehicles were Rowan's red Miata and a Nissan Versa that Niall guessed was his son Harkin's rental.

Nola parked as close as she could to the back door—the better to accommodate the invalid, he thought bitterly—and hurried from the driver's side to the passenger door.

"Is everyone here?" he asked.

"Yes."

"When did Harkin get in?"

"A couple of hours ago."

"Did he bring Kepi?"

"No, he came by himself."

"He should have brought Kepi—that boy has some skin in this game."

"Niall, he's fourteen years old. He has better things to do than fly halfway around the world for a family business meeting."

"Fine." He hauled himself out of the car, then steadied himself on the door, making sure of his balance, catching his breath.

Nola got his cane out of the back seat. "Don't forget this."

He snatched it from her hand, then slammed the door shut. "Let's get this over with."

Nola opened the back door of the Cellar as Niall labored up the few stairs. They passed through the storage room, its walls lined with cases of wine for tastings and retail sales, bales of paper napkins, and boxes of spare stemware. The next space was Rowan and Del's office, with wide, built-in shelves along opposite sides of the room acting as desks. Rowan's desk was tidy—the few items on its surface aligned with the edge of the desk as precisely as the rows in the vineyard she oversaw. A copy of *What to Expect When You're Expecting* sat on top of a squared-off stack of issues of *American Vineyard*. Del's desk was cluttered with the tools of his trade as Lynch's winemaker: a hand-held spectrometer, a glass wine thief stained with residue from the last sample he had pulled from one of the barrels, an all-purpose pocket knife with the corkscrew attachment deployed. Post-its marked with scrawled notes fanned out around the computer monitor. A cork board above the desk held clippings and printouts of reviews of Lynch wines.

Niall continued on toward the tasting room, stopping for a moment in the darkened hallway to catch his breath again.

For many years, he had resisted making any changes to the tasting room. For most of his life, its decor had been much like the decor of the big house: sturdy furniture, long-wearing fabrics, light fixtures whose purpose was to provide light, not ambiance. However, a few years earlier he had overheard a group of well-heeled thirty-somethings comparing the space to a Holiday Inn lounge, and even he understood it wasn't a compliment. He mentioned the comment to Nola, more as a complaint about customers than as an acknowledgement of any shortcomings of the winery's public space.

But over the following week she took him on a tour of spaces in Chester County and Philadelphia—other wineries, restaurants, bars, even the Brandywine River Museum—showing him what the tasting room could look and feel like. She sketched out plans, showed him fabric swatches. She told him that if he gave her the budget, she would manage the project to, as she described it, "haul the Lynch brand, kicking and screaming, into the twenty-first century."

He scowled at one of the swatches, a nubby upholstery fabric in a subtle moss green. "In twenty years, that's going to look just as dated as what we have now."

She laughed humorlessly. "Niall, this will look dated in ten years. If you want to appeal to the kinds of people who will pay top dollar for a flight of Chester County wine, you better be ready to set aside some money to keep the public spaces inviting. God knows you're not setting any aside to keep the *private* spaces inviting."

Now the three people he had come to see were seated under

fashionable pendant lights at the barn board bar that Nola had designed.

As usually seemed to be the case, Del was in the center, a physical and emotional buffer between Niall's children. On one side sat Rowan, her hands laced over her stomach, stray wisps of brunette curls framing a face tanned by her time in the vineyard, her usually bright gray eyes somber. On the other side sat Harkin, brown hair bleached almost blond from his own outdoor life, lines already forming around his hazel eyes. Both his children were fine-boned, like himself, which played out as feminine delicacy in Rowan and a wiry hardness in Harkin. Both were good-looking, although Harkin lacked the normally cheerful demeanor of his much younger sister. It was not only the extra years that marred Harkin's appearance, but the ever-present scowl.

A bottle of Lynch Sapele stood on the bar, a small measure of ruby red liquid in front of Rowan—the quarter of a standard pour per day she had allowed herself during her pregnancy—and an almost empty glass in front of Del. Niall had acquiesced to Rowan and Del naming the wine after the reddish, mahogany-like wood, although it seemed like a flight of fancy to him. And although Sapele was one of the Lynch winery's most expensive bottles, Niall didn't begrudge Del breaking it out for this occasion. After all, it was Del's experiment using Cab Franc grapes that he had purchased from a neighboring vineyard that had produced the award-winning wine.

Harkin took a swig from his infernal bottle of Pepsi. It looked to Niall as if Rowan and Del might as well have been drinking Pepsi for all the pleasure the wine was giving them.

Rowan glanced at her phone where it lay on the bar. "Do you think we should call Aunt Nola? Make sure everything's okay?"

"Let's give them a couple more minutes," said Del. "You know your dad doesn't get around as easily as he used to."

Niall cleared his throat from the doorway and the three at the bar started like guilty schoolchildren. He drew himself upright—as upright as possible—and crossed the room to the bar.

Harkin stood. "Hi, Dad."

"Glad you could make it." Niall extended his hand.

Harkin shook it. "You didn't make it sound optional."

"You could have brought Kepi. I'll bet he'd enjoy another trip back to the winery."

"What about Alana?" asked Harkin, his jaw tightening.

"Of course, Alana would be welcome as well. It's been fourteen years since your son was born. I'd like to meet his mother someday. Bring them both here—make a family vacation of it."

"Dad, we live in Hawaii—we don't need a 'vacation' in Pennsylvania."

"What's Kepi up to?" asked Del, no doubt trying to defuse the situation.

"Scuba lessons," said Harkin, his features relaxing into a smile.

"I thought Kepi already knew how to scuba dive," said Niall.

Harkin's smile disappeared. "He does."

Nola stepped past Niall and gave Harkin a hug. "You tell my great-nephew that if he isn't coming to Pennsylvania soon, I'm going to Hawaii to see how tall he's gotten."

A ghost of the smile returned to Harkin's face. "He'll be taller than his dad pretty soon, that's for sure. I'll probably bring him to the next family meeting, but we'd love to have you visit, Aunt Nola."

Niall stepped behind the bar, thinking sourly that the roster of attendees at the next family meeting would no doubt be a bit different from this one.

Nola took a seat two stools down from Rowan.

Del picked up the open bottle of Sapele. "Nola, can I pour you a glass?"

She raised a hand. "Not for me."

"Niall?"

"Yes. Please."

Del pulled a glass from the rack over the bar, poured, and handed Niall the glass.

Niall took a sip of the wine, sucked in air to release the aromas, then swallowed. He could feel Del's eyes on him—that look of anxious anticipation that the winemaker had whenever someone whose opinion he valued drank one of his wines. Del knew the wine was good—he shouldn't need to keep being told.

Niall felt a wave of the vertigo that had been plaguing him the last few days. He reached out a hand to the bar, hoping the movement would avoid notice.

Rowan knit her brow. "Del, can you get Dad a stool?"

"Sure." Del jumped up and carried a stool around to the back of the bar. He set it down next to Niall, then resumed his seat.

"How did it go at the doctor, Dad?" asked Rowan.

Niall lowered himself carefully onto the stool. "Pretty much what we expected. A year. Maybe a little less."

Rowan's eyes filled with tears. "Oh, Dad."

Del reached over and laid his hand over hers. Harkin kept his eyes resolutely on the bar top.

"I can't complain," Niall said, then attempted a self-deprecating laugh. "At least I shouldn't. I've enjoyed every blessing a man could ask for. The opportunity to spend my life in a vocation that feels more like an avocation ... the satisfaction of continuing a tradition started by my father ... the good fortune to expand Lynch and Son Winery into a thriving business, not only on a sound financial footing but also with a reputation that extends to California and beyond."

"What more could a person want?" muttered Harkin.

Niall clamped his lips over a retort, then continued. "Now is the time to set the stage for the Lynch winery to continue its success into the next generation. Your generation."

"But not our entire generation," said Harkin. "Am I right?"

"You are correct. A business can't have more than one leader just as—"

"—a ship can't have more than one captain," interrupted Harkin.

Niall raised an eyebrow.

"That's what you were going to say, right? That there needs to be one person who will make the decisions and have the ability to enforce those decisions."

"Yes."

"It is Lynch and *Son*," said Harkin, although without much force.

"Jesus, Hark," muttered Del.

"It was named in an earlier era," said Niall. "I think we all now recognize that a woman can be just as qualified to run a winery as a man can. If our father had realized that, a different person might be standing where I am now."

"Evidently, gender trumped seniority," said Nola blandly.

Niall didn't shift his gaze from Rowan, Del, and Harkin. "Regardless of what was driving our father's decision about who deserved control of the winery, Nola and I both did everything we could to make a success of the business. We behaved as allies despite the situation our father put us in."

"That's because by the time you inherited from Granddad," replied Harkin, "Aunt Nola was busy with her own business."

"I doubt Aunt Nola would have started Nolyn Events if she had thought that Grandfather would have let her be involved in the winery," said Rowan. She looked toward Nola. "Right?"

Nola crossed her arms and cocked an eyebrow at Niall. "It's

true that I didn't see much opportunity for myself at Lynch and *Son*."

"The point is moot," said Niall, trying to regain control of the conversation. "By the time our father died, Nola's business was doing so well that I wouldn't have asked her to step away from it to come work at the winery. She and I were already set on the paths that our lives and careers would take us." He took a deep breath and successfully fought off the bout of coughing that seemed to be the inevitable result. He had postponed taking his evening meds so he would be alert for this conversation. He needed to wrap it up so that he could get back to the big house and to the relief of the pills. "Tonight, we're here to talk about the future, not the past." He laid his hands on the bar top. "Harkin and Rowan, I recognize that each of you wants to be the one to determine the winery's direction. Although our personal goals are of course important to each of us, our ultimate goal must be the success of the winery. Obviously, I must make my decision about who will inherit the winery sooner than I had anticipated. I hope you will believe me when I say that my ultimate choice will be an objective one based on what I believe will be best for the business. I expect you to abide by my decision and do your best to help the other if you are not chosen, as Nola and I have done."

"That's easy for you to say," said Harkin. "Your father didn't make it into some oenophile version of *Survivor*."

"It's the survival of the winery, not the success of the individual players, that's important," snapped Niall.

"But the winery might not survive—might not even stay in the family—depending on who inherits it," said Rowan, pointedly not looking at Harkin.

"My will includes a provision that would prevent the sale of the winery by my heir, except to a direct descendant," replied Niall.

Del sat forward. "But what's to stop Harkin from selling the winery to Kepi and having Kepi sell it to someone else?"

"Or," Harkin said to Del, his face reddening, "what's to stop *you* from selling it to your son or daughter and having them do the same?"

Rowan swung in her chair toward Harkin. "The whole point is that we wouldn't do that!"

Niall held up a hand. "I have specified that no one under the age of twenty-one can be the owner of the winery."

Del fell back in his chair. "So Harkin can just hold onto it for seven years and then sell to Kepi, who could then sell it anywhere."

"The winery isn't going to survive seven years of absentee management!" Rowan burst out. "By the time Kepi is twenty-one, it won't be worth anything!"

"What about the one who isn't chosen to inherit?" asked Harkin. "What will they get?"

"Harkin," said Rowan, her voice strained, "now is not the time—"

Niall raised a hand and Rowan dropped her eyes to the wine glass in front of her.

"The winery and the bulk of the financial assets go hand in hand," said Niall. "I've always put the money generated by the winery back into the business, and I will ensure that my heir will do the same. The other will receive an allowance. No one will be out on the street, but neither will they be jetting off for a year visiting the vineyards of France. Or," he couldn't help adding, "kicking back on the lanai with a can of pineapple wine."

Niall could hear the crinkle of the Pepsi bottle as Harkin's hand tightened around it. "Hawaii's not some temporary break from real life, Dad. It's my home. It's my family's home. It *is* my life."

Niall ignored him. "Rowan and Harkin, I realize that I have put you at a disadvantage by not sharing the details of the winery's operation with you. Del understands the production process, and Rowan understands what's needed to manage the vineyard. However, a winery is more than the sum of its parts. I realize now that my failure to expose you to the whole spectrum of activities involved in the operation was shortsighted in terms of succession planning, and I hope to remedy that by sharing my knowledge in the time left to me. But I will not ask you to wait that long to find out who I have selected as my heir. I will make up my mind over the next two weeks. That's why I asked Harkin to stay here for that period." He tipped back the last bit of wine in his glass, held it in his mouth for a moment, then nodded approvingly and swallowed. "I will rely on my heir to continue the success of Lynch and Son Winery into the future, or," his gaze shifted from Harkin to Rowan and back, "to accept responsibility for the decline of a business that is over fifty years old."

The vertigo hit him again and he passed a hand across his eyes.

"Dad, do we need to take a break?" asked Rowan.

"No need. I've said what I came to say." Niall pulled himself up, then dropped back onto the stool.

Nola hurried around to where he sat and took his elbow. "Let's go back to the house."

"Yes, I believe that's best." He struggled to his feet. "I'm sure you all have questions, but I'm afraid the answers will have to wait."

Niall made his way across the tasting room and down the hall, his cane tapping on the rustic floorboards. Nola walked a step behind him, as he had asked her to do. It was far enough to give him space to maneuver but close enough to grab him if he lost his balance. When he reached the storage room, he stopped. How could a walk of a few dozen yards leave him so winded?

"A minute," he wheezed.

"All right."

"That boy ... do you think he'll ever come around?"

"No, Niall, I don't. If you want the winery to continue to prosper—to be headed by someone who actually cares about it—I think you know who your heir should be."

"She's so young."

"She's only a year younger than you were when you inherited the winery from Dad."

"I want to give Harkin a chance to prove himself."

"You tried giving him a chance—in your own inimitable way—and it didn't work. It hasn't worked. In fact, I think you know you've poisoned him against the winery."

"Kepi loves the winery. I thought Harkin might take an interest for his son's sake."

"Kepi's here once a year for the family meetings. Last time he was here, he was thirteen years old."

"It is Lynch and *Son*." He hated the thread of self-pity even he could hear in his words.

"Yes, you and Harkin have reminded us several times."

"You had your event planning business."

"You reminded us of that as well."

He drew himself up. "I'm ready to go."

As he made his way step by breathless step down the steps to the car, he thought of everything he needed to do before he was truly ready to go, ready to trust one of his children to pick up the reins. *End-stage* heart failure. It certainly had a ring of finality to it.

4

Del listened to the *tap tap* of his father-in-law's cane recede down the hall toward the back of the Cellar and a moment later heard the faint click of the door to the storage room closing.

"Harkin," Rowan burst out, "I can't believe how mean you're being to Dad!"

"How mean *I'm* being?" asked Harkin, his eyebrows raised. "He always manages to bring up the fact that Alana and I aren't married, like it's something to be ashamed of. She's always 'Kepi's mother,' never 'your partner.' He dismisses the life I've built for myself in Hawaii—built *by* myself, I should add, since he never sent me a dime after I left home."

"He's sick. He's in pain!"

"He wasn't sick and in pain all the other times he's said the same thing to me in the last dozen years."

"He's just trying to make sure—" Her voice caught, and she cleared her throat. "He's making sure you're ready to take over when he's not around anymore."

"Me? I think it's pretty clear that you have the advantage in terms of inheriting. I don't recall him mentioning that I understood enough to manage *any* part of the business. You and Dad were always two peas in a pod," he gave a harsh laugh, "or two grapes in a bunch. When you talk about the winery, it might be your mouth moving, but it's his voice I hear."

Del sensed Rowan stiffen beside him. Harkin was eight years older than Rowan—thirty-four to her twenty-six—but sometimes he sounded more like a surly teenager than his son Kepi ever had.

Rowan shook her head. "Dad might claim that it was a reflection of the times that Grandfather picked him rather than Aunt Nola to inherit Lynch—even though she's older, even though she would have been great at running the winery—but I think it's pretty clear Dad has that same bias. I'd say you have the advantage being the son." After a moment, she added, "And having a son."

"You might have a son," said Harkin. He shot his sister a look. "Right?"

Rowan was due in a month, and Del's online research suggested that they should be able to find out the baby's gender, but Rowan claimed that the ultrasound was inconclusive. Even before Del had followed her to the house on Larch Street the previous night, he had wondered if she really didn't know, or if she knew and wasn't telling him. And if so, why not?

"A boy or a girl—it doesn't matter to me," she said.

Harkin stood and crossed to the window. When he spoke, his voice was softer. "Being a son, having a son—it's not going to do me any good, Ro. Tell me one time in our lives when Dad cut me any slack because I'm a guy."

She heaved a sigh. "I'm not saying that. In fact, I think he gave you a harder time because he was prepping you to take over."

Del picked up the bottle of Sapele and refilled his glass. "As far as I can see, what your dad said about him and Nola remaining allies through thick and thin is true. She dropped what she was doing to take care of him when he got sick, for God's sake. Let's try to follow their example." He turned to Rowan. "Want something else to drink, Ro? There's Perrier in the kitchen."

"No. Thanks." She climbed off the stool, one hand on her stomach. "As long as we're here, there's some stuff I want to check on my computer. It won't take long."

She disappeared down the hall. A minute later, Del could hear the click of the keyboard.

Harkin scrubbed his hand down his face. "Jesus. I don't *mean* to upset her."

"You were being kind of an asshole." Del tried to keep his tone mild. Part of him wanted to give Harkin a quick shot in the chin, but he knew that the tense relationship between the siblings pained Rowan and he didn't want to do anything to make it worse.

"I know," said Harkin. "Dad always manages to bring out the worst in me." He resumed his seat at the bar.

They sat in silence for half a minute, Del sipping his wine, Harkin scratching morosely at the label on the Pepsi bottle. Then Del asked, "So, Kepi and Alana are doing well?"

Harkin roused himself. "Yeah. It looks like Alana will get tenure this year."

"Really? That's great."

"Yeah—it's sooner than we expected, but it will be nice for her to have some security at the university."

"What about Kepi?"

Harkin smiled. "He's whining about going back to school because it'll interfere with scuba."

"You said he's taking lessons?"

"He's *giving* lessons."

"Really? Is he old enough to do that?"

Harkin shrugged. "Not officially. He's working on a tour boat. He gets the boat ready, keeps an eye on the tourists, gives them ginger drinks when they get seasick. But the scuba instructor lets him help out with the lessons. He says Kepi's a natural."

"Too bad he couldn't come out here with you. I'd love to see him. But I can see how a teenage boy might prefer scuba diving in Hawaii to running bottles through a labeling machine in Pennsylvania."

Harkin snorted. "An *adult* might prefer scuba diving in Hawaii."

"What are you keeping busy with these days?"

"Why—so you can report back to Dad?"

Del raised his eyebrows, but Harkin spoke before he could respond, his tone contrite. "Sorry, sorry. See what I mean about Dad bringing out the worst in me?" He forced a laugh. "I'm working for the tour company, too." He leaned toward Del and said in a conspiratorial whisper, "Try to keep a lid on that intel. It would just feed Dad's assumption that I'm living a beach bum's life."

"Mum's the word." Del took a sip of wine. "You're staying at the big house?"

"Yeah, I didn't want to spend money on a hotel."

"You could stay with me and Rowan."

Harkin rolled his eyes. "I think you better clear that with her before you extend the offer. But thanks." He sat back and stretched. "Fortunately, the big house is so, well, *big* that I could go days without running into Dad. Especially now that he's not so mobile."

"Nola's there as well, right?"

"Yeah, she moved in right before I arrived, but she seems to pretty much stay in her old bedroom trying to keep up with Nolyn Events unless Dad needs her for something."

Del shook his head. "That's got to be tough for Nola, trying to manage a business while she's taking care of Niall."

"It would be tough for anyone to take care of Dad. Although I figure if anyone can handle him, it's Aunt Nola."

"I'm kind of surprised she's devoted enough to him to make the sacrifice."

"I'm betting it's not Dad she's devoted to."

"What do you mean?"

"It's Rowan she's devoted to. Imagine if Rowan had to take care of Dad on top of getting ready for the baby and worrying about the winery falling into my evil clutches. Plus, if Nola's around, she gets to put a bug in Dad's ear about her favored heir."

Del sighed. "Harkin, don't be a dick."

"You don't think Nola has a preferred outcome?"

Del shrugged. "Niall's going to make up his own mind."

Harkin twisted the lid off the bottle and tipped back the last of the Pepsi. "I'm betting Nola thinks that Rowan inheriting the winery would make up for all the shit she's taken from Dad over the years. Even if she didn't have a chance to run it herself, at least she could live vicariously through Ro."

Del was marshaling counterarguments, then realized that Harkin's assessment of the situation was probably more accurate than his own. Del had no doubt that Nola was using her time with Niall to discredit Harkin, and it had to be a bitter pill for Harkin to swallow. Del also had no doubt that the impetus for Nola neglecting her business, moving back into her childhood bedroom, and acting as nursemaid to her brother was Rowan's welfare, not Niall's. That would have been a bitter pill for Niall to swallow ... if he cared about such things. Del found it hard to imagine.

He downed the last of his wine, then refilled his glass and raised it. "Here's to Nola."

To himself, he added, *Taking one for the home team.*

5

Ann tightened the bowline knot on the last of the three tie-down ropes and gave the Piper Warrior a fond pat on the spinner. She had rented the Avondale Airport flight school plane to fly her and Corey to Cambridge, Maryland for lunch at the airport restaurant.

As the two of them crossed the ramp from the tie-down area to the airport office, she groaned theatrically. "I shouldn't have eaten that whole piece of coconut cake."

"Why not? You don't need to worry about your weight."

"Maybe not, but I don't want to worry about spontaneously exploding either. I should really have split it with you, or at least gotten a takeaway container for half."

Ann stopped in the airport office to drop off the key and pay for the rental.

When she emerged, she asked, "What now?" Then she added, "Nothing that will jostle the cake around too much."

"Damn, I was hoping for an afternoon jostle."

Ann laughed. "That will be a lot easier to arrange if I'm not living at the Kinnear and Pate Home for Transient Women."

They went to the parking lot and climbed into her Subaru Forester. "Want to stop by the Lynch winery and get a glass of wine? If I might be living there, it would be fun to check out more than just the tasting room. Maybe we could take our wine out to that little dock over the pond."

"I thought you were worried about spontaneously exploding."

"There's always room for wine."

As Ann started up the Forester, Corey tapped his phone. She glanced over and saw that he was calling up directions on his GPS app.

"I know how to get there," she said.

"Following along on the map helps me get the lay of the land."

When they reached the intersection of Route 1, Ann continued straight, rather than taking the exit onto the highway.

"Taking the scenic route?" asked Corey. "Although it all seems pretty scenic to me."

"There was an accident about a year ago at the next exit. A motorcyclist died. He's still there, trying to flag down passing cars."

"Jesus. Have you ever stopped?"

"I did a couple of times, but I can't communicate with him. It's a little disconcerting—he's all messed up from the accident —so I avoid that exit now."

When they got to the Cellar, the dreadlocked server—whose name they learned was Justin—was behind the bar. Ann was glad it was Justin rather than Del Berendt, since she didn't want Del to feel pressured to show her the guest house before he was ready. Corey bought a bottle of the Cab Sauv, which Justin opened for them, then they wandered down to the pond and lowered themselves into the Adirondack chairs.

Their position gave them a good view of the guest house. It was an elegant little building, clad up to the windowsills in horizontal lengths of wood stained a chocolate brown, above which rough, buff-colored boards ran vertically to the roof. Black-framed windows running up to the eaves walled what was probably the living room. The front porch stepped down on three sides to the ground. Sitting at the edge of the pond, and with its ridged metal roof angling up at each end over front and back porches, it looked like a sturdy boat floating on a tranquil sea.

"The location couldn't be more convenient to Avondale Airport," said Ann. "Plus, wine right next door. And you can't beat the view. I love having water nearby." The tiny body of water wasn't exactly Loon Pond, just down the hill from her Adirondack cabin, but it was every bit as lovely in its own way.

"So, you think that Lynch Winery will be your next home base?"

"Unless the rent is exorbitant, it seems ideal."

"I'd love to have a water view—especially an ocean view. Of course, in L.A., anything with an ocean view is out of my price range."

"You could get a roommate." She grimaced. "Although I can't imagine that the aggravation of a roommate would be worth a glimpse of the ocean."

"Depends on who the roommate was."

"True." She took a sip of wine. When he didn't respond, she glanced over at him. He was looking at her expectantly. "What?"

"Well, I wasn't planning to mention this today—maybe not even on this visit—but I can't pass up that opening." He took a deep breath. "I've been thinking ... you want to get out of Mike and Scott's place, a big city is good because it's near potential business for Ann Kinnear Sensing, you want to be near the water, I'd love a roommate—a very specific roommate—and not just so I can afford a place with a water view. Ever think of L.A. as a possible home base?"

It took Ann a moment to catch Corey's meaning. "Not until this moment."

He sat forward. "Think of all the untapped potential for sensing engagements in the L.A. area. Hell, you might end up with engagements with the rich and famous of Hollywood. And you can't get more water than the Pacific Ocean."

"Corey, just to make sure I'm understanding you—are you suggesting that we get a place together in L.A.?"

He smiled. "It had occurred to me." As the seconds ticked by without a response, his smile faded. "Although it looks like it hadn't occurred to you." He fell back in his chair and turned his gaze toward the pond. "Silly idea, maybe."

"No, no," she said hastily. "It's not a silly idea. I just hadn't thought about it."

He turned back to her. "I know you said you were looking for a place of your own. I wasn't sure if you meant a place where you weren't a guest, or a place by yourself."

"Honestly, Corey, I really hadn't thought about it. I guess I was thinking of a place by myself, but more because I hadn't considered an alternative."

"Is it something you'd consider?"

"Yes. Sure." After a pause, she added, "I'm flattered that *you've* thought about it."

He took her hand and squeezed it, and they both turned back to the water.

Ann took a sip of wine—or apparently more than a sip, because she narrowly avoided sloshing Cab Sauv onto her shirt. Was she really that flustered about Corey's suggestion? Yes, she decided, she was. Not only had it been completely unexpected, but she realized that whenever she visualized herself in a "home base," she visualized herself alone. Not lonely, but with space to herself.

She tipped back the last of her wine.

"Ready for a refill?" asked Corey.

She held out her glass. "Yeah, I am."

6

Sitting at his desk at the big house, Niall Lynch glanced up from the documents before him to the clock on the mantel. Nola had wound it that evening—perhaps the first time anyone had wound it since she had moved out of the house decades before—and he was surprised it still worked. Now, though, he wondered if the time it told was correct. He would have sworn that it had been hours since he last took his pain meds. According to the clock, it had been barely an hour, with several hours to go until his next dose.

He ran his hand down his face and returned his gaze to the documents. The creamy texture of the heavy paper marked them as important, although each was only a few pages. He had never liked tortured legalese and had told his attorney to keep it simple.

He glanced up at a light rap on the doorframe as Nola stepped into the office.

"Are you ready to go to bed yet?" she asked.

"I was ready an hour ago."

"Then you should have called me an hour ago." She stepped toward the desk. "What have you got there?"

"My wills."

She raised an eyebrow. "Wills? Plural?"

"Yes." He turned the documents toward her.

Nola picked up one of the documents and flipped through the few pages. When she got to the last page, she put that document down and paged through the other. then looked up at Niall. "Both of these are executed."

"Yes."

"But they're not identical."

"No. One favors Harkin. One favors Rowan."

She raised an eyebrow. "What did your lawyer think about that?"

"He didn't like it, but I'm the client. He does what I tell him to do. Although he seemed to think he was making some kind of statement by refusing to keep copies."

"And what do you plan to do with your two executed wills?"

"One I will keep and one I will destroy. Harkin and Rowan will decide which is which."

She tossed the document back on the desk. "Niall, good heavens—"

"I want you to know because you're my executor, but also," he scowled, "because you understand them better than I do. I need your advice."

"About what?"

"I don't want to present them with theoreticals. The wills are both executed because I want to show each of them a document that could clearly be enforced. They don't need to know that there are two wills—" He shot her a look. "—and I am relying on you not to share that information with them. As my executor, you have a responsibility to maintain confidentiality regarding the planned disposition of my estate."

She crossed her arms. "Fine."

"So which of the two wills do I show Harkin?"

"What do you mean?"

"I suspect Harkin believes that he has the advantage as the oldest."

"And as the son. But I think you're wrong. I think each of them thinks the other is the more likely heir."

He waved away her comment. "I could show Harkin the will favoring Rowan and tell him that he still has time to convince me to reconsider. It might light a fire under him. Or I could show him the will favoring him, hoping he will recognize the opportunity and step up to his responsibility." He glanced up at Nola. "What do you think?"

"I think it's an awful way to treat your children."

"They may be my children," he snapped, "but it's more important that one of them is going to be the person responsible for ensuring the survival of a business on which dozens of people depend for their livelihood."

"How selfless of you. And which will do you plan to show Rowan?"

"It depends on which I show Harkin. I'm sure they'll compare notes." He shifted in his chair, not meeting Nola's eyes. "If I show her the will that favors her, it might ease her mind."

"To what end? To lull her into a false sense of complacency so that Harkin has a chance to step up to his responsibilities as the next *son* of Lynch and Son?"

"To let Rowan know I appreciate her contribution."

"I'm sure that will be a comfort to her when you tear up her will and leave the winery to Harkin. Because that's what you're hoping for, isn't it?"

He pressed a hand to his chest in an effort to ease its growing tightness. "I'm trying to keep an open mind. I'm trying to make it an even playing field. I'm hoping that now, knowing what they know—about me, about the time I have left—they'll show their true colors. That's why I asked you to get Harkin here. I needed them both here—in person—for this conversation. For what comes next."

"And what do you think Rowan's true colors are?"

They stared at each other, unblinking, across the desk.

Finally, Nola broke the silence.

"You think Rowan will fold under pressure, don't you?"

"She has a baby to think of."

"And how much time do you plan to give her to prove that a woman with a baby is more capable of running a business than a man who has no interest in it?"

"I'll decide in two weeks. Before Harkin leaves."

"And before Rowan has the baby."

"It will be an advantage for her. She can prove herself without the distractions of the baby."

"Niall—" Nola took a deep breath, then continued, her voice careful. "Are you sure you have that much time?"

"I saw the doctor yesterday. I have time. I'm fine."

She stared at him for a moment, then turned and strode toward the door.

"Nola," Niall called after her. "I want to go to bed now. I need to get upstairs."

She turned at the door. "If you're fine, you can get upstairs yourself."

7

Ann entered the dining room carrying her now-refreshed mug and a freshly brewed pot of coffee.

"Anyone else need a top-off?" she asked.

"I'll have some," said Corey, holding out his mug.

"Me, too," said Mike.

"I've had enough already, thanks," said Scott.

Ann refilled Corey and Mike's mugs, then placed the carafe on the dining room table among the remains of the waffles-and-sausage breakfast Mike had made. She settled back into her place at the table.

Each of them was engrossed in his or her own recreational reading: Ann with a copy of *Aviation Safety*, Mike and Corey with their phones, and Scott with a book on dog training. Ursula, who had gotten her own portion of pancakes and sausage, snored contentedly in Scott's lap.

Corey's phone trilled. He pushed his chair back. "That's my mom ... if you'll excuse me for a minute."

He stepped into the kitchen, and a moment later they heard the door to the back porch close.

"See," Mike said to Scott, "Corey takes phone calls at the table. You always yell at me when I do that."

"We were done with our meal and he excused himself," said Scott. "Plus, it's his mother." He turned to Ann. "I recall Corey grew up in Pittsburgh. Does his mother still live there?"

"Yes, but she's spending the summer at the Shore."

"That sounds nice. Cooler than here, I'll bet."

"Maybe you and Corey should visit her there," Mike said to Ann.

Ann looked up from the magazine and raised an eyebrow. "I think it's a little soon for the whole 'meeting the family' thing."

"He's met your family."

"That's because I'm living with you."

"It's been three months."

"It's not like we've spent three continuous months together. I'll bet we've only spent ..." She shifted her eyes to the ceiling for some mental calculation "... a hundred and fifty hours together." She returned her attention to the magazine.

"That's almost a continuous week," said Mike. After a pause, he asked, "What's the threshold for the 'meeting the family' thing?"

"Two hundred hours," she said without looking up.

"Which shore is she at?" asked Scott.

"Ocean City."

"Which one?"

"New Jersey."

They were debating the relative merits of Ocean City, New Jersey and Ocean City, Maryland when Corey returned to the dining room and resumed his seat at the table.

"My mom suggested that since I'm in the Philly area, we could get together for dinner," he said.

"Annie could fly you to Ocean City," said Scott. "The three of us went there a couple of weeks ago. The airport is practically right on the beach."

"Or you're welcome to invite her to West Chester," said Mike. "I could get some lobsters."

"That would be a long round trip for her," said Scott. He turned to Corey. "There's a sleeper sofa in Mike's office. Your mother could stay overnight and go back to Ocean City the next day."

Ann rolled her eyes. "Did you guys ever consider that maybe Corey's mom just wants to have dinner with Corey and not the entire extended Kinnear-Pate clan?"

"Nonsense," said Corey. "My mom loves meeting people." He glanced at Ursula. "Although she might need to stay in a hotel if she came to West Chester for an overnight. She's allergic to dogs. She'd be fine for dinner, especially if we could eat outside, but maybe not for sleeping here."

"Let's go to the Wegman's and see if they have lobsters," Mike said to Scott.

Ann tossed her magazine aside with an exasperated sigh. "Don't you want to make sure Corey's mom's going to be coming for dinner before you stock up?"

"Now I'm in the mood for lobster," said Mike. "If I get enough for five and she doesn't come, I can make lobster salad out of the extra."

"You're going to make me put them in the water, aren't you?" said Scott.

Mike gave a sheepish grin. "Well ... yes. Do you mind?"

Scott waved a hand. "No. If I'm willing to eat a lobster that someone else has put in a pot, I guess I need to be willing to put the lobster in the pot myself."

"That's very grown-up of you," said Mike. "What does that mean about my unwillingness to do it?"

Scott leaned over and patted Mike on the shoulder. "It means you're a wimp, sweetie."

Mike took a sip of coffee and leaned back in his chair. "Your mom has been in Ocean City for a while, right?" he asked Corey.

"Yeah. It's perfect because she knows a lot of the other people who are staying there." He laughed. "I teased her that it was like senior week 'down the shore' but, you know, *senior*."

They joined in his laugh.

"She and my dad used to go for a week—that was all the time Dad wanted to take off from work—but her sister's family always rents a place there for the whole summer, so she decided to make it an extended stay."

"That must be therapeutic for her," said Scott. "Annie told me your dad died last year."

"Yeah. It was unexpected—an aneurysm." Corey got out his phone, tapped, then handed the phone to Ann.

One of the men in the photo was Corey. When Ann had met up with Corey for the Mount Desert Island documentary, he was clean-shaven and his wavy reddish hair was reflecting the ministrations of an L.A.-based stylist. This photo, however, was older, probably taken around the time Ann had first met him during the production of his documentary *The Sense of Death*. At that time, he had sported an unkempt beard and mustache and the beginnings of a beer belly.

The other man in the photo was clearly Corey's father. He had the small paunch that his son was, at least for the moment, holding at bay, but the same red hair and the same infectious grin. The two men stood with their arms around each other's shoulders, each holding up a strikingly small fish.

"That's a great picture," she said, passing the phone to Scott, who smiled at the photo and then passed the phone to Mike.

"I took him out on a fishing charter for Father's Day," said Corey as Mike passed the phone back to him. "Everyone else was catching these enormous fish, and we kept pulling in these guppies." He looked at the photo with a wistful smile, then set the phone aside as his smile faded. "I think Mom really struggled when he died, especially over the winter when she was cooped up at home. I don't think she knew what to do with herself. She and my dad were practically inseparable. I'll bet they didn't spend more than a dozen nights apart the whole time they were married."

Ann shook her head. "I can't even imagine."

"Really?"

Ann was surprised at his surprise. "Yeah. I mean, didn't they have some individual interests?"

"Not really. They both enjoyed golf and boating. Going to movies. Playing bridge."

"You should give her a call and ask her if she has an interest in a lobster dinner in West Chester," said Scott. "There's a darling hotel in town where she could stay."

Corey pulled out his phone. "Let me call Mom and let her know what the proposed plan is." They heard the back door open and shut again.

"I think I have a brochure for the Hotel Warner somewhere," said Scott. He placed Ursula on the floor and disappeared upstairs.

Ann topped up her coffee, then asked Mike, "Do you remember Mom and Dad having their own interests—you know, doing things apart from each other?"

"Mom liked swimming, which Dad hated. Dad liked racquetball, and I don't remember Mom ever playing. They both had their own friends. Remember that time Mom went to Cancun with her girlfriends?"

Ann laughed. "Yeah, now that you mention it. I remember feeling so pleased with myself that I was someone whose mother went to Cancun with her girlfriends."

"You don't want to spend twenty-four seven with your beau?"

"God, no."

Mike raised his eyebrows and glanced toward the kitchen door.

Ann followed his gaze, alarmed. "He's out on the porch, right?" she whispered.

Mike leaned back in his chair so he could see the back door. "Fortunately for you, yes."

She sighed with relief. "It's nothing personal. I really don't want to spend twenty-four seven with anyone."

Mike put his hand to his heart. "Not even your baby brother?"

Ann returned to her magazine. "Are you kidding me? We'd kill each other before lunch."

8

Del didn't bother trying to make conversation with Rowan as she drove the few minutes from their house in Unionville to the winery. He had tried over breakfast, to no avail.

In the three days since he had followed her to Larch Street and watched her slip into the house at the invitation of the Victorian-clad man, he had tried to find ways to broach the topic. But with Niall's news about his prognosis and his plan for determining his heir, exacerbated by Harkin's ever-irritating presence, there never seemed to be a good time.

Del had tried to find out more about 46 Larch Street, but his online searches returned mainly outdated realtor listings showing only a Google Street View image of the house, or sites that looked guaranteed to infect his computer with a virus. He had briefly considered seeing what kind of information paid sites would provide, but Rowan managed their credit card bills and he doubted such a charge would escape her notice.

They arrived at the winery and Rowan pulled the Miata up to the back door of the Cellar.

"Thanks for the ride," said Del.

"No problem."

"Sure you don't want me to come with you to the doctor?"

"It's just a routine checkup."

"Will you be getting an ultrasound?"

"I don't think there's any need, with the baby coming so soon and everything going fine. I think they've done all the ultrasounds they normally would."

"And they couldn't tell if it was a boy or a girl?"

She fiddled with the rearview mirror. "It's not always possible—it depends on the position of the baby. And I'd rather be surprised. Wouldn't you?"

"I'm okay either way."

She leaned over and gave him a kiss. "Thanks, sweetheart."

Del climbed out of the car, then watched as she drove away. He was getting uncomfortably familiar with the rear view of the Miata.

The hour was too early for customers—even too early for the Cellar staff—so he had the building to himself. He passed through the storage room, his and Rowan's workspace, and the tasting room, then pushed through a swinging door into the kitchen.

Niall had been against putting in a kitchen when Nola had renovated the Cellar.

"No one needs a dedicated space to prepare cheese plates and charcuterie boards," he had said during one of the family meetings.

"Just because Lynch isn't offering more than that now," retorted Nola, "doesn't mean you might not want to expand in the future. If you ever want to host events here, you'll need somewhere for the caterer to work."

"It would be perfect for weddings," said Rowan.

Nola shuddered. "I've managed to avoid weddings for Nolyn Events and I don't plan to change that in the future. I've heard enough Bridezilla stories not to want to deal with those myself. But the Cellar would be great for corporate events."

"You don't want to deal with Bridezillas," said Niall. "I don't want to deal with caterers. Or more guests than we already have."

"It's hardly the same thing," said Nola. "Humor me on this, Niall. Maybe the next generation of Lynches won't feel the same way, and it will be cheaper to include a kitchen in the plan now than to try to retrofit it later."

Del knew that Nola had been thinking of Rowan. Like her aunt, Rowan believed that Lynch needed to expand beyond its current offerings: tastings, retail sales, and sales to Philadelphia-area restaurants. Plus, she enjoyed coordinating the larger groups that came for tastings, the closest Lynch currently got to hosting an event. However, pending its use as a caterer's kitchen, Del was using some of its counter space for a makeshift lab.

He had been fiddling for almost an hour with an SO_2 analysis test when he heard a *tap tap* from the tasting room—he recognized it as Niall's cane—and footsteps crossing the room. He was about to pop his head out of the kitchen and ask Niall if he needed anything when he heard Niall's voice.

"Let's sit at the bar. Why don't you open a bottle of the reserve."

"Are you supposed to be drinking?" The second voice was Harkin's.

"It hardly matters."

Del had no interest in joining a conversation between Niall and Harkin—a conversation that would doubtless deteriorate into an argument. He returned to his work.

A few moments later, he heard Harkin's voice again, apparently now behind the bar. "I don't see any of the reserve. How about the Sapele?"

"Yes, that's fine."

Del heard the faint pop of a cork. He imagined Harkin, no doubt armed with a bottle of Pepsi, pouring a glass of the Cab Franc for Niall. A few moments later, Niall spoke again.

"Quite good. An interesting experiment on Del's part."

Del smiled. It would be nice if Niall ever complimented him to his face, but overhearing it was almost better. It hadn't been easy to convince Niall to let him buy the Cab Franc grapes from a nearby vineyard. However, even Niall had to admit that the experiment was fully justified by the awards the wine had won, even when stacked up against the best Napa and Sonoma had to offer.

"Pour a glass for yourself," said Niall.

"It would be wasted on me," said Harkin.

"Come around here and sit. I don't want to talk to you like you're some bartender."

Footsteps. Then Harkin's voice in a tone of forced carelessness. "How *do* you want to talk to me?"

"Like my son. Like the possible heir of Lynch and Son Winery."

Del froze.

Niall continued. "Harkin, my father passed Lynch and Son Winery to me, and I always assumed I would pass it to my son. After all, I spent eight years thinking that you would be an only child before Rowan came along. But as I told you and Rowan, I'm not going to let an outdated tradition stand in the way of the winery's success. If you don't step up to the responsibility, then Rowan will be the first woman to run the winery."

Del stepped carefully to the swinging door that separated the kitchen from the tasting room and peered through the crack to where the two men were seated at the bar, their backs to him.

"That's going to happen no matter what I do at this point, right?" said Harkin. "A tiger can't change its stripes and all that."

"I believe if the stakes are high enough, anyone can change their stripes."

"I can't imagine what I could do that would convince you that I deserve to inherit."

"Move back to Pennsylvania. Get involved in the operation."

"Dad, I'm happy where I am. I'd need a lot more than you dangling what seems like a long shot in front of me to even approach Alana and Kepi with that idea."

"I want to show you something." Niall reached into the inside pocket of his jacket—only someone as sick as Niall would need a jacket on a day as warm as this—and pulled out an envelope. He glanced at it, tucked it back into the pocket, and pulled a seemingly identical one from the other pocket. He removed a document from the envelope, unfolded it, and passed it to Harkin. "That's my will as it stands now."

Harkin unfolded the document and flipped through the pages. He glanced up at Niall, then went through the pages more slowly. "You're leaving the winery to me?"

Del's hands closed into fists and he barely suppressed a groan. Rowan was right—despite everything, Harkin would always be Niall's preferred heir.

"Yes," said Niall. "As things stand now."

Harkin ran his fingers through his hair. "I—" He cleared his throat. "Dad, I appreciate your trust in me—I really do—but I just don't see ..." His voice trailed off. He stood and walked to the window and gazed out across the property. After a moment he gave a short laugh. "I have to say I never gave much real thought to this eventuality."

"Harkin, you're a smart boy—a smart *man*—and you can learn what you need to learn about the winery. We have time to do that. And Rowan and Del will help you."

Del shifted and a board in the kitchen floor squeaked, but

Niall and Harkin were too wrapped up in their conversation to notice.

"You think they'd want to help me out?" asked Harkin, his skepticism clear.

"I hope they would. And you wouldn't need their help forever. Even your willfulness, although it has given me headaches, can be an asset. I know that if you set your mind to it, you can continue the winery's success, maybe even expand it."

Harkin continued staring out the window for another half minute, then returned to the bar and sank down on a stool. "I need to talk to Alana and Kepi."

"What is there to talk about?"

Harkin's features tightened and his lips clamped shut, no doubt against a reflexive retort. But when he finally spoke, his voice was controlled. "Alana has a job she loves. Kepi is at an age where uprooting him would be difficult. They both love Hawaii. We all love Hawaii."

"Teenage boys are adaptable."

"I want to give him stability," said Harkin, his voice a bit less controlled.

"And there are plenty of openings for teachers around here—"

"Professor."

"What?"

Now Harkin wasn't even trying to maintain his calm. "She's a professor. At a prestigious university. She's likely to get tenure." He forced a laugh. "She studies Marine Biology, Dad. How many tenure-track positions in Marine Biology are available around here?"

"She can work at the winery. Maybe in the vineyard—"

This time Harkin's laugh was bitter. "Man, talk about a tiger not changing its stripes. I thought for a minute—was *stupid* enough to think for a minute—that you were going to show me and my family some respect."

Niall raised a hand. "Harkin, I'm just saying—"

"I know exactly what you're saying. Alana's a woman—and on top of that, not even my wife—so how much can what she wants really matter? How much could her career count when I have the opportunity to move back here and live out the rest of my days in a place that has nothing but bad memories for me?"

"Son—"

"Why in the hell would I want to run a winery? I can't even enjoy the fucking product!"

"First of all, don't use that language with me," spat Niall. "Second of all, you don't need to drink wine yourself to appreciate its artistry."

"That's easy for you to say." Harkin dropped his voice to match his father's rumble. "Fruit forward, with hint of sardine. And do I detect ... yes, I think I do ... a finish of Count Chocula on the palate."

"Harkin." Niall's voice was ominous. "You're thirty-four years old—for God's sake, start acting like it. You need to decide what you want to do with the rest of your life."

"I know this is going to come as a surprise to you, Dad, but I'm living my plans for my life."

"And what do those plans entail?"

"You're about the last person I'd share my plans with."

"Why?"

"Because I've tried telling you my plans in the past and you laughed."

"That's because they've never been serious."

Silence.

"Okay, fine," said Niall. "So you don't want to talk to me about what your plans are. But are they providing you with a reasonable income? I always thought that it was Alana's income that was paying the bills. Do you want to keep depending on your wife to support your aloha lifestyle?"

"You son of a bitch."

Niall's hand shot out and slapped Harkin across the face.

Harkin sprang to his feet, his hands balled into fists. Del put his hand against the kitchen door, ready to intercede if Harkin pulled back for a swing at Niall.

Instead, Harkin turned from his father and strode toward the tasting room's front door.

"I have another will," Niall yelled after his retreating son. "It's all ready to go. Another executed will naming Rowan as the heir. I'll destroy one of those wills. It's up to you which one I destroy. And, son, the clock is ticking."

Harkin turned at the door, his face a frozen mask. "You'd better calm down, Dad. If you get yourself all worked up like this, the clock is likely to tick down a lot faster." He yanked the door open, stepped outside, and slammed the door behind him.

Niall struggled off the stool and stood glaring at the door, breathing heavily, his hand pressed to his chest.

Del heard an engine start up, the spinning of wheels as tires sought purchase in the gravel parking lot, then the car speeding away.

Niall stood staring at the door for almost a minute. Del didn't move, knowing that another squeak from the floorboard would give him away. Niall would be livid if he knew that Del had been privy to that scene. And if Niall was angry with Del, Rowan would likely be deemed guilty by association.

Finally, Niall lowered himself onto the stool. He got out his phone and tapped. Del could see his hand trembling even from across the room.

"It's me," said Niall after a moment. "I'm at the winery. In the tasting room. Pick me up out front." A pause. "Yes, the customer entrance." He ended the call and dropped the phone into his pocket.

Several minutes ticked by, Del suddenly all too conscious of the quietness of the tasting room and the loudness of his own breath. Finally he heard a car approach and stop outside the entrance. A moment later, Nola appeared at the door. She crossed the tasting room to where Niall was seated at the bar.

"What happened to Harkin? I thought he was going to drive you back to the big house."

"He left."

"Why?"

"We argued."

"What a surprise. How did your little game with the wills play out? Which one did you show him?"

"I showed him the one favoring him. It seemed promising ..."

"And then?"

Niall scowled. "Evidently suggesting that his *partner* and their son might survive a move to Pennsylvania was the wrong tack to take."

"But now he thinks he's inheriting?"

"I told him about the two wills. I told him it was up to him which one I destroy." He drew shaking fingers across his brow. "That boy is going to be the death of me."

"You're fighting a losing battle, Niall."

"Yes," said Niall, so softly that Del could barely pick up the words. "I think you may be right."

9

Ann glanced out the front window of the West Chester townhouse to see a car slow and then pull into the driveway.

"Corey's mom is here," she called. Mike was in the kitchen putting the finishing touches on mushroom-and-crabmeat appetizers while Scott and Corey debated wine pairings.

"Can you take Ursula upstairs?" Scott called back. "She can stay in Mike's office while Mrs. Duff is here."

Ann scooped up the dachshund from where she was snoozing on Mike's favorite chair and carried her upstairs. Scott had equipped the office with a plush dog bed and new squeaky toys.

Ann placed Ursula on the bed and endured an aggrieved look as she shut the door behind her. She got downstairs just as Corey was leading his mother into the living room.

She was a pretty woman of about sixty who would have looked younger if her clothes had been a little more stylish than the plain shirtwaist dress and espadrilles she wore.

"Mom, this is Ann," said Corey. "Ann, this is my mom, Marsha Duff."

Marsha reached out a hand. "Ann, I'm so pleased to meet you. Of course, I saw the documentary Corey did about you years ago, and he told me all about what happened up in Maine, so I feel like I know you already."

"Really pleased to meet you too, Mrs. Duff."

"Please, call me Marsha."

After Corey introduced Marsha to Mike and Scott, the party moved to the back porch. A patio umbrella shaded the chairs from the still-hot rays of the sun and a few fans circulated the sultry air. Mike served the wine and appetizers, and the five of them chatted about Marsha's summer in Ocean City and her drive to West Chester.

Mike had set up the lobster pot and propane burner in the backyard. When it was time for the lobsters to go in the pot, Marsha excused herself to "powder her nose" and Mike claimed he had vital tasks to accomplish in the kitchen. Ann and Corey stayed outside to give Scott moral support.

During dinner, Ann mentioned Corey's photo of the fishing trip with his dad, and Marsha related how Corey had entertained his father, Carl, by Photoshopping larger and larger fish into the picture, culminating with Bruce the Shark from *Jaws*. Mike described a fishing outing he and Ann had taken with their parents on Lake Champlain, then encouraged Scott to share a story of a goldfish named Goldie Hawn that he had won at a fair. Under Scott's care, Goldie had lived for another twenty years.

Throughout, Marsha complimented the meal, admired the house, laughed at all the right places in their stories and offered some of her own, but she seemed ill-at-ease. As the evening progressed, Ann began to speculate that Marsha would, in fact, have preferred to be dining with Corey alone.

Also as the evening progressed, Ann became aware of an amorphous glow that hovered under the patio umbrella at

Marsha's side. It followed her across the yard when Scott took her on a tour of his vegetable and flower garden, and inside when Mike solicited her advice on a wine to serve with the lobster, although it faded in the brighter light of the yard and the kitchen.

As night fell and Mike served dessert of strawberry short-cake and coffee, Scott pointed to the lawn.

"Look, fireflies! Let's turn off the patio lights so we can enjoy them."

As soon as the lights went out, the glow next to Marsha coalesced into the barely visible figure of a man. He was positioned as if he were sitting in a chair, leaning forward, elbows on knees, hands clasped, posture relaxed. His form was too dim to discern his expression, but as the party commented on the fireflies, the heat of the evening, and the benefits of spending the hottest months of the year near the ocean, his focus never shifted from Marsha. Ann was fairly sure he was the same man she had seen in Corey's fishing trip photo.

"I'm going to start another pot of coffee," said Ann, standing.

Mike moved to stand as well. "There's still some in there. Want more?" He looked at her cup. "You've barely drunk any of that one."

She waved him back into his chair. "Just planning ahead. Corey, can you give me a hand?"

"Sure."

They went into the kitchen, and Ann closed the door to the porch.

"Corey," she whispered. "There's a spirit out there. I think it arrived with your mother."

Corey's eyes widened, and he looked out the window to where Marsha sat with Mike and Scott. "Really?"

"Yes. I'm pretty sure it's your father."

His eyebrows climbed. "My dad?"

"Yes. I saw something earlier, very faint, but I couldn't tell who it was. Actually, I couldn't even tell *what* it was. But when Scott turned out the lights, I could see it more clearly. I'm pretty sure it's your dad."

Corey stepped to the window and looked out. "What's he doing?"

"Just sitting there as far as I can see."

Marsha looked up. Corey waved to her, then stepped away from the window.

"But what's he doing here?" he asked. "Wouldn't you expect him to be back in Pittsburgh? Maybe even at the hospital where he died?"

Ann rubbed her neck. "I would have thought so, too, but I guess it's a case of him being more attached to a person than to a place."

"You think he followed Mom to Ocean City, and then to West Chester?"

"I can't think of any other explanation. I didn't want to say anything in front of your mom until I talked to you. It's one thing to tell someone that the spirit of someone they loved is present if they've paid you to do that. It's another to spring it on someone who hasn't asked."

He looked out the window again, although from a judicious distance so as not to attract Marsha's attention. A few seconds ticked by, then he said, his words slow, "Like I told you guys, Mom and Dad did everything together when he was alive. I think she'd like knowing that he's still with her." After a few more moments, he continued, his voice gaining in enthusiasm. "Maybe we could even talk with him. Has he said anything yet?"

"I don't think so."

"Could you try to mediate a conversation?"

"I could try." She glanced out the window. "I'll get the guys inside so we can have some privacy to tell Marsha what's going on." She opened the door to the porch. "Mike and Scott, can you give me a hand?"

"I never realized that coffee preparation was a four-person job," said Mike, getting to his feet.

"Can I help?" asked Marsha.

"No, thanks, I think we've got it covered," said Ann as Mike and Scott passed her on their way into the kitchen.

She closed the door and said in a lowered voice, "Can you guys pretend to make some more coffee? I'll explain later."

"Uh, sure," said Mike.

Ann and Corey stepped outside and joined Marsha at the table. Corey scanned the area around his mother, then took Marsha's hand.

"Mom, we have something to tell you."

Marsha perked up and looked expectantly from Corey to Ann. "Oh, yes?"

Ann suppressed a sigh. "Not that." She had thought it was too early for family introductions, but evidently Marsha didn't think it was too early for them to get engaged.

Corey laughed quietly, then leaned toward his mother. "You know about Ann's ability."

"Of course. Your father and I went to the premier of your documentary about it." She squeezed his hand. "We were so proud of you."

"Thanks, Mom—it meant a lot to me to have you guys there. And in fact, it looks like the two of you are still visiting me." He reached out and covered her hand with his. "Ann says that Dad is here with you."

Marsha blanched. "Where?"

"On your right," said Ann.

Marsha flinched to the left and scanned the area to her right. "What's he doing there?"

"He wants to be with you," said Corey, squeezing her hand.

"But what's he *doing*?" Marsha repeated.

Corey looked toward Ann.

"He's just sitting next to you," she said to Marsha. "He seems very ..." She cast about for the right word—*placid* didn't seem appropriate. "... comfortable."

"See if he'll talk to us," Corey said to Ann, his enthusiasm clear in his voice.

Marsha looked more stunned than enthusiastic, but presumably Corey knew his mother better than she did.

Ann addressed the amorphous form. "Mr. Duff?"

There was no response.

"Carl?"

Still no response.

"I don't think he can hear me," she said.

Marsha's expression was morphing to something more like active alarm. "Was he with me when I arrived?"

"I believe so. Something was there, but I couldn't see what it was until Scott turned off the lights."

"Is he always with me?" Now Marsha sounded a bit panicked.

"I don't know for sure, but it's possible."

Marsha's voice raised another notch. "*All the time?*"

"It would make sense," said Corey, "considering that you and Dad were always together when he was alive."

"Well, of course, when he was *alive*," said Marsha. She extracted her hand from Corey's, interlaced her fingers in her lap, and drew her shoulders in as if to make herself as inconspicuous as possible.

Corey shifted his chair next to her and put his arm around her shoulders. "Mom, are you okay?"

Marsha ignored him. "Wouldn't it be unusual if he were with me *all the time*?"

Ann was afraid they might have to have Marsha breathe into

a paper bag. "I was just speculating," she said in what she hoped was a calming tone.

"Maybe if we give it a little more time," said Corey, "Ann could mediate a conversation with Dad."

Marsha stood. "No. No, thank you. I should be going." She crossed the porch to the back door, then glanced around her nervously. "Is he still following me?"

"Well ... yes," said Ann.

"I really have to be going." Marsha opened the door and hurried into the kitchen.

Ann and Corey scrambled out of their chairs and followed her.

In the kitchen, Mike and Scott stood next to the coffeemaker.

"Thank you so much for the lovely meal," said Marsha, "but I really have to be going."

"Right now?" asked Mike.

"Is everything all right?" asked Scott.

"Yes. Yes. Fine. Thank you so much for the lovely meal," Marsha repeated.

She grabbed her purse from one of the kitchen chairs and the four of them, plus Carl, trailed her through the living room to the front door.

"Mom, hold on," said Corey. "You seem a little out of sorts. I'll drive you to the hotel."

"Yes, that would probably be a good idea. Mike and Scott, thank you so much for the lovely meal." She gave a somewhat manic laugh. "Although I think I already said that."

"It's been our pleasure," said Scott. "We're so happy you came."

"Yes," said Mike, "really glad you were able to visit."

Marsha was already out the front door, almost running toward her car. She glanced periodically to her right. Carl, who became more visible the further Marsha got from the porch lights, drifted at her side.

Mike turned to Ann. "What just happened?"

"I'll explain later," said Ann.

"Can you pick me up when I've gotten her settled at the hotel?" Corey asked Ann.

"Sure."

"I'll give you a call when she's calmed down." He kissed Ann on the cheek and then hurried after his mother.

Ann, Mike, and Scott stood on the porch and watched Marsha's car disappear down the street, Corey at the wheel and Carl in the back seat.

"What did you guys say to her?" asked Mike.

"I told her that Carl was following her," Ann said, then recapped the exchange on the patio with Marsha.

Mike stuffed his hands into his pockets and glanced in the direction the car had gone. "I suppose not everyone is thrilled by the idea of being followed by a dead spouse."

Scott shuddered. "Certainly not all the time. Everyone wants some privacy now and then."

10

Del opened the backyard grill and transferred the steaks to a pair of blue-rimmed plates that already held potato salad and corn on the cob. He carried the plates to the picnic table, which he had set with Rowan's favorite red-and-white gingham tablecloth and napkins. The sun was low in the sky, but the evening was still hot, and he was glad that the big oak tree provided some shade.

Rowan had half-heartedly suggested setting the table for three and inviting Harkin over, but Del told her he was looking forward to having some time with just the two of them. Considering that they spent most of their waking hours at the winery, he had all too little time alone with his wife. More importantly, he couldn't very well share what he had heard in the tasting room if Harkin was with them.

He went to the living room, where she was lying on the couch. "Dinner's served!"

"You're nice to make dinner." She swung her legs off the couch and tried to push herself up. "I'm stuck."

He took her elbow and helped her up, then, when they got to

the picnic table, helped her swing her legs over the bench and under the table.

She shook the napkin out and laid it across the mound of her stomach. "Steak? What's the occasion?"

The steak had been a splurge. No one would accuse Niall Lynch of overpaying his staff, even his daughter and son-in-law, and they were trying to save money for some finishing touches on the baby's room.

"You've been craving red meat lately," he said, "and that seemed as good an occasion as any."

He opened a red blend from a neighboring winery that they had been wanting to check out. He poured a quarter-sized portion for Rowan and a full-size portion for himself. They sipped.

"Decent," he said gamely.

She wrinkled her nose. "It's way too fruity." She set the glass aside. "I'm saving my remaining daily thimbleful of wine for something that's *really* decent."

Del retrieved a Lynch Cab Sauv from the house and poured Rowan a fresh quarter glass.

He tried to engage her with discussion of an article he had read in *WineMaker*, and questions about the effect of the heat on the grapes, but she seemed tired and distracted. Although one of the things that had first charmed Del about Rowan was the amount of food such a slender woman could put away, tonight she picked at her meal.

He nodded toward her steak. "Too rare? Want me to put it back on the grill for a little bit?"

"No, thanks. It's delicious. I'm just not that hungry."

"Everything okay?"

"Yes, fine." As if to reassure him, she nibbled on her ear of corn, then set it back down on her plate.

When she declared that she had eaten as much as she wanted, Del cleared away the dishes.

He had hoped for an opening in their conversation to describe the argument he had overheard in the Cellar. The moment hadn't arrived, but Del was determined to tell Rowan tonight. It seemed obvious that the likelihood of Niall choosing her as his heir had never been better. With the tension between the siblings and the sad news of Niall's prognosis, she needed some good news.

He returned to the table with a glass of port for himself and a decaf espresso for Rowan and sat down next to her on the bench.

"Niall and Harkin came into the Cellar this morning," he said.

"Oh, yeah?" she asked apathetically. "What were they doing there?"

"I think your dad had brought Harkin there to give him a pep talk."

She grimaced, her eyes on the coffee. "I'll bet."

"They got into an argument—as you might expect. I was in the kitchen, and I didn't want to get involved. They didn't know I was there." He paused. "I think your dad is favoring you as the heir."

She looked up, her expression wary. "Really?"

Del recapped what he had heard, including the fact that Niall had two executed wills.

"He has two wills?" asked Rowan. "Can he even do that? Wouldn't his lawyer object?"

"Even if the lawyer objected, you know how insistent your father can be once he sets his mind on something."

"True." She was silent for a moment, then asked, "He really agreed with Nola when she said he was fighting a losing battle?"

"He did."

She gnawed the corner of her thumbnail. "But if he really has two executed wills and just needs to decide which one to destroy, there's no guarantee that when it comes down to it, he won't choose Harkin. He said he'd make the decision in two weeks. Maybe Harkin will redeem himself."

"Can you imagine that happening?"

"No," she said slowly, "I can't." After a moment, she continued, her voice sad. "Harkin thought he was a shoo-in when Dad showed him the will naming him as the heir, but he threw away his chance because of Dad's attitude toward Alana and Kepi. Harkin has his issues but you've got to admire him for defending his family that way." She picked up Del's glass and took a tiny sip of port. "You're sure about what you heard?" He could tell that she was trying to tamp down a flicker of excitement.

"Yes."

"And are you sure you should be telling me this?" She forced a laugh. "You know what happens when you talk out of turn."

He groaned. "I know, I know. But this isn't the infamous grape debacle. Or near-debacle. And of course I wouldn't tell anyone other than you what I heard," he mustered a smile, "even in casual conversation. But the next two weeks are going to be important, and I wanted you to have all the information you could. I think Niall has finally realized that Harkin will never be a suitable person to run Lynch."

"And Nola also seemed to think that Dad had come to that conclusion?"

Del nodded. "That was my impression."

"It is Lynch *and Son* Winery," she said, still trying to temper her excitement.

He smiled. "There's no reason that the heir couldn't change the name if she wanted to."

She smiled back at him. "Lynch and Berendt."

"Lynch, Berendt, and Berendt-Lynch," he said, patting her stomach.

She raised an eyebrow. "Now it's starting to sound like a law firm. Maybe we should steer away from names entirely."

"How about the One Captain of the Ship Winery?"

She laughed. "We could change the name of the Cellar to the Bridge."

"And the Curragh to the Skiff."

"How about the Ark?"

He thought for a moment. "The Bilge?"

She laughed again, then her smile faded. "But what am I supposed to do with the information? Dad doesn't know you heard the conversation, so I can't really bring it up with him."

"It would be awkward."

"Maybe I'll ask Nola about it."

He stifled a sigh. He respected the close relationship Rowan had with her aunt, but just as he was happier excluding Harkin from dinner, he would have been happier excluding Nola from the decisions that impacted his and Rowan's lives. After a brief hesitation, he said, "Whatever you think is best. I just wanted you to know. I hope that telling you was the right thing to do."

Rowan cupped his cheek in her hand. "I know you always do what you think is right, sweetheart. Or," she said with an attempt at a teasing smile, "at least you never do what you think is wrong."

Del put his hand over Rowan's. He would have believed her not so long ago: believed that she thought only the best of him, trusted him enough to share her secrets. But that belief had been shaken by her unexplained absences and the visit to the darkened house on Larch Street.

"That's what marriage is all about," he said. "Always trying to do right by the other person."

Her smile faded as her hand dropped from his cheek. "Of

course it is." She shifted away from him on the bench, making room to swing her legs over. "Why don't you let me clean up?" She picked up a couple of plates and headed for the house.

"There's ice cream for dessert," he called after her.

"I'll bring it out," she called back over her shoulder.

She stepped inside, and Del could see her through the window over the sink, rinsing the dishes, then disappearing in the direction of the dishwasher. A minute passed, and the next time he saw her through the window, she had her phone to her ear.

She couldn't wait until after dessert to call Nola?

Del turned away from the house and downed the last of his port. As far as he was concerned, the day couldn't come soon enough that his slip up with their grape supplier faded from the family memory … or that he could hear a reference to it without feeling the twinge of resentment that still struck him a month later. If only his father-in-law wasn't the grudge-bearing Niall Lynch.

DEL HAD BEEN at his desk in the Cellar when Niall appeared. Mildly irritated was usually the best Del could hope for from Niall, but now his father-in-law's flushed face and narrowed eyes suggested that he was struggling with a more volatile emotion.

"What's up, Niall?"

"What's up? I hear that Sebastian is looking for buyers for his grapes. For *our* grapes." He leaned over Del, so close that Del could feel the puffs of breath on his cheek. "Would you know anything about that?"

"No!" Del pushed his chair back to clear Niall and got to his feet. "Don't you think that I would have told you if I had heard anything about that? I just saw Sebastian last weekend. I ran into him at Victory, we had a few beers. He didn't mention anything to me."

"And what did you and Sebastian talk about over your beers?"

"The weather ... the Phillies ... his new pickup truck. Nothing important. Nothing about the grapes."

"The fact that you plan to take Lynch and Son organic wasn't important?"

"What? No, I never said that."

"You didn't say that organic was our new direction?"

"Well, yes, *a* new direction—"

"You didn't say to Sebastian, and I was given this as a direct quote, *organic is the way we're going from here on out*?"

"Well, sure, but I didn't mean Lynch specifically."

"And of course Sebastian should have known that by 'we' you didn't actually mean 'we.' Unfortunately, he thought you meant Lynch. And since he doesn't grow organic grapes, he's found new buyers for the non-organic grapes that we had contracted for."

"He can't do that!"

"He can if he thinks that Lynch and Son is backing out on an arrangement that's been in place for decades—a relationship that was established by a handshake between my father and Sebastian's."

"Honestly, Niall, I don't know how he could have thought I was talking about Lynch. He knows I don't make the decisions at this winery."

Niall laughed again, and the laugh had a nasty edge to it. "That's for damn sure. You may be a decent winemaker, Del, but you have shit for brains when it comes to business." His scowl returned. "And now I have to try to sweet talk Sebastian into letting us keep our grapes."

"Well, if anyone could *sweet-talk* Sebastian," said Del, not bothering to keep the sarcasm out of his voice, "you're certainly the man for it, Niall."

Niall stabbed a finger into Del's chest. "You keep your mouth shut—about this winery's plans, about our wines, about our family—and I'll *think* about letting you keep your job."

Niall stormed out, leaving Del shaking with anger and nerves. He had no illusions that being married to the owner's daughter offered any job protection. Niall Lynch had already proven once that one wrong step—if it was a big enough step—was enough to send even the best winemaker packing.

DEL WISHED he had brought the bottle of port out to the picnic table with him, although if the heat didn't lift, he might switch to a cold beer.

Niall had managed to talk Sebastian's grapes back to Lynch, although he made sure Del knew it was not only a humiliating exercise but an expensive one. Sebastian had required a signed contract for the grapes, at a price slightly higher than under the former handshake agreement.

Del was considering going inside to see what was taking Rowan so long when he heard the back door screen squeak open and then clap closed.

She crossed the yard to the table. She had brought a tray out, and began putting the few remaining plates and utensils on it.

"What about dessert?" he asked.

"Oh," she said with a start. "I'm sorry—I forgot. I'm not very hungry. Can we have it later?"

"Sure. What do you want to do now?"

She scanned the table, as though she might see a fork or salt shaker she had missed. "I thought I'd run down to Philly to see Nola."

"Weren't you just talking to her on the phone?"

"Yes," she said, still not meeting his eyes. "But sometimes it's nicer to talk to someone in person."

"Talking in general is nice."

Del had tried to keep his tone noncommittal, but he must not have succeeded.

Rowan shot him a look, then lifted the tray. "I might be a couple of hours. Don't wait for me for dessert."

"I'm not that hungry, either." He stood. "I can get that," he said, taking the tray from her.

"Thanks, sweetheart."

He followed her inside. After Rowan got her purse, they crossed the drive to the two-car detached garage. He hoisted up the heavy door, then stood by as she backed out. She blew him a kiss and disappeared down the road.

After closing the garage door, Del went to the dining room and poured himself a double shot of bourbon. He wandered into the living room and dropped into a chair.

What Rowan said was true—he did always try to do the right thing. It was his tendency to blurt out whatever popped into his head that got him in trouble. If not for that, would Nola always have been Rowan's first choice of confidante? And would his wife have been looking for company at 46 Larch Street?

11

Ann paged through an issue of *Main Line Today*, waiting for Corey's call, when she heard the front door of the townhouse open and he appeared in the living room doorway.

She set aside the magazine. "I thought you were going to call me to pick you up at your mom's hotel?"

"It turns out it's only about a twenty-minute walk, and I didn't mind having some time to clear my head. Any wine left?"

Ann pushed herself off the couch. "There's always wine left."

Corey followed her to the kitchen. She poured him a glass and topped up her own. Then they returned to the living room and settled into the couch.

"How's she doing?" Ann asked.

"She's calmed down a bit." Corey downed a slug of wine. "It turns out that the reason she wanted to see me was to tell me she's thinking of getting remarried."

"Really?"

"Yeah. While she was in Ocean City, she met up with an old friend—actually an old friend of both her and my dad—whose wife died a couple of years ago. They started spending some time together—" He gave a rueful laugh. "I guess I should say 'dating,' although it might take me a little while to think of my mom as someone who dates. Anyhow, they started talking about getting married. She wanted to tell me in person because she was afraid I might be upset."

"Are you?"

"No, I'm happy for her. Larry sounds like a nice guy. I suppose I must have met him when I was a kid, but I don't remember him. In fact, Mom invited me to spend some time at her place in Ocean City so I can get to know him better."

"That's a good idea."

"Yeah. I can do some of the work that's left on the documentary from there."

He took a more moderate sip of wine. "It would be great for her to have someone to do stuff with. Turns out that Larry actually lives not far from her in Pittsburgh, so combining households wouldn't be too disruptive. They'd both still be near their friends and the places they know."

The thought of Corey's invitation for Ann to move to L.A. drifted through her mind. She couldn't get much further from her friends and the places she knew best without leaving the continent.

"But, as you can imagine," Corey continued, "the idea that Dad might have been accompanying her and Larry on their dates threw her for a loop."

"Yeah, that would be awkward."

"I hate to see Mom's budding romance nipped in the bud by my dad being a third wheel." He looked toward Ann. "Maybe you could talk to Dad about it? Encourage him to move along?"

"I can't communicate with him."

"Maybe he can actually hear us and just isn't letting on."

"That's not the impression I got. I suppose it's possible, but I don't know what I'd say to him. I didn't even know him."

"Maybe he could hear me or Mom if we talked to him."

"Maybe."

"But you don't think so."

"I didn't get a sense he was all that aware of what was going on around him."

"He's ignoring us?"

"Not on purpose. Think of all the living people who aren't capable of seeing their dead family members and friends. It doesn't mean they're purposely ignoring them."

"True." After a moment, he continued. "I never thought I'd say this about my own father, but how can we get him away from Mom?"

"I don't know."

Corey gave a short laugh. "If you don't, who would?"

His tone was light, but the words stung.

"I'm not an exorcist," she said, a tinge of irritation creeping into her voice. "I can see spirits if they want to be seen, I can try to talk to them. But if they don't want to hear me, or can't, there's not much I can do."

"Maybe if you had a little more time to try. You could come to Ocean City—Mom said you'd be welcome."

"Corey, I'm not convinced your mom's really ready to try to contact your dad. Maybe it would be better to wait until she's back in Pittsburgh. In fact, I might have better luck if I tried to contact him in the house they shared. Why don't you go to Ocean City and focus on getting to know your prospective stepfather?"

"Yeah, okay," he said, his tone despondent. "Let's give that a try."

She reached over and squeezed his hand.

There were two things that could ruin the rest of her summer. One was to be crowded into a shore house at the height of the summer season with a bunch of people she didn't know. The other was having two of those people expect her to solve a problem she was quite sure was beyond her abilities.

12

"Come!" Niall called in response to the knock on the office door.

The door opened, letting in a wash of noise from the Cellar's tasting room: a late-morning crowd that hadn't let a little drizzle stop them from a pre-lunch wine tasting.

Rowan popped her head around the door. "Ready for me, Dad?"

"Yes. Have a seat."

She lowered herself into a straight-back chair facing his desk. She had always been a graceful person, but he could tell she was starting to struggle with the weight of her pregnancy.

"How are you feeling?" he asked.

"I'm fine." After a moment, she asked, "How are you feeling?"

"Fine." In fact, he had not slept at all the previous night, and had barely been able to catch his breath when he finally gave up and swung his legs out of bed. But there was no need to tell her that. He leaned back and laced his fingers over his stomach. "I wanted to talk with you about the inheritance situation." He paused, giving her a chance to comment. When she was silent, he continued. "I want to give you and Harkin a chance to talk with me individually. Ask any questions you might have. Share any perspectives you might want to share."

She nodded, but still didn't speak.

"So ... do you have any questions? Or perspectives?"

She drew a deep breath. "I wouldn't call it a perspective, just a confirmation of what I think you already know. I believe I'm the right person to head up the winery. I have the expertise, I have the experience, and, most importantly, I have the desire. Harkin has never had the desire to be involved in the winery, and he's built a life for himself in Hawaii—a life, as far as I can tell, that he's quite happy with. I'm afraid of what would happen if he inherited. I don't think Lynch would be around for another generation—maybe not even another year. And, as I said before, if Harkin inherited the winery with the plan to sell it to Kepi when Kepi turns twenty-one, and for Kepi to sell it to cash in, I don't think there'd be anything left to cash in. You can leave the winery to someone who has no interest in selling, whose only interest is to make sure it continues and prospers. Me."

Niall gazed at his daughter and thought back to the day Rowan had been born. Katherine, his late wife, had been so sure that she wouldn't get pregnant again and that Harkin would be their only child. Niall had lived under that assumption for eight years, had grown used to the idea.

When his second child had been a girl, he had had a moment of disappointment, but then he saw the benefit. With a girl who was eight years younger than her brother, there would be no question about the succession plan for Lynch and Son.

Then Harkin had ... turned into Harkin. And his daughter had stepped into the role he had thought his son would fill.

He dropped his eyes to his hands. "I hope you know how much I appreciate your obvious devotion to the business and the effort you've put into making it a success. You've done a wonderful job with the vineyard." He looked up. "Your grandfather would be proud. I'm proud."

He was surprised when tears sprang to Rowan's eyes.

Flustered, he leaned forward. "I didn't mean to upset you—"

She smiled through the tears. "I'm not upset. I don't think you've ever told me that you're proud of me before."

"Ah. Well. I should have."

She leaned forward. "I want to *keep* making you proud. I want to make sure that the winery prospers, and that the wines we produce under the Lynch name keep making you proud, as well."

He quirked his mouth up. "At least you can count on the winemaker."

She returned the smile, if a bit cautiously. "Yes."

"Can you keep him in line?"

Her cheeks flushed. She was silent for a beat, and when she spoke, her voice was steady. "If you're talking about the issue with Sebastian, I know Del feels terrible about the danger he put the business in."

"And the money he cost us."

After a moment, she said, "Yes, that too."

"He needs to be more discreet."

"He would never intentionally do anything to harm the business. I hope you know that."

He waved a dismissive hand. "Yes, yes, I know. Just something to keep an eye on."

She smiled gamely. "I will. Del and I both will."

"And what about the baby coming?" he asked.

Her smile flickered. "What about that?"

"You don't think that will take time away from the winery?"

"I can take care of a baby and the winery at the same time. The fact that Del and I both work here will make it much easier for us than for most parents. I've even thought of how I could set up a place for the baby in our workspace. Customers already love that Lynch is a family business. They would love to meet the baby."

"Do you know the gender yet?"

Rowan's expression closed down like a shade being pulled over a brightly lit window. "No, Dad, I don't know the gender."

He shrugged. "It's no matter. Just curious. We'll all know soon enough. So ... any questions for me?"

"No."

"Any other information you'd like to share?"

"No. I've said what I wanted to say."

He leaned forward and stretched out his hand across the desk.

After a surprised pause, she reached out and took it.

"I'm happy for your baby," he said. "I've probably not said that before, either."

She squeezed his hand. "I appreciate that."

"It puts my mind at rest to know that whoever the heir is, there is another generation behind waiting to pick up the reins."

She forced a laugh and shook her head. "Dad, you know it would be nice if you were happy for me and Del just because we were having a baby, not because it provides a better succession plan."

"Of course. But still."

She sighed. "I'll say it one more time. An extra generation only matters if it's on the side of the family that wants to keep the winery. I don't think Kepi is any more interested in the winery than Harkin is."

He released her hand, dropped back into his chair, and heaved a sigh. "Yes. I think you're right."

13

The day after the abbreviated lobster dinner, Ann puttered around the townhouse, kept inside by a steady drizzle and by the fact that she had loaned the Forester to Corey to take Marsha out to lunch. Ann had passed on an invitation to join them. She not only suspected that Marsha would be more comfortable without her there, but she herself didn't feel like spending an hour either trying to communicate with the uncommunicative Carl, or trying to pretend he wasn't there.

When Corey returned to the townhouse, Ann asked how Marsha was doing.

"She's calmed down a bit, but is still a little freaked out by the situation with Dad. I've decided to accept the invite to spend some time in Ocean City—I'm going to be riding back with her. We'll probably be leaving shortly." After a pause, he added, his voice hopeful, "The offer still stands for you to come along."

"Thanks, but ..." She took a breath, then plowed ahead. "I heard from Del Berendt that Nola Lynch has moved out of the guest house at the Lynch winery and that it's available for inspection."

"Still thinking about that?"

"It's an option."

"A better option than L.A.?"

"I'm still thinking about it, Corey—about *all* the options."

He sighed. "Okay." After a moment, he added, "When are you going to the winery?"

"I can wait until you head out."

He ventured a smile. "You don't want company?"

"Well, sure, but I thought you and your mom were leaving for the shore."

"If we can go to the winery right now, it shouldn't be a problem. Mom commented on how many cute shops there are in West Chester. She can keep herself occupied until we're done."

Ann glanced out the window. "It's still raining."

"Rain will not stand in my mother's way if there's shopping to be had."

Ann wondered whether Corey's interest in accompanying her to the winery meant that he was gaining enthusiasm for that choice or that he saw it as a chance to talk her out of it. "Sounds good."

Half an hour later, Ann pulled her Forester into the Lynch parking lot and parked near a tour bus with *Krapf Coaches* stenciled on the side. She and Corey climbed out into a light drizzle.

Ann hooked the knapsack she used as a handbag over one shoulder. "Del said he'd meet us in the tasting room."

They stepped into the Cellar. All the seats at the bar were taken, all the tables were full. Behind the bar, a woman Ann assumed to be Rowan Lynch was arranging glasses in front of Del; Del was filling the glasses; and Justin was carrying a tray holding several flights to one of the tables.

Del caught sight of Ann and Corey and raised a finger—*one minute*—then spoke to Rowan. She grimaced and replied, Del looked chagrined, then the woman shook her head and hurried across the room to where Ann and Corey stood by the door.

By the time she reached them, a bit breathless, her grimace had relaxed into a welcoming smile. "I'm Rowan Lynch. Del says you're here to see the guest house."

"Yes," said Ann, "but it looks like you have your hands full. I can come back another time."

"It's no problem." She laughed. "At some point, having another person behind the bar isn't that helpful—" She patted her bulging stomach. "—and my tray-carrying duties are temporarily suspended. I can take you over to the guest house."

Ann smiled. "Thanks, I appreciate it."

Rowan pulled a bright yellow rain slicker from a coat rack by the door and shrugged into it, then grabbed a paper bag hidden behind the rack. Ann and Corey followed her outside and to a path off the parking lot marked by a small sign: *The Curragh.*

Corey gestured toward the sign. "What's that?"

Rowan said something that sounded like *KER-ruck.* "It's a traditional Irish boat."

"Perfect name for it," said Ann. "It does look like a boat, and the lawn is the ocean."

"We Lynches do love to tap into our Irish roots to name things. That's why the tasting room building is called *Cellar Fíona*—wine cellar—although everyone just calls it the Cellar. But we're inconsistent. If we followed through, the pond would be called *lochán*, but that sounded a little too grand. We didn't want to be accused of false advertising, so we call it the Tarn, even though that's English."

They reached the Curragh and climbed the steps to the porch, where a pair of chairs and a cafe table provided a view across the Tarn to the vineyard beyond. The building was narrow, about a dozen feet wide, which reinforced its likeness to a boat. Even before Rowan opened the front door, Ann was admiring the interior, which was on full display through the windows and French doors. The three of them stepped inside.

In contrast to the buff and chocolate brown exterior with its black accents, the interior walls were painted a clean, bright white. Along one side of the sitting area was a comfortable-looking leather couch dotted with brightly colored pillows, on the other a pair of puffy upholstered chairs. Between the chairs stood a table fashioned from a round ceramic planter topped with a brass tray. An extension of black soapstone counter separated the sitting area from the kitchen, which was outfitted with white cabinetry and a European-style white enamel gas stove.

"It's a great space," said Ann. "It comes furnished?"

"You could take it fully furnished, or we can remove the furniture if you wanted to bring your own."

"I could never do that good a job myself," said Ann.

"My aunt worked with the architect who designed it," said Rowan. "She also did all the decorating. Feel free to poke around." She raised the paper bag. "I'm going down to the Tarn to feed the ducks. If you need anything or have any questions, just give a yell." She slipped out the door and crossed the lawn toward the dock, around which an expectant group had already formed.

Ann passed from the sitting area into the kitchen and opened a cabinet to find it stocked with a multi-colored inventory of plates, bowls, and mugs. Cabinet facings disguised the refrigerator and dishwasher. The kitchen area was just big enough to accommodate a wooden table surrounded by four rustic wooden chairs.

Corey clicked one of the gas burners on and off. "Nice."

"Yeah. Really nice."

Past the kitchen was a simple but elegantly appointed bathroom, with a laundry area opposite.

"Just a washer?" asked Corey.

Ann peered at the machine. "It's actually a combination washer and dryer."

"No kidding. Fancy."

At the back of the house, a built-in closet and dressers lined one wall of the bedroom and another set of French doors led to a back porch.

"It's a little small," said Corey.

"Are you kidding? It's perfect. Everything I need and nothing I don't."

He looked around the bedroom. "Not much storage space."

Ann sighed. Apparently Corey had insisted on coming along so he could play devil's advocate. "I don't need much storage space. Most of my things are still in the Adirondacks, and I'm sure Mike and Scott would let me keep some stuff at their place. And there's plenty of room for your stuff when you visit."

Corey peered into the closet. "Yeah, there'd be room for my suitcase in here."

"I'll even reserve a couple of drawers for you."

He slid the door shut. "So you like it?"

Ann tried to moderate her enthusiasm. "It is really nice."

"Do you think you'll take it?"

"I really want to get out of Mike and Scott's townhouse. I could stay here for a bit while I decide what to do long-term."

He nodded. "Yeah."

She followed him back down the short hall and through the kitchen to the sitting area. As they stepped outside, she pulled up the hood of her raincoat. They crossed the lawn to the dock where Rowan stood, empty paper bag crinkled in her hand.

"What do you think?" asked Rowan.

"It's a great place," said Ann. "How much is it per month?"

Rowan quoted a price that was steep but not unreasonable for the accommodations and setting.

"Can I let you know tomorrow?" asked Ann.

"Sure. We'd love to have the place go to a couple who comes with the recommendation of customers as loyal as Mike and Scott."

Ann felt her face flush. She didn't look toward Corey as she said, "I would be the official tenant."

"Oh," said Rowan, flustered. "Of course. Sorry. I just assumed ..."

Corey's laugh sounded a little forced. "No problem. How long is the rental term for?"

Rowan glanced at Corey, then said to Ann, "I think Del had planned to make the term a year, but—"

"A year is fine," said Ann. "I'll let you know tomorrow."

Ann and Corey headed back to the parking lot. The drizzle had progressed to a steady rain, and as the tour bus contingent emerged from the Cellar, umbrellas bloomed red, yellow, and blue against the dreary backdrop.

They climbed into Ann's Forester.

"You'd be committing for a year—" said Corey.

"Yeah, I heard."

"Are you mad I asked? It seemed like an important piece of information to factor in."

"Corey, if I decide to move into the Curragh, I'd love to host you here for however often you can get back to the East Coast, but it would be *my* home. I'd feel better asking questions about the terms and conditions of the agreement myself."

He shifted his gaze to the window. "If you're thinking of signing a year-long rental agreement, I guess you've already made your decision about L.A."

She puffed out an exasperated breath. "I haven't made my decision. I have to admit I'm leaning heavily in favor of taking the Curragh. But if my plans changed, I'm sure I could compensate Del and Rowan for breaking the lease."

He raised his hands. "Okay. I don't mean to be pushy about it."

Ann started the engine and turned the Forester toward West Chester.

Corey got out his phone. "I'll let Mom know we're on our way back."

As they approached the Hotel Warner, Corey said, "You can just drop me at the corner."

Ann pulled over. "I hope you have a good time in Ocean City."

"Thanks."

"And I'm sorry I can't give you a definitive answer about L.A. I'm thinking about it. Really."

"Are you going to take the Curragh?"

After a pause, she said, "Yes, I think I will. Temporarily, at least."

He nodded, then heaved a sigh. "Do you need help moving in?"

She marshaled a smile. "I don't think I'll need to bring more than a toothbrush."

"Yeah." He leaned over and gave her a kiss. "Let me know if you change your mind about the shore."

"Maybe I'll rent the flight school plane and fly out for a day."

"That would be great."

He climbed out of the car and Ann watched him walk toward the hotel, his shoulders hunched against the rain.

Did it rain like this in L.A.? She doubted it.

Would she miss these dreary Pennsylvania days?

She thought she would.

14

Nola pulled her BMW up to the back door of the Cellar.

"Niall, are you sure you can't do whatever it is you want to do back at the big house?" she asked, her irritation clear. "The exhibit Rowan and I are going to is in Center City, and we might grab dinner afterwards, so I'll be away for a couple of hours at least. Won't you want to be home before then?"

"I'm tired of being at the house," said Niall. "Besides, aren't you the one who's always saying I shouldn't take my work home with me?"

"This is not exactly the scenario I intended, as you are well aware."

"I'll be fine."

"How are you going to get home?"

"I'll walk."

"You'll walk?"

"I'll take my time. I'll be fine." He opened his door and climbed out.

She gave an exasperated sigh. "Okay. If you need anything, call Del. Or Harkin. He's right up the hill."

"I won't need anything."

"I'm sure you won't," she muttered. She pulled away almost before Niall slammed the door shut.

Niall watched the taillights of Nola's car disappear down the road. It pained him to think that he would spend whatever time was left to him arguing with his sister. He wished she could have stayed in the Curragh. A week ago, that had been ideal: close enough that he could call on her as needed, but far enough away that he had some privacy. Now, the closer the help, the better.

He had intended to go through some of the older winery records, discarding those that were no longer useful, cataloguing those that were. But he came across a box of albums that his mother, and later his wife, had created: snapshots taken on the property, newspaper clippings about Lynch wines, sketches of label designs and examples of the final product. Two hours had slipped away when he put the last of the albums back in the box.

He stood, intending to move it back to the shelf where he had found it, but even the effort of levering himself upright set his heart thumping. He lowered himself back into the chair. He'd ask Del to put the box back tomorrow.

He leaned back, waiting for his heart to quiet. Then he sat forward and pulled two envelopes from his jacket pocket. He removed a document from each and laid them side by side on the desk. He was so tired that the text swam in front of his eyes, but he had read the two documents so many times that he nearly had them memorized.

He thought back to his conversations with Harkin and Rowan.

Niall had thought Harkin was coming around, was starting to see that he could make the winery a success if he just set his mind to it. Then the tenuous connection that Niall thought might be forming between himself and his son had been severed over their argument about moving Harkin's family to Pennsylvania.

Niall had thought the conversation with Rowan was going well—she had obviously been gratified when he expressed his appreciation for the work she had done for the winery—until he asked about the baby.

Maybe he should have had Nola sit in on the meetings. She understood his children better than he did. He drew in a breath and didn't bother to suppress the coughing fit that followed. Almost everyone understood his children better than he did.

He folded the documents and returned them to their envelopes. As he folded down the flap of the second envelope, he felt a tiny sting. Blood welled out of a paper cut on his finger.

He swore under his breath. With the blood thinners he was taking, even a little cut made a mess. He had switched from a razor to an electric shaver when he got fed up with the clean-up needed whenever he nicked himself.

He dropped the envelopes back on the desk and pulled a tissue from a box on the desk and wrapped it around his finger. In the process, he left a smear of blood on the sleeve of his jacket.

"Goddammit," he muttered. Maybe if he got the sleeve in some water before the stain set, he could get it out. He wondered whether he should add some soap to the water and almost picked up the phone to call Nola, but then decided against it. If the stain didn't come out, he'd just throw the jacket away. It wasn't like he needed to preserve his wardrobe.

He pushed his chair back from his desk and stood. He steadied himself, hoping that his racing heart would calm. Thank God Nola had been willing to move into the big house. Much as he hated to admit it, he wouldn't have wanted to be there alone, and he sure as hell wasn't moving into one of those goddamn warehouses for the elderly and infirm. He had spent his whole life on this land. He had every intention of dying here as well.

When he had told Nola he would be fine on his own, he had believed it. Before she had dropped him off at the Cellar, he was fresh from a nap and a dose of pain meds. Now he was no longer sure he could get back to the big house unassisted. Although Del was less than five minutes away in Unionville, Niall didn't want to call him for something as mundane as an escort home. At the same time, he didn't relish the idea of spending the night propped up in his desk chair. Two nights earlier, he had been reduced to sleeping in the chair in his office at the big house after Nola had refused to take him to his room.

Gradually his heartbeat slowed. He would get outside and see how he felt. If necessary, he would call Del.

He was reaching for the desk light when the phone rang. He could let it go to voicemail—after all, business hours were long past—but he was damned if he was going to allow himself the same cavalier attitude about the business that Harkin had. He lowered himself into the chair and picked up the receiver.

"Lynch and Son Winery."

"Hello, Niall." It was a man's voice, low and gruff, vaguely familiar.

"Yes. Who is this?"

"You don't recognize your old colleague?"

Niall floundered for a moment before he realized the caller's identity. He scowled. "Henry Tollman. What a surprise."

"I imagine it is a surprise. It's been some time."

"Twenty years." Jesus—twenty years. He thought back to the last time he had seen Henry. The corded wrists, extending from the sleeves of a worn denim shirt, bound in handcuffs. The usually handsome features twisted in anger not only at the police who had come for him, but at Niall for not interceding.

"Actually twenty-four years," said Henry. "But who's counting."

"You, evidently."

"Well, yes." Henry lapsed into silence. Niall had no intention of filling it.

Finally, Henry continued, his voice softer. "I didn't mean to start out this conversation with an argument, Niall. I wanted to call because I thought it was time we put those twenty-four years behind us."

"I put them behind me long ago." After a pause, Niall added, "I would have thought it would be a little harder for you to put them behind you."

"I did my time—legally and personally. After I got out, I traveled. I learned a lot about the world, and about myself. I straightened myself out. I've been living on the West Coast—San Francisco. Now I'm ready to come home. I haven't had a decent hoagie in years." There was a smile in the voice, but when Niall didn't respond, Henry continued, the voice now sad. "I can't undo what I did, but I can try to lead a life that makes some small amends for it. One of those things is to get in touch with the people I wronged, tell them that I regret my actions."

If he plans to make amends with me, Niall thought sourly, *he'd better hurry.*

As if sensing Niall's thoughts, Henry said, "I heard you're ill, Niall. That's a bitch—I was sorry to hear it."

"Everyone's got to go sometime."

"You have all your affairs in order?"

"That's none of your goddamned business."

A sigh. "That's true. In any case, I'm coming back to Pennsylvania, probably in the next few weeks. And when I get there, I'm coming to the winery and I'm hoping I'll have a chance to talk with you. Nola, too."

"As you well know, the next couple of weeks will be a busy time for us, getting ready for the harvest. Those of us at the winery will be too occupied to entertain a visitor. What you and Nola do is your own business."

Niall was surprised by a soft chuckle on the other end of the line. "Still the same old Niall."

He thought back to his argument with Harkin. "A tiger can't change its stripes, as they say."

"*I've* changed," countered Henry.

"Found a way to keep your temper in line?"

"Yes, I have."

"Got over your savior complex?"

"Is that what you think it was?"

"What else would you call it? Taking the law into your own hands, and over what? A stolen purse."

"Over someone I cared about being hurt."

"She was fine."

"She was fine eventually—at least that's what I understand. I didn't get to hear it from her. That's not the point."

"What is the point?"

"She was your sister—still is, I might add." Now Henry's voice wasn't so friendly. "You didn't care what happened to her. You just wanted to protect your precious winery from a little bad PR."

"A little bad PR? That's what you call a manslaughter conviction?"

"This isn't about me, Niall. It's about you and how you treated the people around you. And if you have no desire to 'change your stripes,' then I suspect it's the way you still treat the people around you. It started with Nola. How about with Rowan? Do you care more about your daughter than you did about your sister?"

"You're the last person who should lecture me about—"

"Are you going to care about your granddaughter? No, because she's not the almighty 'Son' that you're staking your legacy on."

"What are you talking about?"

There was silence for a moment, then a chortle that swelled into a full-throated laugh. Gradually the laugh subsided, but the voice still held a smile. "So you didn't know. And why do you think your daughter didn't tell you she was having a girl?"

"How do you know this?" Before Henry could answer, Niall continued. "You couldn't know that. You're just saying what you think will get my goat. You claim you've changed, but you haven't. Well, you know what my *almighty* legacy is going to be? That the winery continues to uphold the traditions that my father and I established. If you come back to Pennsylvania, don't come to Lynch. You're not welcome here."

He pulled himself forward, slammed the receiver back in the cradle, and collapsed back in the chair.

His heart was thundering. He tried to take deep breaths to calm it, but every breath triggered a spasm of coughing. If the doctor really thought that Niall had a year, he was kidding himself.

Finally, when he could once again breathe easily—or at least not painfully—he picked up the two envelopes. With trembling hands, he extracted the documents they held and unfolded them on the desk.

He had told Harkin and Rowan that he would make his decision in two weeks, but he saw no reason to stretch out the process. He knew what he had to do. He had known it all along.

He bent under the desk and dragged the paper shredder toward him. It seemed such a mundane tool for such a momentous event. A fire in one of the fireplaces in the big house would be more appropriate, but despite Nola's periodic reminders, he hadn't had the chimneys cleaned in years. Plus, it was too warm for a fire. The shredder would have to do.

He turned on the shredder, picked up one of the documents, and watched it disappear between the grinding blades.

fter a dinner of take-out pizza, Mike emerged from the kitchen with a bottle of champagne and three glasses.

"We're having a farewell party for you," he said to Ann.

"A bon voyage party," corrected Scott. "Annie will be so close, we don't need to say farewell. But don't pour a glass for me—I need to go in to work for a couple of hours. I'm covering for one of the other PTs."

"Who wants to do physical therapy this late at night?" asked Mike.

"People who haven't had three gigantic pieces of pizza," replied Scott.

"Sorry it's such a sparse party," Mike said as he removed the foil from the bottle. "We thought about waiting until Corey could join us after his meet-and-greet with Larry, but having a farewell party—sorry, a bon voyage party—after the person has bonvoyaged didn't seem appropriate." He popped the cork and caught a cascade of bubbles in a glass.

Scott went to the kitchen and returned with a glass of Perrier for the toast. After they drank, he came to where Ann sat and gave her a kiss on top of the head. "I think you'll love it at the winery, but if things don't work out, you know you're always welcome here."

She squeezed his hand. "Thanks, Scott."

As Scott took his plate to the kitchen, closely followed by Ursula, Mike gestured at the pizza box. "Want me to put the rest away?"

"No way," she said, dragging another piece onto her plate.

"Well, I can't let you eat alone," he said, taking the last piece.

They finished the pizza and he topped up their glasses with the last of the champagne.

"I'll miss having you around," he said, "but at least you're practically right down the road. How convenient is it that I can visit my favorite sister and stock up on wine at the same time?"

"Good thing you listed your priorities in that order," said Ann.

They drank in silence for a minute, then Ann said, "Are you surprised that you ended up living so close to where we grew up? Did you ever think about moving away? Seeing new things? Meeting new people?"

Mike laughed. "Are you kidding? I planned to live the high life in Manhattan, a regular 'mad man.'"

"Really? You wanted to be in advertising?"

"Advertising. High finance. Whatever would enable me to support myself in the manner to which I planned to become accustomed."

Ann laughed. "What happened that landed you a couple of miles from our childhood home?"

"I met Scott."

"He didn't want to move to the Big Apple?"

He shrugged. "He was already working at Bryn Mawr Rehab.

I like West Chester. The Big Apple is only a couple of hours away by train."

"So you decided the *Mad Men* life wasn't for you. What was Scott's big dream for his life?"

Mike smiled. "To be a physical therapist at Bryn Mawr Rehab."

16

Niall hauled himself up from the desk chair, triggering a bout of weak coughing, then tucked the envelope containing the remaining will into his inside jacket pocket. He grimaced. Only an invalid would need a jacket on a night as warm as this. He picked up the cane, crossed the room, and clicked off the office light. When he reached the end of the hall, he turned right, toward the tasting room.

He brought up the lights just enough to illuminate the rough boards of the bar, the rustic fixtures above it, the paintings by local artists on the walls. It all looked a bit half-finished to him, but he had accepted enough compliments on the room's decor to admit that Nola had known what she was doing. She may never have been an official part of the winery operation, but she had found a way to leave her mark on it.

He clicked off the lights, turned away from the tasting room, and retraced his steps down the hall. He made his way through Del and Rowan's workspace and the storage room, then stepped outside into the staff parking area.

Although the rain that had fallen off-and-on throughout the day was forecast to resume later that night, the sky now was clear. Just as well, since he didn't have an umbrella. He had become far too accustomed to Nola taking care of such details. He couldn't very well complain about people treating him like an invalid if he acted like one.

He stepped away from the security light over the door. As his eyes adjusted, he could pick out the sparkle of moonlight on the Tarn and, beyond it, the tidy rows of the vineyard. Just as the tasting room was Nola's domain, so was the vineyard Rowan's. She had done a good job with this year's grapes, although if the rain continued into September, they risked a harvest of water-logged grapes yielding a weak and unpromising juice.

Rowan and Del had been pestering him to expand the variety of grapes grown at Lynch: Cabernet Franc, Zweigelt, which they argued would do well in the Chester County climate, and even Albariño. Unless they bought more land, it would mean tearing out some of the Cab Sauv grapes, the grapes that had put Lynch on the map. Niall supposed he couldn't stop what the winery's owner chose to grow after he was gone, but Cabernet Sauvignon is what Lynch would grow until the day he died.

He turned from the view across the Tarn and the vineyards and crossed the parking area to the Ark. His own father had called the building *monarcha*—factory—with that Gaelic gargle on the last syllable. When Niall was little, he thought his father was saying "my ark." It had made complete sense to him: a place of refuge from the trials and tribulations visited on the rest of the world. After Niall's father died, Niall had referred to it as "the production building," but one time he had slipped and called it "the ark" in front of Rowan. The name had delighted her for the same reasons it had appealed to him as a child, and the name became part of the topography of the Lynch family compound, along with the Cellar, the Tarn, and the Curragh.

He drew a ring of keys from his pocket, unlocked the door, and stepped into the building.

The front section of the Ark, which housed the fermentation tanks and bottling equipment, was Del's domain, and Niall had to admit he had done a decent job. Thank God he had hired Del four years earlier. Niall hated to think what would have become of winery if he had died without a winemaker in place. And of course it worked out for Rowan, too. She and Del had married two years ago. Niall's mouth twitched up. The Lynch women did seem to love the winemakers.

He breathed in the yeasty aroma, contemplating the processes—hidden from view but carefully managed—occurring within those tanks. As he walked past the equipment, his posture became more erect, his step more confident, his breathing easier. He opened the door to the backmost space, stepped inside, and flipped on the light.

If the building was the Ark, then the barrel room was the *lasta*—the cargo. The Ark was built into the side of one of the hills that rolled across the Lynch property, the room's rock walls helping to maintain a constant, cool temperature. Orderly rows of barrels, stacked four high, stretched a dozen yards into the hillside. The brick ceiling arched overhead.

The Cellar might be Nola's territory, the vineyard Rowan's, the fermentation tanks and bottling area Del's, but the barrel room was his own. It represented everything he and his father had worked to build.

He lowered himself into the chair at the desk where he worked on the inventory sheets. He considered when—and to whom—he would explain his system and cryptic notations. He glanced at the photos lined up across the back of the desk: a Lynch family tree tracing the line from Niall's father to Kepi. Niall straightened one of the frames and thought back to what Henry had said. Did he really know that Rowan was going to have a girl? Then Niall shook the thought away. He himself would know in due time.

He slowly spun the chair toward the barrels. He almost wished he had thought to have a cot set up in the room. The quiet of the space, the scent that spoke of wine coming into its own, the pleasant play of subdued lights and shadow. Maybe he wouldn't need a sleeping pill if he could spend his nights here.

But it was too cold. His illness was robbing him even of the ability to enjoy this space where he had spent the happiest hours of his life.

He glanced at his watch: ten o'clock. He pushed himself to his feet. The cool of the room had revived him a bit. He'd take the path through the woods. It was a steeper climb than the drive, but a shorter distance.

He'd enjoy the walk to the house—it might be the last he'd take unassisted—and when he got there, he would open one of the last remaining bottles of the Cabernet Sauvignon from the first year of Lynch and Son Winery—a name Niall's father had given the business when Niall was barely a year old.

The doctors had told Niall not to drink, but to hell with that. He was a winemaker.

17

D el sprawled on the couch in the living room, flipping through channels whose offerings he barely registered.

Rowan was at an art exhibit in Philadelphia with Nola, and he had to admit he was vaguely relieved. She had been irritated with him about going ahead with the plan to get Ann into the Curragh, an irritability he knew was worsened by her discomfort in this last month of her pregnancy.

"Del," she had said, rubbing her back, "I appreciate that you think that there will still be a Curragh for us to rent out when we find out who the heir is, but wouldn't it have been better to wait until we know for sure?"

"But she wants a place now. If things really hit the fan and she has to move out, I'm sure she'll understand. She can just move back in with Mike."

Rowan shook her head. "Okay, but I hope we're not setting her up for disappointment."

He flipped the channel again and glanced at the time on his phone. He would have expected Rowan to be home by now. The knowledge that she was with Nola didn't entirely set his mind at rest.

He was about to put the phone aside when it buzzed. He checked the caller ID, then hit *Accept*.

"Hey, Nola—what's up?"

"Del, do you know where Niall is?"

Del had never heard Rowan's aunt sound anything other than calm, cool, and collected—or, especially when dealing with Niall, irritated—but her voice was taut with concern.

"Isn't he at the Cellar?" he asked. "I thought he was going to stay there until you got home or call me if he wanted to leave."

"That's what I told him to do. I just got back and went to the Cellar but he's not there. He's not at the big house either. I tried calling him but he didn't pick up. Can you ask Rowan if she knows where he is?"

He sat up. "She's not home yet." He paused to see if Nola would respond, but she was silent. "If she left the exhibit at the same time you did, she should be home by now." He wasn't sure whether to be worried by the fact neither he nor Nola knew where Rowan was, or to be suspicious that she was back at 46 Larch Street.

After a pause, Nola said, "She probably stopped at the store on the way home—she told me she was in the mood for potato chips." Before Del could quiz Nola further on Rowan's possible whereabouts, she continued. "Maybe Niall didn't feel well and called 911 and they took him to the hospital. I'm going to call Mercy and see if he's there."

"Okay. I'll try to track down Rowan, then I'll head over to the big house."

Del ended the call and hit Rowan's number.

The call rang to voicemail.

"Ro, call me when you get this." He grabbed his car keys and headed for the door. Maybe Rowan was somewhere on the property with Niall. Maybe she was in an ambulance with him on the way to the hospital. He would almost prefer one of these explanations to thinking she was back in West Philly.

The rain, which had let up earlier in the evening, had moved back in. A steady drizzle slicked the roads, but it still took him only a few minutes to reach the Lynch property. As he started up the drive to the house, he could see that the Ark and the Cellar were dark except for the security lights in the staff parking area. However, through the strip of woods, he could see the shimmer of lights at the big house.

He pulled the Escape up beside Nola's BMW. He jumped out and started for the front door, but then heard a call from the woods.

"Del, I'm down here!"

He couldn't quite identify the tone of Nola's voice. She didn't sound panicked, but there was a thread of some strong emotion running through it.

He ran for the path that linked the big house and the winery. "I'm coming, Nola!"

He headed toward an eerie glow about halfway down the path. Almost immediately, he caught his foot on a rock or root and went sprawling, hands skidding along the muddy ground. He scrambled up, swearing, then fumbled his phone out of his pocket. Using the flashlight app to light the way, he continued down the path.

A flashlight propped against a rock illuminated the scene. Nola sat on the ground, twigs tangled in her usually perfectly coiffed hair, tears and dirt streaking her hands and face, her muddy skirt hiked up around her thighs. Niall was stretched out on his back beside her, his head in her lap, eyes closed, features slack.

"Oh my God," said Del. "Have you called 911 yet?"

"No."

"I'll call now—"

"No, Del."

The dull insistence of her voice stopped him. "No?"

"No. He had a do-not-resuscitate order. He specifically said no CPR." Her voice caught on the last word.

Del squatted down beside her. "What happened?"

"He must have tried to get back to the house on his own and fell. He was lying off the path—I almost didn't see him. I think he hit his head."

Del swung the light in the direction Nola indicated. Blood stained one of the many rocks that poked up out of the ground on either side of the path, although the rain that dripped through the branches overhead was already washing it off in runnels of red.

"But—" He was trying to get a handle on the situation, trying to wade through the torrent of possible responses and reactions swirling through his head, when his phone chimed with Rowan's ringtone. He stabbed *Accept*. "Rowan," he managed, forcing the word through a throat tight with anxiety.

"Del, what's up? Is something wrong?"

"Where are you?"

"I'm on my way back from Philly. What's wrong?"

"It's ..." He didn't want to give Rowan the news of her father's death over the phone, especially since it sounded like she was driving. "It's an issue at the big house." His eyes drifted to the blood-stained rocks. "It's a leak. We're trying to fix it."

"Del—"

"Come to the big house. But don't hurry. Or I can come get you."

"No, I'm not that far away," she said, and now her tone was steely. "I'll be there soon."

She ended the call.

"Shit." He glanced toward Nola, then dropped his eyes. "I can't imagine she believed me about a leak."

Nola reached over and squeezed his arm. "I think you should call her back and tell her what's happened. It's better that she knows that there really is no need to hurry." She dropped her hand from Del's arm. "Tell her Niall is gone."

18

Vehicle lights moved slowly up the drive, and Del was relieved that Rowan was heeding the advice not to rush. He scrambled up the path and reached the driveway just as Rowan levered herself out of the Miata.

"He's on the path?" she asked, heading in that direction.

"Yes. We figured it was better if the EMTs brought him up." He had explained to her on the phone about Niall's DNR order. "Do you want to wait in the house until then?"

"No, I want to see him."

"It's slippery."

She hurried past him. "I'll be careful."

He took her arm as they made their way down the path, although he barely avoided falling again himself. He helped her onto the ground next to Niall. Nola slipped her arm around Rowan from one side, Del from the other. Rowan took one of Niall's limp hands in hers, her tears mixing with the rain that dripped down her cheeks.

Eventually Nola and Rowan agreed that it was time to call someone to take Niall's body away. Del called the police nonemergency number and described the situation. While they waited for an ambulance to arrive, he retrieved umbrellas from the big house, even though they were already soaked.

The ambulance arrived, lights strobing but sirens silenced, and the EMTs strapped Niall's body to a stretcher and hauled him up the path.

Despite the warmth of the night, Rowan was shivering. Del found one of Niall's old raincoats in the entrance hall closet and draped it over her shoulders. He and Nola stood on either side of her by the front door, watching as the lights of the ambulance and a police cruiser disappeared down the drive.

"So Dad had a do not resuscitate order?" asked Rowan. "I never knew, but I'm not surprised."

"Yes," said Nola. "Niall would never have countenanced the idea of ending up helpless in a hospital bed." She smiled wanly. "He wanted to be the captain of his voyage to the very end."

Rowan's hand flew to her mouth. "Oh my God—where is Harkin? Does he know?"

Del and Nola exchanged looks.

"No," said Nola, "I didn't think—"

"It's no wonder neither of us thought of him," said Del. "He's so rarely here. He must be asleep. Let's get inside. I'll get Harkin and, Nola, why don't you take Rowan to the kitchen and get her something warm to drink."

Nola led Rowan toward the back of the house while Del climbed the stairs to the second floor.

The door to Harkin's room was closed, and Del knocked, first lightly, then a bit harder.

"Yes?" came a bleary voice through the door. "Dad? Do you need something?"

"It's Del. Can I come in?"

"Sure."

Del stepped into the room.

Harkin sat on the bed in boxer shorts, squinting into the light from the hallway.

Harkin's eyes widened. "What happened?"

Del realized the picture he must paint, sodden and mud-smeared.

"I'm sorry, Harkin. Niall's dead."

Harkin stood. "Dead? What happened?"

"It looks like he tried to walk back from the Cellar and fell on the path and hit his head."

"Jesus." Harkin stood, grabbed a pair of shorts off a chair, and stepped into them. "Are you sure? I mean, maybe he's just knocked out—"

"No, he's dead."

"You can't be sure." Harkin headed for the door, obviously expecting Del to step aside, but pulled up when Del didn't move. "You can't be sure," he repeated.

"The police and the EMTs have been here and taken him away."

Harkin stared for a long beat, mouth hanging open, then said, "And you're just telling me now?"

"I'm really sorry, Hark—we were all in shock ... we didn't think ..."

Harkin walked unsteadily back across the room, sat heavily on the bed, and dropped his face into his hands. "God almighty."

"I'm really sorry." Del heard footsteps approaching. He stepped back into the hallway. Nola was standing at the top of the stairs.

"I need to get some dry clothes for Rowan," she whispered, glancing toward the open door to Harkin's room. "Is he ..."

Del looked back toward Harkin. He hadn't lifted his face from his hands.

"Fine," Harkin said dully. "I'm fine."

"Do you want a minute by yourself?" asked Del, hoping the answer was yes.

Harkin straightened but didn't look at Del. "Sure. A minute by myself."

"We're in the kitchen when you want to come down."

"Okay."

Del eased the door shut.

Nola had found one of her nightgowns and a robe that was loose enough to fit over Rowan's belly, and by the time she had changed into dry clothes herself, Harkin had emerged from the bedroom. They convened in the kitchen, and Harkin gave Rowan an awkward hug and listened without comment to their recap of the discovery of Niall's body. Afterward, Nola brewed a pot of decaf and the four spent a miserable half-hour hunched over their mugs of untouched coffee, the silence interspersed only occasionally by a comment about the weather or a half-hearted remembrance of Niall.

Finally, Nola said, "Rowan and Del, I expect you would be more comfortable back at the Unionville house—and that Del would be more comfortable in dry clothes."

Rowan roused herself and looked toward Del. "I'm sorry, sweetheart—I didn't think."

"It's no problem. It's not like it's cold."

He was relieved Nola hadn't suggested that he borrow some of Niall's—it would have felt like grave robbing—and was unsurprised that Harkin hadn't offered his.

They all stood, and Nola collected the mugs and put them in the sink. "I'll tidy up in the morning," she said.

"It's okay," said Harkin. "I'll take care of it."

"Oh. Okay. Thank you."

Rowan and Del started for the hallway then turned back at Harkin's voice.

"It hasn't been two weeks," he said. "I suppose Dad still had both the wills."

After a brief hesitation, Nola said. "Let's worry about that in the morning."

19

Del spent a wakeful night at home in Unionville. Rowan lay on her side, her back spooned against Del's front, but even when her soft crying subsided, her breath never achieved that slow, steady rhythm that comes with sleep. He suspected that both of them resisted tossing and turning to avoid disrupting any rest the other might get. By the time the first of the morning light filtered through the bedroom curtains, Del's legs were beginning to cramp, and he thought they might have been better off not bothering with bed and just continuing their vigil in their own kitchen.

Just before ten o'clock, when most of the staff was scheduled to arrive, they drove to the winery. The rain had ended during the night, and they found Nola waiting under the overhang at the front door, shaded from sun that was already hot. She got into the back seat of the Escape.

"I guess Harkin's not coming along," said Rowan, her tone carefully neutral.

"He did offer," said Nola, "but the staff barely knows who Harkin is—I thought it might be an unnecessary distraction. I asked him to choose a suit of Niall's we can use for the burial."

Rowan nodded. "That's a good idea. Thanks."

As they rolled down the driveway, Del saw a half dozen vehicles in the staff lot between the Cellar and the Ark, and a few more, mainly pickups, parked near the vineyard.

"What's the plan?" he asked.

"Why don't you drop me off at the vineyard," said Rowan, "and I'll round up whoever's there. Can you get anyone who's working in the Ark this morning?"

"Sure. Where do you want everyone?"

"I think the Cellar will be the best."

"If you can give me a key," said Nola, "I'll make sure it's open."

Ten minutes later, the permanent staff and temporary vineyard workers were assembled in the tasting room. Nola stood at the back of the room. Rowan stood in front of the bar with Del at her side. Her eyes were red and swollen, but when she spoke, her voice was soft but strong.

"I wanted to let you know that Niall died last night. I wanted all of you to hear it from me."

A number of those in the group bowed their heads.

"I suppose it's not a huge shock," she continued. "You all know how ill he was. But I suspect we all thought we had a little more time with him. It looks like, after working late in the Cellar —" She paused and mustered a sad smile. "*Still* working late on winery business, even as sick as he was—he took the path up to the big house. He must have gotten dizzy. He fell and hit his head on one of the rocks along the path. We found him there last night."

"So sorry, Rowan," said Sam Griller, the assistant winemaker.

There was a murmur of condolences.

"Thank you, Sam. Thank you, everyone." Rowan pulled a

tissue from her dress pocket and blotted her nose. "I don't have anything else to say right now. Obviously, the Cellar won't be open to customers for at least a few days."

"I'll put something up on social media," said a woman standing toward the back. "And a sign up on the door as well."

"Thanks, Cecily. For now, just say that we're closed—not why. Del and I will call the rest of the staff to let them know about Niall, and I don't want them to find out from Facebook."

"Sure," said Cecily. "Just let me know when you've gotten in touch with everyone, and what you want me to post."

"Thank you." Rowan turned back to the group. "If anyone would like to take the rest of the day off, I totally understand— full pay for anyone who chooses to do that. But grapes and wine don't care what's happening in the lives of the people who tend them, so I'm hoping that as of tomorrow, you'll be ready and willing to get back to work and—" Her voice caught, and she cleared her throat. "To get back to work and make sure that this year's harvest and this year's vintage are up to the Lynch family standards—the standards we've held ourselves to for over fifty years."

A man in the front, hands crusted with vineyard dirt, said, "I'm not waiting until tomorrow to get back to work, Miss Lynch."

Rowan smiled through the tears glistening in her eyes. "Thank you, Luis."

A chorus of *absolutely* and *me, too* echoed through the room.

"Thank you all. I'll let you know as soon as we have plans for the funeral and memorial service."

The small crowd dispersed, a few of them stopping to give Rowan a hug or to grasp Del's hand.

When the room was empty save for the three family members, Del folded his wife in his arms.

"That was wonderful, sweetheart."

"Thanks," she said, her voice muffled against his shoulder. "I guess we should start making those calls."

"I hate to say it," said Nola, "but I don't think it makes sense for me to help with that since most of the staff doesn't know me that well."

"Yes, I agree," said Rowan. "Del and I will make the calls."

"If that coffee maker's still in the kitchen, I'll brew up a pot," said Nola.

"Decaf for me," said Rowan.

Del and Rowan went to their work area and divided the winery's staff roster between them, she calling the vineyard staff and he the winemaking staff. Nola arrived periodically to top up their coffees, then pulled a chair in from the coat check room.

When they were done, Rowan pushed back from her desk with a sigh. "That wasn't as awful as I thought it would be. I don't think anyone was too surprised." She paused. "Although a couple of them did ask me what the plan was for the winery."

"What did you tell them?" asked Del.

"I told them we would let them know as soon as things settled down." She looked toward Nola. "What does it mean that there are two wills?"

Nola placed her mug carefully on Rowan's desk. "I'm not a lawyer, but I imagine that in the case of two wills, the winery would end up being split between you and Harkin."

"Could be worse," said Del.

"In fact, it is worse," said Nola. "I can't find either of the wills."

Rowan sat forward. "Really?"

"Yes. I checked his office at the big house this morning. While you two were making the phone calls, I checked his desks in the Cellar and the barrel room. Nothing. I even called his lawyer, and what Niall told me was true—he didn't keep copies because he didn't approve of Niall having two executed wills."

"Maybe he was carrying them," said Del. "I saw him take them out of his jacket pocket when he was talking with Harkin in the Cellar."

Nola shook her head. "Before the ambulance took him away, I checked his pockets. Nothing. But ..."

"What?" asked Rowan.

"I did find paper in the shredder in Niall's office that looks like the paper the wills were printed on."

"So he already chose the heir?" asked Rowan, her voice spiking.

"It looks that way."

"Can we tell what name was on the shredded will?" asked Del.

"No—the shredder did a thorough job. But even if we could piece it together, I don't know that it would do us any good, at least from a legal point of view. No matter whose name was on it, Niall obviously didn't want that will to be executed."

"What happens in the case of no will?" asked Del.

Nola sighed. "I suppose the same thing as two wills—probably the winery will be divided between Rowan and Harkin. The thing that concerns me is that we don't have any evidence that Niall wanted to prevent the sale of the winery outside the family."

"I'm certainly not selling my half," said Rowan.

"No, of course not. But conceivably Harkin could sell his half."

"Does Harkin know all this yet?" asked Rowan.

"No. The sooner we tell him we can't find any wills, the better." Nola grimaced. "Especially after we managed to forget to tell him about Niall's death until after the ambulance left. But I think mentioning the shredded will is more trouble than it's worth. We can't tell which one it is, and it seems like an unnecessary complication. Let's not mention that to Harkin."

They locked up the Cellar, climbed into the Escape, and drove up to the big house.

They found Harkin in the kitchen, the smell of burnt toast in the air.

"That toaster belongs in a museum," he said as they entered. "How did it go with the staff?"

"Rowan did a great job," said Del. "And they plan to keep working today despite what's happened. Which is a good thing, considering the harvest is coming right up."

"Did you pick out a suit for Niall?" Nola asked Harkin.

"Yup. Suit, tie, socks, shoes. I didn't know if you would want him buried with those cufflinks he liked or would rather keep those as a memento. Let me know and I'll find the right kind of shirt."

"Thanks, Hark," said Rowan. "I'm okay burying him with the cufflinks. Unless you want them ..."

"No, thanks. I'm not really a cufflink kind of guy." Harkin stood. "I'll find a shirt with cufflink cuffs."

"Actually," said Nola, "before you do that, we have something important to talk with you about."

"Oh?" Harkin's tone was wary. "What's that?"

Nola waved them toward the table. It took her only a few minutes to update Harkin on the missing wills.

Harkin sat back and crossed his arms. "All I know is that Dad showed me an executed will leaving the winery to me."

"He had two wills," said Nola. "They were both executed. He showed them to me."

"We only have your word for that."

"Harkin!" exclaimed Rowan, aghast.

"I'm sorry," he mumbled. "I'm just saying that I only ever saw one will, and it left the winery to me."

"He told you he had another one favoring Rowan," said Del.

"What are you talking about?"

"I was in the kitchen when you and Niall argued. I heard him tell you that there were two executed wills, and that he was going to destroy one based on what happened over the next two weeks."

Harkin leaned forward. "You were spying on us?"

"I was in the kitchen. I didn't want to get involved. I didn't intend to eavesdrop."

Harkin ran his fingers through his hair. "So, according to Nola, Dad had two wills and today he doesn't have any?"

"It looks like he might have had one," muttered Del.

"What do you mean?"

Del caught Nola's glare and flushed. "Nothing."

Harkin drew his eyebrows together. "Don't tell me 'nothing.'"

Del looked to Nola for help.

She sighed. "There's paper in the shredder in Niall's office in the Cellar. It looks like the same paper the wills were printed on."

Harkin opened his mouth, but Nola held up her hand. "It's impossible to tell which will he shredded. It's just fluff."

"I'd like to see it for myself."

"Help yourself."

They were silent for a few moments, then Harkin said, "So you're telling me Dad didn't have a will?"

Nola gave an exasperated sigh. "As I said, Harkin—"

"No, I mean Dad *never* had a will? He was the sole owner of a large and important—to him, at least—business and he never wrote a will before the two we're talking about?"

Nola paled.

Harkin's eyes narrowed. "There *is* another will."

"Not that I'm aware of."

Harkin stared at her for a long moment, then sat back again and recrossed his arms. "Well, you are his executor. If anyone was aware of another will, it would be you." After a pause, he added, "Wouldn't it?"

He got no response.

20

Ann dropped the last article of clothing into the suitcase on the guest room bed and pressed the lid closed. That one suitcase held everything she had brought with her to Mike and Scott's townhouse. She certainly wouldn't have to worry about storage space at the Curragh, at least until she brought her winter clothes down from where they were stored in Walt and Helen Federman's basement in the Adirondacks.

She looked up at a light knock. Scott stood in the bedroom door.

"I just saw an announcement online," he said. "Niall Lynch died."

"Damn. I'm sorry to hear that. I remember Del mentioning he was ill."

"Yes. Heart failure."

Ann furrowed her brow. "Ugh."

"I'm going to send flowers. Do you want me to add your name to the card?"

"Sure. Thanks." Ann glanced at the suitcase. "I wonder if I packed prematurely?"

Scott stepped into the room. "You think the plans for the guest house might change?"

"I don't know. It seems a little cold to just show up at their doorstep right after the dad dies."

"They might appreciate knowing the guest house is in good hands—and earning them some rent. I've never sensed that the winery is in any trouble, but a couple of times Del has dropped hints that he and Rowan are watching their finances."

"True. I have to say I'd be disappointed if it fell through. I was getting excited about it." After a self-conscious laugh, she continued. "I never thought of myself as the nesting type, and Rowan's aunt did a fantastic job on the decor, but I was thinking about what things of my own I'd want to bring there."

Scott sat down on the bed. "Like what?"

She sat down next to him. "My favorite mohair blanket."

"The one you used to have hanging over your couch at the cabin?"

"That's the one. That woven basket I got on the trip to Sedona with you and Mike." She smiled. "The super-classy snow globe from Key West."

Scott laughed. "I remember the store I bought that in. What a dive that was!" He shook his head. "That won't qualify you for a spread in *House Beautiful*."

"True. But it would make it more homey."

"Want me to ask Del what would work best for him and Rowan in terms of you moving into the guest house?"

"That would be great, thanks."

"I'll give him a call. Maybe they need someone to run some errands for them or pick up some takeout." He stood and went downstairs.

She flopped back on the bed. She didn't want to impose on the Lynch family in the aftermath of Niall's death, but her growing enthusiasm for having a place of her own made the possibility of a postponement that much more disappointing.

And the more her excitement grew for a place that wasn't a guest room, the more she realized she also wanted a place alone. She had spoken with Corey a couple of times since he had left for Ocean City the previous day. He reported that Larry seemed like a good guy, and that there was plenty of room in the rental house if she decided to join him. She reported on her bon voyage party and conveyed her wish that he had been there. They agreed to host their own follow-up party the next time they were together. She was relieved he hadn't brought up the possibility of her relocation to L.A. She wanted to have that conversation in person.

From downstairs, she could hear the hum of Scott's side of the phone call. She realized that even if Del Berendt gave the go-head for Ann to move into the Curragh, there was another consideration: whether the guest house was free of spirits. If she was balking at the idea of sharing a space with Corey, how much worse would it be to share a space with the dead former owner of the Lynch winery?

———————

21

Harkin sifted the cream-colored fluff from the shredder's bin through his fingers. It could very well have been the will Niall had shown him, or one just like it except with Rowan's name on it. But Nola had at least been telling the truth about the machine having done its job too well to be able to tell which it was. He snorted cynically. If Nola had been able to reassemble the shreds of the destroyed will, she would no doubt have brought it to their attention if it showed Harkins name, or hidden it away if it showed Rowan's.

The thought saddened him. He had never fooled himself into believing that his aunt was impartial in her feelings toward her niece and nephew. Nola had always been Rowan's champion. But before today, he would have trusted his aunt, especially in her role as Niall's executor. It hadn't been until he had asked about an earlier will and seen her face go pale that he believed she might hide information that would favor him. If Niall had drawn up a will before Rowan was born, then it certainly would have named him as the heir. And based on Nola's reaction, it seemed possible that such a will existed.

The aftermath of that conversation had been almost comical: the three younger family members searching the places they knew Niall had stored official documents, and then expanding to places they imagined he might have stored them. Del and Rowan searched together, Harkin searched on his own. As far as Harkin knew, Nola had stayed in the kitchen.

Harkin pushed the shredder back under Niall's desk, then hurried to the Cellar's customer entrance. If Nola left the big house, he planned to follow her. He had a vague memory of Niall having a safe deposit box at a bank in West Chester, but it was also possible that Nola had kept any official documents Niall had given her at her own bank, probably in Philadelphia.

When he stepped outside, he caught sight of a flicker of light through the trees: the bright noon-time sun glinting off the windshield of a vehicle headed down the drive. For a moment, he thought he had missed his chance to follow Nola. Then he saw the vehicle was Del's Escape, and it appeared that there were only two occupants. Well, he couldn't follow everyone. He waited until the Escape reached the road, then trudged up the drive, relieved to see Nola's BMW still parked out front.

He paused in the entrance hall for a moment, listening for footsteps or other sounds that would indicate where Nola might be. The house was silent. Might she have been in the Escape after all? He thought he would have seen her unless she had hunkered down in back, but he couldn't imagine Nola resorting to that extreme, even for her beloved niece. He went to the kitchen and poured a glass of Pepsi from the bottle he had picked up at the Wawa.

Glass in hand, he went to the library, which not only had the least uncomfortable chairs in the house, but also gave a view of the entrance hall and front door. Although he wasn't much of a reader, he was tired of surfing the web on his phone. As he scanned the shelves, his eyes lit on the tattered spine of James Michener's *Hawaii*. He was surprised his father hadn't purged the book from the collection, just as he had tended to purge anything he found distasteful. But Niall probably had not known it was there, since reading was one of the many things he had deprioritized in favor of a laser focus on the winery.

Harkin pulled the book off the shelf and settled into a chair. He was only a few paragraphs into the first chapter when he heard a muffled thump. He closed the book and strained his ears. A moment later, he heard the sound again, apparently coming from the basement. Setting the book aside, he rose, made his way to the door to the basement, and eased it open.

The lights at the top and bottom of the stairs were on. He heard a delicate grunt, a sound like something sliding across the floor, then another thump and a quiet *Damn!*

He made his way slowly down the stairs, testing each step for squeaks before putting his weight on it. When he reached the bottom, he could see that a far corner of the basement was illuminated by a cone of light. There was a squeak of wood on wood —maybe a drawer opening—the light shifted and steadied, then silence.

He approached the corner via an aisle created by the castoffs of three generations of Lynches.

Nola was standing with her back to him, facing a hulking cabinet, glass-fronted shelves on top, drawers below. One drawer was open. In her hand, she held a document.

"Whatcha got there?" he asked.

She gave a little shriek and whirled to face him. "Harkin—don't do that! You almost gave me a heart attack!"

"Sorry about that," he said. "So ... whatcha got there?"

She regarded him in silence for a moment, then sighed. "A will. Niall gave it to me right after he inherited the winery from your grandfather."

"Interesting. And what does it say?"

"It leaves everything to you."

He held out his hand and, after a brief pause, she handed him the document.

As with the document Niall had shown him just two days earlier, it was only a few pages long, and he quickly found the passage he was looking for.

After payment of all of personal debts, expenses and liabilities, I assign ownership of Lynch and Son Winery to my son, Harkin Niall Lynch.

His heart thumping, he scanned the rest of the document, then looked up at Nola.

She returned his gaze, her face impassive.

"No mention of limiting sales to family members," he said.

"No."

"Or of any restrictions on the ability to sell based on the owner's age."

"No," she said, her voice tired. "I imagine at the time it didn't occur to him that would be necessary." She paused. "What are you going to do now?"

"I guess we need to get in touch with Rowan."

"Yes. I guess we do."

He stepped aside to let her precede him up the aisle, then followed her up the stairs.

"Do you want to call her?" he asked.

Nola nodded. She retrieved her phone from her purse in the kitchen and placed a call.

"Hi, Rowan, it's Nola. Can you come back to the big house?" She shot Harkin a look. "There's been a development."

She ended the call, and they both sat down at the kitchen table.

"So," asked Harkin, "would that will ever have seen the light of day if I hadn't gotten to the basement when I did?"

She regarded him for a moment, her face expressionless. "I guess we'll never know."

22

Del and Rowan left their lunches half-eaten in Unionville and drove back to the big house.

The family convened once again in the kitchen. The conversation that followed was painful—especially so since it was clear that Harkin believed that Nola would have destroyed the will that favored him if he hadn't interrupted her.

"What now?" Rowan asked, clearly trying to hold back tears.

"I'm going to sell," said Harkin, not meeting the three pairs of angry eyes.

"Can't we work something out?"

"Are you in a position to pay me what the winery is worth?"

"You know I'm not." She clamped her lips together, then burst out, "You know that Dad wanted to prevent exactly what you're threatening to do."

"I'm not *threatening*, Ro," said Harkin, keeping his voice steady with obvious effort. "I'm acting on the terms of a signed, dated, and witnessed will. I'm accepting my inheritance and doing with it what I think will be best for me and my family. It's exactly what you would be doing if you had inherited."

"What are you going to do with the proceeds from the sale of the winery?" Nola asked.

"I think that's my business."

"I think it's all our business!" said Rowan. "Maybe not legally, but ... for God's sake, Harkin, if you're going to throw away a business that has been in our family for over half a century, don't you think you owe it to us to tell us what you're planning to do with the money?"

"I'm not *throwing it away*," said Harkin, his voice just shy of a shout. "There are people who will keep the winery going. People who might even do a better job of it than our sainted father."

"You know this for a fact? That there are people interested in keeping it going?"

"I do."

Rowan's voice raised a notch. "How?"

"I've asked around."

Her voice spiked. "You've been planning this?"

"I wasn't making official inquiries, just feeling people out."

"For how long?"

Harkin's face reddened. "For my whole goddamned life, Ro —ever since it became clear that I'd never be a winemaker. Ever since I managed to crush Dad's dreams for me."

"If you think Dad—" began Rowan.

"Stop it!" Nola glared at them.

Harkin dropped back in his chair. Rowan crossed her arms and turned her head toward the window, tears sparkling in her eyes.

Nola continued. "Let's continue this conversation when tempers aren't so high." She turned to Harkin. "Harkin, you'll be here at least for the next few days?"

"Yeah, I'll be here." He pushed back his chair and stood. "Ro ..."

Rowan refused to shift her stare from the window.

"Fine," said Harkin. "Let me know when you want to meet." He strode across the kitchen and disappeared down the hall.

Del reached out and squeezed Rowan's arm. "Sweetheart—"

She jerked away as if she had been stung. "You told me Dad said I was the heir!"

"I'm sorry," said Del, taken aback, "but it's what I heard."

"But you didn't have to tell me!" she sobbed as the tears finally fell. "You didn't have to get my hopes up. It was a conversation you weren't even supposed to hear." She jumped to her feet and her chair tipped, clattering, to the floor. "If it wasn't for you and your complete inability to keep anything that pops into your head from popping out your mouth, Dad might have left the winery to me." She disappeared down the hall.

Del stood.

Nola touched his arm. "Let her go, Del. She needs some time by herself."

A few moments later, Del heard the front door slam. He fell back onto his chair with a groan. "Goddammit. Will I never learn?"

Nola marshaled a smile. "Your enthusiasm is one of your most endearing traits. You and I both thought that when Niall admitted he was fighting a losing battle, he meant he had finally realized Harkin was not the right heir. In fact, I think that *is* what he meant—at least in that moment, when he and Harkin had just argued." She squeezed his hand. "You told Rowan what you heard because you wanted to share what you thought was good news with her. She'll see that once she's calmed down."

"What do you think Harkin's going to do with the money?"

She sighed. "I have no idea. Harkin may be my nephew, but I know less about his personal life than I know about my accountant's. Nothing wine-related, obviously."

"Bastard," said Del, although without much energy.

"Don't be too hard on him. Niall tried so hard to chain

Harkin to the winery, but it was Niall himself who turned Harkin against it."

They sat in silence for a few moments, then Del looked toward the door through which Rowan had disappeared. "I wish there was something I could do for her."

Nola patted his hand. "Just let her calm down. Then she'll be looking for someone to talk to."

Eventually he received a text from Rowan saying that she had taken the Escape back to Unionville and asking Del to get a ride home from Nola. When he got to the house, he found the bedroom door locked and could hear soft sobs from the other side.

"Rowan? Sweetheart?" he called through the door.

"I don't want to talk to you right now, Del."

He retreated to the dining room and poured himself a bourbon, the first swallow burning his throat.

Nola might be right that Rowan would be looking for someone to talk to, but that someone obviously wasn't Del—at least not yet.

23

Rowan seemed no more in the mood to talk to Del when she emerged from the bedroom a few hours later.

They spent the rest of the afternoon and early evening in an awkward silence, interspersed only occasionally by overly polite exchanges. Eventually Del escaped to the baby's room, where he spent an hour trying to fix a squeaky floorboard.

A little after seven, Rowan appeared in the door, the strap of her purse slung over her shoulder.

"I'm going to run down to Philly. Nola and I are going to have dinner."

He stood from his task. "Okay."

"There's some leftover steak and potato salad in the fridge."

"I'll be fine."

He thought she was going to say something else, then she sighed. "I'll be back by ten."

She descended the stairs and he almost let her go—*let her open the garage door herself*—then thought how he'd feel if she strained her back hauling up the heavy door. He trudged down the steps behind her and followed her to the garage.

He returned her wave as she pulled out of the driveway and watched the Miata disappear down the road.

Then he went inside, grabbed his car keys, got the Escape out of the garage, and followed her.

He spotted the Miata as he pulled onto 95 North, and it soon became clear that she was not headed toward Nola's Center City neighborhood. Del dropped back. He wasn't worried about losing her—he had his GPS set to 46 Larch Street.

Even if Rowan wasn't ready to talk to him, he needed to talk to her. They needed to discuss what the sale of the winery meant for the two of them. If Rowan was willing to relocate, he was sure she could get a job as a vineyard manager, although with the baby due in less than a month, she would probably want to postpone looking for a new job. He also felt confident that he could get a job as a winemaker or assistant winemaker. However, the possibility that they could both get jobs in their respective areas of expertise at the same winery was practically zero. If they moved to California, they might improve the chance that they could at least get jobs at wineries within commuting distance of each other, although Del doubted whether Rowan would be willing to move that far away from Nola.

But even that discussion could wait. What he really wanted to talk about with Rowan was where she had gone after leaving the art exhibit that she and Nola had attended the night of Niall's death. Nola had confirmed that she and Rowan had left the Center City gallery at the same time, so Rowan should have arrived in Unionville at almost the same time that Nola arrived at the big house.

Had Rowan made a trip to Larch Street the night of her father's death?

Del made the final turn to his destination, number 46 just down the block. He planned to park in the same unlit space he had used on his earlier reconnaissance mission, but it was occupied. He debated whether it was better to circle the block and risk passing Rowan, or to back up.

She appeared around the far corner just as a vehicle turned onto the street behind the Escape. Del, blinded by the other vehicle's headlights, couldn't see what it was, but the lights were high—probably some kind of jacked-up pickup truck.

His heart hammering, he put the Escape in reverse and began backing up. The other vehicle was still a dozen yards behind him, but the driver leaned on the horn. Del stopped. Not only was the horn attracting Rowan's attention, but its headlights were lighting up the Escape. He took his foot off the brake and began coasting backwards again.

He just caught the other driver's shout—"Hey, buddy, you got someone behind you!"—through his closed windows.

Del hit the brakes again and looked toward Rowan in a panic.

She had raised a hand to shield her eyes from the headlights. No doubt intent on avoiding any involvement in an incipient road rage incident, she dropped her hand and hurried toward the house. She stepped through the gate, ran awkwardly up the steps, and knocked on the door.

The horn of the car behind him blared again. "Buddy—move it or lose it!"

Del looked toward the clock on his dash. 7:59.

"Come on, come on," he muttered, his hands white-knuckled on the steering wheel.

A moment later, he saw the gradual illumination in the panes of the door of number 46. He also heard the thunk of a vehicle door closing behind him and, in his mirror, saw a man almost as wide as he was tall lumbering toward him.

The door of the house opened to reveal the man in Victorian garb. Rowan slipped inside, the man closed the door behind her, and the light in the panes faded to blackness.

"Sorry about that!" Del called through the window just as the man reached his door. Throwing the Escape into drive, he hit the gas and leapt forward with a squeal of rubber on pavement. He glanced back long enough to see the man throw his arms up in frustration, then turn and lumber back to his truck.

Del briefly thought about driving down the alley and seeing what cars were parked in back. However, he not only didn't want to give Rowan another opportunity to see him, but also wanted to put some space between him and the truck. The driver had seemed more irritated than angry, but you never knew.

Del made his way back to 95, driving with the exaggerated caution of a drunk.

When he pulled into the driveway of the Unionville house, it was just a few minutes shy of an hour since Rowan had disappeared into 46 Larch Street. He parked the Escape, went to the dining room, and poured himself a shot of bourbon.

The time on his phone showed 8:59. He stared at it until it showed 9:00. Then he jabbed Rowan's number.

When she answered, she was a little breathless. The ambient sound made it clear she was outdoors.

"Hello, Del."

"What are you up to?" he asked.

"I told you, Nola and I had dinner."

"Where?"

He heard the thunk of a car door and the sound modulated.

"What?"

"Where did you have dinner?"

"Is something wrong?"

"I'm just wondering where you had dinner."

"An Italian place. I forget the name."

"How was it?"

"Del, I'm going to be home soon," she said, her voice

combining fatigue with irritation. "If you really want to know about my dinner, I'll tell you then."

She ended the call.

Del went to the living room and fell into a chair—one of a set of two that had been his and Rowan's first purchase when they moved into the Unionville house.

Rowan must not have recognized him at Larch Street, because she surely would have said something if she had—wouldn't she?

He got out his phone again and hit another entry in his Favorites list.

"Hello, Del."

"Hello, Nola. Is Rowan with you?"

"No. We had dinner, but she left a little while ago."

"How long ago did she leave?"

"I don't know—not long."

"Where did you go?"

"A new Italian place near my apartment."

"Sounds nice."

After a brief silence, Nola asked, "Del, is there anything I can do for you?"

"No, I'm fine." He sat forward and rested his forehead in one hand, the glass of bourbon dangling between his knees in the other. "No, I'm *not* fine. You said Rowan would be looking for someone to talk to when she calmed down."

"Yes." Nola's voice was cautious.

"I hoped that would be me."

After a pause, she said, "Del, this is such a difficult time for her. You need to give her some space."

He stood and took a swallow of bourbon. "How much space am I expected to give her?"

"I can't say." When he was silent, she continued. "Do you want me to talk with her? Find out what's up?"

He heaved a sigh. "No. Thanks, Nola, I appreciate it, but ... never mind." He gave a hoarse laugh. "Maybe she'll tell me all about dinner when she gets home."

"Yes. Maybe."

"I'll let you go. Bye."

He ended the call, finished the bourbon, and went to the dining room to pour himself another shot. Then he hit redial on his call to Rowan.

It went to voicemail.

He hit redial on his call to Nola.

Also to voicemail.

On the phone with each other, no doubt.

Had they agreed ahead of time on *an Italian place near Nola's house* as a location he couldn't possibly fact check? Were they even now comparing notes about their conversations with Del—poor, stupid Del, home alone in Unionville? He gave a bitter bark of a laugh—*Union*ville. Wasn't that ironic.

He downed the shot and, leaving the glass on the dining room table, went to the guest room and shut the door.

24

M ike was in the kitchen pouring a cup of coffee when he heard a thump from the stairs. He found Ann carrying a suitcase down and trying unsuccessfully to keep it from knocking against the walls.

"Any more to bring down?"

"Nope."

"Heading out now?"

"Yeah."

He set his cup on an end table. "I'll help you move in."

"I have one suitcase."

"I'll carry it inside for you."

"Gee, thanks."

By the time he got his car keys and made a quick detour to the basement wine cellar, Ann had loaded the suitcase into the Forester, which was parked at the curb.

He got his Audi—affectionately named Audrey—out of the garage and caught up with Ann a minute later. He was right behind her most of the way from West Chester to Kennett Square, but much to his annoyance, he missed the light at Birmingham Road. While he waited for the light to change, he rolled up the window and turned on the AC. Although it was only late morning, the day was a scorcher, and he was glad that there wasn't more to move into the Curragh than a suitcase.

When he pulled into the parking area behind the little guest house, Ann was just closing the rear door of the Forester.

"The movers have arrived," he announced as he climbed out of the car.

"I already got my *one suitcase* inside."

"Then we should toast your new digs," he said. He pulled a bottle of Sapele out of the back seat and presented it to her with a flourish.

"It's a little early in the day," she said.

"Okay, we can toast with coffee."

Ann took the bottle of Sapele from him. "I said it was early. I didn't say it was *too* early."

They went inside and she poured two glasses, which they took out to the cafe table on the front porch. The sun glistened off the water of the Tarn, beyond which they could see a few figures moving among the vineyard's orderly rows of vines. Up the hill, the Lynch family home was visible through the band of woods.

Mike took a sip of wine and looked out over the scene. "Think you'll be here for a while?"

"I certainly hope so."

"If you wanted to buy a place, you wouldn't need to sell the Adirondack cabin or the studio to afford a down payment. The rental income you're getting from the cabin is good, so I'd recommend holding onto that, just in case you decide you want to move back there. But I think it would be good to have the studio off the books just to avoid the taxes and expenses for general upkeep." Ann was Mike's last remaining client from the

financial planning business he had wrapped up once managing
Ann Kinnear Sensing became a full-time gig.

"Yeah. I really don't see myself getting back to painting
anytime soon," she said.

"Especially with your interest in flying."

"Exactly."

"Do you think you'll want to buy a plane?"

She contemplated the brilliantly blue sky. "Maybe."

"How pricey would that be?"

"Actually, for some of these older, more basic planes, it's not
the purchase that's the expensive part. Ellis, the manager at
Avondale Airport, got his Stinson for not much more than a nice
used car. It's the care and feeding that gets expensive."

"Yeah—well, you don't want to skimp on that."

"That's for sure."

"Do you think you want to buy a place around here?"

Ann laughed. "Mike, I haven't even unpacked my *one*
suitcase."

"I know. It's just that if you think you might need a bundle of
cash for a down payment—or an outright purchase—I'll factor
that into your financial plan."

She shrugged. "I don't know. I'll give it some time here and
see how things are going."

Del emerged from the Cellar carrying a vase of flowers and
turned up the path to the Curragh.

Mike leaned toward Ann. "He got you flowers? I've hooked
you up with a full-service landlord."

"Hi, Del," Ann called as he approached them.

"Hey, Ann. Mike." He reached the porch and handed the
vase to Ann. The flowers were a riot of reds, purples, oranges,
and yellows. "That came in for you this morning. I didn't look at
the card at first—just put them with the condolence flowers

we've been getting. Although I should have noticed that the colors were a little more boisterous than the others."

"I was really sorry to hear about your father-in-law," said Ann. "My condolences to you and Rowan."

"Yeah, really sorry to hear that, buddy," said Mike.

Del ducked his head in acknowledgement. "Thanks. I saw the flowers you guys sent—we appreciate that."

Mike cast a mystified glance toward Ann, who mouthed, *Scott.*

"I know that having a glass of Sapele is probably not as exciting for you as it is for us," Ann said to Del, "but can I get you a glass?"

"No, thanks." Del ran his fingers through his hair. "This isn't exactly the 'welcome to the neighborhood' message I hoped to deliver, but we just found out that Harkin has inherited the winery. He plans to sell, and I'm not sure what that will mean for the Curragh. I should have called you when we found out, but we were all a little bit rattled."

Ann set aside her glass. "Does that mean you need me to move out?"

Del waved his hand. "No, that's not necessary, at least not for now. Who knows how long it might be before someone else takes over."

"And a new owner might appreciate having a tenant for the Curragh," said Mike.

"That's right," said Del.

"Any chance the brother will keep the winery?" asked Mike.

"No chance. Not only does he have no interest in wine-making—or in wine, for that matter—but he doesn't have the fondest memories of the place. Dicey relationship with Niall." He sighed. "Niall had this whole crazy thing going with two wills —one favoring Rowan and one favoring Harkin. Now both those wills have disappeared and the only will we have is one that

Niall drew up before Rowan was even born ... so it's no surprise it favors Harkin. But worse than that, there's no provision that keeps him from selling the winery. We've been looking for a more recent will, but we've exhausted all the places we can think of where Niall might have put it." He jammed his hands into his pockets and scuffed the ground with a boot-clad foot, then looked up at Ann. "We'd love you to stay as long as possible. I promise to keep you up-to-date on developments."

Ann nodded. "Just let me know if I need to vacate."

As Del made his way back to the Cellar, head down, Ann opened the card tucked into the bouquet.

To a woman who can often be found on *the water (ahhh) or* in *the water (brrr!)—remember that L.A. offers the biggest water (and it's a lot warmer than Maine!). Happy housewarming! Corey*

With a sigh, she tucked the card back into the bouquet and set it on the cafe table.

Mike took a sip of wine. "Are you thinking what I'm thinking?"

"World's most convenient sensing engagement?"

"Yup."

"I'm surprised you didn't make the pitch on the spot, although I guess that proposing a business engagement right after offering condolences to someone on the death of their father-in-law really isn't good form."

"Actually, the reason I didn't bring it up was that I figured if I wasn't supposed to be turning down business without consulting you first, maybe I wasn't supposed to be accepting it either."

"Hey, you *are* trainable!" Ann said with a laugh.

Ignoring her comment, Mike continued, "And if Del and Rowan are interested in seeing if they can find out from Niall about the existence of another will, then I think time is of the essence."

"Yeah, I think you're right," said Ann, her expression more sober.

"I'll stop down at the Cellar and talk with Del—and Rowan, if she's there—before I leave," said Mike.

While they finished their wine, they speculated about what the sale of the winery might mean for Del and Rowan. Then Ann went inside to unpack her suitcase and Mike followed the path Del had taken to the Cellar. A sign hung on the door: *Due to the death of Niall Lynch, head of Lynch and Son Winery, we will be closed until further notice. Please check our website for updates.*

The door was unlocked, and he stepped inside.

The tasting room was empty, but a bank of flowers in subdued hues lined the top of the bar. He could hear the clack of a keyboard from the hallway beyond.

"Hey, Del," he called as he crossed the room. "It's Mike."

"Hey, Mike. Come on back."

Mike found Del in a workroom, seated at one of two built-in desks.

"Everything okay with the flowers?" Del asked.

"Sure—we appreciate the personal delivery ... although I can see why they might have gotten mixed in with the others. Niall must have had a lot of friends."

Del's mouth quirked up. "I think folks sent them more as a comfort to Rowan than a tribute to her dad. I just brewed a pot of coffee. Want some?"

"Sure, if it's no trouble."

"No trouble. Have a seat. I'll be right back."

Mike pulled out the chair from the other desk and sat.

A moment later, Del was back with a mug for Mike and the coffee carafe. He settled back into his chair.

"I'm sorry to hear about the situation with the winery," said Mike.

Del heaved a sigh. "Yeah."

"Do you think Niall intended for Harkin to get the winery?"

"I can't imagine he did. I think he realized that having Harkin as the heir wouldn't end well. He had a provision in the missing wills that would have limited the heir's ability to sell outside the family, but the will we found doesn't have any limitation. After all, Harkin would have been just a baby when Niall made up the will, and I'm sure he never considered that any son of his would want to sell." He took a sip of coffee and shook his head. "Niall must be spinning in his grave. I can't imagine what he would think about this mess."

Mike figured he wouldn't get a better opening than that. "Well, if you're interested in what Niall thinks, or in finding out anything he could offer to resolve the mix-up with the wills, I know someone who may be able to find out. I've told you about Ann's ability, right?"

"Sort of a ... psychic medium?" Del asked tentatively.

"Sort of like that. She communicates with the dead."

"For real?"

"For real."

"She's done this before?"

Mike ran through his standard recitation of Ann's résumé, including pulling up samples of media coverage of some of Ann's engagements on his phone.

Del's expression morphed from skeptical to cautiously hopeful as Mike spoke.

When Mike had wrapped up his spiel, Del asked, "And she could talk with Niall?"

"It's possible. Just to set the expectations appropriately, some spirits just aren't available to be contacted. But if he's available, she'll contact him."

Del sipped his coffee, mulling over the offer, then asked, "What does that kind of thing cost?"

Mike quoted a price on the low end of the friends-and-family rate. "No contact, no charge," he added.

Del nodded. "It's not something Rowan and I had considered before, but I figure it can't hurt, and I appreciate that you're probably cutting us a break on the price. I'll check with Rowan, but I think she'd be up for it." He topped up their mugs from the carafe. "One of those articles you showed me was about the Philadelphia socialite case?"

"Yup. Brought in by Detective Joe Booth." That police connection was Mike's ace in the hole for potential clients in the Philadelphia area. Occasionally, one recognized Joe's name, which was all the better.

"Does she do other police-type work? You know, investigative work?"

"She has worked with a few police departments. It's always behind the scenes because no police department is going to want to admit that they had to rely on her to solve a case."

Del shifted uncomfortably. "Actually, there's something else she might be able to help me with."

"What's that?"

"There's someone I need to have followed. I've been doing it myself, but let's just say I'm not cut out for that kind of work. Plus, I'm known to the ..." He cast about for a word. "... subject, so it's harder for me to avoid being spotted."

"Who is it?"

"Off the record?"

"Sure."

Although they were clearly alone, Del leaned toward Mike and lowered his voice. "It's Rowan."

"Ro—" Mike began, louder than he intended. He lowered his voice to match Del's. "Rowan?"

Del's cheeks flushed, and he dropped back in his chair.

"Yeah. She's been secretly going to this derelict house in West Philly. I want to find out what the deal is."

"Did you ask her about it?"

Del dropped his eyes. "Not yet." He was silent for a moment, then continued. "I thought maybe she was angry with me about something I did about a month ago that pissed off Niall. It was all just a big mix-up—a misunderstood conversation I had with our grape supplier—but Niall was furious. I think Rowan thought it was a mark against her in terms of inheriting the winery. Then, just the other day, I overheard Niall talking with Harkin. Based on what I heard, I thought Niall was going to leave the winery to Rowan. I told her what I had heard. But when that didn't happen, I think it was twice as disappointing to her because she had almost convinced herself she would be the heir. I'm still in the doghouse for that screwup." He met Mike's gaze for a moment, then dropped his eyes again. "I think she might even have been lying about where she was the night of Niall's death. She and her Aunt Nola were supposed to be at an art exhibit in Philadelphia. Nola said they left the exhibit at the same time, but Nola got home way before Rowan did. I want to know where she went after the exhibit."

"And you think she's ..." Mike trailed off. Even if he acknowledged that there was no accounting for tastes, he was having a little trouble picturing the very pregnant Rowan Lynch engaging in an affair.

Del sighed. "I don't know what to think. I've followed her to this place in West Philly twice, but there were other times in the last month or so when she went out alone in the evenings. I didn't think much about it at the time, but now it seems suspicious. She never used to go out so much in the evenings. At least not without me."

Del told Mike what he had seen on his own reconnaissance missions, including the surprise of the older, Victorian-garbed man and the fact that visitors to 46 Larch Street arrived at the front entrance at the top of the hour and apparently left by the back entrance. "I'm worried about her." He dropped his eyes to his mug and spoke more quietly. "I'm worried about us."

"Del, tailing people, it's not really our thing—" Mike began, then stopped.

It certainly wasn't Ann's thing, but obviously Del didn't need a spirit senser to tell him where his wife was going and what she was doing. Mike didn't mind playing second fiddle in Ann Kinnear Sensing, but it would be fun to have a job that was strictly his own—an engagement that didn't require him to get someone else's approval before accepting or rejecting.

"It's not Ann's thing," he said, "but if you just need to find out what's up with Rowan, I could do that."

Del considered, then nodded. "That would be good. To tell you the truth, I'd feel kind of funny about Ann knowing. If she does stay in the Curragh for a while, she and Rowan might become friends."

"I'll see what I can find out."

"I think I'd only need coverage in the evenings." After a pause, Del asked, "What would that cost?"

Mike sensed that a payout beyond Ann's fee might put a strain on Del's resources, especially since it sounded as if he might be out of a winemaker job soon.

"I'm not coming to this job with a sheaf of references," said Mike. "No charge."

Del looked relieved. "That's great, Mike. I really appreciate it."

Mike swallowed the last of his coffee and set the mug aside. "As far as Ann's sensing engagement goes, once you get the okay from Rowan, I'll let Ann know."

"I'll call Rowan right now. If she and Ann are both agreeable, we could get started right away. Just give me one minute." Del got up and headed for the tasting room, pulling his phone from his pocket as he went.

Mike put his hands in his pockets and leaned back, humming softly. Not only did it seem like he had landed Ann the world's most conveniently located sensing gig, but he couldn't wait to get home and talk to Scott about the PI job he had lined up for the two of them.

W hile Mike was down at the Cellar drumming up business for Ann Kinnear Sensing, and after Ann had transferred her clothes from her suitcase into the built-in dresser, Ann called Corey.

"Thanks for the flowers," she said when he answered. "That was sweet."

"My pleasure. How's it going?"

She flopped back on the bed. "It's a mixed bag. The downside is that we just found out that Del's brother-in-law, Harkin Lynch, inherited the winery and plans to sell it.

"Man, that sucks."

"The upside is Mike is working on a hyper-local engagement for me: trying to contact Niall and finding out if there's a way to avoid having that happen. And even if Harkin sells, it's not clear what will happen to the Curragh. I might just get new landlords."

"Should you find yourself in the market for new water-view digs, just let me know."

"Will do," she said, keeping her tone upbeat. She heard the

shriek of multiple youthful voices in the background of Corey's call. "How's it going there?"

"Good. Larry and I took a bunch of the nieces and nephews out for miniature golf."

"That sounds ..." *Awful*, she thought. "Festive."

"It was fun. Turns out Larry is a pro at mini golf. And a really nice guy. I hope that he and Mom can work out this issue with Dad ... hopefully with your help."

"We'll give it a try when your mom gets back to Pittsburgh. Maybe Carl will be more receptive on his home turf." Ann heard the front door of the Curragh open and close. "Mike's back. Maybe he has an update on that engagement with the Lynch family. Can I give you a call later?"

"Sure thing. Let me know if I can bring you a housewarming present from the Shore."

"How about some saltwater taffy?"

"You got it."

When she emerged from the bedroom, Mike said, "We're on for the engagement. Del got the okay from Rowan." He sat down on a stool at the kitchen's soapstone counter. "Sounds like Rowan's aunt, Nola Lynch, is also onboard, although I got the impression that Del hadn't counted on her being involved, much less polled for her opinion. They're asking if you can start right away—or at least as soon as Nola gets here."

Ann grimaced. "All three of them want to be in on this?"

"I know. It's not optimal. I explained to them that the more spectators who tag along, the less likely it will be for Niall to put in an appearance. We agreed to try one recon with them there, and that if it doesn't work out, you'll try on your own later."

"It's not just the crowd—it's the time of day. Did you explain to them that I'll be more likely to contact Niall at the time of his death?"

"I did." He shrugged. "I figure if you have to make a few passes to find Niall, it's not like it's a long commute."

She sighed. "True. I guess Harkin's not going to participate?"

"That's my understanding. He hardly has any incentive to look for a more recent will."

"Are you going to stay for the show?"

"No, I'm going to head out. I figure Niall is even less likely to show up if the crowd includes someone he doesn't even know."

An hour later, Ann got a text from Del that Nola had arrived. Ann took the path from the Curragh to the Cellar and stepped into the tasting room.

Del and Rowan sat at one of the customer tables with an older woman who looked much the way Ann imagined Rowan would look in another thirty years.

Del stood. "Ann, this is Rowan's aunt, Nola Lynch. Nola, Ann Kinnear."

Nola nodded to Ann. "Pleased to meet you."

Ann guessed that "pleased" was overstating Nola's enthusiasm, but dealing with skeptical family members was all part of the job.

Rowan rose. "I really appreciate you giving this a try," she said to Ann. In Rowan's face, Ann read cautious excitement.

"I appreciate you giving me the chance to try," Ann replied with a smile.

"So, how does this work?" asked Del.

"Since we're here," said Ann, "why don't I look around the Cellar first. Is it okay if I walk around by myself? I can call you if I see anything."

After a pause, Rowan nodded. "All right."

Del reached for Rowan's hand, but Rowan, perhaps not noticing the gesture, walked to the window that gave a view across the parking lot to the vineyard beyond. Del took a step after her, hesitated, then redirected his steps to rejoin Nola at the table.

Ann scanned the tasting room but didn't see any sign of Niall Lynch. She stepped through a swinging door into a large but sparsely outfitted kitchen area, then made a cursory trip up a short hallway that led to the restrooms. One never knew where a spirit might appear.

Another short hallway led to a workspace with built-in tables on two sides acting as desks. Based on the photo of Del hanging on the corkboard over the tidier desk and the photo of Rowan over the messier one, she guessed these to be the couple's desks. On the far side of the room was a door leading to a storage area. Ann returned to the hallway and followed it past a room that she guessed was intended to be used as a coat check.

At the end of the hall was an office that must have been Niall's. If she contacted him at the Cellar, she guessed it would be here. She lowered herself onto the desk chair, then sat quietly, keeping her senses on alert for a ghostly presence. While she waited, she scanned Niall's desk.

It was topped with a sheet of glass, under which were newspaper clippings and printouts of online articles related to the winery. Pride of place was given to an article that contained two photographs.

Ann had seen pictures of Niall in online coverage of his death and she didn't have to read the captions to recognize in him the photos. In the first, a much younger Niall stood next to an older man, identified as his father, who rested his hand on Niall's shoulder. The men were smiling. Standing on the other side and slightly apart was a young Nola Lynch, looking very much like Rowan except for her somber expression.

The other photo was more recent, although almost identically posed. In this one, Niall was now in the center, flanked by a teenage Harkin and an even younger Rowan. In this version of the scene, the boy scowled at the camera while the girl displayed a ready grin.

Ann stood and wandered around the room, looking at other pictures and articles hanging on the walls: celebrations of the winery's fiftieth anniversary, an enthusiastic review of its Cabernet Sauvignon in the *Philadelphia Register*, a somewhat less enthusiastic but respectful article in *Wine Spectator*, praise for Lynch and Son Winery's Sapele. The photos accompanying the articles usually showed the winery itself rather than the people who ran it, although Ann was interested to note that the Sapele review included a photo of Niall rather than the winemaker, Del Berendt. She returned to Niall's desk chair.

After another twenty minutes of spirit-free waiting, she returned to the tasting room.

Rowan was now seated at a table by the window, still staring outside and absently rubbing her stomach. Still seated at the table with Nola, Del played with one of the cardboard tent signs that described the wines on offer. Nola looked up from her phone.

"Nothing so far," said Ann, "but I'll check the Cellar again later if we don't find him elsewhere. Is the building behind the Cellar where you make the wine?"

"Yes," said Rowan, pushing herself out of the chair. "That's where the fermentation tanks, the bottling equipment, and the barrel room are."

"Did Niall spend a lot of time there?"

"Yes, he—" Rowan began, then pulled a tissue from the pocket of her dress and blotted her eyes.

Nola stood, went to Rowan's side, and gave her arm a squeeze before turning back to Ann. "It was Niall's favorite part of the winery."

"Let's check that next," said Ann.

Rowan nodded. "We can go out the back way."

She led them down the hallway and through the workspace and the storage room to the back of the Cellar. They crossed the small staff parking area to the Ark and stepped into a room that was pleasantly cool, especially after the rising afternoon temperatures. Stainless steel tanks dotted with gauges and dials and sprouting neatly coiled tubing stood on a concrete floor that looked as clean as a countertop.

A man appeared from behind a tank, and Del introduced him to Ann as Sam Griller, the assistant winemaker.

Rowan glanced at her watch. "Sam, will you be taking your lunch break soon?"

"I can," said Sam, "or I can wait if you need me for anything."

Rowan glanced toward Ann.

"Now would be a good time for the lunch break," said Ann.

Rowan nodded and turned back to Sam. "Maybe Lee and Bradley, too, if it's not inconvenient."

"Sure thing," said Sam.

As he rounded up the other two Lynch staffers, Ann scanned the room. Although Rowan, Del, and Nola stood in a corner and their brief exchanges were infrequent and muted, Ann was increasingly certain that she wouldn't see Niall Lynch on this reconnaissance. Even if Niall wasn't put off by their presence, Ann found it distracting.

After a few minutes—all it took to check the space—she went to where they stood and shook her head. "I'm not getting anything here. Are there more rooms?"

"Yes, the barrel room," said Rowan.

She led Ann to a pair of heavy doors and pulled one open. An even cooler waft of air slipped out.

"Can I go in by myself?" Ann asked.

Rowan nodded. Ann stepped into the barrel room and the door closed behind her.

The air, cooler here than in the fermentation room, held an

earthy ripeness. Racks of stacked barrels stretched away in the dim light. It seemed like a space that might draw the spirit of a devoted winemaker, but despite a careful check of every aisle, despite Ann calling Niall Lynch's name, the barrel room appeared to be as free of spirits as the other locations.

Before leaving the room, she detoured to a battered desk with a row of silver-framed photos arranged across the back. She expected more mementos of winery milestones, but instead they were headshots. On the left was Niall's father in a formally posed studio portrait, then a younger but still stern-looking Niall, followed by a stiffly uncomfortable Nola, an unsurprisingly sullen Harkin, a quite glamorous Rowan, and a dark-haired teenager whom Ann guessed was Harkin's son. Based on the regularity of the photos' spacing, Niall might have used a ruler to arrange them.

When she stepped out into the fermentation room, Del asked, "Anything?"

Ann shook her head. "No. Not yet."

"Should we check the vineyard?" asked Nola.

"Sure," said Ann, feeling it was the route of least resistance to let the family accompany her on this preliminary search of the property. At least it would give her the lay of the land when she set out on what she was sure would be a more fruitful solo examination.

"Let's go through the Cellar," said Rowan. "I can check the schedule and see if anyone is likely to be in the vineyard."

They reentered the Cellar by the back door. Rowan stopped at the tidier of the two desks in the workspace and tapped some keys on its computer. "Actually, if we want some privacy, now wouldn't be the best time. Sean and Anita are fixing the cordon wire that popped when that limb fell over in Block C, and I don't want to interrupt their work."

"Should we try the path to the big house now?" Del asked

Rowan tentatively. "If we only go partway up, I don't think Harkin will see us, and I don't imagine he's spending much time strolling the grounds."

The four jumped at a nasal voice from the hallway. "Yeah. Heaven forbid I should go anywhere on the property other than the house."

Harkin leaned against the doorframe, arms crossed.

"What are you doing here, Harkin?" asked Rowan, her tone brittle.

"Why shouldn't I be here? It's my winery."

Rowan's face reddened, and Harkin must have regretted his response because he delivered his next words in a more conciliatory tone. "I need to get some papers. I figured they'd be in Dad's office." After a pause, he said, "Giving the new tenant a tour?"

Nola answered. "Del and Rowan have hired Ann to try to contact Niall. She has some experience in that area. You can read about her in the *Register*."

Harkin raised an eyebrow. "I'll do that. But what about you, Nola? Not in on the gig to summon Dad?"

"Niall and I said everything we needed to say to each other before he died. But I think we all believed we had at least a few more months with him. I imagine that Del and Rowan would like an opportunity to say goodbye."

Del nodded uneasily. Rowan glared at her brother.

Harkin pushed himself off the doorframe. As he turned and disappeared down the hall toward Niall's office, he called back, "If you see Dad, say hi to him for me."

26

On the way from Kennett Square back to West Chester, Mike called Scott to update him on the conversation with Del Berendt and the assignment to follow Rowan Lynch and find out what she was doing in West Philly. When Mike arrived at the townhouse, Scott was jotting on a notepad.

"What are you up to?" Mike asked.

"I'm making a list of provisions we'll need for the stakeout."

"I can't imagine we'll need much. According to Del, we only need to be on duty in the evenings. If we need a snack, there's a Landhope Farms store right down the road from Del and Rowan's house, and if we get really hungry, we can get takeout from Kennett Bistro."

"We can't be leaving our post to get snacks."

Mike looked over Scott's shoulder at the list: *Water, cheese, crackers, grapes, Hershey Kisses, kibble, water bowl*

"Kibble? Water bowl?" asked Mike.

"I figured I'd bring Ursula, so she doesn't get lonely." After a moment, he asked, "You don't think it's going to be dangerous, do you?"

"Not unless Rowan Lynch is a lot more formidable than I would expect from the wife of the mild-mannered Del Berendt."

"Sometimes opposites attract."

"We're not opposites."

Scott raised an eyebrow. "Okay. Sometimes likes attract."

Mike went to the refrigerator. "I'm making a sandwich—want me to make you one?"

"What kind?"

"Haven't decided yet."

"Tuna fish?"

"Sounds good." Mike got mayo and celery from the fridge and a can of tuna from the cupboard. "Del doesn't want Ann to know—I think he has visions of her and Rowan becoming buddies. And we obviously want to keep it as quiet as possible. If I thought my spouse was stepping out on me, I wouldn't be interested in broadcasting it, either."

"Does he know I know?"

Mike began chopping celery. "No, but Ann was the only person he specifically didn't want to know. I need your help, and you're not going to tell anyone." He hurried on before Scott had a chance to reply. "Their place in Unionville is just a few minutes from the winery. Where can we wait? We can't wait at the Lynch property without having to explain to Ann what we're doing there. We can't just park down the road from Del and Rowan's house, at least not on that road—it doesn't have much of a shoulder."

"If she goes from Unionville to West Philly, she'll go right past Longwood Gardens. We could wait in that picnic area across Longwood Road."

"What if she goes the other direction?"

"If Del can let us know if she turns the other way, we still might be able to catch up with her ... especially if you, the man to whom speed limits are a mere suggestion, are the one doing the driving. You said Rowan drives a red Miata, right? It would be easy to spot on the road."

"Okay," said Mike, getting out his phone. "I'll ask Del to let us know what direction she goes when she leaves the house."

"To let *you* know," corrected Scott. "Remember, I'm the silent partner."

27

H arkin's footsteps receded down the hall toward Niall's office, and Ann heard the click of the door closing behind him.

Rowan's face was red and Del looked as if he was barely restraining himself from pursuing his brother-in-law down the hall, and not just for a chat. Nola, her lips pressed into a thin line, gestured them out of the work area and down the hall, away from Niall's office.

When they reached the tasting room, Rowan said in a strained whisper, "Aunt Nola, I don't know how you can be so patient with him. He's being awful."

"It's a hard time for everyone," said Nola, her voice equally quiet. "I don't know how long he'll be in Niall's office, but I guess there's no impediment to walking up the path, or even checking out the big house."

"Except it's Harkin's house now," said Rowan bitterly.

"I don't care what the will says," Nola replied. "It's the family home and I intend to treat it as such." She turned to Ann. "Do you want to check the path and the house now?"

"Sure."

They stepped out the front entrance of the Cellar. As they crossed the parking lot, Rowan slowed, then stopped.

"I thought I was ready for this—for going to where we found Dad—but I don't think I am. I have some things I want to check out in the vineyard. Why don't I meet up with you at the Cellar afterwards. Hopefully Harkin will be out of Dad's office by that time."

"Want me to come with you?" asked Del.

"No, that's okay. Just text me when you're done." Rowan turned and headed for the vineyard.

Del watched her retreating form for a moment, then sighed and turned to Nola. "Since you're the one who found him, do you want to lead the way?"

"Certainly."

Nola led them up the path, and they entered the lightly wooded area that ran between the winery buildings and the house. The path itself was well maintained—clear of fallen branches or engulfing vines—but the ground on both sides was dotted with rocks poking up through the soil. The entire area must have been similarly rock-studded at one time, based on the low stone walls that snaked through the property.

As they walked, Ann kept an eye out for any sign of Niall, but even if he was in the area, the dappled sunlight that found its way through the canopy of leaves would make him difficult to see.

They were about halfway up the hill when Nola stopped. "This is where I found him."

The ground was churned up, low branches broken or trampled into the ground.

"Was it like this when you found him?" Ann asked, gesturing.

"I don't think so. It was dark. I suspect a lot of the mess was caused by the EMTs when they brought him up to where the ambulance was parked."

"Did you find him right on the path?"

"Just off it." Nola pointed to a spot a few feet from the path. "It looked like he had hit his head on that rock."

"The front of his head?"

"No, the back. He was lying on his back when I found him."

Ann raised her eyebrows. "He tripped and hit the back of his head?"

Del spoke up. "We figured that he stopped to catch his breath, got dizzy, and fell backward. It wasn't unusual for him to have dizzy spells, although as far as we know, he had never fallen before."

"Even if he had fallen before that night," said Nola, "he might not have told us."

Ann stepped off the path and picked her way among the rocks, looking for an angle that would put a patch of undergrowth behind the area where Niall had fallen. Perhaps a darker background would reveal a presence that the sunlight disguised. But she still saw no sign of a spirit.

As she returned to the path, Nola gestured up the hill. "It looks like Harkin finished up at the winery."

Ann turned to see a man walking up the drive toward the house.

"Let's wait and check the house when Harkin isn't there," continued Nola, "especially since Ann will have to try at the Cellar and the Ark again when we aren't all tagging along."

"And I might have better luck at the time of Niall's death," Ann said. No reason for Del and Nola to think that their presence was the only reason that Niall wasn't putting in an appearance.

"Do you want to try again tonight?" asked Del.

"Sure."

He pulled a keyring from his pocket and handed it to her. "These are to the Cellar, the Ark, and the big house," he said, pointing to each of the three keys. He glanced up the hill. "I don't know what Harkin's plans are. We might have to wait for another day for you to check the house."

"That's fine with me," said Ann, pocketing the keys. She was happy to avoid another unpleasant encounter with Harkin Lynch.

Del pulled out his phone. "I'll let Rowan know that Harkin's out of Niall's office, and that we're going back to the Cellar."

As they reached the parking lot, Rowan emerged from the vineyard, her dress fluttering in a slight breeze, her sandals hooked over her fingers.

The four met at the front door of the Cellar.

"So, no luck?" said Rowan.

"No," said Del. "Ann's going to try again tonight."

"Do we need to be available?" Rowan asked Ann.

"It's better if I'm on my own. But I can give you a call and let you know what I find."

"I may be out for a little while this evening," said Rowan.

Based on Del's expression, Ann guessed that Rowan's plans were news to her husband.

"If I can contact Niall," said Ann, "I'll get a piece of information from him that it's unlikely I could get elsewhere."

Rowan said, "That's not necessary—" at the same time Nola said, "That would be helpful—" The two women exchanged surprised looks, then similar rueful laughs.

"It's no problem," said Ann. "It's a usual practice, just so you can feel comfortable that I've actually spoken to him. Assuming I can contact him tonight, I could meet up with the three of you tomorrow to give you an update."

"I have a meeting in the morning with a Nolyn Events client that I can't change," said Nola. "But if you keep Rowan—and

Del, of course—updated, then they can pass on any information they think I need."

Del nodded. "That sounds like a plan. But let's meet somewhere other than the winery." He turned to Ann. "Rowan and I live just a few minutes away. Let's meet at our place if there's anything to report." He glanced up the hill toward the house. "At least we won't have to worry about Harkin making an unexpected appearance there."

28

That evening, Mike and Scott were in position in Longwood Garden's picnic area when Mike's phone pinged.

Mike read the text. "Del says that Rowan told him she's going to an expectant mothers' support group meeting."

"That seems plausible," Scott said as he lifted Ursula off his lap and buckled her into her booster seat in back.

Mike started Audrey the Audi. "I guess we'll find out." The phone pinged again. "He says she turned left out of the driveway."

"That's toward Philly," said Scott.

A few minutes later, the red Miata passed them, easy to pick out even in the waning evening light. Mike pulled out of the parking lot, about fifty yards behind her.

Half an hour later, as they followed her onto 95 North, Mike said, "It's a long way to go for an expectant mothers' meeting. I wonder if we're supposed to send Del updates."

"You couldn't very well text him while you're driving—at least you shouldn't—and he doesn't know you have an assistant."

"Partner. But you're right."

The heavy traffic on 95 meant that they could stay fairly close to the Miata and not attract any unwanted attention, but when Rowan exited 95 just north of the airport and traffic became more sparse, they dropped back. They crossed the Schuylkill, skirted South Philly, West Passyunk, and Grays Ferry, then recrossed the river and headed northwest.

When the Miata turned onto Larch Street, Scott said, "It looks like she's headed for the same place Del followed her to."

As they approached the block that had been Rowan's destination on her previous trips to Larch Street, the Miata turned left. When they reached the intersection, they saw it disappear into the alley.

"Now what?" asked Mike.

"Drive by and I'll see what I can see."

As Mike rolled past the alley, Scott said, "She's pulling into a parking area next to one of those little delivery vans like a florist would use and some kind of silver four-door sedan."

Mike turned right at the next intersection and then made two more rights to put them back on Larch. He pulled up a few dozen yards from 46, in a space unlit by the widely spaced streetlights. Just as he killed the engine, Rowan Lynch rounded the far corner, hurrying up the street. She glanced at her phone, then went to the house door and knocked. After a moment, a light illuminated the small glass panes at the top of the door, which opened to reveal a man carrying an oil lamp.

"Same old-fashioned clothes Del described," said Mike.

The man dipped his head to Rowan and stepped aside to let her enter. The door closed and a moment later, the light faded away.

Scott glanced at his watch. "Exactly eight o'clock." He turned to the back seat, unbuckled Ursula from her booster seat, and lifted her into his lap. "I wish our first job wasn't following Rowan. It's going to be terrible if we end up having to bring Del bad news about what's going on."

"Yeah, but I'm guessing PIs are rarely hired to catch people behaving themselves." Mike got out his phone. "I guess I should let Del know we're at Larch Street."

"That *you're* at Larch Street."

"Right."

Mike tapped out an update to Del, then they sat in silence, gazing at the seemingly empty house on the deserted street.

After a few minutes, Scott said, "Del never saw Rowan leave. Maybe we should check to make sure her car's still there. I could go back there while you watch the front."

"What if she comes out the back while you're there?"

"There are a bunch of trash and recycling containers. I can hide behind one of those."

"This neighborhood is sort of sketchy—I don't like the idea of you wandering around on your own. At least let's hold off on that approach unless we really need it. We can drive by the alley periodically to see what's up."

Mike started up the Audi, drove to the end of the street, turned right, and coasted past the alley.

"Rowan's Miata and the florist-type van are still there," said Scott, "but the sedan is gone."

"If the van belongs to the Victorian guy, I guess it's just him and Rowan in the house now."

Mike circled the block and pulled back into the space on Larch Street.

On their second circuit, Scott talked Mike into turning into the alley, where he hopped out of the car and peered into the passenger window of the van.

"Nothing of interest in the front seat," he said when he

climbed back into the Audi. "It's too dark to see anything in back."

As nine o'clock approached, Scott said, "Since people seem to arrive at the front door at the top of the hour, maybe I should just happen to be walking Ursula when the next visitors show up."

Mike glanced up and down the street. "I don't know ... doesn't this neighborhood give you the creeps?"

"What do you mean? We haven't seen anyone who looks threatening. In fact, we haven't seen anyone, period."

"I know. Maybe that's why it gives me the creeps—it's like the street that time forgot."

Scott patted Mike's arm. "If I run into any trouble, I have my knight in shining armor to rescue me."

Mike snorted. "More like your knight in shining armor to call 911 from the safety of the car."

"I don't believe that for a minute," said Scott. "While I take a walk, you should drive past the alley and see if Rowan leaves as a new group shows up."

"I thought I was supposed to stand by to rescue you."

"I'll put my phone in my shirt pocket and keep it on speaker. But you should keep your phone muted unless you really need to tell me something. We don't want to spook someone with a mysterious voice emanating from my pocket."

Mike chewed the corner of his thumbnail. "I wonder if I'm supposed to have a license of some kind in order to follow people."

"No one will know. We're undercover."

"What if Rowan sees you?"

"We haven't heard about or seen anyone come out the front. They must all leave by the back door and then go to their car in the parking area. I'll stay out of the alley, so even if we cross paths, she won't see me up close. And even if I ran into her, I don't think she'd recognize me. I've never actually talked with her."

"Maybe take your glasses off."

Scott sighed. He removed his chunky black glasses and slipped them into his shirt pocket.

"And put on my baseball hat," said Mike.

"I don't look good in a baseball hat."

"It's not a fashion show," said Mike, rummaging in the back seat for the hat. "It's an undercover job."

Scott put on the hat, then placed a call to Mike's phone, turned his phone to speaker, and slipped it into his shirt pocket.

"What if I see her driving away?" asked Mike. "I won't be able to follow her if you're still cruising the neighborhood with your attack dachshund."

"It sounds like Del didn't have any reason to think she went anywhere other than back home after she left here. I think it's more important to see if we can get any information from other visitors than to follow Rowan when she leaves."

"Makes sense."

Scott pulled an item out of Ursula's bag of supplies and clipped the dog's leash to her harness. Then he climbed out of the car and set the dachshund on the sidewalk.

"Wish me luck!" he said and swung the door shut and crossed the street.

"Luck," Mike said with a grimace.

Mike set his phone on the dash, speaker on and mic muted, then started the car and pulled away from the curb. When he reached the corner, he looked back to see Scott and Ursula passing under a streetlight. As usual, Ursula seemed driven less by a philosophy of "stop and smell the roses" and more by a belief that the next thing she came to might be something to eat. As she towed Scott along, Mike thought it would be a miracle if

Scott managed to intercept anyone else who arrived at number 46.

Mike turned right at the intersection—and almost yelped as Rowan's car appeared at the mouth of the alley ahead of him. He fought an urge to slide down in the seat as he rolled past the alley, less than a dozen feet from the Miata. However, a quick glance suggested that Rowan was occupied with checking for any other traffic on the otherwise deserted cross street. By the time she pulled out of the alley, Mike was already turning at the next intersection. A moment later, his rearview mirror showed the Miata buzzing past.

Mike decided that Rowan's departure didn't merit breaking radio silence with Scott. He continued his circuit of the block and pulled into the same parking space on Larch. Scott was picking his way along the cracked and heaved sidewalk toward number 46.

Just as Scott reached the house, a man and woman appeared around the same corner from which Rowan had come, walking toward him. They were both dressed in black, the streetlight picking up the glint of metal from piercings on the woman's eyebrows and nose and the sheen of leather on the man's pants.

Mike did a mental calculation—Scott would be past the house when he encountered the couple.

However, as Scott and Ursula approached number 46, the dachshund began towing even more enthusiastically against the harness. When Ursula reached the house, she flattened herself on the sidewalk and began gobbling something off the ground.

The couple reached Scott, who was waiting for Ursula to finish consuming whatever trove she had found.

The man glanced uncertainly toward number 46. "You here for the cabinet?" Mike heard from his phone's speaker.

"Just out for a walk," answered Scott. "Are *you* here for the cabinet?"

Before the man could respond, the woman said to him in a stage whisper, "You're not supposed to talk about it!"

The man folded his arms and rolled his eyes.

"It's the worst kept secret in the neighborhood," said Scott conspiratorially. "Is this your first time?"

"Yes. But they told us not to talk about it," the woman said sullenly. She hooked her arm under the man's elbow and tugged him toward the gate. "Come on. We don't want to keep them waiting."

"Well, have ... a satisfying time," Scott called after them, then turned and continued up the street. Ursula must have cleared the sidewalk of consumables because she trotted into the lead and began once more to tow Scott in her wake.

The couple pushed through the creaking gate of number 46 and climbed the stairs to the porch. Mike couldn't hear what they were saying, but the tone was argumentative. He checked the time: 8:59.

At exactly 9:00, the woman knocked on the door. The sequence that Mike and Scott had observed played out: a light illuminated the panes of glass in the door; the door opened to reveal the frock-coated, oil lamp-carrying man; the couple entered; the light dimmed; and the house was dark again.

A few minutes later, Scott and Ursula reached the Audi. Scott scooped Ursula up and got into the passenger seat.

"Could you hear?" Scott asked.

"Yeah. What's the cabinet?"

"I didn't understand it either. But it does look like whatever is going on inside is supposed to be a secret."

"It's a secret and super-exclusive furniture store?"

"I suppose weirder things happen in Philly."

"Rowan headed out." Mike got out his phone and tapped. "I'm going to let Del know. At least she was headed in the direction of home." As he slipped the phone back into his pocket, a few drops of water hit the windshield. "Glad that held off. By the way, what did you do to get Ursula to stop in front of the house?"

"On my first pass, I dropped a handful of kibble on the sidewalk."

Mike grinned. "You have a flair for this PI work."

29

Ann unlocked the front door of the Cellar and stepped inside. A steady rain had moved in earlier in the evening, and she hung her dripping umbrella on the coat rack next to the door. It was ten o'clock, about an hour before the time Nola had found Niall's body on the path between the winery and the house. The path, as the location of Niall's death, was a strong candidate for a successful contact, and she had stopped there before coming to the Cellar. Her evening would be a more comfortable one if she could locate him indoors.

Although a light, turned low, had been left on over the bar, much of the tasting room was in shadow. She locked the door behind her, then made a circuit of the room. She popped her head into the restrooms, although she could think of few things more depressing than finding that a spirit had chosen to haunt that location. The kitchen, Del and Rowan's workspace, the storage room, and the coat check were all free of spirits.

She wasn't surprised. If Niall was going to appear in the Cellar, his office was the most likely place. She would use that as her base.

She went to the office, settled into the desk chair, and set the alarm on her phone for twenty minutes.

She hoped she would be able to contact Niall, and not only to help Del, Rowan, and Nola locate a will that would supersede the one that left the winery to Harkin. She had her own motivation. Even though she had been at the Curragh for less than a day, she already loved it: the elegant space that was just right for her needs, the delightful view across the Tarn to the vineyard, and of course easy access to a virtually endless supply of excellent wine.

Another draw was the people. Although Nola's evident skepticism about Ann's ability didn't predispose Ann to feel chummy toward her, she did like Rowan and Del.

Ann had plenty of male friends. Mike. Scott. Joe. Her charter pilot, Walt Federman. And Corey? She thought he would be happier if she counted him in a category other than "friend." Although maybe he *was* just a friend, albeit a friend with benefits. Otherwise, she thought ruefully, she might be more enthusiastic about the idea of moving to L.A. to be with him.

She didn't feel a need to add to her roster of male buddies. But female friends? It had been a long time since she had one of about her own age. If Ann stayed at the Curragh and became friends with Rowan, how might that pan out? Would they meet up for lunch at Kennett Bistro? Would they chat over coffee at the Curragh or Rowan's Unionville house? Would they ... ? She cast about for what other things women did with their girlfriends.

Then she thought of Rowan's impending baby. Would Rowan see her as a potential babysitter? Ann was more interested in a friendship that involved cocktail napkins than one that involved spit-up rags. An expectation that she become "Aunt Ann" and take an interest in baby-related activities would definitely reduce the attraction of living on the Lynch winery property.

The chirp of the phone's alarm saved her from further brooding. She made an unproductive circuit through the other rooms in the Cellar. After retrieving her umbrella, she rechecked the path, then made her way to the Ark.

She walked slowly through the space containing the fermentation tanks, the tile floor throwing back whispery echoes of her sneaker-clad steps. In the barrel room, she walked up and down each of the aisles, although she doubted it would improve her chances of encountering Niall. She sensed the room was empty of spirits in the same way one might sense a house was empty of people. She returned to Niall's office in the Cellar and set the alarm for another twenty minutes.

She was on her third patrol when she found Niall in the barrel room.

He was at the desk, gazing at the row of photos ranged along its back. He turned with a scowl, the chair turning slowly in a delayed reaction to his movement.

The toll that Niall's heart condition had taken on his body was clear. His face was gaunt, eyes sunken between jutting brows and cheekbones, his hair was neatly combed but lusterless, his hands trembled. Ann wondered if Niall's spirit could control how he appeared to her. She guessed not. Otherwise she would have expected to see the handsome and hale man memorialized in the photographs in his office.

"Hello, Mr. Lynch."

He stood. "Who are you?"

"My name is Ann Kinnear, and your family hired me to contact you."

"Mike Kinnear's sister?"

Since her minor celebrity was one of her least favorite

aspects of her profession, it was a refreshing change to be thought of as *Mike Kinnear's sister*. "Yes."

"The psychic? I guess that's why you can see and hear me."

It was a term she disliked, one that suggested gaudy signs over narrow doorways sandwiched between stores selling tourist tchotchkes. "I prefer 'senser,' but yes. I'm also a tenant. I'm living in the Curragh now."

He glanced toward the photo of his sister. "I'm guessing Nola was happy to get back to her own apartment."

"I imagine so." She waited to see if he would say more. When he didn't, she continued. "I was here earlier, with Nola and Rowan and Del. Did you know that?"

"No." His expression changed again, this time to guarded uncertainty. "Why wouldn't I have seen you?"

Ann shrugged. "Spirits aren't always aware of what's going on with the living, just like the living aren't always aware of what's going on with the dead."

"I'd like to think I'd know what's going on at my winery."

Ann restrained herself from pointing out that, strictly speaking, it wasn't his winery anymore.

"You say the family hired you to contact me?" he asked.

"Yes. In fact, it's sometimes helpful for the spirits I contact to give me a piece of information I can convey back to the clients to convince them that we actually spoke. Is there something like that you could tell me?"

Niall considered for a moment, then said, "Barrel 44 is Hungarian, not French. I borrowed it from Ed Kujala at Pocopson Winery and forgot to return it. I wanted to see if there was a difference besides the price. There isn't."

Ann got out her phone. "Can you say that again?"

Niall repeated the information.

"I can't imagine they'll accuse me of making that up." Ann tapped the information into her phone, then slipped it back in her pocket. "The reason they asked me to speak with you is that they've only been able to find one copy of your will—one that you gave Nola years ago, before Rowan was born. They're wondering if there's a more recent one."

"How about the one I was carrying?"

"You were carrying one?"

"Yes. It was in my jacket pocket."

"They didn't mention that."

"I suppose it could have fallen out when ..." His voice trailed off.

"When what?"

"When I was on the path."

"What happened on the path?"

"I wanted to get back to the house. I thought the path would be easier than the drive because it's shorter, but I forgot how steep it is. I stopped to rest, and suddenly there was pain and then ..." Confusion flickered across his face. "Well, I suppose I fainted. Or my heart gave out." His eyes narrowed. "Why?"

"Nola found you next to the path. She said it looked like you had fallen backwards and hit your head. Do you remember anything like that?"

"No. But I might have gotten dizzy and fallen. There are plenty of rocks along that path—it's more likely than not that I would have landed on one."

"And when you started back to the house, you had a more recent will with you?"

"Yes."

"And who did that will favor?"

"Harkin." When she was silent, he added, his tone defensive, "He is the oldest."

She sighed. Not the information she had hoped to bring back to her clients.

"The will they have leaves the winery to the heir you

intended, but it doesn't have any provision to keep Harkin from selling. And that's what he's planning on doing."

Niall's jaw tensed, and he looked away. "Ungrateful little bastard."

She hoped she'd never have to mediate a conversation between this unpleasant man and his equally unpleasant son. "Would Harkin have known that he was the heir?"

"I don't see how. He knew I had two executed wills, and that I was going to destroy one of them."

"Is it possible that someone hit you?"

The surprise on his face seemed genuine. "Why?"

She shrugged. "Family turmoil. Disappearing wills."

Niall's laugh had a harsh edge. "You think Harkin knocked me over the head so that he could get his hands on the winery a couple of months sooner?"

"It doesn't sound like you believe that's likely."

"I suppose anything's possible, but I can't imagine Harkin taking that kind of decisive action."

Decisive action seemed an odd way for a possible murder victim to describe his own murder. Each of Niall Lynch's pronouncements gave her a better sense of the kind of father he must have been.

"He might have wanted to get rid of the will that included the limitation on selling the winery," she said.

"I can't imagine he knew about that earlier will. Even I didn't realize that Nola still had it. And I imagine that if she had remembered, she would have destroyed it. She was always pushing Rowan as the heir."

"Is there anyone who would have known about that will—someone who knew that Harkin would get the winery if the more recent wills were gone?"

"No. It's not like Harkin had a lot of supporters ..."

She waited him out, and after a moment, he continued.

"Although there was one supporter," he said slowly. "I got an unexpected phone call right before I left to go back to the big house. It was from Henry Tollman. He was the winemaker at Lynch many years ago."

"Did he call regularly?"

"No. I hadn't heard from him for twenty years." He glowered. "Twenty-four, to be precise."

"Why did he call?"

"We had a falling out back then. He said he wanted to make amends."

"Could he have come to the property after you talked?"

"He said he was in San Francisco."

"He could have been lying."

"I wouldn't put it past him."

"Maybe if we went back to the path, you'd have a clearer memory of what happened there."

His features tightened. "No."

"You don't want to leave the Ark?"

"No." The flicker of confusion again. "I'm ... settled here. I don't want to leave."

She raised a hand. "No problem." It was not unusual for spirits not to want to leave the place they had found themselves after death.

"But if Harkin sells the winery," his expression morphed toward one of panic. "What will I do? Where will I go?"

"I'm afraid I don't know."

Niall turned and glared at the photo of Harkin on the desk. "'How sharper than a serpent's tooth it is to have a thankless child.'"

"You're casting yourself as King Lear?"

Ignoring the comment, Niall continued. "I spent his whole life grooming him to take over Lynch and Son. What young man wouldn't jump at the opportunity to head up a winery? Tracking the evolution of the grape, urging it one direction or another to express the best qualities of the fruit to create something unique. Something sublime. But he had no interest, and he wouldn't take the steps that might have enabled him to develop an interest." He waved a hand. "I don't blame him for having limitations to overcome," the hand clenched into a fist, "but I do blame him for failing to take the steps that would have enabled him to surmount those limitations."

He turned from the desk and began pacing the room. "And after I had paved the way for him to attend one of the California universities specializing in viticulture, he told me he was going to the University of Hawaii. Who knows what he studied." He grimaced. "Probably sun, surf, and pretty girls. And then his girlfriend got pregnant and he would only come back to Chester County for the family meetings. He even asked to hold the meetings via videoconference." He shook his head. "Ridiculous! Running a winery is a physical, tactile endeavor: tracking the status of the grapes, monitoring the fermentation process, assessing the result by eye, nose, and tongue. There was nothing wrong with Harkin's eyes, at least. I wasn't about to relegate the operation of the business to talking heads on a computer monitor." He turned to Ann. "He never stepped up to his responsibility."

"In what way didn't he step up?"

"He didn't take the steps necessary to equip him for his role."

"What steps should he have taken?"

Niall's mood shifted, and Ann tried to interpret the new state. Irritation? Embarrassment?

After a few seconds, he spoke, his tone reluctant. "Harkin suffers from anosmia."

"What's that?"

"It means he lacks any sense of smell. And, as a result, has almost no sense of taste."

"What causes that?"

"Nasal polyps."

Ann thought back to the nasal twang she had heard in Harkin's voice when he had surprised them in the Cellar.

"And nothing could be done about his condition?" she asked.

"Of course something could be done," snapped Niall. "Nasal sprays, medication, we tried them all. Some of them worked for a time but never long-term. I suggested surgery, but Harkin balked."

"How old was he?"

"I don't remember exactly. Seven? Eight? Old enough."

"What happened without the surgery?"

"I told you, he didn't have any sense of smell or taste."

After a beat she asked, "That was it?"

"He couldn't appreciate the product of the family business!"

"He was just a child—"

"He was destined to be a winemaker," he said, angry spots of color appearing on his pale cheeks. "To be able to direct the production of the product, to understand its subtleties, to tell good from bad." He glared at her. "To tell red from white without looking."

"He wouldn't even be able to enjoy the product for over a decade!"

Niall dismissed her comment with a slash of his hand. "I wasn't insisting he have the surgery immediately. He could have waited for a few years. But he kept refusing, right through his teens until he left for college."

"Well, if the only thing surgery would have done was equip him to run a business he wasn't interested in, I can't blame him for refusing to do it."

Niall took a step toward Ann, and she took a hasty step back. "With surgery, he might have been interested!" he thundered.

"And the game with the two wills—?"

"I was trying to motivate him. I thought under the circumstances he might step up to his responsibility—might understand the importance of carrying on the family tradition."

"Which family tradition is that?"

"It's Lynch and *Son* Winery!" he burst out.

"Ah, *that* tradition. Because if you had meant the family tradition of winemaking, I think Rowan would have been a better bet."

He glared at her for a moment, then, in what Ann guessed was Niall Lynch's best attempt at a conciliatory tone, said, "Maybe if you help me talk with Nola, we can figure out a way to change the terms of the will."

"I think the horse is out of the barn on that one."

"I could write a new will."

"It doesn't work that way."

He threw up his hands. "How can you stand there and tell me you won't help when it sounds like you were hired specifically to make sure the winery went to someone who would carry on the family tradition?"

"They hired me to talk with you. They didn't hire me to bilk your son out of an inheritance that you yourself left to him."

Niall gave a snort of disgust. "Women."

Ann summoned a smile, but she knew it wasn't a warm one. "I know a male senser you could talk to. I can guarantee you'd get the same answer from him."

30

T he next morning, Ann arrived at Rowan and Del's Unionville home, a small, neat Victorian with a freshly painted white picket fence in front. The two-car detached garage looked like it had also had a recent coat of paint, but a slight list to one side suggested that some structural work was needed as well. Summer-themed wreaths hung on the cherry red front door.

When Rowan answered Ann's knock, she looked less tense than she had the day before, although no less sorrowful.

"Come on back to the kitchen," she said, leading Ann down the center hallway. "Del had to go back to the winery. One of the temperature gauges was acting funny. Hopefully he just needs to replace the batteries in the thermostat. If it's a problem with the HVAC system..." She shook her head. "Although I guess it's not our problem anymore."

Ann wondered if Niall Lynch would be looking over Del's shoulder, providing pithy commentary on Del's efforts to remediate the issue.

Rowan waved her to a chair at the kitchen table. "I just

brewed some herbal tea—would you like some? Or I could make you coffee."

"Tea's good—thanks."

Rowan brought a teapot and mugs to the table. She poured two steaming cups—more appealing, despite the already hot morning, than Ann would have expected—and lowered herself onto a chair. "How did it go last night?"

"I was able to contact Niall."

Reading from her phone, Ann told Rowan about the Hungarian Barrel 44 borrowed from Pocopson Winery and Niall's interest in how it compared to its French counterpart.

"I guess we should get the barrel back to Ed at Pocopson," said Rowan. After a moment, she added with a sad smile, "I didn't really disbelieve that you could do what you can do, but hearing the proof ... what a skill to have."

Ann slipped her phone back into her knapsack. "It can be a mixed blessing, but it has its benefits."

Ann recounted her conversation with Niall, playing down her impression of Rowan's father as an insensitive bully and softening his obsession with the winery passing to his son. She conveyed his belief, at least initially, that his fall must have been caused by his heart condition, and his surprise about the disappearance of the will he had been carrying.

"'Will,' singular?" asked Rowan. "So the shredded document in his office was one of the two wills?"

"Yes." Ann hesitated. "The one he destroyed was the one favoring you."

Rowan drew a deep, trembling breath, then puffed it out. "I guess I shouldn't be surprised."

"Harkin has the benefit of gender *and* seniority, and I guess Niall thought he could get him interested in the business right up to the end. Beyond the end, in fact. Your father is obviously a ... challenging personality."

Rowan gazed into her mug. "He could be difficult, but I suppose he did what he did because he thought it was for the best."

"I can imagine some people might not be as understanding as you are." She took a sip of tea while she considered how to approach the next topic. "Niall is confused about the circumstances of his death. He assumed it was due to his illness, but he doesn't remember specifically. Do you have any reason to doubt that Niall's fall was caused by his condition, or maybe the medications he was taking?"

"No. Why?"

Ann sat back in her chair. "There's so much bad feeling swirling around this whole situation. I'm wondering if there might have been some kind of altercation on the path. Especially because the will he thought he was carrying is missing."

Rowan's eyes widened. "You think someone killed Dad?"

"Not necessarily on purpose, but if there was an argument, if someone pushed him—"

"You're not thinking of Harkin, are you?"

"I don't know." After a pause, Ann asked, "Are you?"

"No!" Rowan gnawed her thumbnail, then shook her head. "No. I think Harkin is happy with the life he's built for himself in Hawaii with Alana and Kepi. I think if he had gotten mad at Dad —madder than usual—he would have just driven to the airport and flown back to Hawaii, not followed him up the path to argue with him. And certainly not to intentionally hurt him. Especially when he knew Dad wouldn't be around that much longer in any case."

"Assuming he thought Niall's will favored him."

"Yes. But I guess we all should have assumed that all along."

Ann sipped her tea, thinking that if she were Rowan Lynch, she might have been tempted to crack Niall over the head. "How do you want to let Del and Nola know what I learned from Niall? Do you want me to tell them? Or to be there?"

"No, that's okay," said Rowan. "I'll tell them."

Ann heard the ping of a text and Rowan pulled her phone out of her pocket and glanced at the screen. "Ah, good. The thermostat just needed new batteries." She dropped the phone back into her pocket. "Good news for the new winery owners, I guess."

"If I can get in touch with Niall again, do you want to try to talk with him? Not necessarily about the will, but about anything else?"

Rowan stared into her tea. "I'm not sure. Let me talk to Nola and Del—and maybe Harkin, too—and see what they have to say." She glanced up at Ann. "I think Harkin might not be comfortable with you being there. Even as dicey as things are in the family, I think he would prefer to keep it private—especially if we're able to communicate with Dad. Do you think it would be possible for us to communicate with him without you there, especially now that we know where to look?"

"It's not unheard of."

"How would we go about that?"

"I suppose just hang out in the barrel room, call his name, talk about things you think he would be interested in."

"No Ouija board?" asked Rowan, perhaps only half joking.

Ann smiled. "You never know, but I'd try just talking first."

"And ... he'll talk back?"

Ann shrugged. "Maybe. I can make a living by communicating with the dead because not many people can do it, but there are plenty of stories of people who don't normally have that ability seeing or even hearing a dead friend or family member. Sometimes the dead send some signal, like a whistling or tapping noise. I heard of one case where a pencil would roll across the deceased's desk at exactly the same time every night.

Being able to communicate with them is much rarer, but not unheard of. But you should try soon. I can't tell how long he might be there."

"I'll talk to Del and Nola and Harkin today." She brightened. "Actually, Aunt Nola was planning to come out here to have dinner with me and Del anyway. We can meet up at the winery instead." Her hand drifted to her stomach and she smiled. "Pretty soon we'll have a new picture to add to the collection on his desk. Maybe Dad will stay around long enough to see it."

fter wrapping up her meeting with Rowan in Unionville, Ann headed toward West Chester. She was meeting with Mike for breakfast to update him on the progress of the engagement.

When she arrived at the Main Line Diner, she found Mike in a booth working on his laptop.

"Were you waiting long?" she asked as she slid across the vinyl bench.

"I got here early to get some work done."

The waitress came by with the coffee carafe to fill Ann's cup and refill Mike's. They both put in orders for omelets.

Ann once again recapped her conversation with Niall. "Rowan's going to talk with Del, Nola, and maybe Harkin about whether they want me to try to mediate a conversation with Niall. In the meantime, she's going to give it a try herself."

"You're letting amateurs do your job?"

"Don't be a snob. It's not impossible that she could contact her father. Maybe Niall would like to have a final conversation with the only member of his family who seems really broken up that he's gone. And if I can avoid having to deal with Harkin Lynch, that's okay with me."

"Sounds like none of the Lynch men are going to be winning any congeniality awards."

"At least Del seems like a good guy. He seems very protective of Rowan." She lowered her voice. "Did you ever think that maybe something happened on the path other than Niall keeling over onto a rock? Especially since the will he said he was carrying is missing?"

Mike raised his eyebrows. "No. He was terminally ill—it wouldn't have been surprising if he was unsteady on his feet. And he might have been taking blood thinners for his heart condition, so if he hit his head, it would bleed more than normal —externally and internally. It seems like an accident waiting to happen. Why?"

"I don't know. There's a lot going on in that family. And he had gotten a call from a former Lynch winemaker that evening. Niall said they had a falling out."

"Recently?"

"Well, no. Over twenty years ago. But it sounded like there was no love lost there."

"Sounds like you could say that about pretty much everyone who knew Niall Lynch—except maybe Rowan. I'd look at Harkin before some long-ago winemaker. After all, he's the one who ended up with the winery, even after all the shenanigans with the wills."

"If we're sizing up suspects, what about Nola? She and Rowan seem very close. Maybe she thought she was defending Rowan's interests."

"If she did, it sure backfired."

They suspended their conversation when the waitress arrived with their omelets.

When she had left, Ann said, "What about Del? You know him better than I do."

"I really can't see Del Berendt as a cold-blooded killer ... or even someone who could get mad enough to push his terminally ill father-in-law onto a rock in the middle of the night."

"Maybe whoever pushed Niall wasn't the initiator. Maybe Niall encountered someone on the path, attacked him, and the other person just lashed out in self-defense."

Mike chewed thoughtfully. "I suppose I can imagine that. Del did mention that he had gotten the winery into some trouble shooting his mouth off about the business—or at least about something that the person he was talking to assumed to be the winery's business—and that Niall was none too pleased with him about it. And if Niall was at all sensitive about people who have no filters between their brains and their mouths, he might have reason to take a swing at Del." He sipped his coffee. "Back when I was working as Del's financial planner, I found out about a microcap stock that I thought was going to move because the company had a new patent coming out. I only told a few of my clients—including Del—because it was a bit of a risky investment, but honestly, he didn't have enough money with me for it to be much of a risk for him. I told him not to spread the news any further because I wanted to get a few other clients in before the stock price went up as more people noticed the news." He sighed. "Del happened to mention it while he was shooting hoops with a couple of his buddies, who then bought the stock and moved the price up before I could get the rest of my clients to buy."

"Michael Kinnear, are you engaging in insider trading?"

"Nope. All the information I was basing my recommendations on was in the public record. It's just that not a lot of people were following what the company was doing."

"That was kind of a jerky move on Del's part. Why did he do that?"

Mike shrugged. "I don't think he deliberately ignored my request for him not to mention it. I think he just forgot in the moment and blurted it out because he thought it would be useful, or maybe just interesting, to the people he was with."

"He does seem kind of—"

"Clueless?"

She laughed. "I was going to say 'guileless,' but 'clueless' works, too." Her expression became more somber. "I can't imagine Niall Lynch being as forgiving as you are. I'm guessing that it was another strike against Rowan in the inheritance sweepstakes that she's married to someone who's indiscreet with confidential information."

"It seems like Rowan has her own indiscretions to worry about—" Mike stopped and took a swallow of coffee.

"What do you mean?"

"Nothing."

"Nothing?"

Mike glanced around for the waitress. "Want a top-off?"

She raised an eyebrow. "Mike—"

He sighed. "It's a secret."

"A secret? What are you—twelve?"

"It's a confidential assignment."

"Ah. You're not twelve. You're 007."

Mike groaned. "Okay. But you have to promise not to tell."

Ann extended her hand. "Pinky promise, Mikey."

"Don't be a jerk," he muttered. He leaned forward. "Rowan Lynch has been going to this creepy house in West Philly—she thinks she's keeping it a secret from Del—and Del hired me and Scott to follow her and try to find out what's up."

"You and Scott?"

"Well, Del just hired me but I ... subcontracted with Scott."

"And you got Scott involved in this why?"

"He's better at this kind of thing than I am."

"He might also have held up better under the brutal interrogation I subjected you to."

Mike scowled.

"So, you're tacking on extra work to the engagements?" Ann asked. "Like 'would you like fries with your burger'?"

"It's not part of the engagement. It's completely separate."

Ann raised an eyebrow.

"Hey, you're the one who told me I needed to get a hobby other than my business."

"True." They sipped coffee in silence for a few moments, then Ann asked, "So what was Rowan doing at the creepy house in West Philly?"

"That's what we're trying to find out."

Mike described what he and Scott had seen, and what Del had reported to him.

"A guy in Victorian clothes?" she asked.

"Yup."

"Weird. Do you think this has anything to do with what happened to Niall?"

"I don't know."

Ann tapped her fingers on the tabletop for a moment, then smiled. "I know who might be able to help us out."

32

A nn opened the door of Mike and Scott's townhouse to Philadelphia Detective Joe Booth. She had first met him when he arrived at her Adirondack cabin to solicit her sensing help, having exhausted more traditional means of investigating the Philadelphia Socialite murder. Joe's observant hazel eyes and prematurely graying blond hair were just as they had been then. What was different was that he had dropped some weight, and the button of his navy sport coat didn't strain at his waist as it might have a year earlier.

"You're looking sharp," she said as he stepped inside.

"Thanks. You, too."

Joe had suggested that they get "a little dressed up" for the evening's outing, so she had added a necklace and bracelet to her one dress that wasn't in storage: an all-purpose sleeveless black cotton knit that she had once pressed into service as a beach coverup. Other than the need for dressiness, and the fact that their destination was Larch Street, he hadn't shared any other information about the plan for the evening.

They stepped into the living room where Mike and Scott were waiting for them.

"Hey, Joe," said Mike. "Long time no see. You're looking good —have you been working out?"

Joe blushed. "Not so much working out as eating fewer fries and hoagies."

"What was the impetus?" asked Scott. "Smartening up for a lady?"

Joe's blush deepened. "Reconnected with an old friend."

Ann was surprised by a tiny twinge of jealousy.

"Thanks for picking Ann up in West Chester," said Mike. "I figured this would be more discreet than at Lynch and Son Winery. The family's planning to meet at the winery this evening to talk about whether they want Ann to mediate a conversation with the late owner—maybe even to try to contact him themselves."

"Which means that Rowan Lynch isn't likely to make a surprise appearance at 46 Larch Street," said Scott. "And if she does leave the winery, Del will let Mike know. By the way," he asked Mike, "when are you going to tell Del that you've enlisted a whole team to find out what's going on at Larch Street?"

"I'm putting you in charge of PR at *Pate and Kinnear Investigations*," said Mike. "'Enlisted a team' sounds so much better than 'blabbed the secret and got a Philly cop involved.'"

"I'll take the blame—or the credit, as the case may be—for involving Joe," said Ann.

"And based on what I've heard about Del," said Scott, "if anyone would sympathize with a blabbermouth, it would be him."

"I guess whatever I tell Del—and when—depends on what Ann and Joe report after their visit. Why does everyone have to be so secretive about everything?" Mike laughed. "I guess I should be asking how *can* everyone be so secretive about everything?"

"Don't look at me," said Ann. "I'm as much in the dark as you are."

She headed for the door with Joe, followed by Mike and Scott.

"Are you sure you don't want us to come with you as back-up?" Mike asked.

"I don't think we'll need backup," said Joe, "and I promise to give you guys the full rundown when we get back."

Joe followed Ann to his elderly Accord.

"I'm surprised they didn't bring out a corsage and ask to take pictures of you pinning it on me," said Ann.

Joe laughed as he opened the passenger door for her. "At least I didn't have to wear a powder-blue tux for the occasion."

"What *is* the occasion?"

"You'll see," he said cheerfully. He swung the door shut, then got into the driver's seat.

As they headed for Philadelphia, she filled him in on what Del, Mike, and Scott had seen at the Larch Street house.

"Del wants to know what Rowan is doing with some guy who's dressed up like a Victorian gentleman."

"It is quite mysterious," he said with a smile.

As they neared their destination, Joe deviated from the GPS's route and turned onto Woodland Avenue and then onto South 43rd Street.

"Mike showed me the house online," said Ann, looking around. "I wasn't expecting the neighborhood to be this busy."

"We're not there yet," said Joe, "but we'll get there too early if we drive right there."

He pulled into a space across the street from a park. The light was just shading toward dusk and the temperature had moderated from the heat of the afternoon to a balmy warmth. Parents sat on benches watching children play in the grass. A group of teenage spectators whooped as two young men, one rail thin, one rotund, played a vigorous game of hacky sack.

Joe rolled down the windows and turned off the engine.

"So, you have a girlfriend," she said.

"'Girlfriend' sounds so high school."

"Significant other?"

"Not quite that either."

"Squeeze?"

He laughed. "Definitely not."

"You said she's an old flame?"

"Old *friend*."

"Oh, come on," said Ann in exasperation. "You won't tell me what's going to happen when we get to Larch Street—at least throw me a crumb with some scoop about your relationship status."

Joe sighed. "Like I said, she's an old friend. Actually, she dated my best friend in high school. We ran into each other at the courthouse. She's an attorney. We got together for drinks to catch up. We've been out to dinner a couple of times since then. Went to see a movie last night."

"What did you see?"

"*Rashomon*."

"How was it?"

"It won an honorary Oscar in 1952."

"That's not exactly what I asked."

He shrugged. "It was a little too much like a day at the office —trying to sort through a bunch of different perspectives on the same incident, everyone trying to paint themselves in the best light possible."

"Yeah, I can imagine that might be a busman's holiday."

"How about you? Any boyfriend, significant other, squeeze, or flame on the scene?"

"I've been seeing Corey Duff. He's the guy who directed *The Sense of Death* documentary."

"He lives around here?"

"He lives in L.A., but he's been in Maine for the last couple of months working on another project. Right now he's in Ocean City, New Jersey."

"A long distance relationship. Serious."

"I don't know. I'm not sure what will happen when he moves back to the West Coast."

"Maybe he's planning on sticking around here."

This had not occurred to Ann. "Maybe."

They switched to a discussion of other movies they had seen recently, which segued into a debate about Clint Eastwood's filmography. Joe was a fan; Ann was on the fence.

"*Dirty Harry* isn't too much like a day at the office?" she asked.

He laughed. "Not my office." He glanced at his watch, then started the car. "I lost track of time. We better get going."

A few minutes later, they pulled into an alley that paralleled Larch Street and parked in a space between a Ford Transit Connect and a Porsche. They climbed out of the Accord.

A six-foot stockade fence separated the parking area from the house. Ann couldn't see anything below the home's second floor, but the windows were dark, and even in the dimming evening light, she could see paint curling off the wooden window frames. A broken branch hung from a gnarled tree.

"We better hustle," said Joe. "Three minutes to go."

"Three minutes to what?"

"You'll see."

"You're not even going to give me a hint?"

"Nope."

They hurried to the end of the alley and turned toward Larch. "Scott isn't the only one who enjoys covert operations," she said. "If the new gig doesn't work out for Mike, you and Scott can form *Booth and Pate Investigations*."

They turned onto Larch Street. There were no other pedestrians, and most of the other houses on the street looked uninhabited, only one light glowing dimly from a window half-way down the block.

When they reached number 46, Joe held the creaking gate open for Ann, then they crossed the tiny and disreputable front yard and climbed the steps to the porch. The condition of the paint on the doorframe was no better than on the windows in back. One of the floorboards was missing.

Joe glanced at his watch. "Right on time." He knocked on the door.

After a few moments, Ann saw a dim glow in the door's glass panes. Then the door opened and a tall man in the full regalia of a Victorian gentleman stood before them. A protuberant belly stretched the buttons of his frock coat. His short hair was speckled with gray, his eyes were a pale blue, and behind a neatly trimmed beard and mustache, his skin was pocked with the signs of long-ago acne. He carried an oil lamp.

"I'm Joe, and this is my friend Kay." Mike had suggested that she use an alias to lower the already low chance that someone would make the connection between the visitor to 46 Larch Street and the new tenant of the Curragh.

"Of course," said the man with a slight bow. "Please come in." His voice was thin and reedy—not what Ann would have expected from someone of his height and girth.

He stepped back, and they entered a vestibule. An empty coat rack stood against one wall, a yellowing stack of *Philadelphia Registers* bound with twine leaned against another.

The man flipped a deadbolt and fastened a security chain mounted high on the door, then turned back to them.

"I'm the Professor, your host for the evening. Please follow me."

Ann and Joe followed the Professor out of the entrance hall. The man had a slight limp, and the light from the oil lamp swung irregularly with his gait, sending shadows dancing across the walls.

They stepped into a space that must have served as a reception area, a tiled fireplace anchoring one wall, a staircase with elaborately carved balusters leading upward into the darkness. Heavy drapes covered the windows. Dust carpeted the floor, except for a path scuffed clean by the Professor and his visitors. Ann got a sense of another room opening off this central space —likely what the Professor would refer to as the parlor— furnished with bulky, sheet-draped shapes. He led them further into the house, through a room that was completely unfurnished, although Ann suspected that it would have been used as the dining room.

They passed into a narrow hallway. In the kitchen at the end of the hallway, barely visible in the light of the oil lamp, Ann could see the stained enamel of a refrigerator door standing slightly ajar.

Before they reached the kitchen, however, the Professor slid open a pocket door on the right and stepped back.

It seemed likely to Ann that it was a pantry, or even a broom closet.

"In there?" she asked uncertainly and glanced toward Joe.

He was trying to hide a grin.

"Yes, miss," said the Professor with a smile.

Ann shrugged and stepped into the small space.

The Professor held the oil lamp low so that it illuminated only the floor and the lowest tier of shelves and cupboards lining the walls.

"Please have a seat on the bench in back," he said.

He raised the lamp slightly. This room didn't have the dated refinements of the other rooms. The floor was scuffed wood, the shelves sturdy but plain. Along the back wall, raised on a platform to barstool height, was an upholstered bench just wide enough for two. A water pipe ran along the wall, although the bench had been cleverly designed to keep visitors from having to lean against it.

Ann stepped up on the platform and lowered herself onto the bench. Joe sat beside her.

The Professor placed the lamp on the floor. He grasped a panel that Ann would have expected to be a cupboard door and pulled it down in front of Ann and Joe as a bar top ... or as an inescapable barrier.

The room was so quiet that she could hear the click and whir of a CD player spinning up and a moment later, very faintly, the strains of a Victorian music hall song.

"Welcome to the Cabinet of Curiosities," said the Professor, and a string of fairy lights near the ceiling glowed to life.

33

D el unlocked the door to the Ark, and Nola and Rowan followed him inside. The evening was warm but as always, the Ark was a cool oasis. As they passed through the fermentation room, Nola shrugged into a jacket, and Del realized that he should have reminded Rowan to bring a sweater. When they got to the barrel room, he pulled Niall's old sweater from the back of the desk chair and draped it over Rowan's shoulders.

"Did Harkin say whether he was coming?" asked Nola.

"He said he would," said Rowan. "I told him about the conversation Ann had with Dad. Harkin said he wasn't interested in talking about the winery, but I promised him that if he came tonight, we'd steer clear of that topic."

"I don't know why we should go out of our way to make him feel comfortable," grumbled Del.

Rowan sighed. "Because it isn't going to make any difference to what happens with the winery. We're not about to change his mind now."

Nola crossed her arms. "Well, I hope he doesn't keep us waiting long."

Del pulled out the desk chair for Rowan to sit in. Nola perched on the edge of the desk. Del busied himself collecting some plastic cups that had been used to sample the wines. A few minutes passed, Nola's expression becoming increasingly sour and Rowan's more downcast. Then the door opened, and Harkin stepped in.

Rowan stood. "Hello, Harkin."

Harkin stuffed his hands in the pockets of his shorts. "Hey, Ro. Aunt Nola. Del."

"Thank you for coming," said Rowan. "I know things have been rough lately, but I talked with Ann Kinnear this morning and I'm convinced that she contacted Dad. She brought back some information she could only have gotten from him."

"What was that?"

"That Barrel 44 is Hungarian and borrowed from Pocopson Winery."

"Well, I'm convinced," said Harkin sardonically.

Ignoring his tone, Rowan said, "Ann obviously has a special talent for communicating with people after they've died, but I thought that if she could do it not even having known Dad, maybe we could do it, too. She seemed to think it was possible. Not *likely*, but possible. We could give it a try and, if we're not successful, and if anyone is interested, we can ask her to mediate a conversation for us."

"Rowan, are you sure you want to do this?" asked Nola. "Even if we can contact Niall—or even if Ann can mediate a conversation between us and him—I'm not convinced it's a good idea. We've spent all our lives trying to talk with Niall and look where it's brought us."

"I think Nola's right," said Del, turning to his wife. "If the winery is a taboo subject, what else is there to talk about?"

Rowan rested her hand on her stomach, teary-eyed but smiling. "I want to tell Dad I'm having a girl. I wanted to tell you all."

"Sweetheart, that's wonderful news!" said Del. He folded her in his arms.

"Congratulations, Ro," said Harkin. "I'm sure Dad would be happy for you guys. I know Alana and Kepi will be."

Del looked toward Nola, waiting for Rowan's aunt to offer her congratulations.

Nola was smiling indulgently, obviously pleased but not, as far as Del could tell, surprised.

He loosened his hold on Rowan and stepped back so that he could look into her eyes.

"Really wonderful news," he said. "So, when did you find out?"

Rowan's eyes drifted to Nola, and Del followed her gaze.

Nola flushed, obviously realizing she had not held up her part in the charade.

Del's arms dropped and he stepped back. "When did you find out?"

"I ..." Rowan wouldn't meet his eyes.

"You've known for a while, haven't you?" he said, trying to keep his voice steady.

"Yes," she said, the tears falling. "I've known for a little while." She raised her eyes to his. "I didn't want to tell you because I was afraid you'd say something in front of Dad. And if he knew I was having a girl, it would be a strike against me while he decided who would inherit."

"And what about after he was dead?"

"At first, I was angry that you had told me about the argument Dad and Harkin had in the Cellar, that you had gotten my hopes up that I would inherit. And then when Ann told me that Dad was in the Ark, I thought—" She looked from Del, his mouth pressed into a thin line, to Nola, still struggling with the embarrassment of giving away Rowan's secret, to Harkin, who was clearly having second thoughts about his agreement to a family meeting. Rowan gave a sob and dropped her eyes. "I thought it would be a happy moment to share. Maybe our last time together at the winery."

"I thought the winery was off-limits as a topic," muttered Harkin.

Del wheeled on him. "Harkin," he said through gritted teeth, "can you try not to be a bastard just for one evening?"

Harkin stuffed his hands deeper into his pockets. "Sorry. I shouldn't have said that."

"You're goddamn right you shouldn't have said it," said Del, advancing across the room, his hands balled into fists at his sides. "You know what you might have done instead—not just tonight but through your whole miserable life? You could have been grateful that your father cared enough about you to entrust you with the family business. You could have done your best to get involved, to get interested. And when you inherited—which it now seems clear was Niall's plan all along—you could have turned the winery over to Rowan, and someday to our daughter, to run. Then you could have run away to Hawaii to do whatever the hell it is you do there."

Harkin took a step forward. He was half a foot shorter and a couple dozen pounds lighter than Del, but it was clear that if Del threw a punch, he would be happy to return the favor. "Don't put this on me. I would have been thrilled to have my gender be an excuse for getting away from this godforsaken place. And it's your fault, not mine, that your wife didn't trust you enough to tell you she's going to have a girl."

Del began to draw back his arm, and Harkin to raise his fists.

Rowan grabbed Del's wrist. "Stop it! Just stop it! Both of you!"

Del turned to her, and Harkin took a cautious step back.

Rowan's face was splotchy with anger and sorrow. She stepped away and swiped a hand across her eyes. She gave a bitter laugh. "Well, if you wanted to convince me that trying to get in touch with Dad was a bad idea, you certainly succeeded."

She turned and ran awkwardly across the room, yanked the door open, and disappeared.

Del followed her to the door, but before he stepped through it, he turned back to Harkin.

"If you ever hurt Rowan again, I'll kill you."

34

The shelves along one wall of the Cabinet of Curiosities held a collection to intrigue the most enthusiastic amateur naturalist: the stark white skulls of small mammals, brightly colored coral, delicately patterned seashells, sparkling geodes, preserved butterflies affixed to a twisted segment of branch. There were manmade objects as well: a voodoo doll with a strand of hair protruding from its head, an intricately carved ivory fan, a framed design created with brilliantly colored butterfly wings. Meticulously rendered drawings of birds lined the backs of the shelves.

On the opposite wall were ranks of bottles and decanters filled with liquids of almost as many hues as the butterfly wings. Another shelf held glassware—stemmed and unstemmed, delicate and chunky, colored and clear—with only two of each variation.

It was a tiny bar—by far the tiniest bar Ann had ever seen.

Ann laughed with delight. Joe grinned at her.

"What in the world is this place?" she asked.

"As I said, miss," said the Professor with a smile, "you are in the Cabinet of Curiosities."

She looked toward Joe, who was still grinning. "How ...?"

"Let's just say I happened upon a happy guest of the Cabinet who arranged our reservation," he said.

"A guest whom the Cabinet is most grateful to count among its patrons," said the Professor.

"So, who's your contact?" Ann asked Joe.

"Our benefactor would prefer to stay anonymous," said Joe, matching the Professor's formal diction, but when their host turned away for a moment to adjust the volume of the CD player, Joe mouthed *city council* to Ann.

She gave him a surreptitious thumbs up. If she had had any remaining concerns about the safety of the situation, they were assuaged by the fact not only that her date for the evening was a Philadelphia police detective but also that the bar was frequented by a Philadelphia city council member.

The Professor turned back to them and gestured to a cross-stitched sampler that hung near the bench where Ann and Joe sat. "If I may ask for your indulgence?"

The Professor wishes to transport you back to a less complicated time and requests that you silence your telephone and refrain from photography.

"Good idea," said Ann as she and Joe turned off their phones. As the sister of the amateur private investigator responsible for learning about 46 Larch Street, she wished she could snap a few photos. However, as a guest of the Cabinet, the idea of a device-free hour charmed her.

"The four cocktails I'll be serving you this evening," said the Professor, "are from a little New York cafe-bar named the Café des Beaux Arts that was run by the Bustanoby Brothers. Unlike many bar owners of the day—this would be the days of the late nineteenth century—the brothers welcomed ladies with open arms. The first cocktail of the evening is one the brothers served to their dainty-but-bessemer-steely clientele," he turned to Joe, "if you don't object, sir."

"I would never turn down a cocktail worthy of being served to a steely clientele, regardless of gender," said Joe.

"This is the most complex of the drinks I will be serving tonight: the Pousse Café." The Professor took from the shelf two tiny glasses that looked like stemmed, footed test tubes, then began selecting bottles of liqueurs and arranging them on the bar top for Ann and Joe's inspection: a bottle of grenadine, its label in French ... an opaque bottle of something called Advocaat ... an emerald green bottle of Crème de Menthe ... Crème de Noyaux ... sloe gin ... Curaçao, the bottle wrapped in rattan ... a dusty Cognac.

He placed a delicate glass straw into each glass, then opened the first bottle and poured a thin layer of the ruby liqueur. "Actually, the Pousse Café refers to an entire class of drink, all requiring the same arduous layering of ingredients." He set the first bottle aside, pulled a bar spoon from a crystal vase, and picked up the second bottle. "The order in which they are added is vital. Each liqueur must be added based on its specific gravity." Holding the bar spoon backside up, he carefully poured the second liqueur over the back of the spoon and into the glass, adding a thin layer of creamy white. "It's the bartender's solemn duty not to allow the ingredients to mix."

The layers built up: brilliant green, amber, rose, blue, golden straw.

Ann found herself holding her breath, willing the layers not to mix, but she needn't have worried. The Professor's pour was sure.

When he had filled the glasses, he put linen cocktail napkins in front of Ann and Joe and placed the drinks carefully on top, the brilliant white of the napkins highlighting the kaleidoscopic hues of the drinks.

"The guest as well as the bartender has a part in ensuring the experience is as it should be. You must sip the drink, being careful not to mix the layers, enjoying the taste of each liqueur as you reach it."

Ann brought the straw to her lips and sipped: pomegranate ... egg nog ... mint ... almond ... plum ... orange... and the smoky leather and tobacco of the Cognac.

She put the glass on the bar top and leaned back on the bench. "I'm guessing there's not another place in Philly I could get that."

The Professor smiled. "I suspect not. The Pousse Café would normally have been served after an elaborate meal, followed by or served with coffee, but I can't resist starting our evening with it ... perhaps a metaphor for the multi-layered experience I hope to provide for you this evening."

"An impressive feat of bartending," said Joe.

The Professor dipped his head to acknowledge the compliment. "There's an even more complex version—the Pousse l'Amour—made with a raw egg yolk floating, centered, as the middle layer, but I have found that guests are not as enthusiastic about that variation."

Ann wrinkled her nose. "Good call."

As they drank, the Professor regaled them with stories of the provenance of the glassware and the difficulty of sourcing some of the more obscure liqueurs.

When they had finished their Pousse Cafés, the Professor removed the glasses and offered them a palate cleanser of a few oyster crackers served from a tiny sterling bowl.

"Our next cocktail is the Mamie Taylor, named for a Broadway actress of the early 1890s." He took two limes from a basket on one of the shelves, sliced them open, then used what looked like a sturdy crystal teacup with a spout and topped with a fitted juicer to extract the juice. "You may be familiar with the

Moscow Mule, which was created in Los Angeles after the Second World War. But whereas the Mule uses vodka, the Mamie Taylor uses Scotch."

Using a pair of silver tongs, he extracted a few chunks of ice from a silver bucket and lowered them into a a silver cocktail shaker, then added the lime juice and Scotch. He capped the container and shook it vigorously, setting his belly shaking as well, then tapped the now frosty shaker on the edge of the bar. He removed the cap and strained the solution into two stemmed cocktail glasses, added some fizzing ginger beer, stirred gently, then placed the drinks in front of Ann and Joe.

They drank, the Professor sharing some stories of popular Broadway shows of the Mamie Taylor era.

After a few sips, Joe set down his still half-full glass.

"Not to your liking, sir?" asked the Professor.

"I wouldn't have expected to enjoy that combination," said Joe, "especially Scotch with lime, but it's very good."

"You didn't finish it," said Ann.

"I'm the semi-designated driver."

"That's very responsible of you."

"No—having *no* drinks would be very responsible."

"But no fun."

"I believe you've hit on just the right balance of responsibility and fun, sir," said the Professor. "But I must say I'm relieved you instituted that policy after finishing your Pousse Café. Even the most sophisticated drinker would be hard-pressed to find a way to drink only half of a layered drink while still enjoying the full scope of the experience."

Joe laughed.

When Ann finished her drink, the Professor cleared away the glasses.

"Next is the Fluffy Ruffles," said the Professor. He cocked an eyebrow at Joe. "Perhaps the drink least likely to be ordered by a gentleman, but you seem game, sir."

"Count me in," said Joe.

"The Fluffy Ruffles first appeared in 1907, so I must admit it's a bit late to be truly Victorian." He pulled bottles of Cuban rum and sweet vermouth from the shelf. "It does pre-date the Great War, which is the clearest before-and-after marker of the era. As best we can tell, Fluffy Ruffles is named after a popular comic strip of the era, featuring an independent, savvy, and willful heroine of that name." He added ice and the liquors to a mixing glass, stirred, then strained the drink into what looked like squat Champagne coupes with heavy hexagonal bases. He garnished each with a lemon wheel and placed them on napkins trimmed with a ruffle of lace.

Ann sneaked a look at her watch. The drinks seemed to be coming every fifteen minutes, and although the portions were smaller than normal, she had to admit she was feeling a little tipsy. She was glad Joe was driving.

The Professor accompanied the Fluffy Ruffles with a description of the various types of vermouth, and for which types of cocktails each was best suited. When Ann had finished her drink and Joe had finished half of his, the Professor cleared the glasses.

"And finally," he said, "our last cocktail of the evening: the Pink Lady, another concoction from the early twentieth century." He removed a cocktail shaker that had been chilling in an ice bucket and added gin, applejack, a few dashes of pomegranate grenadine, lemon juice, and, much to Ann's surprise, an egg white. After a shake, he strained the opalescent, delicately rose-colored liquid into two delicately proportioned coupes.

"Very similar to the more masculinely named Clover Club Cocktail, except for the addition of the applejack, which makes it not only stronger but tastier without adding sweetness."

Ann realized that she was running out of time to find out information that would be useful to Mike. "Do you ever get individual guests rather than couples?" she asked.

Did she imagine a slight pause before the Professor answered?

"Almost exclusively couples. An individual would still have to pay for two seats, so that's a bit of a deterrent."

"Do you open up any other areas of the house to guests? It would make a great haunted house at Halloween."

"Oh, no. Guests only come here to the Cabinet."

"I'm guessing there may not be many trick-or-treaters in any case. The neighborhood certainly is quiet."

"Yes, admirably quiet." He launched into a description of the neighborhood as it would have looked in 1925, when the house was built.

As Ann finished her Pink Lady, and Joe finished his half portion, the Professor pulled a gold watch from his vest pocket. "I'm afraid that brings us to the end of our hour."

He cleared the last glasses from the bar top, then lifted it and latched it to the wall.

Joe took an envelope out of the inside pocket of his jacket and handed it to the Professor. The envelope disappeared discreetly into one of the pantry's drawers.

"It's been a pleasure having you join me this evening," said the Professor. "Let me show you to the door."

They stepped out of the Cabinet, but instead of turning left, toward the front door, he led them to the right. They passed through the kitchen, and the Professor opened the back door for them. "I hope you have enjoyed yourself this evening."

"I certainly have, Professor." said Ann. She laughed. "That sounds so awkward. Is there some other name we can call you?"

He gave a polite smile. "You may call me John."

"Thank you for a lovely evening, John."

"Entirely my pleasure, Kay."

"Yes, great evening," said Joe.

The Professor's smile became a bit warmer. "I hope that the rest of your evening proves equally satisfactory."

Ann and Joe stepped outside, and the Professor closed the door behind them. They found themselves in a small, untended backyard, its rough condition serving to highlight the charm of the Cabinet. A pile of bricks in one corner spilled broken fragments across the yard. Bare patches of lawn were dotted with a few bright blue Bud Light cans, no doubt tossed over the stockade fence from the alley.

They descended a set of rickety wooden steps and crossed the yard to a gate. Unlike the front door, where the locks were mounted high, perhaps to prevent young children from letting themselves out, the latch that opened the back gate was mounted low, no doubt so that passersby couldn't reach it over the stockade fence. After fumbling with it for a moment, Joe got the gate unlatched.

Joe's Accord and the Transit Connect van were the only vehicles in the parking area. They climbed into the Accord.

"That was fantastic," said Ann.

"Yes, definitely a once-in-a-lifetime experience." He backed out of the space and headed down the alley toward the street. "Trying to pump him for information there at the end?"

"Yeah, but finding out that his name is John is hardly a help. Other than letting Mike and Scott know about the decor and all the great drinks, what can we tell them?"

"That it seems unlikely that Rowan Lynch was getting up to too much trouble at 46 Larch?" He turned onto the cross street.

"Maybe ... but what *was* she getting up to? The fact that Rowan is weeks away from giving birth makes it hard to imagine that she was meeting a lover at the house—plus, I'm having trouble picturing the Professor as anyone's lover—but it's equally hard to imagine that she was sitting around for an hour pounding back cocktails. That's a lot of drinking to pack into an hour." She watched the passing scenery for a moment, then said, "Maybe there's something going on in some other part of the house."

"We saw all the first-floor rooms, and I didn't see any recent footsteps in the dust on the stairway."

"So probably not a drug den or Victorian bordello." Her mouth twisted in a smile. "Although it would give an interesting spin to the council member's visit if it was. That's who got you the reservation?"

"Yeah. I asked around at work about the address and pretty soon I got a call from the person in question. It turns out he's a happy customer of the Cabinet and he suggested that I had better things to spend my policing time on than busting a speakeasy. I told him it was purely a personal interest, and he set me up with a reservation."

"Well, other than the fact that it sounds like they don't have a license to be running a bar, everything else seems on the up-and-up." After a pause, she added, "Although I'm surprised the neighbors don't care."

"I'm guessing that the neighbors are willing to look the other way. They're probably happy to have the visitors be well-heeled connoisseurs of exotic cocktails and not addicts looking for a place to shoot up."

"True. By the way, how much did it cost?"

"Why do you want to know?"

"Mike can reimburse you—it was a business expense."

He grinned. "I don't need Mike to reimburse me. It was worth it just to see your expression when the lights came up."

35

———

Harkin glanced with bleary eyes at the time on his phone: after midnight. He fell back in the chair and rotated his head, trying to ease a crick in his neck.

It had been a day of ups and downs. The up was that he had a handshake agreement with Ed Kujala of Pocopson Winery for the purchase of Lynch and Son. He was glad that it would continue to be run as a winery. In fact, he hadn't pursued other buyers, although he suspected he would have gotten more money from a developer. Once the dust settled, maybe Rowan and Del would be glad as well, although he wasn't holding his breath for any thanks. He had even felt Ed out about keeping Rowan and Del on, but Ed already had a winemaker and vineyard manager who would fold oversight of the former Lynch property into their existing responsibilities.

Even assuming he would get less for the winery from Ed than he might have elsewhere, there'd be more than enough money from the sale to bankroll the dream that he, Alana, and Kepi had spun around the dinner table in Lahaina. And there would be enough left over for him to help Rowan and Del transition to whatever they decided to do next. If a change had to

happen, now was as good a time as any. They could spend a few
months at home with the baby while they assessed their
options. Once everyone had a chance to cool down, he'd talk
with Rowan about it.

Ed, who was on a business trip in Napa, had asked for copies
of some winery records that he thought would be in Niall's desk
in the Cellar. So a couple of hours after the family meltdown in
the Ark, and checking that the parking area was free of any
family members' cars, Harkin had gone to the Cellar and spent
an hour on the phone with Ed. Ed described the documents he
wanted, and Harkin scanned and emailed the ones he found. It
was convenient that Niall had been old-fashioned enough to
have most of his records in hard copy, saving Harkin the trouble
of having to wait through whatever process would enable him to
access online accounts. The downside was that now ledger
boxes and file folders littered the desk, floor, and guest chair in
Niall's Cellar office. He'd straighten it up later.

The down of the day, of course, was the blow-up at the Ark.
Harkin could have kicked himself—he was no better than Del
when it came to keeping his thoughts to himself. But he was
damned if he was going to take the rap for Rowan not trusting
her husband enough to tell him the gender of their own baby.

He gathered up a few files he wanted to take another look at,
locked up the Cellar, then trudged up the hill to the big house.
In the kitchen, he tossed the files onto the table, then got a glass
from a cupboard and poured himself some Pepsi from a two-
liter bottle in the fridge. Kepi had convinced him it was a
marginally more ecological choice than always drinking from
single-serving bottles.

With his mind still jangling from the day's events, he wasn't
ready for bed. It would be early evening in Hawaii. Alana and
Kepi would be sitting down to dinner—maybe talking about
what movie they wanted to watch, unless Kepi was going out

with his friends. If Harkin was still up in an hour, he'd call then. He toyed with the idea of asking them if they wanted to fly out to Pennsylvania. It looked like they could afford it, but he didn't plan to stay long enough to make the trip worth their while.

He couldn't even watch a movie on a decent screen. Considering all the money that passed through the winery business, Niall hadn't been in the habit of diverting any of it to personal expenses. The television in the den was the same boxy Panasonic Harkin had watched as a child.

He left the kitchen and walked through rooms that felt cold and drafty even on this hot August night. His footsteps echoed hollowly through the empty house. *The big house.* He was surprised someone hadn't come up with some cute Gaelic take on the name, although as far as he was concerned, the name was appropriate—he had certainly felt like a prisoner when he had lived here.

He found himself in the library and noticed the copy of Michener's *Hawaii*, still where he had left it when he had heard Nola banging around in the basement. It seemed like an appropriate way to pass the time until he called home.

He settled into a chair and was deep into the first chapter when his phone rang. The caller's information was blocked. He normally didn't answer blocked calls, but it was possible it was Ed or one of his representatives calling back with more questions. He hit *Accept.*

"Hello?"

"Hello, Harkin," said the caller, the voice low and gruff. "This is Henry Tollman."

Harkin drew a blank for a moment, but then the name clicked into place: the winemaker at Lynch when Harkin had been a boy. He put the book aside and pinched the bridge of his nose. "Oh. Hello, Henry."

"I just heard about your father's death. I wanted to call and give my condolences."

Harkin stifled a sigh. After the scene in the Ark, he was even less enthusiastic than usual about talking about his family or the winery, but Henry Tollman had been an ally to him in his childhood. "Thanks, I appreciate it."

"You're living in Hawaii now, am I right?"

"Yup. Went for college and never looked back."

"Will you be going back to Pennsylvania for the funeral?"

"Things are a little busy here with the harvest coming up—I suspect they'll hold a memorial service after that's done—but I'm in Pennsylvania now. I was already here for one of the infamous Lynch family business meetings when Dad passed."

"Oh, man, Harkin, I'm sorry. I thought you were still in Hawaii. It must be ridiculously late there."

"Lucky for me I'm still on Hawaii time."

"Ah, that's good. I ended up out west, too. I'm in the Bay Area, waiting tables." He gave a rueful laugh. "Sometimes a customer will ask for a wine recommendation, so I tell myself I'm keeping a hand in the game." His laugh trailed off. "I heard that Niall had been ill."

"Yeah. Heart trouble."

"Ironic it was his heart that got him in the end."

"How so?"

"He always seemed a little heartless to me."

Harkin was silent. He wasn't sure if Henry meant this as a joke—tasteless as it was—or as an acknowledgement of the treatment both of them had suffered at Niall's hands.

After a moment, Henry asked, "Was the heart trouble the cause of his death?"

Harkin rubbed his eyes. "He wasn't so steady on his feet. He fell and hit his head. The blood thinners he was taking probably made the bleeding worse than it would have been otherwise.

Internal bleeding or external—I'm guessing that one of those did him in."

"I'm very sorry to hear that."

There was silence again, and Harkin thought there would be an opportunity to extract himself from the conversation, but then Henry continued. "And now you have the winery."

"How did you hear that?"

There was a soft chuckle. "I think it's only appropriate that the wine business has the world's most extensive *grapevine*, at least where gossip is concerned."

"Yes, I got Lynch and *Son*."

"Going to be making any changes?"

"That news hasn't hit the grapevine yet?" asked Harkin, not bothering to keep the irritation out of his voice.

"No."

"Well, a man has to have a few secrets."

Harkin hoped that would bring the conversation to a close, but Henry continued. "I understand Rowan had some ideas about expanding beyond Cab Sauv, and that her husband wanted to go organic." The chuckle again. "Little Rowan with a husband ... it doesn't seem possible. She was just an infant last time I saw her."

"Yeah, well, the organic thing was just a flight of fancy that Del managed to indulge in with the wrong person—namely, the supplier of Lynch's non-organic grapes. That's what Del's known for."

"For being pro-organic?"

"No. For being an idiot."

"It sounds like life in the Lynch family is just as turbulent as it used to be."

"Henry, I don't see how this is any of your business."

"I'm sorry, Harkin, but I can't imagine it's not a bit of a relief to you, not having Niall judging you, judging every choice you made. You and I, we were in the same boat."

Harkin had had enough. He had tried to be patient with Rowan—although look how well that had gone—and for Rowan's sake had tried to be patient with Del. His patience was wearing thin, and he didn't see any reason to expend the few remaining shreds on Henry Tollman.

"In the same boat? You could have left anytime, but you didn't until you were forced to—forced to by the piss-poor choices you made. Don't compare your choices with mine."

"Sorry, Harkin, I didn't mean—"

Harkin jumped out of the chair and strode to a window. In the daylight, it would have given a view through the trees to the winery. Now the darkened glass gave Harkin back his own reflection. "Like hell you 'didn't mean.' You come sniffing around here like some tabloid reporter, trying to rake up details that you, of all people, should know would be painful."

"Harkin—"

"He was my father, Henry. We never saw eye-to-eye—hell, he might have died hating my guts—but he was my father. And you call me and laugh about the industry grapevine and pump me for information about my *turbulent* family life."

"Harkin—"

"My family isn't in Pennsylvania. My family is in Hawaii, and it has never been turbulent. I left Lynch behind and made a life for myself. It sounds like we both ran away, but you never left Lynch behind. Get a goddamn life, Henry, and leave me alone."

He stabbed off the call, regretting that slamming down a receiver was a thing of the past, and threw himself back into the chair. He leaned his head back, staring at the ceiling, trying to slow his breath and his heartbeat.

He had always thought of Henry as an ally but looking back with the perspective that time—and a more stable family life—

provided, he realized it was more likely a case of the two of them having a common enemy in Niall.

A scene sprang to his mind: an eight-year-old Harkin trailing Henry through the fermentation room a few weeks after Rowan was born, trying to act interested in Henry's explanation of why periodic sampling of the wine to monitor its sugar content was so important.

Harkin could understand why his mother and even his father were distracted by the baby, but even Henry seemed obsessed with the little girl, finding excuses to visit the big house and quizzing Harkin about how much time Niall was spending with his daughter.

"Do you like Rowan best now?" Harkin asked Henry.

"I don't like her best, but the women in this family need all the help they can get."

"Why?"

"Because of your father." Henry laid aside the wine thief he had been using to siphon off samples of wine from the fermentation tanks. "But no woman has it easy. It's a man's world. And the *good* men need to make sure women aren't taken advantage of. Aren't hurt."

"Who are the good men?"

"I've tried to be one."

"Have you kept women from being hurt?" Harkin stretched his arms toward the ceiling. "Like Superman?"

When Henry spoke, his voice was harsh. "It's not like rescuing a girl tied to the train tracks, Harkin."

Harkin dropped his arms. "But you rescued them, right?"

"Yes."

"Who have you rescued?"

"Your Aunt Nola, for one." His gaze shifted from Harkin back to the wine thief, although Harkin didn't think he was seeing it. "My mother, for another."

"Who was taking advantage of your mother?"

"My father."

"What was he doing to her?"

Henry looked back at Harkin, and the anger in his eyes made Harkin take a step back. "He was hurting her."

"But you helped her?" Harkin wanted to ask a question that might replace Henry's look with a less scary one. "You made him stop?"

Henry's face darkened, and a chill ran up Harkin's spine, like being suddenly in shadow when the sun goes behind a cloud. "For a while."

After that conversation, Harkin steered clear of Henry. When Henry disappeared a few months later, Harkin was relieved ... and hopeful that, with his father picking up Henry's winemaker responsibilities, he might have a chance to spend time on his own interests: mainly baseball and dinosaurs. But Niall's attention, like a compass needle swinging to the north, quickly shifted back to his efforts to equip Harkin for life as a winemaker.

Harkin thought back to those arguments about the surgery to remove the nasal polyps: Niall's tone alternating between wheedling and hectoring, Harkin sitting with shoulders hunched and arms crossed, just riding out the harangue like a small boat riding out a storm. For a time, his mother had made a timid effort to deter Niall from his insistence on the surgery, but she had died not long after Rowan was born.

Harkin picked up the copy of Michener's *Hawaii*. He'd give it a few more minutes—long enough for him to simmer down—then call Alana and Kepi.

He paged through the book, not reading so much as looking for references to the much-loved landmarks that he now knew better than those in Chester County. Whenever he found a passage that he wanted to read to Alana or Kepi, he dog-eared the page.

The wind picked up and was at just the right angle to draw from the house the low moan that used to keep young Harkin huddled under the covers, waiting for angry monsters to arrive.

Then he heard another sound. A click? A thump? He listened for a few seconds but didn't hear it again. He returned to the book. There was almost no end to the odd sounds the house could make, especially at night.

After a few more minutes, he pushed himself out of the chair. He'd get into bed and call home from there, then it would be lights out as soon as he wished Alana and Kepi a good night.

With the book tucked under his arm, he took his empty glass to the kitchen. He put the glass in the sink, then noticed that a half-full glass sat on the counter. He must have poured two by accident. No point letting it go to waste. He downed the drink, thinking of Alana's disbelief that the amount of caffeine Harkin consumed never interfered with his sleep.

As he climbed the stairs to his childhood bedroom, he thought back on the day. Was it possible for him to have a conversation with anyone associated with Lynch and not have it turn into an unmitigated disaster? Despite the weird direction Henry had taken with what had started out as a condolence call, he had done his best to look out for Harkin, at least until he had left Lynch. He'd call Henry back in the morning and apologize.

Maybe after he had called Rowan—and even Del—to do the same.

But tonight, what he needed was a chat with his wife and son and a good night's sleep.

36

A nn stood in the Curragh's kitchen in her underwear and a T-shirt, sipping a cup of coffee and waiting for the toast to pop up. Corey was in the shower, belting out what sounded like a college fight song in quite a pleasant baritone.

Ann had picked up a voicemail from Corey as Joe drove her back to Mike and Scott's townhouse. Marsha Duff and Larry were flying back to Pittsburgh, and Corey planned to drive his mother's car back for her. He'd pass near Kennett Square—did she fancy an overnight guest? When Ann called him back, he was already on the road, and she told him she'd meet up with him at the Curragh.

When she got back to the guest house, she told him she had been out for drinks—to explain her uncharacteristically dressy outfit—and hanging out with Mike and Scott. She excused her lie of omission as the easiest way to keep yet another person from knowing about Mike's theoretically top-secret PI assignment.

Ann grabbed a piece of saltwater taffy from the box Corey had brought her. As she unwrapped it, a movement outside the

Curragh caught her eye and she looked out the window to see Rowan Lynch headed toward the Tarn, a paper bag in hand. Her yellow sundress fluttered in the slight breeze that was all that was left of the previous night's winds. She walked along the dock, tossing food to the ducks that paddled over to greet her. When she got to the end of the dock, she stood looking across the Tarn toward the vineyard. It made a pretty scene.

The toast popped up, and Ann turned her gaze from the window.

Then a scream rent the air. Ann whirled back toward the window just in time to see Rowan leap into the water, scattering surprised ducks.

"Corey, something's wrong!" she yelled, not at all sure he would hear her over the shower and the song.

Not bothering to add pants to her outfit, she ran out the door and across the lawn that separated the Curragh from the Tarn, wincing as tussocks of grass jabbed her bare feet. Rowan had ducked under the water but now reappeared, spluttering, hauling something to the surface. She saw Ann.

"Help me!" she screamed.

Ann shot off the end of the dock and into the water. The something that Rowan was wrestling with was a person, face-down in the water. Ann grabbed the other arm.

"Rowan, let me," she gasped. She didn't like the idea of a pregnant woman tussling in waist-deep water with that dead weight. And based on the unnatural stiffness of the arm, the weight was decidedly dead.

Rowan ignored Ann, her words an almost breathless chant. "No. No. No, no, no ..."

Together, they hauled the body toward the edge of the pond.

Just as they reached the edge, Corey, dressed only in boxer shorts, burst out of the Curragh and raced across the lawn toward them.

The bottom of the pond was slick, and Ann's feet slipped as she tried to pull the body out of the water. Corey waded in up to his knees, grabbed the collar of the shirt, and pulled the body out. He turned it over.

Harkin Lynch's skin was gray and mottled, his arms locked in the position they must have been in when he sank to the bottom of the pond. His T-shirt was hiked up under his arms, and blood had pooled under the skin, a dark bluish purple, along the front of his torso.

Rowan crawled out of the water on her hands and knees, her voice rising to a keening pitch. "No ... no ... no!"

Corey had turned back to the water to help Ann out when Del appeared from the Cellar, took in the scene, and sprinted across the parking lot and lawn. Ann hoped he reached Rowan before she tried to give Harkin CPR, which she appeared about to do despite the fact that she seemed close to hyperventilating.

Del reached Rowan and knelt by her side. His face twisted at the sight of Harkin's body, and he drew Rowan into his arms.

"Sweetheart," he said, stroking her hair, "I don't think there's anything we can do for him."

COREY HELPED Ann clamber out of the pond while Del called 911, his arm around his sobbing wife.

Ann and Corey retired briefly to the Curragh—Corey to add shorts and a T-shirt to his outfit, Ann to put on dry clothes.

By the time they got back to the Tarn, Del had removed his shirt and put it over Harkin's face. Ann could hear the wail of approaching sirens and a moment later, an ambulance and a fire truck wheeled into the driveway.

The following minutes were a blur. Someone had tossed Del's shirt to one side—Ann noticed that Del picked it up but didn't put it back on—but it was clear to everyone that Harkin was beyond help. Despite Del's best efforts, Rowan wouldn't leave the scene, although her brother's disturbing appearance was clearly feeding her growing hysteria. After a brief consultation with the police officers, the EMTs covered the body with a blanket.

More vehicles arrived, including a police cruiser, and an officer began stringing yellow crime scene tape around the area where Harkin's body lay. Two men, one older and one younger, stepped out of a nondescript sedan. The older went to Del and Rowan, while the younger approached Ann and Corey.

"Good morning, I'm Detective Brady Plott. And you are ...?" he asked, pen poised over a notepad.

"Ann Kinnear. I live in the guest house," she said, pointing out the Curragh.

"And I'm Corey Duff," said Corey.

"You also live in the guest house, sir?"

"Just visiting," said Corey.

The detective ran through a list of questions and Ann and Corey answered. Yes, they had both been at the Curragh the previous night, but not until quite late. No, they hadn't seen Harkin Lynch last night. No, they hadn't seen anything unusual at the Tarn or elsewhere on the property.

When Plott had exhausted his list of questions, he got their cell phone numbers.

"Don't leave the area without checking in with us," he said.

"I was on my way to Pittsburgh," said Corey.

Plott glanced toward the other detective. "Just give us a little time to see what's what, then I imagine you'll be able to leave."

Ann and Corey went to where Rowan was sitting in the back of the ambulance, wrapped in an orange blanket. Del sat beside her, his arm around her shoulders. The older detective, who

introduced himself as Bruce Denninger, stood beside the ambulance. A solicitous EMT hovered nearby.

"How are you doing, Rowan?" asked Ann.

"All right," said Rowan, in a small voice that made it clear
she was anything but.

"It would be best to take you in for a quick check-up,
ma'am," said the EMT.

"I don't need to go to the hospital," said Rowan, in a tone that
didn't brook argument.

"Do you want to go home, sweetheart?" Del asked. He
glanced toward Denninger. "We only live a couple of minutes
away."

Denninger nodded. "That would be okay."

Rowan glanced toward the blanket-covered body still lying
next to the dock, then down at her hands. "I don't want to leave
Harkin."

"Maybe you'd be more comfortable at the Curragh," said
Ann. She caught Denninger's eye and gestured to the guest
house.

He rubbed his neck. "There's going to be a lot of ... activity
around here for a while, and that's going to be front row seating.
Maybe not the best place for the young lady."

"There's a porch in back," said Ann. "We can sit there and
still be close, but not too close."

"That would be better than waiting here, right, Ro?"
asked Del.

"But what about Harkin?" sobbed Rowan.

"We'll take care of him, ma'am," said Denninger. He looked
toward Ann. "Do you have clothes she could borrow?"

"I'm sure I can find something," said Ann, wondering what
she had that might accommodate Rowan's enormous belly.

"I can give Del a change as well," said Corey. Ann noticed

that a considerable amount of mud had transferred from Rowan's clothes to Del's.

"We'll need the clothes they were wearing," said Denninger. "I'll send someone over in a few minutes to bag them."

Rowan gave Denninger a bleary look of surprise. "Bag our clothes?"

"I'm sure it's just standard procedure," said Del.

"That's right," said Denninger. "Just standard procedure."

Del helped an unsteady Rowan out of the ambulance and guided her across the lawn to the Curragh.

Ann hung back until they were out of earshot, then turned to Denninger. "What will happen now?"

"The coroner's on his way. Once he's here, we'll take photos, measurements. Then we'll bag the body for transport to the morgue."

"You don't think it was an accident?"

"I don't have a feeling one way or the other, miss."

When Ann reached the Curragh, Corey was emerging from the bedroom with a T-shirt for Del.

Ann took Rowan's elbow and Del slipped out of his mud-smeared T-shirt, which he draped over one of the porch chairs.

"Let's find some dry clothes for you," Ann said to Rowan.

"I'll get a fresh pot of coffee going," said Corey.

"Maybe not high test for Rowan ..." said Ann as she led Rowan through the kitchen toward the bedroom.

"I think Nola might have left some herbal tea," she heard Del say and she closed the bedroom door.

Ann got Rowan, still wrapped in the orange blanket, seated on the bed. She opened the closet, surveyed the options, and got out the black dress she had worn to the Cabinet. "How about this?"

Rowan glanced up. "That looks nice. I don't want to take your nice things. Plus, I'll stretch it all out."

Ann appreciated that Rowan recognized that the dress was, in the context of Ann's wardrobe, a "nice thing."

"It's no problem. Another exactly like it is just a call to L.L. Bean away."

Rowan attempted a weak laugh, ending in a little sob.

Ann sat down next to Rowan. "I feel like a dry dress and tea is small consolation for what you're going through. Is there anything else I can do? Anything any of us can do?"

Rowan pulled the blanket more tightly around her shoulders. "Did you see Harkin? You know, his ghost?"

"No, but it's not the best circumstances. You remember what I said about a crowd making it less likely that a spirit will appear. I can check later if you'd like."

Rowan nodded.

After a moment, Ann asked, "Did you guys meet at the Ark last night like you planned?"

Rowan pressed her hand to her mouth and hiccuped back a sob. She nodded.

"Was Harkin there?"

Rowan nodded again.

"How did it go?"

Rowan dropped her hand into her lap. "Not good. We had a huge argument. I thought Del was going to hit Harkin. Del said ..." She twisted her hands in her lap and turned her gaze out the glass doors to the back porch.

"Said what?"

"I forget."

"Did you tell the police about the meeting?"

"No. I didn't think of it. I'll tell them later. I need to call Nola." She absently patted the pocket of her dress, then said, "I think my phone's in my bag in the Cellar."

"You can use my phone."

Rowan gave a weak smile. "I don't know her number—it's just an entry in my contacts."

"We can get your bag for you."

"Thank you. It's at my desk."

Ann waited a moment to see if Rowan would say more, but she was silent. Ann gave her arm a squeeze. "Let us know when you're changed and then we'll bring you tea and you and Del can sit out back."

Rowan emerged from the bedroom a few minutes later. It was clear that Ann's black dress would never resume its original shape. Ann steered her back through the bedroom to the porch, which gave a pleasant but innocuous view across the drive that led to the big house. She got Rowan and Del settled in the porch's two chairs, and Corey brought out two mugs of tea.

"I'll get your bag," said Ann to Rowan.

"I'll come along," said Corey.

They detoured to the Tarn to get the okay from Denninger to retrieve Rowan's bag, then followed the path to the Cellar.

"How long do you suppose he was in the water?" asked Corey.

"I don't know." Ann shivered and crossed her arms, even though the morning was already warm. She thought back to Harkin surprising her, Rowan, and Nola in the Cellar during their first, fruitless search for Niall's spirit. "I haven't seen him for a couple of days, but Rowan's trip to the dock to feed the ducks seems like a regular ritual, so he probably hadn't been in the Tarn for more than a day."

When they reached the Cellar, Ann retrieved Rowan's purse from her desk in the workroom, then they headed back up the path to the Curragh.

"It can't be an accident," said Corey, "him dying so soon after his father." He looked toward Ann. "Right?"

"Niall Lynch was a sick man, and even he thought his death

was an accident. But I've got to believe this is going to make the police look at Niall's death a little more carefully."

"Do you think you just moved to a winery where two murders took place?" Corey was trying to keep his tone light, but his expression reflected his concern.

"I certainly hope not. That would kind of ruin the ambiance."

When they reached the Curragh, they stood on the porch for a few minutes, watching the activity near the Tarn.

"I'm going to give Joe Booth a call," said Ann. "If there's any investigation into Harkin or Niall's deaths, this wouldn't be in his jurisdiction, but he might have contacts who could give him some inside scoop."

"The Philadelphia detective? You're still in touch with him?"

"Yeah, actually—" She was about to tell Corey about her trip to the Cabinet with Joe, but there was no way she could tell him that now without raising the question of why she hadn't told him the previous night. In fact, even Del still didn't know about Ann and Joe's trip to the Cabinet. "Now and then," she concluded.

"I guess it's good to have contacts in the police force," he said, his tone carefully neutral, "but if this is a police matter, I think you should step back." After a pause, he added, "I could stay here for a while, so you don't have to be here alone."

"Corey, that's sweet, but I'm sure it's not necessary. Plus, I thought you were on your way to Pittsburgh."

"I could adjust my plans."

"What are the plans?"

He smiled sheepishly. "Mom and Larry are getting married the day after tomorrow. Larry wants me to be the best man."

She turned to him. "That's great!" After a pause, she added, "Isn't it?"

"Yeah, it is. I really like Larry, Mom obviously loves him, and he's been shockingly understanding about the situation with Dad."

"What are they going to do about your dad?"

Corey shifted uncomfortably. "They went to this woman in Atlantic City and she ... exorcised him."

Ann's eyebrows rose. "Some woman in Atlantic City exorcised your father's ghost?"

"That's what she said, and Mom and Larry believed her, which I guess is all that really counts."

Ann gave a short laugh. "Well, that would be one way to go about it. I hope it works out for them."

"Yeah. Me, too. Much as I loved Dad, even I wouldn't want him around all the time."

She slipped her arm around his waist. "You're not missing your mother's wedding—and being her new husband's best man—to stay here and babysit me. If I start feeling uncomfortable here, I'll just move back in with Mike and Scott." She stood on tiptoe and gave him a kiss. "In fact, let's call them once everything settles down. They'll want to know about this."

37

"So I can go now?" Del asked Detective Denninger.

"Yes. I appreciate you taking the time to talk with us. We'll be in touch if we have any further questions."

Del glanced at his phone: 7:00. He pushed himself out of the chair, stiff from the several hours he had spent there, and wondered if police departments intentionally furnished their interview rooms with uncomfortable chairs.

Although Denninger had framed their conversation as "just a little chat," not as a formal interview, Del suspected it didn't make much difference from a procedural point of view.

"Is Nola Lynch still here?" Del asked.

"She left about an hour ago."

"Rowan isn't here, is she?"

"No. We know she's had a tough time, and we figured we could wait to talk to her. Not that you haven't had a tough time yourself," Denninger added, "but with her having just lost her dad and brother, and being pregnant ..."

"Yeah," said Del, "I appreciate you being willing to give her some time."

Del trudged out to the Escape, feeling far more tired than he would have expected after an afternoon of sitting and drinking coffee. Denninger had been polite but dogged, and as the interview wore on, his questions made Del increasingly uncomfortable. The police obviously didn't think Harkin had just tumbled into the pond. Did they think Del had helped him in?

Del had told Denninger about the argument in the Ark—*of course he had*, he thought, his mouth twisting in irritation—although not his parting shot that if Harkin ever hurt Rowan again, Del would kill him. Even he had managed to keep his mouth shut about that one, although it wouldn't look good if Nola had mentioned it. He knew from experience that Nola could keep a secret if she wanted to ... but would she want to? What might be in it for her to point the police's attention toward Del?

And what about Niall's death? It seemed possible that someone could have snuck up behind Niall on the path and hit him over the head. Harkin? He had little apparent motivation other than his fraught relationship with his father. And, Del thought with a shudder, if Harkin had killed Niall, who had killed Harkin?

As Del started up the Escape and pulled out of the police station parking lot, his speculation drifted to Nola. Had Niall really had a do-not-resuscitate order? Del didn't recall ever hearing about it before. On the other hand, it was easy to imagine Niall rejecting the idea of being kept alive by beeping monitors and hissing pumps. He made a mental note to find out if there was a way to confirm Nola's claim.

The drive to Unionville took less than fifteen minutes, but it was long enough for Del to commit to the decision that had been developing during his time at the station. He needed to talk with Rowan, and he had to hope that if he shared his secrets with her—told her about following her to Larch Street, and about hiring Mike to follow her when he was afraid that he himself would bungle the job—she would share her secrets with him. He would commit to being more careful with the information he got, and more circumspect with the information he shared. He wasn't going to let his tendency to blurt out the first thing that entered his mind stand in the way of his wife sharing the important parts of her life with him ... including the fact that they were going to have a daughter. He could feel his anger and sorrow as a knot in the pit of his stomach.

If he could convince her that he could keep his mouth shut if he needed to, maybe she would tell him what she had been doing at 46 Larch Street.

And what, he thought suddenly, would Denninger make of those visits if he found out?

Would Rowan tell the police more about Larch Street than she had told her husband?

He pulled into the driveway of the Unionville house. In the list of improvements he and Rowan wanted to make, adding automatic garage door openers was always near, but never quite at, the top. In his rush to get inside, to ask Rowan what she was doing in West Philly before he lost his nerve, he yanked the door up harder than he intended and barely avoided getting caught by the rebound. However, before the door slammed down, he saw that the other bay, where he had expected to see the Miata, was empty.

Leaving the Escape in the driveway, Del hurried into the house, already pulling his phone out to call Rowan, when he saw the note on the kitchen table: *Out for a drive. Be back soon. XOXO R.*

Del ran his fingers through his hair. Out for a drive? She couldn't have let him know where?

He hit her number. It rang to voicemail.

"Dammit!"

It hadn't occurred to him that Rowan would disappear on an

unexplained outing just hours after finding her brother's body in the Tarn, so he had called Mike off his tailing assignment. He opened his contacts and scrolled to Mike's entry. Then he paused.

He was tired of sneaking around, tired of having another man keeping tabs on his wife.

He was going to Larch Street, and he was going to find out for himself what was going on there.

38

A t seven o'clock that evening, Ann, Mike, Scott, and Joe Booth sat in the sitting room at the Curragh, discussing the mysterious deaths at the Lynch winery. Ann had opened a bottle of Lynch Cab Sauv, although Joe had opted for a bottle of Victory Dirtwolf Double IPA. Corey had left a few hours earlier for the drive to Pittsburgh for his mother's wedding in two days.

"I knew Bruce Denninger when he worked in Philly," said Joe. "He's heading up the investigation. He told me that in view of Harkin Lynch's death, they're looking at Niall's as well."

"It's too bad they didn't do it sooner," said Scott. "If someone attacked Niall on the path—or attacked him somewhere else and moved him to the path—they won't find much evidence after all this time and all the rain we've had."

"I don't think they would have found much even if they had investigated immediately," replied Joe. "From what I heard, Nola, Del, and Rowan disrupted the scene quite a bit."

"What are the police saying about Harkin's death?" Mike asked Joe.

"No obvious signs of a struggle, but it's hard to tell from a visual inspection of a body that's been in water."

"Maybe he was drinking and went out on the dock and fell in," said Mike.

"Niall told me that Harkin wasn't able to smell or taste wine," said Ann.

"That doesn't mean he didn't drink," said Mike. "Or take drugs."

"The tox screen will show any drugs or alcohol," said Joe.

"Is it possible someone drowned him in the Tarn? With Ann a couple of yards away?" asked Mike, knitting his brow.

"It's more than a couple of yards," said Ann. "And the bedroom is on the far side of the Curragh. I don't think I would have heard a commotion at the Tarn unless there was a lot of yelling. Maybe he was killed somewhere else and dumped in the pond."

"We'll have to wait for the autopsy," said Joe, "but he probably wouldn't have sunk to the bottom unless he was alive when he went in and breathed in water."

"The water can't be more than three feet deep," said Ann. "He must have been unconscious."

"Or someone held him under," suggested Mike.

"Maybe," said Ann. "He wasn't a big guy, but he looked wiry, like he could put up a fight if someone tried to overpower him." She turned to Joe. "Can they tell about what time Harkin died?"

"Best estimate is after midnight, but there again, we'll have to wait for the autopsy."

"I suppose you haven't encountered Harkin since he died?" Scott asked Ann.

"No—although I haven't been back to the Tarn since this morning."

They were silent for a few moments, sipping their drinks, then Mike sat forward.

"So who would want to be knocking off members of the Lynch family?"

"Not just any old members of the Lynch family: the current owner," she said.

"And does it have anything to do with Rowan Lynch sneaking off to a speakeasy in Philadelphia?" added Scott.

"I don't know," said Ann. She turned to Mike. "Have you told Del yet about the Cabinet?"

He sighed. "No. I'm still trying to figure out how to explain to him how you and a Philadelphia detective ended up there. I'm hoping I can get a reservation for me and Scott so that I can describe it to him based on personal experience. That way, I don't have to admit that I let his secret slip."

Ann raised an eyebrow. "I think we have bigger issues to deal with."

"Just let me try to salvage a shred of dignity, okay?" Mike said peevishly. He turned to Joe. "Could whoever got you your reservation hook me up, too?"

"I think I tapped out that resource," said Joe.

"Actually," said Ann, "considering all the weird things that are going on, maybe it's better that we tell anyone associated with the Lynch family as little as possible. Who knows who's involved in what? Rowan mentioned that there was a big family blow-up last night, although she didn't give me any details."

"You think Del, Nola, or Rowan got so mad at Harkin that one of them drowned him in the family pond?" asked Mike.

"They were pretty upset about Harkin's plan to sell the winery ... but killing him does seem extreme." She rose from her chair. "I need a top-off." She refilled her glass in the kitchen, then, since Mike was holding out his glass expectantly, brought the bottle back to the sitting area. "Maybe all three of them were in on it, although it's a little gruesome to imagine the three of them wading into the pond and holding Harkin under." She leaned over to refill Mike's glass when a knock on the door made her jump, sending a splash of Cab Sauv onto the floor.

The three men stood.

"Let me—"

"I'll get it—"

"Better let me—"

Ann set the bottle down, irritated with herself for the mess and with the men for their alarm. "I think I can handle opening the door myself."

"Ann?" came a voice from the front porch. "It's Rowan Lynch."

The four exchanged looks. The blinds on the sitting room windows were closed, but the windows themselves were open. Had Rowan heard them speculating about the possibility that she, her husband, and her aunt had murdered her brother?

"Mike, can you clean that up?" Ann said, gesturing to the spilled wine. Then she threaded her way to the door and opened it.

If Rowan's red-splotched and puffy face was any indication, she was too deep in her grief to pay attention to an overheard conversation. In fact, her look of surprise when she glanced past Ann into the crowded sitting room suggested that she hadn't realized that Ann had company.

"I'm sorry," said Rowan, flustered, "I didn't mean to intrude." She thrust a black fabric bundle toward Ann. "Here's your dress. It's a little stretched out—I'll get you a new one—but it's clean now and I thought you could use it for ... maybe rags?"

Ann took the bundle and put it on a table next to the door. "Thanks, but you don't need to get me a new one. Maybe I'll branch out into another color—or if I'm really feeling crazy, a new style. Do you want to come in?"

"No, no. I can come back later," said Rowan, turning away.

"Hold on," said Ann. She turned back to the roomful of concerned men. "I'll be right back."

She stepped outside and closed the door. "How are you doing?" she asked Rowan.

Fresh tears began leaking from Rowan's eyes. "Not too good."

"You look like you need to sit down." Ann glanced at the chairs on the porch, but she didn't feel like having three sets of ears straining to overhear their conversation. There was a bench halfway down the path to the Cellar, but unfortunately it looked out over the Tarn. She briefly thought of shooing the men out of the Curragh, but where would she send them?

"Do you want to go to the Cellar or the big house to talk?" she asked.

"Let's go to the vineyard—there are benches there."

Ann followed Rowan down the path. For the first time, her movements seemed ungainly. When they reached the customer parking lot, Ann glanced back long enough to see the door of the Curragh open and someone—she thought it was Joe—slip out and follow them. Ann supposed that since they had just been discussing the possibility that Rowan Lynch was knocking off her family members, she shouldn't be surprised that they had sent out a chaperone.

Ann followed Rowan across the customer parking lot to the vineyard. The waning light glowed along the tops of the vines and the heavy clusters of grapes that hung thick along the rows. By the time they reached the far side, Rowan was a bit breathless. She led Ann to a pair of seats that had been fashioned from wine barrels. She dropped onto one and waved Ann onto another, then pulled a tissue from her pocket and blew her nose. "I can't stop crying."

"I don't blame you. You've gone through—are going through —a terrible time."

"I thought I could hold it together long enough to talk to you."

"Don't worry about me," said Ann.

Rowan nodded and took a deep breath, rubbing the small of her back. After a few moments, she continued. "You haven't seen Harkin yet, have you?"

"No, but I haven't looked for him yet. The police were at the Tarn for most of the day, and it looked to me like they were up at the big house, too."

"Harkin wasn't at the Tarn when we walked by just now?"

"No."

"Can you try to contact him? Ask him what happened?"

"I'll try." After a pause, she added, "Although spirits don't always hang around."

Rowan dabbed her eyes. "I guess they're more likely to stay if they have good memories of a place?"

"Good memories, bad memories. Anything that ties them to a location, especially if they feel there's unfinished business."

Over Rowan's shoulder, Ann could just see Joe, watching them from the corner of the vineyard.

Rowan gave a sad laugh. "Well, 'bad memories' would cover Harkin's feelings for sure. He never loved the winery like Dad and I did." She drew a deep breath and rubbed her back again. "Even when I was little, this was all I ever wanted. The house, the woods, the vineyard, the Cellar, even the Ark—it was like a fairytale come to life for me. The vineyard manager, Reynaldo—I called him Uncle Rey—used to let me follow him around and 'help' him judge when the grapes were ready for picking. He'd let me hold the clips when he was clipping up the thinned vines, or the basket of laundry pins when he put up the bird netting. His wife Maribelle let me sit in her lap while she drove the tractor, and then later taught me how to drive it."

She turned toward the vineyard, and Joe disappeared back

into the rows. "The vineyard is where I spent most of my time. Nola said that Harkin used to like to play in the Ark, and it made Dad angry because he felt it was disrespectful. He wanted Harkin to be paying attention, not playing. One day Harkin was trying to climb up the barrels and fell and broke his wrist, which I suppose Dad felt was poetic justice." A look of consternation crossed her face. "I wonder if they're arguing. *Still* arguing." She looked at Ann. "Could they do that? Run into each other?"

"It varies. I think Niall's spirit is tied to the Ark, but even if he could wander the property, he might not encounter Harkin. I've been in a room with spirits of family members who said they couldn't perceive each other, and others who have claimed to be able to communicate with each other across miles or years." She reached over and squeezed Rowan's hand. "I'll look for Harkin tomorrow, and if I can contact him, I'll ask him. Is there anywhere on the property he *did* like—or disliked less? I can start there."

After a moment, Rowan said, "The kitchen in the big house. He told me he used to hang out there with our mother. Could you check tonight?"

"Sure."

"You think it will be better for you to look for him alone, right?"

"Yes, I think so. Del gave me keys to the big house as well as the Cellar and the Ark."

Rowan nodded. "You'll have to let us know how much we owe you. Maybe we can suspend rental payments on the Curragh for a while ... except I don't know whether we'll be around 'for a while.'" She blotted her nose.

"Don't worry about it. No charge for me trying to contact Harkin."

"Thank you." Rowan marshaled another smile. "As long as

Del or I have anything to say about it, drinks are on the house for you."

Ann laughed. "Don't make any rash promises. I can put away a lot of wine."

Rowan's smile looked a little less forced this time. "I'm willing to take the risk."

She tried to stand but fell back with a grimace.

Ann helped her to her feet.

"Thanks," said Rowan. "My center of gravity is all screwed up."

"How are you feeling?"

"I've been having some back cramps, but the doctor says it's nothing to worry about." She waved a hand toward the Curragh. "Sorry again about interrupting."

"No problem. I'll let you know what I find tomorrow."

Rowan led them back through the vineyard to the parking lot.

"Where are you parked?" asked Ann.

"Behind the Cellar, in the staff lot."

"Let me walk you to your car."

"You don't have to do that. I've walked these grounds so often I could do it in my sleep."

"I'm sure you could, but ..." She couldn't think of any way around saying what she was thinking. "Bad things are happening to the Lynch family. I don't want anything bad to happen to you."

Rowan's eyes widened. "Do you think someone would ..." She glanced around the darkening parking lot.

"Let's err on the side of caution."

Ann accompanied Rowan to the Miata, then watched as it rolled down the drive and turned toward Unionville.

She heard Joe's voice call from behind her. "I'd give a password if I knew one."

She turned to see him strolling across the parking lot, hands in pockets.

"Thanks for standing guard," she said. "Although I'm still finding it hard to picture Rowan Lynch as a cold-blooded killer. Admittedly, I've only met her a few times, but she seems like a nice person. I like her."

"I hate to say it, but a lot of the killers I've met have seemed like nice, likable people."

Ann sighed. "Yeah. Although she did want me to see if I can get in touch with Harkin. Doesn't seem like something a killer would do. I told her I'd check the big house tonight."

"Want an escort?"

Ann didn't really think she needed a bodyguard, but the company would be nice. "Sure, if you don't mind waiting for me by the door. Don't want Harkin scared away by a crowd of two."

"Always happy to help out Ann Kinnear Sensing."

39

W hen Del got to Larch Street, he pulled into the alley. There was no red Miata behind number 46, but there was a Mercedes and the usual Ford Transit Connect. He pulled into the third parking spot and got out of the Escape.

The cargo area of the Connect was windowless, but he peered in the driver's window. Would it give him a hint about what was going on in the house? A small duffel bag sat on the floor of the passenger side, and on the seat was the usual detritus of a personal vehicle: crumbled receipts, a pair of sunglasses, a water bottle. As far as Del could see, the back contained only a few cardboard boxes and what looked like a folded tarp.

He turned to the gate in the stockade fence that separated the parking area from the back of the house. A small sign read *Please Use Front Door*. Even if he had wanted to ignore the request, there was no visible handle on the outside of the gate. He considered climbing the fence—hell, he considered kicking in the gate—but then rejected that idea. He didn't want to sneak up on the occupants of the house. He was tired of all the sneak-ing. He would go to the front door and demand that the man in the frock coat admit him, just as he had admitted Rowan and her fellow visitors.

He strode down the alley to the cross street and made two lefts. When he reached number 46, he glanced at his phone: 8:32. If experience was a guide, the two people who had arrived in the Mercedes had been inside for half an hour, and another two would arrive in another half hour. It seemed as if only Rowan arrived at the house alone.

He climbed the steps to the front porch and thumped the door with his fist, shaking it in its frame. He waited for almost a minute, then banged again. After a few moments, he saw the telltale illumination in the door's panes.

"May I help you?" a male voice called through the door.

"My name is Del Berendt, and I need to talk to you."

He waited a few seconds, then raised his fist to hammer on the door again.

"Very well," he heard from inside. "One moment."

He heard the rattle of a chain and the click of a deadbolt, then the door swung open to reveal the man in Victorian garb.

Del pushed past him into a vestibule dimly lit by the oil lamp the man held.

"You can't just barge in," the man said, although without much energy.

"I want to know what's going on in here," said Del.

The man raised his hands. "I can explain, if you'll just give me a chance."

Del heard another man's voice echo back his own ques-tion—"What's going on out there?"—from deeper in the house.

Del stepped out of the vestibule and into a central room. A man stood in a hallway leading further back into the house, silhouetted against the light from what Del guessed to be the kitchen.

"Is this part of the show?" the man asked.

"No, I'm afraid this is unscripted," said the Victorian-clad man from behind Del. "I'm terribly sorry. If you'll just give me a few moments with this gentleman, I'll be right back with you. No charge for tonight's reservation."

Del glanced around the space. A doorway led to a front room containing sheet-draped furniture. The room beyond the central space was empty. A heavily carved staircase disappeared into the darkness above.

What kind of business could Rowan have in this seemingly abandoned home?

A woman's silhouette joined the man's in the hallway, and Del heard a quickly whispered conference between the two. Then the man said, "I think we'll be leaving now. I wasn't wild about coming to this neighborhood to begin with, and I'm not going to wait around while you two argue."

The Victorian man spared a moment to scowl at Del, then hurried toward the couple, a hitch in his step that suggested an old injury. "I totally understand. I'm terribly sorry the evening hasn't turned out as you wished. If you'd ever like to return, your entertainment will of course be complimentary."

As the man escorted the couple down the hall, Del stepped further into the house, into an empty space that had probably once been a dining room. He heard a few more murmured exchanges and the click of a closing door, then the man reappeared in the hallway.

"You'd best come back to the kitchen," the man sighed. "We can talk there."

Del's self-righteous anger was giving way to confusion and curiosity. The home's empty rooms were certainly not like any house of ill repute he had ever imagined. Its tidy, if dusty, condition didn't suggest a drug den. He followed the man without a word.

The kitchen was a dreary time capsule, its metal cupboards hanging askew, its porcelain sink and built-in drainboard stained, the linoleum floor tiles curling at the edges. A scarred but clean butcher block island sat in its center. The man lowered himself onto a stool at the island and gestured Del onto another.

Del sat.

"So," said the man, "you're Rowan Lynch's husband."

Del raised his eyebrows. "Yes."

"And you want to know what your wife has been doing here?"

"Yes."

The man puffed out a bushel-sized breath. "My name's John Derkammern, although my guests call me the Professor."

"Your guests?"

"Yes. I run a little bar here. The smallest bar in Philadelphia, I feel confident saying. An unlicensed bar. A speakeasy, you might say."

"Where is the bar?"

John gestured toward the hallway. "You passed the door on your way back here. Would you like to see?"

Del nodded, and John stood and led him back to the hallway. He slid open a pocket door and stepped aside. Del peered in.

Where the rest of the house was decrepit, this room was a little jewel, artifacts and natural objects on shelves on one side, liquor bottles and glassware on another, all illuminated by a string of fairy lights. A pair of intricately etched crystal glasses holding a purplish liquid sat on a wooden bar top. Behind the bar top was a raised bench that was just wide enough for two people.

"Heavens," John said with a sigh, "they must have slid under the bar top to get out." He picked up the glasses and set them aside, next to a few other pairs of equally elegant glassware, then swung the bar top up and latched it to the wall.

"It's tiny," said Del.

"The former butler's pantry."

"And you serve two people at a time?"

"That's right."

"Just cocktails?"

"Yes."

"For one-hour reservations."

"That's right. How did you know that?"

"I saw people enter at the front door at the top of the hour."

"You've been watching the house?"

"I followed Rowan here. I even hired someone else to follow her when I thought she had spotted me."

John frowned. "You hired some kind of private investigator?"

"Not exactly a private investigator—a friend. Actually, he used to be my financial planner. Now he—" Del stopped himself before he launched into a description of Mike's current job as business manager of Ann Kinnear Sensing. "Now he's just a customer at Lynch."

"And it seemed advisable to hire a friend—a Lynch Winery customer—to spy on your wife? You couldn't have just asked her what she was doing?"

The words carried a reprimand but John delivered them in a tone that suggested he was sympathetic to Del's plight.

Del flushed. "Yes, of course I should have done that."

"Perhaps you had some other idea about what might be going on in here," John said with a smile.

"Well ... yes."

John gave a soft laugh. "I can hardly blame you. It's not as if the home's actual use would occur to anyone."

"I never saw her come out. I suppose the customers—"

"The guests."

"—the guests always leave from the back, like that couple just did?"

"Yes. It helps retain the illusion that the Cabinet is only for them."

"The Cabinet?"

"The Cabinet of Curiosities." John waved at the items on the shelves. "Amateur natural scientists and anthropologists would use them to display their collections. Very popular in Victorian times." He patted his frock coat. "Hence the costume."

Del nodded and stepped back from the butler's pantry. John slid the door closed, then led him back to the kitchen where they resumed their seats.

"But you have it set up for two people," said Del, trying to process what he was learning, "and I only ever saw Rowan come alone. Unless ..."

John raised a hand. "Rowan always came alone. And left alone."

"So it was just the two of you sitting around drinking fancy cocktails?"

"I never drink myself when I'm entertaining guests. And I only made Rowan non-alcoholic drinks." He chuckled. "I have to say that finding a way to prepare a non-alcoholic Tantalus was quite a challenge."

Trying to keep his tone light, Del asked, "So Rowan came here so she could drink Shirley Temples in a butler's pantry with a guy in costume?"

"We chatted."

Del didn't bother trying to lighten his tone for his next question. "About what?"

"About the winery. About her father. About her brother. About the difficulties she had with them."

"And did you chat about why she felt she couldn't discuss that with me?"

John's smile was gentle. "No, we never chatted about that. But I've been a bartender in one form or another for many years, and I've learned that there are some things you can say to a virtual stranger much more easily than to those you're close to. Plus, with you being not only Niall Lynch's son-in-law but also his winemaker, I suspect she felt it would put you in an awkward position for her to complain to you. Being both a member of the family and an employee—it's a tricky situation to be in."

Del raised an eyebrow. "Spoken like someone who knows from experience." He lowered his eyes. After a moment he said, "I'm thinking that Rowan might have had another reason to come here. She might not have thought I could keep her secrets."

"You were in the habit of betraying her confidence?"

"Not just hers, and never on purpose. And not always a confidence." Del felt his face redden. "Let's just say I don't always think before I speak." He waved a hand. "Never mind. You don't need to become the unofficial psychiatrist to more than one member of the family. But how did Rowan even know about the Cabinet? I've certainly never heard of it, and if it's unlicensed, it means it's illegal ..."

John regarded him for a moment, then said, "If you'd allow me to make a phone call, I think I can explain."

Del nodded, and John pulled a cell phone—a jarring anachronism—from his vest pocket. He tapped and held the phone to his ear. After a moment, Del heard the faint sounds of a woman's voice on the other end.

"The Professor here," he said. "We got an unexpected visitor tonight. Del Berendt."

Del heard a response.

"He followed her," said John. He smiled at Del. "With a little help from his friends."

There was another response, then John said, "Would you like to speak with him?"

After a moment, Del heard a single-word response. John nodded and extended the phone toward Del.

Del took the phone and put it to his ear. "Hello?"

"Hello, Del," said a voice he knew all too well. "This is Nola."

40

The Lynch family home had a blocky central structure with wings extending from either side. Ann unlocked the front door, and she and Joe stepped into a two-story entrance hall whose impressive size was offset by the pedestrian nature of the furnishings: a distinctly ungrand coat rack and a patterned runner that looked more Costco than Karastan.

"Harkin?" she called.

There was no answer.

She wandered around the entrance hall, looking into the connecting rooms and periodically calling Harkin's name. Getting no response, she turned to Joe. "I'm going to check the kitchen. Do you mind waiting here?"

"No problem. If you need a hand, yell."

She set off to find the kitchen. As one room led to the next, Ann found it hard to believe that Niall Lynch had inhabited this house alone, at least until Nola had moved in to care for him. Why had Rowan and Del gotten a separate place when they could have rattled around in this house for days without running into another occupant? Then she thought back to her interaction with Niall and decided perhaps the expense was worth the benefit of having an ensured break from the Lynch family patriarch.

Not only that, the house itself was unwelcoming. Rugs curling at the edges created an obstacle course of tripping hazards, the upholstered chairs looked lumpy, and the rooms were dark without being atmospheric.

When she finally found the kitchen, it was no more updated than the rest of the house, but Ann could understand why it might have been a refuge for Harkin. The curtains that hung at the windows would once have been a cheerful yellow, and a dusty row of vases on top of the cabinets suggested that someone might at one time have decorated the table with bouquets of flowers. But there was no sign of Harkin. She made a quick tour of the few first-floor rooms she had missed, then the second floor, as well.

She returned to the entrance hall. "Nothing."

"Can you get into the other buildings?" Joe asked.

"Yeah, Del gave me the keys."

"Want to check them tonight?"

"Sure. Although we should let Mike and Scott know what's up."

"I texted them."

"Thanks."

They checked the Cellar, then the Ark, Joe staying by the entrance each time.

In the barrel room, Ann gazed for a moment at the line of family photos along the back of Niall's desk. Someone had draped a black ribbon across Niall's picture, but Harkin's was not similarly decorated. She suspected that if she encountered Harkin in the Ark, he would point to it as yet more evidence of his status as the Lynch family outsider.

As she and Joe took the path up to the Curragh, she texted Rowan an update that neither Harkin nor Niall was in evidence. She wished she had some news for Rowan, but she was relieved not to have found Niall and Harkin locked in an argument that might now have no ending.

41

When Del got back to Unionville, Rowan was lying on the living room couch talking on the phone. Her eyes were puffy and a pile of tissues lay on the floor beside her.

When she saw Del in the doorway, she said into the phone, "Del just got home. ... I'm sure it's nothing—the baby isn't due for another three weeks." She listened, then said, "I'm sure we won't be going anywhere." She glanced up and must have noticed Del's worried expression. "Nola, let me call you back. ... Yes, I'll let you know if things change."

She ended the call and shifted uneasily on the couch. "I didn't expect you to be at the police station this late. What in the world took so long?"

"They had a bunch of questions. What's wrong? Have you been crying?"

She scowled. "Yes, Del, I've been crying. My father and brother are both dead."

"Of course, of course—stupid question." He went to the couch and perched on the edge of a cushion. "What did you mean by 'I'm sure it's nothing'?"

"My back hurts. Nola doesn't think it sounds like labor."

"What does she know? She's never had a baby."

"Well, none of us have, have we? So her guess is as good as anyone's." She sighed at his stricken look. "I called the doctor earlier. She said hold tight."

"Hold tight? What is that supposed to mean?"

"That we don't need to be rushing off to the hospital. It might not even be labor." She nudged Del with her leg and he jumped up to let her stand. "I'm going to take a bath and see if that helps." She shuffled across the room and made her way slowly up the stairs.

By the time Del checked on her half an hour later, she was in bed and snoring loudly.

Once again he had missed an opportunity to come clean with Rowan.

42

Ann woke the next morning to heavy rain drumming on the roof of the Curragh.

She made periodic circuits of the property throughout the day and, despite her raincoat and umbrella, barely dried out from one patrol before it was time for the next.

It was dusk when she stepped into the kitchen of the big house and yelped at the sight of a man seated at the table.

Harkin Lynch looked as present, and as unwaterlogged, as when Ann had seen him lounging in the doorway in the Cellar, eavesdropping on Del, Rowan, Nola, and herself.

"Sorry about that," he said in the nasal voice she remembered from their earlier encounter. "Didn't mean to scare you."

"You just startled me. I was starting to think this was a wild goose chase."

"I guess it would be a bit of a professional impediment to be afraid of ghosts."

"Did you hear me calling just now?"

"Yeah, but I figured if you really wanted to talk to me, you'd get here eventually."

"Did you know I was here earlier?"

A look of confusion passed over his features. "Were you? No, I must have been ..." He considered for a moment, then shrugged. "Not paying attention, I guess."

She nodded toward one of the other chairs at the table. "May I?"

He waved toward it. "Be my guest."

She sat.

"I thought Rowan was crazy to hire you to contact Dad," said Harkin. "I figured Del and Nola were just going along with it to humor her. Silly me."

"Seeing is believing."

He laughed. "That's for sure. Is this visit for the Lynches, or on your own account?"

"Rowan asked me to look for you."

"Wondering what's going to happen to the winery now that I'm gone?"

"No. She expects it to go to your son. She wanted to know what happened to you."

Harkin's expression softened. "Good old Rowan."

"She seems very sweet."

He gave her a lopsided smile. "You're wondering how two siblings could grow up into two such different people, right?"

She smiled back. "Sort of." Her smile faded. "Although, after talking with your dad, I can see how it would happen. It seems like you, as the son and the oldest, had the benefit *and* the curse of his expectations."

Harkin raised his eyebrows. "What was the benefit?"

"You inherited the winery."

"Ah, right. Although fat lot of good that did me." He crossed his arms and leaned back in his chair. "And what, from your point of view, was the curse?"

"That he wanted you to follow in his footsteps."

He snorted. "Primogeniture is alive and well in Kennett Square. Might as well have been a feudal manor."

"He told me about your lack of taste and smell. It seems like the curse was the fact that he was so obsessed with fixing it. And it seems like he had some pretty extreme ideas for how to deal with a condition that sounds like it wasn't a serious health problem."

Harkin sat forward. "It wasn't a health problem at all! I'll never get a job as a radio DJ, and maybe I get sinus infections more often than most people, but as far as I'm concerned, the biggest downside is that my wife has to poke me in the ribs when I snore. She says I sound like an elephant trumpeting." His lips crept up in a smile, then his expression darkened. "Dad got me steroid spray. When that didn't work, he tried to put me on oral steroids, although the doctors wouldn't go for that. I hadn't even hit puberty." He shook his head. "He wanted me to have surgery. Do you want to know how they remove nasal polyps surgically?"

"Not particularly."

"Suffice it to say it's gross. And did he do all this for my benefit? No. He did it to fix a condition that didn't even bother me—that wasn't in any way harmful to me—to equip me for a lifetime sentence in a job I didn't even want!"

"Did Nola ever intercede with you and your dad?"

He shrugged. "Not much. She was more Rowan's protector. The only person I had in my corner wasn't even a family member—just one of the winery staff." He was silent for a moment, then his expression brightened. "Although Nola was the person who introduced me to Hawaii—took me on a trip there when I was eleven. I was hooked. The scenery, the weather, the water, the people. Ever been?"

"Briefly. I had a sensing engagement on a cruise ship sailing between Hawaii and Vancouver."

"Nice work if you can get it."

Harkin waxed poetic about Hawaii for a few minutes, and although Ann was all for establishing rapport with the spirits she was engaged to contact, she did have an assignment to discharge.

"So," she said when an opportunity presented itself, "how did you end up in the Tarn?"

His eyes widened. "In the Tarn?"

"That's where your body was found."

"Jesus," he said, his eyes wide. "Who found me?"

"Rowan."

He puffed out a lungful of air. "Poor Ro. But how did I end up in the Tarn?"

"That's what we're wondering."

He jumped up and walked to the window. After a moment, he turned back to Ann. "Is it weird that I haven't thought of this before? That I just 'woke up' dead and didn't wonder how I got that way?"

"Not really. It seems like there's a period of reorientation after a person dies, where their conscious thoughts are catching up with their situation. It sounds like that's what you were experiencing." She didn't add that it sounded like Niall had experienced that as well, the circumstances of his death vague in his mind. "But if you could remember what happened, it would be helpful. I take it you didn't decide to take a midnight stroll from the house to the Tarn?"

"I don't think so."

"Were you drinking? Or taking some medicine that would make you forget?"

With a scowl, he said, "I don't drink, and I don't take *medicine* or do drugs, which is what I assume you meant."

"Is it possible someone drugged you and took you to the Tarn?"

"You mean carried me down there from the big house?"

"Carried you down, or led you down if you were drugged. You could have been conscious but unaware of what was going on and suggestible."

He ran his fingers through his hair. "I don't know. I was heading up to bed and then ..." His voice trailed off.

"And then?" Ann prompted.

Half a minute ticked by, Harkin's brow knotted in thought, then he shook his head. "I don't remember."

"Were you eating or drinking something that someone might have drugged?"

"I was drinking Pepsi, like I always do."

"Was the bottle sealed?"

"No. It was a two-liter bottle I had in the fridge."

"Is it possible someone drugged the bottle?"

"I suppose it's possible." He glanced toward the door that led from the kitchen to the backyard. "You know, I thought I heard something from the back of the house. I checked and didn't find anything. Everything was locked up."

"Did you drink out of the bottle of Pepsi in the refrigerator after you heard the noise?"

"No," he said absently, then his features tightened. "No, because when I got to the kitchen, there was a glass of Pepsi sitting on the counter. I figured I had accidentally poured two, so I drank it."

"Did you notice any weird taste?"

He raised an eyebrow. "I *never* notice any weird taste. I never notice any taste at all." He ran his fingers through his hair again. "Jesus. You think someone drugged me and then dropped me into the Tarn? Who would do it?"

"I don't know. Any ideas?"

"No. I mean, I know I wasn't everyone's favorite Lynch, but

drowning me in the Tarn seems extreme. Was I—" He cleared his throat. "—dead when I went in the water?"

"We don't have the official word on that, but it appears you were alive but not struggling."

He shuddered. "Makes me kind of hope for the 'drugged and unaware' scenario."

"If you got to the Tarn under your own steam, it doesn't do much in the way of narrowing the field of suspects. If you didn't get there under your own steam, we'd need to find someone who could carry you—or at least get you into a wheelbarrow. I imagine the only family member who could do that would be Del."

"Dudley Do-Right? I don't think so." After a pause, he added. "Although he was certainly mad enough at me the last time I saw him."

"When was that?"

"That last night. Family conclave in the Ark. I ..." He looked down at his hands. "I said something that upset Rowan, and Del got pretty angry about it."

"What did you say?"

He sighed and dropped back into his chair. "It doesn't matter, does it?"

"I suppose not—unless what you said would make Del killing mad."

Harkin considered. "I still can't see it."

"Why not?"

"Whatever damage Del Berendt does, he does unintentionally."

"I don't see how it would be possible, but just to cover all the bases ... could it have been your father? I spoke with his spirit in the barrel room. He acted as if he couldn't move beyond the Ark, but he might have been lying ... or his range might have expanded since then."

Harkin gave a bark of a laugh. "You think my father's ghost roofied me and schlepped my unconscious body or unaware self to the Tarn?" His expression sobered. "Is that even possible?"

"I've never seen it happen, but I suppose anything's possible."

They were both silent for a few moments, then Harkin said, "My dad could be a bastard, but he was usually a bastard in pursuit of a goal. Obviously killing me wouldn't make me more likely to keep the winery. And the will we had—" His features twisted. "—the will Nola had hidden away—didn't impose any restrictions on the sale."

"Might he have thought that having the winery go to Kepi would keep it in the family?"

"If he thought that, he was wrong. Kepi never thought of the winery as anything but an interesting place to visit. Scuba is his life." If a ghost's face could be said to become paler, Harkin's did. "But I barely told Dad anything about what was going on with me and my family in Hawaii, and he did have this idea that Kepi was interested in the winery—maybe more interested than he actually was. Jesus. I suppose ..." His voice trailed off.

"I'm just considering all the possibilities," said Ann.

Harkin sat forward. "My son has a dream, to have his own scuba training and tour business," he said, his voice rising. "Not only would he be good at it—he's a natural teacher, a natural people person," his laugh was harsh, "unlike his dad, obviously —but he's working incredibly hard at it. He's fourteen years old, and he's already saving his money to make his dream a reality. You know what my dream was when I was fourteen? Not to be part of the winery. That's not pursuing a dream—that's just escaping a nightmare."

"If Niall wanted to keep the winery in the family, Rowan and her line might have been a better bet than you and yours."

She instantly regretted voicing the thought, expecting

Harkin to be angry. Instead, he fell back and heaved a sigh. "I hate to say it, but only if she was going to have a boy. She told us at our little get-together at the Ark that she's having a girl. I guess she figured that at this point, Dad's inevitable disappointment couldn't matter that much."

"Did you and Nola know she was having a girl?"

"I didn't. I'm not sure about Nola."

"Del must have known."

Harkin snorted. "Oh, no. She had especially kept it a secret from Del 'Loose Lips Sink Ships' Berendt."

"He's really that bad?"

He shrugged. "He means well."

"That sounds like damning with faint praise."

Harkin gave a tired smile. "He's just ... unguarded. And naive about how people will take the things he says, and what they'll do with them." His smile faded. "My first couple of years in Hawaii were pretty wild, and I used to tell Rowan stories about what her big brother was up to. I knew she'd never tell Dad. When I found out Alana was pregnant, I even told her that. Even though she was only eleven, she kept it a secret for months before I got up the nerve to tell Dad myself. Later, when she and Del got together, she asked me if she could tell him the stories— I think she thought he would get a kick out of them. I said sure —what did I care?" He sighed. "The stories about my wild times got back to Dad and he would use them as ammunition in our fights—threw them in my face as examples of how irresponsible I was. I'm sure he died thinking that the frat boy version of Harkin Lynch was still the man I am." He grimaced. "Or maybe I should say, the man I was."

"How do you know it was Del who told your dad?"

"He 'fessed up. He always felt terrible when he realized what damage he had done by having no filter between his brain and his mouth."

"Do you think there's a connection between Del's lack of discretion and what happened to you and your dad?"

Harkin waved a dismissive hand. "No, I'm just spouting off." His mouth twisted in a cynical smile. "See, I'm no better than Del is."

"But better than you led me to believe when I first met you."

He looked at her, surprised.

"Hearing you defend Rowan and even Del, hearing the way you talk about your family back in Hawaii ... it's not what I would have expected."

He gave her a tired smile. "Not the nasty frat boy after all?"

"Not once you didn't have your father pushing you toward a life you didn't want. Rowan had Nola—and later Del—to help her deal with Niall. You have Alana and Kepi."

"Yes, I have—" His voice caught, and he dropped his eyes to his hands. Then he drew a deep breath and met her eyes again. "I *had* Alana and Kepi."

43

Rowan's back cramps continued throughout the day, and the obstetrician continued to advise her to hold tight, and to let her know if the situation changed. Afterwards, Rowan told Del that she hated the term "hold tight," that she knew for a fact that the doctor had never had a baby, and that the next time she had a baby, she was damn well going to find an obstetrician who had gone through labor herself. She complained about the fact that the rain was doing nothing to reduce the mugginess, and that they needed to move the addition of air conditioning way up on the list of home improvements.

Del thought that if ever there was a time for him to exercise his vow to think before he spoke, it was now.

He had expected Nola to join them in Unionville, but Rowan told him that Nola was meeting with the lawyers to figure out how to execute Harkin's will without requiring Alana and Kepi to come to Pennsylvania.

"She seems very intent on saving them the trip," Rowan said as Del rubbed her feet. "I imagine it can all be done long-distance, but it would be nice to see them. I feel like I barely know Alana."

By evening, the situation was unchanged, except that the living room was now equipped with several oscillating fans Del had picked up at Target.

Rowan tossed aside the copy of *Vogue* that she had asked Del to pick up along with the fans. "I'm never reading another magazine that shows such emaciated women." She hauled herself to her feet with a groan. "God, I'm going to be glad when I'm not so rotund."

"Rotund but radiant," Del said gamely, and was pleased to earn a tired laugh from Rowan.

"I think I'll take another bath."

"You're going to turn into a prune."

"But a prune with a less sore back."

He followed Rowan to the stairway, which was too narrow to allow him to help her up. "How about a heating pad?"

"I'm not putting anything hot next to my body." She stopped halfway up to catch her breath. "I think this baby is taking up most of my lung space."

When he heard the pipes clanking as the tub filled, he went to the dining room and poured himself a bourbon. He swirled the liquid in the plain glass tumbler, thinking back to the elegant glassware at the Cabinet. After the call with Nola, John had prepared two glasses of something called a Clover Club cocktail that they drank at the kitchen island. An hour later, after a second round of cocktails, Del could understand what had drawn Rowan to the Larch Street house. John was an excellent listener. Del wouldn't have minded a sympathetic bartender of his own to talk to.

He puttered around the house—straightening the pillows on the couch, unloading the dishwasher, refreshing his drink—

until he heard Rowan's tired call from the upstairs bathroom. "Del, I can't get out of the tub."

He hurried upstairs and helped her out.

She dried off and put on a fresh cotton nightgown. "I think I'll just lie down up here," she said. "It'll save me a trip up and down the steps if I want to take another bath."

Del got her settled in bed, propped up with a mound of pillows, and brought her a glass of water. He went to the door and was pulling it shut when Rowan said, "Will you keep me company?"

He stepped back into the room. "Of course." He lowered himself onto the side of the bed and took her hand in his. "What do you want to talk about?"

"I don't know." She wrinkled her nose. "Anything except the winery."

They discussed whether they would need to get a new car when the baby came, or if the baby seat-appropriate Escape was sufficient. Rowan was skeptical that they could afford a new car without trading in her beloved Miata. Del said that they should crunch the numbers before discounting the possibility of keeping the little sports car for date nights.

Rowan squeezed his hand. "This is nice. We don't get enough time to just sit and talk."

Del decided he wouldn't get a better opening than that.

"Ro, I went to Larch Street."

She looked at him blankly for a moment, then placed the location. She blushed. "You know about Larch Street?"

He looked down at her hand where it rested in his. "I followed you there. Twice. You didn't know?"

She shook her head.

"Remember the time some jacked-up pickup started honking at a vehicle blocking the street?"

Her eyes widened. "That was you?"

"I was the blockage. I even asked a friend to follow you and see if he could figure out what was going on."

"A friend? Who?"

"Mike Kinnear."

"Ann's brother?"

"Yes ... but Ann doesn't know about it."

"Good heavens, Del," she said, her tone vacillating between embarrassment and indignation, "you had me tailed?"

"Yes. I'm sorry, but I was really at my wit's end. I wanted to know what was going on, but at the same time I was afraid to ask you. Afraid to find out."

She sighed and leaned her head back against the pillows. "I guess I'm the last person who should be angry about you sneaking around."

"I finally went to the house myself. I met John."

"John?"

"The Professor."

"Oh. I didn't know his name was John—I always just called him the Professor."

"He told me why you went there. He said you needed an impartial third party to talk about family stuff with."

She raised her head. "Winery stuff, not family stuff. At least not *this* family."

"But the Cabinet was a bit of a family affair, wasn't it? I know Nola is involved. John—the Professor—made a call and then handed the phone over to me. I couldn't believe it when I heard her voice."

"She didn't tell me about that."

"I asked her not to. I promised her I would let you know that I had been to the Cabinet, but that I had a lot to think about and didn't want to be rushed into it." He gave a rueful laugh. "Look at me, being all circumspect."

She smiled. "Did she tell you how it all came about?"

"She said you would tell me."

She nudged him and he stood so that she could swing her legs off the bed. She patted the bed beside her and he sat down next to her.

"She and I used to joke about wanting a bartender all to ourselves for an hour. Someone who was cheaper than a psychiatrist and more discreet than a girlfriend. Someone to talk about our whole screwed-up family with. We even talked about what the setting would be. In our version, it was always a tiny Irish pub." She squeezed his hand. "This was before we got married —it was before I even met you—and what we wanted to talk about was Dad and Harkin and the winery. And in fact, that's all I ever talked about with the Professor."

"And you couldn't talk to me?"

"I needed someone with a little distance." She sighed. "But now it's a moot point, isn't it? Dad's gone. Harkin's gone. The winery's gone." She marshaled a smile. "And we have better things to talk about—like the baby."

"Our daughter."

Her smile faded. "Yes, our daughter. I'm sorry I didn't tell you the gender, Del. I really thought that it would count against me if Dad found out it was a girl."

"And you thought he might find out from me."

"Well—"

He waved her comment away. "I can't blame you. I might have done the same in your position."

She laughed. "You would have told everyone as soon as you knew, consequences be damned."

He laughed with her. "Yes, I probably would have done that."

"And then when it seemed possible that we might be able to contact Dad—either ourselves or with Ann's help—I had this vision of being able to tell you all at once. Dad shouldn't care any more about whether we had a boy or a girl. And I started to be afraid that ..." She put her hand to her mouth, then took a deep breath. "I was afraid that once Harkin sold the winery and went back to Hawaii, he might not come back." She dropped her hand into her lap. "I had this vision of a happy family event. I should have known that was too much to ask for, even without Dad there."

He took her hand. "I don't blame you for trying."

She squeezed his hand, lost in thought.

After a moment, he prompted her. "You were going to tell me how the Cabinet came about."

She roused herself. "One day Nola told me that she thought she might be able to make our dream of our own bartender for an hour come true. She knew someone who was looking for work, and who she thought would be just right for the job. She found the house on Larch, and once it was all set up, she started carefully spreading the word to her event planning clients."

"For an evening in a Victorian Cabinet of Curiosities."

"The Victorian theme was the Professor's idea."

"It is a charming place."

"It was a refuge for me. Away from the winery." She looked up at him. "Not away from you. But even the drive there and back was therapeutic. A couple of hours where I didn't have to worry about anyone or anything."

"Will you be going back?" Del asked tentatively.

"No. I don't need to go back. But even if I wanted to, Nola is shutting down the Cabinet. She never meant it to be a permanent thing—more like a pop-up event—but it was so popular that she kept it going for longer than she intended."

"When is it closing?"

"Soon—I'm not sure exactly when."

"I'm sorry to hear that—I was sort of looking forward to sending Mike Kinnear there."

"You should call the Professor—I have his number. I think he and Nola were canceling reservations, but as far as I know, they haven't dismantled it. Maybe they could fit him in as their last guest."

44

Ann dropped her eyes, giving Harkin a moment of privacy as she considered the legacy—actual and emotional—that Niall Lynch had bestowed on his children.

She was trying to decide where to take the conversation next when Harkin said, "You know, there was another weird thing that happened that night. I got a call from the former wine-maker, Henry Tollman."

Ann sat forward. "Really? Henry Tollman called Niall right before Niall died."

Harkin's eyebrows climbed. "No shit."

"Why was he calling you?"

"It started out as a condolence call—he had heard that Dad died. When I told you that the only person in my corner when I was a kid was one of the winery staff, it was Henry I was talking about."

"He didn't stop by in person?"

"He hasn't been on the Lynch property for years ... actually, for decades. He said he was calling from San Francisco, although he could easily have been lying about that."

"You said you heard something from the back of the house that night. Would Henry have been able to get into the house? For example, might he have known where there was a spare key?"

"Actually, he might have kept a key from when he worked here. Henry was always a collector of odds and ends, and I don't think the locks have ever been changed."

Ann crossed her arms and gazed at the ceiling. "You said that Henry was your champion when you were little. Did your relationship change when you got older?"

"Our relationship changed when he went to prison."

Ann dropped her gaze back to Harkin. "He went to prison?"

"Yeah. He and Nola had gone out for dinner. Nola was waiting in front of the restaurant for Henry to bring the car around—" His mouth twisted in a smile. "That tells you how long ago it was—I certainly can't imagine her waiting for someone to bring a car around these days." The smile faded. "Anyhow, some kid ran by and grabbed her purse, knocked her down. She broke her wrist when she fell. Henry was just pulling up, and after he got someone from the restaurant to take care of Aunt Nola, he took off after the kid. Found him a couple of blocks away. The kid had ditched the purse but had Nola's things in his pocket. Henry made the kid take him to where he had thrown Nola's purse in a dumpster, then he ..." Harkin trailed off, looking uncomfortable.

"He ... what?" asked Ann.

"He beat him up. Henry had been a boxer in college, and he didn't hold back. Henry was twenty-nine, the kid was a scrawny teenager." He paused again. "The kid died."

"Jesus," breathed Ann.

"Yeah. The fact that Henry attacked him after they had walked to the dumpster to retrieve Nola's purse made it a little hard to argue it was a crime of passion. Henry was convicted of manslaughter and went to prison."

"Did Niall stay in touch with him after that?"

"No. Dad was determined to distance the winery from any blowback. He cut Henry off completely. I guess I can imagine Henry might have resented Dad for not at least visiting him in prison. After all, as far as Henry was concerned, he had ended up where he was because he was defending Niall's sister's honor."

"You said Henry and Nola were out to dinner together. Were they dating?"

Harkin smiled grimly. "They were engaged."

"Holy hell." Ann considered for a moment, then shook her head. "I don't know your aunt very well, but she doesn't strike me as someone who would go for the bad boy type, much less the murdering type."

"Yeah, I always thought that, too. I sometimes think that Aunt Nola got involved with Henry as much to piss off Dad as because she was madly in love. After all, as far as I know, she didn't keep in touch with Henry afterwards."

"But if Niall hired Henry as the winemaker, he must have thought he was okay."

"You hire a winemaker for his nose, his palate, and his ability to get great wine out of the grapes, not because you want him as a brother-in-law."

"Or as a son-in-law," said Ann.

Harkin snorted. "Yeah, Dad might have had second thoughts if he realized when he hired Del that Rowan would be smitten." He drew a deep breath. "Anyhow, the kid had some friends inside, and they caught Henry in the exercise yard one day and returned the favor. He was in pretty bad shape by the time the guards broke it up."

"But Henry's out of prison now?"

"Yeah. I think he ended up serving just a couple of years."

"I wonder what he's done since then?"

"Some traveling."

"You stayed in touch with him?"

Harkin shifted in his chair. "Not really."

Ann raised her eyebrows.

"Until that evening, I hadn't spoken with him. I was only eight when the whole thing with the purse snatcher happened. I found out the details over the years, bit by bit. After he left, he sent me postcards on my birthday, always from a different place —all over the U.S., a couple of times from France or Argentina or Australia—usually from some history museum. For a while, the cards just wished me a happy birthday, but on my eighteenth birthday, he wrote that now that I was an adult, he hoped I'd get in touch with him. He included a contact number—I think it was in California."

"And did you get in touch?"

"No," said Harkin, not meeting her eyes. "I really didn't want to revisit that part of my life. In fact, I wasn't eager to revisit any part of my childhood. I was getting ready to go to college in Hawaii and really didn't want to have anything to do with him."

"Did you get any cards after that?"

"I don't think so. I didn't give him my address in Hawaii, and I never heard that any cards showed up here, although if Dad had found them before Rowan or Nola did, I'm sure he would have thrown them away." Harkin rubbed his forehead. "I hoped Henry was seeing all the places he used to tell me were on his bucket list. He was a student of life, was the Professor."

Ann felt her heart clutch. "The Professor?"

"Yeah, that's what I used to call Henry—the Professor."

"You said Nola didn't stay in touch with him?"

"Not that I know of."

"Did Rowan know Henry?"

"No. She was just an infant when he left."

"Would she know what he looks like? Are there photos of him she might have seen?"

"I don't think so. Dad got rid of any evidence that Henry ever existed. Why?"

"I think I know where Henry is."

Harkin leaned forward. "What are you talking about? Have you seen him?"

"I'm not positive," said Ann. "Del hired my brother to follow Rowan. I think he thought she was having an affair—"

"Rowan? Cheating on her husband? I have never met two people more nauseatingly in love than Rowan and Del."

Ann laughed. "Yeah, that's my impression as well, but as everyone keeps reminding me, looks can be deceiving. Anyhow, Rowan kept going to what looked like a derelict house in West Philly. We eventually found out that it's a tiny bar—just two customers and the bartender. It's called the Cabinet of Curiosities, and the bartender said his name was John but he calls himself the Professor. He dresses in Victorian clothes—frock coat, vest, ascot."

Harkin nodded vigorously. "I recall Henry being interested in that time period. In fact, he used to volunteer as a docent at some museum in Philly that was all done up as a Victorian mansion."

"What did Henry look like?"

"Tall, thin. Brown hair."

"Beard and mustache?"

"Not when I knew him."

"Scars, maybe from acne?"

Harkin shook his head.

She tapped her fingers on the table. "All that would be easy to change ... except maybe for the scars." She pulled out her phone and opened a browser. "Maybe I can find a picture of

Henry Tollman online. Maybe from news coverage of the incident. The person at the Cabinet has a beard and a potbelly, but if I saw a photo of Henry, I might be able to tell if it's the same person."

"I doubt you'll find one. I've tried and never been able to find a photo. It was a while ago—before online news and social media were so common."

Ann tapped and scrolled for a few minutes, then sat back with an irritated exhalation. "Nothing. Damn."

"You said this place was called the Cabinet of Curiosities?" asked Harkin.

"Yes."

"I think I know where there might be a photo of Henry ..." Harkin said slowly.

"Where?"

Harkin stood. "Come with me."

45

"Scott!" Mike called as he emerged from his second-floor home office.

"What's up?" Scott called back.

Mike hurried down the stairs and into the kitchen, where Scott was stirring a pot of spaghetti sauce. "We have reservations for the Cabinet!"

"Really?" Scott put down the spoon. "How did you manage that?"

"Del just called me. He went to Larch Street and says he found out what's going on there but won't say anything else."

"Did you tell him about Annie and Joe going?"

"No. He was in such a good mood, I didn't want to rain on his parade."

Scott raised an eyebrow. "How thoughtful of you."

"Not realizing that we had sent in our own reconnaissance team, he said I should check it out for myself."

"He just invited you?"

"Yeah, but I'm not going without you."

"Mike—"

"Oh, come on, remember how excited you were when Ann described it?"

"Well, that's true ..."

"Perfect. Del got us a reservation at eight o'clock. We need to leave right now, especially because it looks like the rain is moving in again."

Scott turned the burner off. "I think a trip to the Cabinet is worth sacrificing a pot of sauce for. What are you wearing?"

Mike looked down at his outfit: a collared knit shirt, jeans, and docksiders. "I was planning to wear this."

"Oh, come on. Remember, Joe was wearing a sport coat and told Annie to dress up—we should, too. Let's make an event of it."

Fifteen minutes later, they were in Audrey the Audi, headed for West Philly. Although a heavy gray overcast blanketed the area, the rain held off and they made good time. When they reached the Larch Street alley, Mike maneuvered Audrey into a space next to the Transit Connect. The third spot was vacant.

As they made their way to the front door, Mike could hear traffic from the cross street and kids shouting good-naturedly in what sounded like a pickup basketball game. But Larch Street itself was as quiet and dark as when he and Scott had followed Rowan there three nights ago.

"Remember that Joe and Annie said they only use first names," said Scott.

"Right. Good memory."

They arrived at number 46 at the top of the hour. They climbed the steps to the porch and Mike knocked. A moment later, the familiar illumination appeared in the door's panes and the door opened to reveal the Victorian-clad man carrying the oil lamp.

"You must be Mike," said the Professor. He turned to Scott. "And this is ...?"

"Scott," he said, extending his hand.

"Good evening. I'm the Professor. Please come in."

They stepped into a vestibule that was just as Ann had described it.

"Welcome to the Cabinet, gentlemen."

The Professor reached up to lock the deadbolt and slide the security chain into place, then led them through dusty, deserted rooms to a small room off the back hallway. He directed them to the bench along the back wall, lowered the bar top into place, started up a murmur of Victorian-era music, then brought up the lights. Even though Ann and Joe had described the setting, a grin split Mike's face as he took in the naturalist artifacts, the colorful bottles of liquor, the sparkling glassware.

"Just lovely," said Scott.

"Very cool," agreed Mike.

The Professor gestured to a cross-stitched sampler hanging from a shelf. "If I may ask for your indulgence?"

The Professor wishes to transport you back to a less complicated time and requests that you silence your telephone and refrain from photography.

"That's an excellent idea," Scott said as he and Mike got out their phones and turned them off. "I'll be happy to have a call-and text-free hour." He shot an arch look at Mike.

"I thought we'd start out with a classic gin and tonic," said the Professor, taking a lime from a basket and slicing off two wedges. "When Del called me to make your reservation, he told me that you, Mike, are the person he hired to follow Rowan."

Mike sighed. "Yeah. Although 'hired' is probably putting too professional a spin on it. More like a favor for a friend."

The Professor pulled from the shelf a bottle of gin, another labeled *Extra Bitter Quinine Tonic*, and a club soda dispenser. "It would have been alarming for Rowan if she had seen someone following her—especially in this part of Philadelphia."

"We made sure she didn't see us."

The Professor took two heavy crystal glasses from the shelf and ran the lime wedges around the rim. "But I thought you weren't professionals."

"We are not," said Scott, shooting Mike a look. "I certainly hope we never gave her cause for alarm."

"Of course," said Mike. "although she wouldn't have been in this part of Philadelphia—at least not alone—if she had told her husband what she was up to." He glanced appreciatively around the small room. "I imagine Del would have enjoyed this, too. In fact, I understand that he eventually came to the Cabinet himself."

"Oh, yes," said the Professor. "I believe he was quite relieved when he realized what was happening," he waggled his eyebrows theatrically, "behind the closed doors of 46 Larch Street."

He finished preparing the drinks, put brightly colored cloth cocktail napkins in front of Mike and Scott, and placed a glass on each. "A gin and tonic might seem an odd choice for an establishment that prides itself on the uniqueness of its cocktails, but I have prepared these in the style that Englishmen living in the tropics at the turn of the last century might have used—extra bitter to mask the taste of the quinine they used to combat malaria. A special preparation for the last guests of the Cabinet."

46

"We need to go to the basement," said Harkin to Ann. "There's a flashlight under the sink—you'll probably want that."

"What's down there?"

"I'm hoping the photo of Henry Tollman that you said you want."

Ann retrieved the flashlight, and Harkin led her down a hallway to a nondescript door.

"In there," he said. "Light's on the left."

Ann opened the door and found herself at the top of a narrow wooden staircase. She flipped the light switch, which illuminated two unshaded bulbs—one at the top of the stairs and one at the bottom.

She stepped back. "I always feel more comfortable letting someone else take point."

He rolled his eyes and descended the stairs. Ann followed.

The basement contained a jumble of old furniture and disintegrating cardboard boxes stacked among ancient wooden posts that hardly seemed equal to supporting the weight of the house above. Spider webs festooned the corners, and Ann thought she heard the scrabble of tiny rodent feet from one corner.

"Spooky, huh?" said Harkin over his shoulder as he made his way toward the back of the space. "I was always trying to talk Dad into letting me set up a haunted house down here for Halloween."

"And now here you are—" Ann had second thoughts about the appropriateness of the comment and morphed the rest of the sentence into an unconvincing cough.

Harkin laughed. "And I'm equipped to provide the world's most convincing haunted house experience." His good humor seemed a bit more forced as he continued. "Maybe Rowan and Del's little girl can bring her friends here a decade from now and Uncle Harkin can rattle some chains and make moaning noises." He was barely visible in the far corner of the basement. "Do you want to see this or not?"

Ann switched on the flashlight and followed the path Harkin had taken.

"There," he said when she reached him, pointing to the corner.

The flashlight beam illuminated a huge, glass-fronted cabinet.

"Henry built it for Nola," said Harkin. "Her very own cabinet of curiosities. I remember him telling me they were very popular in Germany in the sixteenth century—they were called *wunderkammern*—but they were still a thing with amateur naturalists in Victorian times."

Most of the cabinet's shelves were empty, but one contained a twisted branch on which perched a few preserved butterflies.

"After the shit with Henry went down," continued Harkin, "I guess Nola didn't want something around that would remind her of him every time she walked past it. Also, not really her style." He indicated a drawer under the glass cabinet. "The photos are in there."

Ann propped the flashlight on a nearby box and opened the drawer to find a shoebox of yellow Kodak envelopes. She picked up one near the front and pulled out a stack of photos. They showed children in party hats posing around a birthday cake, their clothing suggesting the photo must have been taken fifty years earlier. The background was a bright, colorful home that couldn't have been less like the Lynch house.

"Too early," said Harkin. He pointed to the middle of the box. "Try one of those."

The next envelope showed a pretty and surprisingly cheerful twenty-something Nola, her expression making her look even more like her niece than she had in the more somber photos Ann had seen in the Cellar and the Ark. In one, she raised a glass of champagne to the camera. In another, she twirled, arms outstretched, the skirt of her emerald green dress belling out around her. In a third, her laughing face appeared in a photo cutout board of a mermaid on some sunny boardwalk.

"Still too early," muttered Harkin, looking over Ann's shoulder. "Go further back."

A few minutes later, they found the photo that Harkin had been looking for. Nola and a tall, thin, clean-shaven man stood with their arms around each other's waists, the Tarn forming a picturesque backdrop.

"That's him," said Harkin. "Henry Tollman. As I recall, that's where the wedding was going to be held. Is that who you're looking for?"

Ann turned the photo toward the light. "It's hard to tell. The man I met at the Cabinet introduced himself as John, although obviously that doesn't mean anything, but he had a potbelly, and with the beard ..." She turned to Harkin. "You said that Henry was attacked when he was in prison?"

"That's right."

"Do you know if his face was injured?"

He drew his eyebrows together. "I don't know, but it's certainly possible."

"If he had scars on his face from the attack, he might have grown a beard and mustache to hide them. Maybe that's what I was seeing—not acne at all." She looked from the photo to the twisted stick and dead butterflies that were all that was left of the contents of the cabinet that Henry Tollman had built for Nola Lynch. "Plus, what are the chances that this connection with a cabinet of curiosities is a coincidence? There was a branch with butterflies on it in the house on Larch Street as well."

"So Henry Tollman comes back to Pennsylvania, sets up a speakeasy, and invites Rowan but no one else in the family?"

"We don't know he hasn't invited anyone else." She considered. "Did Henry and Nola part on good terms?"

"I never heard one way or the other."

"Any promise from Nola to wait for him to get out of jail?"

"Not as far as I know."

"Obviously Henry and Niall didn't part on good terms."

"No." He raised his eyebrows. "Do you think Henry killed Dad?"

She tapped the photo against her hand as she gazed up the aisle formed by the detritus of the Lynch family lives. "If Niall cut Henry off after he killed the purse snatcher, it sounds like Henry had a motive—at least in his eyes." After a pause, she continued. "I can understand why Henry might want to kill Niall, but why would he want to kill you? You said you were buddies, right?"

"Well, 'buddies' might be stretching it, but we were friendly. And I was only eight—I can't imagine he would blame me for him becoming persona non grata at Lynch."

"Could he have been angry about your plan to sell the winery?"

"I can't think how he would have known. When he called, he knew I had inherited and he asked what my plans were, but I didn't tell him. Who else would have told him? As far as I know, nobody knows except Nola, Del, and—"

"—Rowan," they said at the same time.

Harkin's expression tightened for a moment, then his features relaxed and he shook his head. "I don't know. Rowan is visiting the disgraced former Lynch winemaker at a Philadelphia speakeasy and passing on details of the family business?"

"It does seem hard to explain." Ann shook her head. "I need someone else's brain on this." She got out her phone. She saw that Corey had left a voicemail message while she was talking with Harkin. She glanced at the automated transcript. He had arrived in Pittsburgh and was helping Marsha pick out the dress she would wear the next day for the justice-of-the-peace wedding. Ann smiled—it sounded as if Corey was serving not only as best man but as the maid of honor as well.

She replied with a text—*Making my rounds at Lynch, will call later*—then opened her contacts and punched a number. After a moment, voicemail picked up.

"This is Joe's voicemail," intoned the recording. "Leave a message and I'll get back to you as soon as possible."

After the beep, she said, "Hey, Joe, it's Ann. Can you call me when you get this?" She ended the call and turned to Harkin. "If the man at the Cabinet is Henry Tollman, and if he's the person who killed you, and might have killed your father, there's a chance Rowan doesn't know who he is. But I've been giving her updates about my search for you and she's been at home with Del all day. Sounds like the baby is about to make an appearance, or is just making her life difficult at the moment." She tapped out a text to Rowan.

Still no luck. How are things going there?

Still the same here too. Can't wait for the baby to get here!

Resting up at home with Del?

Yup. Trapped in the house—probably too big to fit through the front door anymore.

Ann sent back an *LOL*, then held up the phone so that Harkin could read the messages. "I don't think either one of them is going to be going to Larch Street anytime soon." She tapped her phone against her hand. "I'd like to get some confirmation of whether the Professor is Henry Tollman. If I can get to Larch Street near the top of the hour, when the Professor opens the door for another set of guests, I'll try to take a photo of him. Then I'll bring it back here and you can see if you think it's him. If I do it tonight, I won't have to worry about Del or Rowan showing up unexpectedly. I could even give the photo to my brother and he could turn it over to Del as part of his secret PI assignment. No need for Del to know that it wasn't Mike who took the picture." She brightened. "In fact, there's no reason for Mike not to be the photographer."

She hit Mike's number. It rang to voicemail. Same with Scott's number.

"Damn. Where is everybody?" She looked up at Harkin. "I'm guessing you can't come with me?"

"I don't think so." He paused, then continued, his words halting. "When I 'came to' after I died, I was in the kitchen, and somehow it doesn't feel good to think about going too far from here. Certainly not off the property. Does that make sense?"

"Yes. Best not to risk moving beyond where you feel comfortable."

"'Comfortable' might be putting too positive a spin on it—

more like something bad would happen if I tried to leave." He gave a harsh laugh. "A whole goddamned life trying to get away, and now it looks like I'm here for eternity."

47

D el returned to the bedroom with mozzarella sticks and raspberry iced tea for Rowan. She was propped up on pillows, tapping her phone.

"Ann's still looking for Harkin," she said. "And I let Nola know you lined up a reservation at the Cabinet for Mike."

"Okay. I'm going to get a beer and chips for myself."

Rowan made a face. "Beer. Blech."

He returned a minute later with his snack as well as a kitchen chair. He maneuvered it into the bedroom and put it down next to the bed.

Rowan was still looking at her phone, her expression concerned.

"News from Ann?" he asked, settling himself on the chair.

"No. It sounds like Nola doesn't want Mike to go to Larch Street. She says that because they're closing it down, she's not even sure that the Cabinet is still set up for customers."

"When I talked to John, he didn't mention that as a problem."

Rowan tapped back a response to Nola, and a minute later, her phone pinged again.

"She says one of the reasons they're closing down is that the neighbors started to complain."

"John didn't mention that either," grumbled Del. "If it's okay with him to host Mike for a couple of cocktails, I don't see why Nola should care."

"I don't know, but can you call Mike and ask him not to go?"

Del looked at his watch. "He's probably already there."

"Just give it a try."

Del called Mike, but the call went to voicemail. "No answer."

Rowan chewed her thumbnail. "There is that sign in the Cabinet about turning your phone off." Her phone pinged and she read the message. "Nola says she's going down there. I wonder if she wants some company."

"I hope you're not planning on driving—or even being driven—to Larch Street tonight."

Rowan smiled. "No." She looked up from her phone. "But would you mind going down there?"

"I want to stay here with you."

"Yeah," Rowan laughed, "it's so riveting, sitting here watching me eat mozzarella sticks." Her expression became serious again as she read the next text. "She says she doesn't need help."

"There you go."

"Del, you know her. She's not likely to admit she needs help. Would you go down there? Just make sure everything's okay?" She smiled winningly. "And you can pick up some more ice cream on your way home."

"I can get you ice cream without having to drive all the way into Philly. Plus, you might need something—something more important than ice cream. You might need to go to the hospital."

"Del, I've been feeling exactly the same for twenty-four hours. I promise that if anything changes, I'll call you and you can come back."

Del groaned. "Oh, all right. But call me *right away* if anything changes."

"I will. Thanks, sweetheart." As he headed for the stairs, she called after him, "Don't forget sprinkles! I used up the last batch."

48

W hen Ann reached Larch Street, the clock on the
dashboard of the Forester showed 8:45—fifteen
minutes until she could expect John to open the
door for the next set of guests. She pulled into a parking space
across the street from number 46. The house was dark, but she
knew that didn't mean it was uninhabited.

She'd get another look at John and try to take a picture she
could show Harkin. If it seemed likely that Professor John was
Henry Tollman, she'd convince Mike that he needed to provide
a full update to Del about the goings-on at Larch Street, despite
whatever embarrassment it caused him.

She tried calling Mike and Scott again, but both calls went to
voicemail. Ditto Joe. She noticed another voicemail from Corey
and briefly considered calling him back, but she didn't want him
to worry if she told him she was in West Philly by herself after
dark.

She decided to check the alley to see if the normal comple-
ment of cars was there. She climbed out of the Forester. The rain
had been building in intensity during the drive, and she zipped
her raincoat and pulled the collar more closely around her neck.

On the dark street, and with the patter of raindrops a possible mask to any sound of approaching footsteps, the idea of having her peripheral vision blocked by the raincoat's hood was unappealing. She kept it back, periodically wiping droplets from her eyes. Fingers of water found their way into the neck of the coat and crept down her back.

When she reached the alley, she saw two vehicles in the parking area.

One she expected: the Transit Connect.

The other she didn't: Audrey the Audi.

Her mind awhirl, Ann stepped from the weak sodium vapor light of the street into the murky darkness of the alley. She squatted behind a trash bin that shielded her from view from the house, then got out her phone and called Mike's number. Voicemail. Scott's number. Voicemail. Joe's number. Voicemail.

"Shit," she hissed under her breath as she listened to Joe's outgoing message. When the beep sounded, she whispered, "Joe, it's Ann. I think something weird is going on at Larch Street. It's too complicated to explain on voicemail, but I think that the Professor is actually the former Lynch winemaker—who was apparently not a nice guy—and that Mike and Scott are inside." She paused, illogically wishing that he would hear the message and pick up. "Anyhow, call me when you get this message."

She ended the call and switched her phone to silent mode. She cautiously straightened from behind the trash bin and stretched up on her toes, trying to see over the stockade fence. Unlike the darkened front of the building, a dim light shone in the kitchen.

From the cross street, she heard voices approaching, a group of teenage boys by the sound of it, interspersed by the pinging thumps of a basketball.

"I'm just telling you what I saw!"

"You have an overactive imagination, man."

"Okay, you tell me what it means."

"It doesn't necessarily mean he's stealing from you."

"Doesn't mean he's not."

"Just saying—if you're looking for proof that he's stealing from you, then you're going to find proof, whether it's there or not."

The voices were so close that she expected the group to pass by the mouth of the alley at any moment. However, the trajectory of the voices changed, then the slam of a door cut off the rest of the argument.

Ann straightened from behind the trash bin and tried again to look over the fence. The dim light in the kitchen still glowed, the house was quiet.

She was suddenly uncomfortable about having called out the cavalry. She wasn't sure what was going on inside, or even if the Professor was Henry Tollman. Was she looking for proof of something that was a product of an overactive imagination, triggered by two possibly unrelated deaths? Mike had been trying to score a reservation at the Cabinet so that he could describe it to Del from his own experience rather than from Ann and Joe's description. She had thought it was unusual when her calls to Mike and Scott went to voicemail, but then she remembered the cross-stitched sampler over the tiny bar. If they were in the beautifully decorated butler's pantry, enjoying a Pousse Café or a Mamie Taylor, then they would no doubt have complied with the request to turn off their phones.

She checked the time on her phone: 8:55. If the Professor stuck to the usual schedule, Mike and Scott would emerge from the Cabinet in just a few minutes. On the other hand, since there wasn't a third vehicle in the parking area, they might be the last clients of the evening. Would the Professor extend their visit if there were no other guests waiting?

She'd give it five more minutes and, if no one had emerged, she'd knock on the front door, claiming that she had understood she was to meet her brother for a return visit to the Cabinet. If she got a bad feeling about the situation, she wouldn't go inside, but she could call to Mike from the front porch.

She was so engrossed in watching the minutes tick down on her phone that she yelped when a beam of light engulfed her.

"Police!" called a male voice from the mouth of the alley, sounding as Philadelphia-born as a Mummers string band. "Who's back there?"

She raised her arm to shield her eyes. "My name's Ann Kinnear."

"What are you doing back there?" He approached her slowly, no doubt on the lookout for an ambush.

"I'm ... looking for someone." She straightened and started to slip her phone into her jacket pocket.

"Hands up!" barked the cop.

She popped her hands in the air as he advanced on her. "I think something weird might be going on that house and I can't get in touch with my friend, Detective Joe Booth." A little name-dropping seemed in order.

"And what do you want with Detective Booth?"

"I want his advice. Give him a call. He'll vouch for me." She attempted a laugh. "I'm not usually a lurker."

He was only a few steps away when the flashlight beam shifted away from her face and she could see him more clearly. He was wearing not a police uniform but a frock coat, vest, and ascot. And although his face no longer wore the jovial expression she remembered, he was clearly John, her host at the Cabinet.

He saw the recognition in her eyes and crossed the few feet separating them in a heartbeat, the beam of light sweeping across the alley as he drew back the arm holding the flashlight.

Ann had barely opened her mouth to scream, had barely raised her arm to ward off the blow, when the flashlight connected simultaneously with her arm and the side of her head, her phone went flying across the alley, and she dropped to the ground.

Her vision flashed white then black, and a dagger of pain drilled into her brain. John grabbed her around the waist and hauled her to her feet. Just as she was sucking in air for another attempt at a scream, he slapped something over her mouth, sealing it closed, and began dragging her toward the stockade fence gate.

She reached up to tear the seal from her mouth, but her fingers had lost their coordination. John shifted his hold, pinning her arms to her sides, then fumbled at the top of the gate with his free hand. He pushed it open, pulled her through, and kicked it closed behind them.

As he dragged her across the small lawn, she tried to get her feet under her, but she could find no purchase on the rain-slicked ground. Then she realized that easing their progress toward the back door was the last thing she should do. She let her body go limp and sagged against his arm.

He lost his grip on her and she dropped to the ground. She tried to crawl away, at the same time groping at the gag over her mouth, but he pushed her down, mud smearing across her face and into her nose. He grabbed her arms and pulled them together behind her back. Something slipped over her hands, sharp metal tightened around her wrists. Handcuffs. Her panic spiked as the fog from the blow to her head cleared.

He bent and, with one arm under her shoulders and the other under her knees, lifted her with a grunt. She thrashed and he lost his hold on her. She thumped onto the ground, the tape over her mouth muffling her shout of pain.

He grabbed her around the waist again, hauled her up the few rickety stairs to the back door, and jerked the door open.

Ann tried to hook her leg around the edge of the door—anything to prolong for even a few seconds her time outside the house. Someone might walk down the alley, someone might look over the stockade fence and see this oddly dressed man trying to drag a gagged and trussed woman into the derelict house.

But he kicked her leg free, pulled her inside, and slammed the door behind them.

As he dragged her across the kitchen, she screamed behind the tape, not in pain, but at the sight of two black body bags laid out next to each other on the floor, their contours showing the shapes of human forms.

49

D el pulled into a spot across the street from 46 Larch Street. He had bypassed the parking lot in back because he recalled the stockade fence gate that provided no apparent means of entry from the alley. If Nola wanted to avoid attracting attention, then he could hardly stand in the alley and yell for John's attention.

He realized with surprise that the vehicle parked in front of him was a Subaru Forester that he thought he had seen in the tenant parking space behind the Curragh. Had Ann accompanied Mike on his visit to the Cabinet?

He heaved a sigh. Nola was closing the Cabinet to avoid the ire of the neighbors, and here he was bringing even more people to Larch Street.

He checked the time: almost nine o'clock. If Mike, and possibly Ann, had stuck to the schedule Del had arranged with the Professor, they would be almost at the end of their hour-long visit. He tapped out a text to Rowan.

I'm at Larch Street. Can you send me the Prof's number?

He got a response a moment later.

Just tried calling him. No answer.

Del supposed that since the Professor asked his guests to turn off their cell phones during their visit to the Cabinet, it made sense that he would turn his off as well.

He texted back a thumbs up, climbed out of the Escape, and crossed the street to number 46. He stepped through the creaking gate and climbed the stairs to the door he had first watched his wife enter over a week before. He thought he heard some thumps, like furniture being moved, from inside. Maybe John really was dismantling the Cabinet. He knocked lightly, expecting to see the light from the Professor's oil lamp illuminate the door's glass panes, but they remained dark.

The sounds suggested the Professor wasn't in the butler's pantry with Mike and Ann, but Del was hesitant to knock louder for fear of attracting unwanted attention from the neighbors.

He'd give it a few minutes and try again. But if avoiding the attention of the neighbors was important, he doubted Nola would want him hanging out on the porch.

He descended the steps and returned to the Escape.

50

J ohn dragged Ann into the hall leading off the kitchen, showing none of the unsteadiness of gait that had set his oil lamp swinging when he had escorted Ann and Joe to the Cabinet. She kicked at his legs, but he must have been wearing heavy boots, because she felt sure that the kicks hurt her sneaker-clad feet more than they did his shins.

He hauled her into the butler's pantry and tossed her onto the bench in back. He grabbed her neck, his fingers digging painfully into tendon and muscle, and held her in place as he pulled another pair of handcuffs—Victorian, by the look of them—from a pocket. He reached behind her, she heard two metallic clicks, then he stepped back.

Ann tried to move her arms, but the cuffs were secured to something. She flashed back to the pipe running along the wall behind the bench where she and Joe had sat.

John leaned against the door frame, glaring at her as he caught his breath. She noticed that the vest that had stretched over a pot belly the last time she had seen him now hung loose around his waist.

"I see Detective Joe's date decided to make a repeat visit to the Cabinet, although I'm suspecting that Kay is actually Ann Kinnear." His gaze slid toward the kitchen, then back to her. "I must say the Kinnears are a most aggravating family."

He stepped back and slid the door shut, cutting off the dim light from the kitchen. His steps retreated toward the back of the house. A moment later, she heard movement in the kitchen, an oath, then a scraping sound like something large being pulled across the floor. She felt a tiny movement of air that suggested John had opened the back door. There was more grunting and swearing, then the back door clicked closed.

She fell back against the bench, struggling to breathe through nostrils clogged with snot and tears. She tried to yell, but the tape was stuck tight over her mouth. She leaned to one side, thinking that she might be able to scrape the tape off on the corner of one the shelves, but the cuffs brought her up short. She kicked the door of one of the cupboards but realized that no one would hear those dull thumps coming from the center of the solid old building. It was more likely that the noise would serve only to further irritate her captor, assuming he came back. And she was quite sure he was coming back.

She tried to summon an image of the room that had seemed so welcoming when she had shared cocktails with Joe and enjoyed the stories told by the soft-spoken Professor: heavy crystal decanters she could swing like a club, bottles whose broken edges would provide a weapon. She'd gladly bite the head off the voodoo doll if she could replace the hair on its head with tufts of John's. But all these were useless as long as her wrists were cuffed and her mouth gagged. She thought with a stab of regret of her phone, lying in the rain somewhere in the alley.

As her eyes adjusted to the dark, she became aware of a glow emanating from the bottom shelf—an area that the bar top would have hidden during her earlier visit. The glow suggested an electronic display. Did John monitor the arrival of guests with a security camera?

With the handcuffs digging painfully into her wrists, she stretched her foot toward the glow. Her shoe tapped the source of the glow, pushing it a half inch further away. She groaned in frustration behind the tape. She levered one of her sneakers off and, with her bare toes, snagged a cord extending from the back of the device. Slowly, slowly, she worked it around until she could see its display.

As she had hoped, it was a security camera monitor, the images on a split screen rendered in the somber blacks and grays of infrared.

One image showed the parking area, the back doors of the Transit open. The other showed the front porch and a stretch of Larch Street. Just across from 46 she could see a familiar-looking Escape—and it looked like someone was sitting in the driver's seat. Was it Del?

As she strained to make out the driver's identity on the grainy display, she saw movement in the parking area.

John appeared on the screen, a body bag slung over his shoulder. He heaved it into the back of the Transit.

Ann screamed in rage and anguish.

She flung herself forward. The cuffs dug into her wrists and wrenched her arms backward.

But she had felt a slight tremor in the pipe to which she was attached.

She threw herself against the handcuffs, and didn't even bother crying out. She threw herself forward again. She could feel the pipe loosening. With each excruciating lunge, the pipe gave a little more, the stressed metal creaked a little louder.

Squinting against the pain she knew was coming, she threw herself forward with her full weight and felt her left shoulder pop out of its socket. She went sprawling on the floor as a geyser of water erupted from the broken pipe.

She struggled to her feet, then turned her back to the door and scrabbled at the handle with her right hand, her left twitching uselessly behind her. After a few frantic seconds, she found the handle and slid the door open inch by inch. When she could squeeze through, she stepped into the hallway, the tears of pain that stung her eyes further dimming the already dim light from the kitchen.

She turned left, toward the front of the house, and just barely recovered her balance when her foot slipped on the already wet floorboards. She shuffled carefully down the hall. The faint illumination from the kitchen lit her way to the empty dining room, but didn't reach the reception room beyond. At least she didn't have to worry about walking into any furniture in the dark.

Trying to ignore the spasming of her shoulder muscles, she made her way to the vestibule. She backed up to the door and turned the handle, but the door wouldn't open. She felt behind her for a lock mechanism. Nothing. Then she remembered the deadbolt and chain mounted high on the door. She had thought it was to keep young children from making their way onto the street. It trapped her as well. The lock and chain were too high for her to reach with her manacled hands, or even with her teeth if her mouth hadn't been taped shut.

She faced the door, checking her balance and readying herself to give it a kick in the hope that Del would hear her. Then she hesitated, trying to pull her thoughts away from the clamor of pain in her shoulder. Had the windows of the Escape been open? John might come back inside at any moment, and if he heard her kicking the door, he could certainly get to her faster than Del could. There was no point making a racket if Del would sit through it, oblivious, in the Escape. Her stomach flipped at her next realization: in that rain, no one would sit in their vehicle with their windows down.

And who else might be out there to hear her? She thought of the street that had been pedestrian-free when she and Joe had arrived at the Cabinet. She thought of the houses on either side that looked as uninhabited as number 46 did.

Surprise might be the only weapon she had against her captor, and she wasn't about to give it up for what seemed like a slim chance of rescue.

She left the vestibule and made her way back through the rooms, shuffling crablike, right side leading to protect her left shoulder. She got to the hallway without mishap.

But she had forgotten about the water from the broken pipe, and this time she couldn't recover her balance when she slipped. She landed on her left side, and now she was grateful for the tape over her mouth, which silenced her scream. As she struggled to get to her knees, she realized that the impact had popped her arm back into the socket, although it was hard to think of the pounding throb as an improvement.

The water had reached the kitchen, spreading out across its linoleum tiles. One of the black plastic bags was in her line of sight, and as she watched, the water reached it and began to pool around its edges.

Still on her knees, she shuffled down the hall until she was kneeling next to the bag. Who was it—Mike or Scott?

She thought she was sobbing, but it was hard to tell. She leaned over the black bag, as if to protect its occupant from further indignities. Then she caught her breath.

The bag moved.

Scarcely allowing herself to believe it, she leaned closer.

There it was again—a slight movement of the plastic. The person in the bag was breathing, the plastic moving as he inhaled and exhaled.

And if the person in the kitchen was still alive, it was possible the one in the van was as well.

51

D el checked the time: nine-fifteen. There had been no sign of life from 46 Larch: no visitors coming or going, no light in the doors glass panes. If John was really dismantling the Cabinet, maybe he was serving Mike and Ann their cocktails in the kitchen, as he had with Del.

He climbed out of the Escape, locked the doors, and headed for the alley.

In the dim light that reached into the alley from the street, Del saw movement behind number 46. There were two vehicles in the parking area: an older model Audi and the ever-present Transit Connect. A man stood at the open back doors of the Transit, and although Del couldn't see his face, he wore the same Victorian garb John Derkammern had worn as the host of the Cabinet. The man stepped back from the Transit, then bent over to catch his breath, hands resting on his knees.

"Everything okay?" called Del.

The man jerked upright, snatched something out of the van, and spun toward Del.

It was definitely John, although without the paunch that Del recalled straining the buttons of his vest, and holding not the oil lamp but a tactical flashlight.

John's expression of alarm morphed into irritation when he recognized his visitor.

"Del. You startled me." His tone was reproving.

"Sorry about that." He gestured toward the flashlight as he approached. "Fast reflexes."

John swung the back doors of the Transit shut, then turned back to Del. "You never know who might be wandering through the alleys after dark around here."

Del reached the vehicle. "Doing some hauling?"

"Yes. As Nola may have told you, we've decided to close the Cabinet. Just packing up the furnishings."

"Any more to bring out? I'd be happy to give you a hand."

"Just one more thing, and I can take care of it myself. In fact, I'm thinking that I might just leave it until tomorrow. I have some other things I need to take care of." He stepped away from the Transit and under a branch that extended from the backyard over the stockade fence, although the ragged leaves provided little protection from the rain.

Del stepped under the branch as well. "Was Mike Kinnear already here?"

"No, he never showed up."

"I'm sorry to hear that—I hate no-shows. But good news in a way. Nola asked me to come by and see if I could head him off at the pass. I understand you're getting some heat from the neighbors."

"Nothing we can't handle. Well," John continued, his tone brisk, "now that you've discharged your errand for Nola—"

"Actually, I wanted to talk to you anyway."

"Oh?"

"I wanted to let you know I came clean with Rowan."

"Did you? I'm glad to hear it. Honesty is always the best policy."

"That's for sure." Del nodded toward the Audi parked next to the Transit. "Nice car. I like those older models, and someone has taken good care of that one." He gave John a sympathetic smile. "At least you won't have to worry about strangers using your parking spaces anymore."

"Very true. Speaking of which ... where did you leave your car? Is it nearby? It's not safe to be walking these neighborhoods after dark."

"I'll be fine." Del glanced toward the stockade fence. "You've got things pretty buttoned up back here. That would be a hard fence to climb, and no latch on the gate."

"Oh, there's a latch—you just need to know how to find it." John pulled a pocket watch from his vest. "Well, I really must be on my way. Please give my best to Rowan."

"I will. What's next for you?"

"I'll move on. This was never intended to be a long-term arrangement. Maybe I'll head back to the West Coast. I've never been to Hawaii. Maybe some international travel."

Del looked down and shuffled his feet. "I'm glad I got to see you before you moved out. And sorry again about Mike skipping out on his reservation. Best of luck to you wherever your travels take you, John." Del turned toward the mouth of the alley but tripped as he took a step. He looked down to where the laces of one of his shoes trailed into a muddy puddle. "Oh, man," he muttered. "Figures."

"Better to take the time to tie it—you wouldn't want to take a tumble in the dark," said John.

As Del bent to retie his shoe, he heard John's footsteps move toward the gate, the metallic click of the latch opening, then the squeal as the gate opened and then started its closing swing.

Del jumped to his feet and caught the gate just as it was about to click shut.

John was climbing the stairs to the back porch.

"John!" Del called.

John flinched at the sound of his name and turned back to Del. "What is it now?" His demeanor was a bit less cordial than it had been during the conversation in the alley, and far less cordial than when he and Del had shared cocktails in the kitchen outside the Cabinet the previous evening.

"I was wondering if you ..." Del cast about for an excuse to continue the conversation. "... had a piece of paper I could borrow. And a pencil." He crossed the yard, his voice becoming more confident as his story gelled. "I love those old Audis, and I just realized that with the baby coming, we'll probably have to replace Rowan's Miata." Del reached the bottom of the porch stairs and stood looking up at John, who was now openly glaring at him. "I'd love to leave a note under the wiper, see if the owner might be willing to sell." He climbed the stairs.

"I doubt if a note would survive in the rain." The last vestiges of good humor were gone from John's face.

Del gave a self-deprecating laugh and dropped his eyes to the porch. John's eyes followed Del's, and when they snapped up, Del knew that he had also seen the evidence that all was not well inside: the stream of water leaking from under the back door and spreading across the rotting boards of the porch.

John drew back the flashlight to swing, his face contorted by a grimace Del would never have imagined on the face of the jolly old man Nola had hired to entertain guests at the Cabinet. Del barely had time to let out a yelp and draw his fist back when the back door of the house swung open and Ann Kinnear came spinning out and slammed into John Derkammern.

52

A nn's momentum carried her and John across the porch and into its decrepit wooden railing, which barely slowed their descent to the ground. He landed first, his body providing some cushion for her impact, but her shoulder screeched with pain nonetheless.

Del leapt off the porch after them, but John was already throwing Ann to one side, scrambling to his feet and drawing back the flashlight. Ann had a vague impression of John swinging and of Del juking to the side, almost but not quite avoiding the blow.

Ann rolled toward John's feet, hoping to knock them out from under him. She realized the error of her timing when Del's fist went whistling past its target as John went tumbling to the ground.

"Hey! Somebody help!" shouted Del as he tried to grab John's flashlight-wielding arm.

It was good that someone could yell, thought Ann. With the stockade fence blocking the view of the backyard from the alley and the rain drumming down on the scene, it would be all too possible for someone to walk by without realizing what was playing out in the backyard.

Ann kicked at John, but she could only connect with his arm and shoulder. John swung the flashlight and caught her in the stomach.

She rolled away from him across the muddy ground and tried to suck in air through her nose. Her body was screaming for oxygen, but she felt as if someone had slipped a plastic bag over her head.

Or as if someone had zipped her into a body bag. Whoever was in the kitchen—Mike or Scott—might be breathing now, but how long would it be before he used up whatever oxygen was in a bag that must be designed to be airtight?

She was vaguely aware of John scrambling to his feet, of the two men circling each other, of Del's shouts for help. She had no sense of the shouts being heeded: no calls from the other side of the fence, no approaching sirens. If John caught Del in the head with the flashlight, she would be its next target. It would take John only a minute to dump them both into the back of the Transit van, perhaps along with the body still in the kitchen. She didn't want to think what their next stop would be.

She kicked toward where John had been standing. Her foot connected with a leg, but it was not a leg encased in the heavy boots she had encountered before—she must be kicking Del. She realized that John had maneuvered to put her between him and Del a second before a heavy boot connected with her ribs.

Ann screamed ... and sensed a puff of air and sound make its way through. She gulped in a breath and drew in air through her mouth as well as her nose.

The corner of the tape covering her mouth was coming loose.

She rolled onto her stomach and dragged her face across the ground, mud clogging her nose, uneven tussocks of spiky grass and fragments of broken brick scraping her nose, cheeks, and chin.

But it scraped the tape as well.

She dragged her face along the ground again, and the tape tore off one side of her mouth. Once more, and it peeled away.

She rolled over just in time to see John swing the flashlight and catch Del in the side of the head. Del dropped to his hands and knees. John advanced on him, flashlight raised.

"Henry Tollman," she yelled. "You murdering bastard!"

He wheeled on her.

Behind him, Del rose to his feet, a brick in his hand, and brought it down on the back of Tollman's head.

Tollman staggered, reeled, and dropped. Ann barely managed to roll out of the way of his falling body.

Del was at her side instantly, the rain washing a trickle of blood from his hairline down the side of his face. "Oh my God, are you okay?"

"Get the flashlight away from him," she gasped. "Then get these cuffs off me and onto him. Check his pockets for the key."

Del patted the unmoving man's pockets until he found the small key. He grasped Ann's arm to maneuver her onto her side to reach the cuffs.

"My arm!" she yelped.

"Oh, God, I'm sorry." Del scrunched down next to her to reach the cuffs, then her hands were free. She cradled her left elbow in her right hand as Del helped her sit up.

She gestured toward Tollman. "Hurry, before he comes around."

Del bent over Tollman and attached the cuffs to his wrists.

"Check the van," she croaked. "There's someone in the back in a body bag. He might be alive."

She hauled herself to her feet. As she labored up the steps to the back porch, she heard an approaching siren, joined a moment later by a second, then a third. She pulled open the back door, staggered inside, then lowered herself to her knees next to the bag. With her good hand, she wrestled it open.

Mike lay inside, looking ... well, looking a whole hell of a lot better than she imagined she herself looked. His eyes were closed, his breathing steady if a bit shallow, his face, as best she could tell in the dim light, pale but not alarmingly so.

She shook his shoulder. "Mike?"

No response.

The sirens reached the alley, red and blue lights strobing across the kitchen walls. She heard the thunk of car doors and Del yelling, "There's a man in here—he's alive but unconscious."

She lowered herself to a seated position next to Mike, into the deepening puddle on the kitchen floor. "Hang in there, Sleeping Beauty—the cavalry has arrived."

53

Ann's eyes fluttered open, then squinted shut against the fluorescent lights over her bed at William Penn Hospital. The ER doctor had checked out her shoulder, confirmed that it had, in fact, popped back into the socket on its own, and provided her with a sling. He confirmed that her ribs were bruised but not broken, bandaged the lacerations the handcuffs had inflicted on her wrists, and cleaned up the scrapes she had inflicted on her face. Although she had gotten some pretty potent painkillers, she felt so banged up that she hadn't put up an argument when he suggested she be admitted overnight.

And who, she thought groggily, would have taken care of her if she had insisted on being driven home? Mike and Scott must be sleeping off the effects of whatever sedative the Professor had given them. Corey was in Pittsburgh, getting ready for his mother's wedding. And Joe ...

She opened her eyes at a light knock. Joe was standing in the doorway, Del peering anxiously over his shoulder. She raised her good hand to wave them into the room.

"You do seem to be a lightning rod for trouble," Joe said with a sympathetic smile.

"Completely unintentional."

"How are you feeling?"

"Like a lightning rod." She turned to Del, who had come to the other side of the bed. "Actually, I'm fine, thanks to your timely arrival. How about *you*? It looked to me like you took a flashlight to the head." She noticed a row of stitches near Del's temple.

"Just a scratch."

"No concussion?"

"Nope ... although I think he thought he hit me harder than he actually did."

"But you were on the ground. I thought you were out."

Del smiled. "I hoped he would think that as well. When I got to the alley, I recognized Mike's Audi—he had that car back when he was my financial planner—but John claimed he never showed up for his reservation. I wanted to get in the back gate to see if I could get an idea of what was going on in the house, but I couldn't see a latch on the outside. I stepped on my shoelace so it would come untied. That gave me an excuse to still be nearby when John went back through the gate, and then I caught it before it closed. When I got to the porch, I saw water leaking out from under the door—so something was wrong. And then you popped out," he concluded cheerfully.

She gave a surprised laugh. "And you faked being knocked silly so that the Professor would turn his back on you."

Del smiled ruefully. "I figured that since I have a reputation for being a little clueless, I might as well use it."

Ann turned to Joe. "How are Mike and Scott?"

"They're fine. They were coming out of it by the time they got to the hospital."

"What did he give them to knock them out?"

"I don't know—the doctor wouldn't tell me—but it doesn't seem to have done them any harm. The ER doc didn't even admit them—he kept an eye on them for a couple of hours, then let them go. They got a room at a hotel nearby so they could rest up a bit but still be close by when you came around. Want me to give them a call? Ask them to come by?"

"No, they could probably use some rest. Some non-drug-induced rest," she amended. She pulled herself up in the bed and winced at a twinge from her ribs. "Not that I care very much, but how is the Professor doing?"

"He *does* have a concussion," said Joe, "although he's conscious now. He's in custody, and the police are questioning him."

"And by 'him,' am I right in assuming that he's actually Henry Tollman, the old Lynch winemaker?"

"It looks that way," said Joe. "Although he's giving his name as John Derkammern."

Ann turned to Del. "And how is Rowan doing?"

"Still at home, and getting increasingly crabby. Nola's with her. Rowan asked me to come and see how you're doing."

"Tell her I'm doing fine. And make sure she knows what you did at Larch Street. I don't want to think about what would have happened to me—not to mention Mike and Scott—if you hadn't shown up. Thank you."

"Hey, you wouldn't be in this mess if you hadn't gotten involved with our screwed-up family. Don't thank me. I owe you —seriously."

"You better get back to Unionville and see if your family is any closer to having a new member."

He smiled. "Yeah, I better." He gave Ann and Joe a farewell nod and hurried from the room.

"You don't have to stand," said Ann, waving vaguely to the guest chair.

Joe pulled the chair over and sat.

"John Derkammern ... that sounds familiar," said Ann, searching her trauma-addled brain for the connection. Then she smiled. "*Wunderkammern.* It's German for 'cabinet of curiosities.'"

"Clever." He leaned forward, elbows on thighs, hands clasped loosely between his knees. "I'm sorry I didn't get your voicemail sooner."

"Out with your squeeze?"

"Yeah. Late dinner."

"Where did you go?" She was getting sleepy, but the normalcy of the conversation was soothing.

"The Moshulu."

"Fancy."

"I barely knew which fork to use."

She gave a little snort of laughter. "You're not that much of a rube."

"Work from the outside in, right?"

"Exactly. See, you're a veritable Emily Post."

They were silent for a few moments, and she felt her eyelids drooping.

"Do you want to call Corey and let him know what happened?" Joe asked.

"No. I'll call him in the morning. Actually, what time is it?"

"Four a.m."

"That means it's the day of his mom's wedding. He's the best man. I don't think I'll interrupt the festivities with a call about what happened at Larch Street. I'll call him tomorrow." She yawned.

He stood. "I should let you get some rest."

"Can you ..."

"Yes?"

"Can you stay with me until I fall asleep?"

He smiled. "Sure." He sat back down.

As her lids drifted shut, she felt Joe's hand on hers where it rested on the blanket, and she closed her fingers around his.

54

Whe Ann woke again, a bright mid-day sun shone outside the hospital window. The pain in her shoulder, ribs, wrists, and face had moderated to a generalized ache. And the hand that had previously been held by Joe Booth was now held by Corey Duff.

"What are you doing here?" she asked groggily. She tried sitting up, but the pain in her shoulder flared. She winced and lay back. "How did you know I was here?"

Corey straightened a pillow she had knocked askew. "I was worried when you didn't return my calls, so I tried calling Mike and Scott. When I couldn't get in touch with them either, and with all the stuff that's been going on at Lynch and Son, I tried the main winery number. It went to voicemail, and about an hour later, Del called me and told me what had happened."

"How did you get here so fast?"

"Drove."

"From Pittsburgh?"

"Yeah."

"Corey, I'm sorry. I didn't want to mess up your mom's big day. I was going to call you after the wedding."

He managed a smile. "And tell me what? 'Someone tried to kill me, I'm in the hospital, but don't go to the trouble of coming here'?"

She blushed. "Well, yeah, something like that." She found the bed control and buzzed herself to a more upright position. "What's your prospective stepfather doing for a best man?"

This time his smile looked less forced. "They postponed the wedding."

"Did they postpone it because you had to come out here? You should have stayed in Pittsburgh!"

"They encouraged me to come. Honestly, I think they were getting cold feet, not least because they were banking their relationship on the word of an Atlantic City exorcist. And you know what?" He gave a rueful smile. "Mom said that the more she thought about it, the more it seemed best for the two of them to keep their own places and take things slow."

"Sounds like a good plan," Ann said carefully.

"Yeah, I think so." He squeezed her hand. "So you just have to concentrate on getting better."

"I'm fine, really. I'm just taking advantage of insurance-subsidized room and board as an excuse to lie around."

"Now we can relocate you to a more comfortable room and you can let me take care of the board."

"You don't have to do that."

He leaned forward. "I want to do it. And you don't have to worry about feeling beholden to me. I've come to terms with the fact that this isn't a super-serious thing for you. I think if it was, you would have called me and not Joe when you were in the West Philly alley."

"I called him because I thought there might be a crime going on and he's a cop."

"I know. But I'm not going to pretend I'm not a little jealous. I'd like to be the one you call when you need help—badge or no badge." He squeezed her hand. "I need to be getting back to L.A. pretty soon. I don't expect you to come with me, but I hope you'll come out to visit me. There are sights I want to show you and places I want to take you. But you do it if and when you feel like it."

She squeezed back. "I'd like to see those sights and go to those places." She released his hand and gingerly touched her face. "Once I'm a little more presentable."

"You look great to me."

There was a knock at the door, and Ann looked up to see Mike and Scott hovering in the doorway. Mike held a cardboard tray with four coffee cups, and Scott carried a white paper bag.

"Holy crap, look at you!" said Mike as he stepped into the room. "You're a mess!"

Ann laughed and Scott swatted Mike's arm as they moved to the side of the bed not occupied by Corey.

"At least pretend to have some bedside manners," said Scott.

The men exchanged greetings. It turned out that the three of them had already caught up while Ann was still asleep.

"I can't believe we finally got into the Cabinet only to get roofied," said Mike.

"We didn't get 'roofied,'" said Scott. "The Professor put mida-zolam in our drinks. The doctor told us it has a bitter taste, and he did serve us a very bitter-tasting drink, probably to cover the taste of the drug. I believe he described it as 'a special prepara-tion for the last guests of the Cabinet.'"

"Special preparation for sure," said Mike with a scowl. "It gave me a headache."

"We would have had a lot worse than a headache if it weren't for Annie and Del," said Scott. He opened the bag. "We got pastries. We didn't know if you'd be hungry or not."

"I'm starving," said Ann.

"Good. We got you a chocolate croissant and a latte."

Scott and Mike handed out pastries and coffees, then tracked down two more chairs.

"So what did I miss while I was asleep ... again?" she asked.

Mike answered around a mouthful of sticky bun. "Nola Lynch arrived at Larch Street right after the police got there. The police questioned her, but we don't know what came out of that."

"I wonder how deeply she was involved in ... whatever the Professor a.k.a. John Derkammern a.k.a. Henry Tollman was up to."

"Even Del started getting suspicious of her," said Mike. "He told me that when he went to where Nola had found Niall's body on the path, Nola said she hadn't called 911 because Niall had a do-not-resuscitate order. No one else knew about that, but the police did confirm with Niall's lawyer that what she said about the DNR was true."

"Have they talked to Rowan yet?" asked Ann.

"Not yet. Seems like bad form with her being in labor."

"For real?"

"That's the rumor."

They finished the coffee and pastries, then Mike said, "I imagine you can go home if you want to. Want me to track down a doctor to discharge you?"

"Absolutely. But where ..." Her voice trailed off.

"You can come back to the townhouse for a few days and let us take care of you," said Scott. Then, as if afraid he was overstepping his bounds, he looked toward Corey. "Unless ..."

"Let's all spend a couple of days spoiling Ann," said Corey, "and then I'll need to head home."

"And I wouldn't mind being spoiled at the townhouse," said Ann. "God only knows what's going on at the Lynch property."

55

Ann sat in a molded plastic chair pulled up to the desk of Detective Harry Deng. He had worked with Joe Booth on the Philadelphia Socialite murder, the case for which Joe had unofficially enlisted Ann's help. Now he was working on the case known in the station as the Cabinet of Dr. Derkammern.

"Turns out that after Henry Tollman got out of prison for killing the purse snatcher," said Deng, "he kept getting in trouble. Knocked a guy unconscious who was putting the moves on a woman in a bar and who wouldn't take no for an answer. Broke the nose of a guy who was hassling a girl in a convenience store. Did a couple more short stints in prison."

"He thought he was rescuing damsels in distress?"

"Looks that way. We found out from Nola Lynch that he grew up in an abusive household. Teenage Henry came home one day and found his dad beating up his mom—not for the first time— and gave him a pretty severe beating in return. Saved his mom that time, but of course that wasn't the end of it. A couple of years later, his dad shoved her out of a moving car. She died."

"And he's trying to make amends."

"Yup. He didn't mind talking about the incidents where he was the hero, but he didn't tell us about his mom, and he's not admitting to Niall or Harkin Lynch's deaths, although he's dancing around a confession in a most aggravating way. We're not getting much from forensics to tie him to the murders. Of course the scene of the dad's death was a mess by the time we started investigating it as a possible murder—ground churned up, rain washing evidence away—and if Tollman did kill the son, he was careful. No sign of forced entry. No identifiable footprints in or around the house. No fingerprints. No traces of midazolam, or any other drug, in anything in the fridge. We thought we could take advantage of his apparent preference of women over men by having a female detective interview him, but no luck. We thought he might talk with Rowan, but she won't see him."

"How about Nola?"

"She volunteered to try talking to him—she's been cooperating with us—but he's refusing to see her."

"How cooperative has Nola been?"

"She's admitted she was telling Tollman what was going on at the winery. Niall's health condition. The game with the two executed wills."

Ann's hand drifted to the sling supporting her arm. "She was in on this?"

"We don't have any reason to think that. She says that she hadn't been in touch with Tollman until he got in touch with her about six months ago, and we don't have any evidence to the contrary. He told her he had heard Niall was sick and called to offer moral support. They talked a couple of times. He convinced her he had turned over a new leaf. She mentioned the idea of the speakeasy, and he was enthusiastic. She decided to hire him as the bartender." He rubbed his neck. "He can be a charmer if he wants to be, as you probably saw in his guise as the Professor. I think Nola really believed Niall's death was an accident—although when both the wills disappeared, she must have started to get suspicious."

"What about Harkin's death? Was she involved in that?"

"She says not, and that Henry wasn't telling her anything, which would make sense. If he fancies himself the knight in shining armor, he wouldn't want to implicate her."

"But when Harkin died, Nola must have believed that Henry was involved. Withholding information about a murder—that's got to be a crime, right?"

"A *suspected* murder." Deng sighed. "There's no law that says that you have to report the suspicion that someone committed a crime. Of course, if we find she lied to us in an interview, that would be another matter. Obstruction of justice. Aiding and abetting. But we haven't been able to shoot any holes in what she's told us."

"If Henry Tollman was working his way through the Lynch winery owners, that means Harkin's son Kepi would be next up. Wasn't Nola worried about him?"

"I think she was. The day everything went down at Larch Street, she was working with the lawyers to arrange for the transfer of ownership of the winery to Kepi without him and his mom having to come to Pennsylvania. Tollman's bank account wasn't too flush. I'm guessing she figured that as long as Kepi was in Hawaii, it would be hard for him to get to them."

"And what about Del Berendt? He wasn't an heir, but I can imagine Henry Tollman might have lumped him in with the other Lynch men."

"Nola must have figured that Berendt was glued to his wife's side until the baby came—although, as it turned out, that wasn't the case."

"Yeah. Luckily for me."

Deng leaned back in his chair. "It seems obvious that Nola

Lynch suspected what Tollman was up to, but if she didn't have any actual knowledge of what he was doing, then she didn't break the law by not telling us. She was closing down the Cabinet and says that Tollman said he would hit the road after that. She probably figured she had done all the damage control she could."

"And she was never worried about Rowan?"

"Nola never believed Tollman was a threat to her or Rowan —remember, knight in shining armor. And he might have seen Rowan as even more a damsel in distress than Nola. Young woman under the thumb of her father, bilked out of her rightful inheritance, denied her dream, that sort of thing."

"And no sign that Rowan was involved in the murders," said Ann, half statement, half question.

"Not even any sign that she knew that Professor John Derkammern was actually the former Lynch winemaker." He sighed and leaned forward. "Anyhow, we think that playing on his knight complex is our best bet and you're the only damsel we've got to try to get him to talk."

She raised an eyebrow. "Great." After a moment, she said, "But obviously he wasn't acting like much of a knight in shining armor toward me on our last encounter."

"I agree it's a long shot, but still worth a try. Our job gets a whole lot easier if we have a confession on the record. Maybe you can rattle him by dropping in some comments about stuff you claim you learned from Niall and Harkin Lynch."

Ann tried to keep her expression neutral, wondering if "claim" reflected Deng's skepticism about her ability or encouragement to expand on what she had actually learned from the two Lynch men.

As if sensing her thought, Deng added, "No issue with making things up."

"Okay." She considered. "Maybe something Harkin said ..."

After a moment, she sighed. "If I'm the best you've got, I'll give it a try."

Deng slapped the desk with the flats of his hands and levered himself up. "Let's do it."

He led Ann through the hum and bustle of the station to a door flanked by two uniformed officers.

"If at any point you want to leave," he said to Ann, "just say the word and we'll bring you out."

"What's the word?" asked Ann.

Deng shrugged. "'Get me out.' 'I'm done here.' 'Screw this, I have better things to do.' Whatever strikes your fancy."

Ann managed a smile. "Gotcha."

"Ready?"

"Ready."

He nodded to one of the officers, who unlocked and opened the door.

Deng stepped in and Ann followed.

56

Henry Tollman regarded Ann with a mixture of amusement and curiosity.

Deng said, "For the record, here in the room we have ..." He nodded to Ann.

"Ann Kinnear."

"And ..." Deng nodded to Henry.

"John Derkammern."

Deng rolled his eyes. "Let the record show that the subject is Henry Tollman." He gestured toward a camera mounted on the ceiling. "Henry, you know that we'll be watching and listening to your conversation with Miss Kinnear, right?"

"Yes."

"And that a couple of my larger colleagues will be right outside, ready to intercede should you act up."

"Yes."

Deng turned to Ann. "Sit or stand, whatever makes you feel comfortable. Just stay on this side of the table."

"No problem," she said.

Deng stepped outside and closed the door behind him.

Henry's wrists were manacled to the table, his ankles to the chair. He was clean-shaven, and the scars from the prison yard attack—one that ran from ear to chin, another that ran from the corner of his nose to his lip—were clearly visible.

"You look a little worse for wear," said Henry.

Her own scars, including the scrapes on her face, hadn't quite healed, and her left arm was still in a sling.

He gestured to the chair on her side of the table. "You'd probably be more comfortable sitting."

Ann lowered herself onto the chair.

Henry gestured with his head to take in the interview room. "Not quite the Cabinet, is it?"

"No."

"If I had known Detective Joe's date was a famous psychic, I might have asked you to get in touch with some dead Victorians who could give me their cocktail recipes first-hand."

"I might have had to look beyond number 46—it seemed free of spirits to me ... at least spirits of the dead kind. Although if Del Berendt hadn't shown up, that might have changed."

He regarded her for a moment, then asked, "What made *you* show up?"

"When I contacted Harkin's spirit at the big house, he mentioned that he used to call you 'the Professor.' He showed me the cabinet of curiosities you made for Nola. He told me about you killing the purse snatcher. It sounded to me like the Professor and Henry Tollman might be the same person."

"Harkin's ghost told you that, eh? Good material for your sales brochure." He shook his head. "When Nola first told me that Rowan and Del had hired you to get in touch with Niall's ghost, I was surprised that they were gullible enough to believe you could actually do it."

Ann didn't answer.

"I guess we both rely on spirits for our livings. Mine the intoxicating kind, and yours the—"

"Informative kind?"

He snorted. "Convince me."

After a pause, she said, "It was lucky for you that Harkin was drinking Pepsi from the container in the refrigerator at the big house. And you must have known that his addiction to Pepsi made it likely that he would drink the glass you left on the counter. How did you get into the big house to drug it? Did you keep a key? He said you were a collector."

She thought she saw a flicker of surprise on Henry's face, but he quickly resumed his look of smug self-confidence. "I don't know what you're talking about. Although I must admit I am a collector. Once I have something, like a key, I rarely get rid of it."

"How did Harkin get from the big house to the bottom of the Tarn?"

"You're asking me? Why don't you ask your new dead friend?"

"He doesn't remember."

"Convenient."

"Not from my point of view."

"Or the cops'."

"You must know that the cops can't do anything with any information I get from the spirits I contact."

He leaned back in the chair and Ann felt certain that if his hands hadn't been manacled, he would have laced his fingers behind his head. "But I've heard that the cops found Rohypnol in his system. I understand that people who take Rohypnol can be very suggestible, and later may not remember what they did."

"So he walked to the Tarn himself?"

A smile twisted the corners of his mouth. "If he did, he would have gone right past the Curragh. Hey, if you had been awake, maybe you could have stopped him."

"Maybe *you* could have stopped him."

"If I had been there, I wouldn't have had any reason to stop him."

"Charming. Did Nola know she was sending her pregnant niece to a derelict house in West Philly to chat with a man who wouldn't bother to save her brother from drowning? Someone who was fired from the Lynch winery because he killed a man. No, killed a *boy*. According to what Harkin told me, that kid wasn't a threat to Nola by the time you caught up with him."

"You could have found that out from the news coverage."

"I could have, but I didn't."

Henry waved a dismissive hand. "That kid was a punk. He needed to be taught a lesson."

"Like Niall needed to be taught a lesson?"

"Niall needed to learn that the world didn't revolve around his every whim." He smiled. "Not that *I* necessarily taught him any lessons."

"I think you did—or at least tried to. And that you had a damn unfortunate way of going about it."

Henry leaned forward. "The only 'lesson' I tried to teach Niall Lynch was how he should treat the women in his life."

"Nola and Rowan?"

"Yes."

"What is it with you and Rowan? She was just a baby when you left Lynch. Why would you care so much about her?"

Henry's expression hardened. "Because when I see Rowan, I see Nola thirty years ago. I saw what it did to Nola to be shut out of the family business, and I saw the same thing happening to Rowan."

"And not only Rowan being shut out of the family business in favor of Harkin," said Ann, "but in favor of Harkin's teenage son."

"A teenage son who lives in Hawaii. Seems likely that he would need some help with his inheritance. Seems likely that he would ask his aunt to run it for him. Rowan might not have owned the winery, but she could have been the hand at the wheel ... or the captain of the ship, as Niall enjoyed saying."

"If I were a teenage boy, I'd rather have the money than a winery, regardless of who was running it."

"Sure, grab the money, head for the beach, and leave the family high and dry. Sounds like the son is cut from the same cloth as the other Lynch men. When I called to give my condolences on the death of his father, Harkin proved he was as much of a bastard as Niall. I was sick of the Lynch men." He gave a short bark of laughter. "Sick to death, you might say."

"So you killed them both."

"I've never claimed credit for that."

"Credit?"

"My hat's off to whoever took care of them."

Ann waited, hoping that Henry would say more, but he was silent, a self-satisfied smile on his face.

Dangling bits of information she had learned from Harkin didn't seem to be doing much in the way of rattling Henry. She tried another tack.

"Assuming that Rowan really didn't know who you were, you went to some trouble disguising yourself. The fake beer belly, the beard and mustache, the limp."

"I create a world for the guests who come to the Cabinet—a world away from the nastiness that goes on outside. John Derkammern with his pot belly and unsteady gait—he set them at ease."

"And the beard and mustache?"

He gestured, as best he could, to the scars on his face. "I didn't want to distract them with this."

"I guess that isn't a problem anymore."

"No, not once Nola decided to close down the Cabinet."

"And what did you plan to do with the last visitors you hosted that night?"

"Mike and Scott? I'm not denying I drugged them."

"It would be a little hard for you to deny that. But why? What were you planning to do with them?"

"I guess we'll never know."

"What about me and Del?"

"What about it? You showed up, you were combative. I put you in the Cabinet while I decided what to do with you—maybe call the authorities and ask them to deal with you. Then Del showed up and tried to break in."

"I'm not sure that's what the video recording from the cameras will show."

He grinned. "Live feed only—no recording. And I have a concussion from the attack the two of you launched."

"I have a dislocated arm to prove that you did a little more than lock me up until you could call the police to take me away."

"I had no intention of hurting you—it was you thrashing around that caused that injury."

"Fine. I'll be interested to see how that explanation flies in a courtroom."

He shrugged. "I know I'm going back to prison. I drugged Mike and Scott—I'm not denying it. And I held you against your will, but only for a short amount of time. I like my chances for being out in a few years." He smiled. "I have a lot of experience being the model inmate."

Ann's blood chilled. Was it true that one day soon, Henry would be a free man again, or was he playing her the way she was trying to play him?

She cast about for another approach she could take. He would never see her as the damsel in distress ... but maybe she didn't have to be the damsel in question to get a rise out of him.

"How do you think Nola felt when she realized that the only reason you wanted to marry her was to piss off Niall?"

"That's not true. She knew I cared for her."

"Harkin told me otherwise." Harkin had told Ann he thought the goal of annoying Niall had been Nola's, but there was no one who could contradict her version of their conversation.

"I don't believe you," said Henry. "Now if you told me you had heard that from Nola—"

Ann laughed. "Nola? She's not likely to say a word against you. She's terrified of you."

"She is not. She was happy to hear from me when I contacted her—"

"Ever wonder why she didn't stay in touch after you left the winery?"

Henry opened his mouth, shut it, then took a deep breath. "That was my choice. I didn't want to make her life harder than it already was. But when I heard Niall was dying, I thought she and Rowan might need some help. I got in touch. We chatted. She told me about the idea for the bar. I suggested the Victorian theme. The more we talked, the more enthusiastic she got."

"And then you made her take you on as the bartender."

"I didn't make her do anything."

"She went along with you because she was afraid of what you'd do to her if she refused to have you back. What you would do to her ... and to Rowan."

He leaned forward, his face flushed. "That's a load of crap. Everything I did was for her and Rowan."

She gazed at him for a few moments, then said, "Maybe it's the truth. You obviously care what happens to Rowan."

"She's a sweet girl who deserves better." He leaned back and smiled, relaxed again. "It was just icing on the cake that I became Niall's daughter's closest confidante. In some ways, I was closer to her than Nola was. I just wish he had known before he died." He smirked. "Maybe you can let him know."

"Maybe." She heaved a sigh. "But whoever killed Niall certainly didn't do Rowan any favors. Whoever did it robbed her of the chance to prove to her father that she was a more deserving heir than Harkin."

His smile faded. He flexed and unflexed his fingers.

"Harkin," she continued, "who evidently walked to the Tarn, jumped in, and held his own head under water until he drowned." She shuddered. "Not a pretty sight. Did you know that Rowan would be the one who found him?"

"I was sorry to hear that."

"Quite an unpleasant shock for her, as you can imagine." Ann shook her head sorrowfully. "It would have been better if it hadn't been Rowan. Better for her ... and the baby."

His fingers stilled, then curled into fists. "What do you mean?"

"It would have been better for both of them if the baby had come to term."

"What are you talking about? Rowan was all but nine months along. Nola told me."

"Yeah, that's what Nola thought. That's what everyone thought." Ann lowered her voice and leaned toward him "Isn't anyone telling you anything?"

"No." He glanced toward the ceiling mounted camera, then said with forced nonchalance, "What aren't they telling me?"

She sat back. "I'm surprised you let it unfold the way you did. Detective Deng told me about your mother—"

"What does this have to do with Rowan and her baby?"

"—and what your father did to her."

"My father was a bastard—he should have been the one to go out that car door. If I had been in the car with him, I would have been happy to do the honors. But the baby—"

"It's too bad you didn't. Of course, it was different when you were a child. You couldn't be expected to take on an adult. But once you grew up, you didn't have size as an excuse anymore, did you? At that point, all you needed was a sense of honor. And the guts to act on it."

"I did! I gave him the beating he deserved!"

"And then left your mom to deal with him alone."

"I couldn't take care of her for her whole life!"

"Yeah. I guess thinking of yourself as the knight in shining armor is a lot more fun than actually being the knight. As Nola and Rowan—and the baby—found out the hard way."

"What are you talking about?"

"You certainly made a clean sweep of the Lynch women. Nola with a broken heart, Rowan with her hope of convincing Niall that she should inherit dashed by his untimely death, the baby ... well, neonatal technology has come a long way." Her gaze was stony. "Sounds like you're not the knight in shining armor. Sounds like you're no better than the men—and teenage boy—you killed."

She could hear his breath rasping in his throat. "If something happens to that baby girl, it's not my fault—it's the fault of the men in that family."

"You're suggesting that Niall and Harkin managed to jeopardize the life of an infant girl who wasn't even born when they died?"

"They laid the groundwork for everything that happened, back then and now."

"And what groundwork did they lay?"

He lunged forward, his features twisted, and she tried to keep herself from sliding her chair back. "The men in that family didn't care about anything except themselves. Nola's father abandoned her, and Niall let him do it. Niall abandoned

Rowan. Harkin ran away to Hawaii and left Nola and Rowan to deal with Niall all by themselves."

"Harkin was trying to make a life for himself."

"He was trying to take the easy way out."

"Doesn't sound to me like it was easy. Although," she added, "it sounds like he did find a good life in Hawaii, including a wife and son he obviously loves. A son who will now inherit the winery. Thanks to you. And a little girl who—if she lives—will have nothing." She shook her head. "Too bad you didn't take care of Niall and Harkin before this disaster was set in motion. Like it's too bad you didn't take care of your father before he pushed your mother out of a moving car."

"I did take care of them!"

"When you pushed Niall into the rocks? A terminally ill man who could barely walk? Aren't you the big man."

"I didn't push him into the rocks, like two little boys in a playground spat." said Henry, his voice dripping with disgust. "There are rocks all over that goddamned property—it's not hard to find a loose one."

"So you snuck up behind him and bashed him on the head?"

"He didn't need to suffer. He just needed to be out of the way."

"So that you could destroy the will favoring Harkin."

He glared at her.

"But you didn't know that Niall had already made his choice —that he had destroyed the will favoring Rowan." She leaned back. "But all was not lost. You just had to take the remaining will. With no will, the winery would likely be split between the children. Not ideal for Rowan, but better than nothing."

"She would have gotten half, if Nola hadn't found the old will."

"And Harkin? You drugged his Pepsi, then walked him down to the Tarn."

"Him and his infernal Pepsi."

"And when he got there, you drowned him."

"People are suggestible with Rohypnol, but not suggestible enough to kill themselves."

"Why did Harkin have to die?"

"With him gone, there was a chance that Rowan could get the winery."

"You didn't know it would go to Kepi?"

"He's a boy. He's in Hawaii. It was the last chance to make it right for Rowan."

"So you killed them both."

Henry dropped his head. His breathing, which had been ragged, slowed. Half a minute ticked by.

Ann thought he wasn't going to answer. She wondered what was going on wherever Harry Deng was monitoring the conversation, wondered if he would come into the interview room and end this conversation with Henry if he thought she had gotten everything she would.

Then Henry spoke, his voice barely audible. "Yes. I killed Niall. I killed Harkin. I killed them both."

Ann leaned toward Henry, her face a foot from his downturned head. "You know who you *almost* killed?"

Henry's head snapped up.

"My brother and my brother-in-law. I wish Del Berendt had really nailed you in the head with that brick. I wish I had been able to do it myself."

Henry's scars were a vivid red against the pallor of his face. "I never meant for Del and Mike to get involved ... and I didn't realize your brother was bringing a date. I'm not that much of a bastard."

"You're way more of a bastard than Niall Lynch. At least he never killed to get what he wanted."

"And look how it turned out for him," Henry spat. "Harkin's family still plan on selling?"

"As far as I know."

"And Rowan's little girl has nothing." His voice was filled with self-loathing.

Ann straightened. "I wouldn't worry about it too much. I imagine that with parents like Rowan and Del, she'll make a name for herself."

"If she survives."

"Oh, that shouldn't be an issue. She was already charming the staff in the nursery before she went home."

"Went home?"

"I've seen a picture of her. She's adorable. And quite the bruiser—over eight pounds."

His face blanched. "She wasn't premature?"

"Oh, no. I've never seen a baby look as healthy." She stood. "I'm done here."

57

The following days were busy ones.

Ann met the newest member of the Lynch family, a robust baby girl with a riot of strawberry blonde curls. Rowan and Del had named her Rose.

At Rowan's request, Ann accompanied the three to the Ark, where they toured the fermentation room and barrel room looking for Niall, without luck.

"It's possible that he comes and goes," said Ann. "I can keep an eye out for him."

"Thanks, I'd appreciate that," said Rowan, her disappointment clear. She arranged the blanket in which Rose was bundled more snugly around the sleeping baby. "I was hoping to show him Rose in person, but we brought a picture of her in case he wasn't here."

Del showed Ann the silver-framed photo—Rose propped up against a wine barrel—then positioned it prominently in the middle of the desk.

Ann stopped back that night. There was no sign of Niall, but the photo of Rose had been moved to the end of the row of family portraits, the others rearranged to maintain their precise spacing.

She returned the photo to the middle of the desk and stuck a Post-it to the frame: *Lynch staff, please don't move this.*

The next morning, Rose's photo was back in line with the rest of the family.

Niall Lynch might have been a bastard, but it seemed he had accepted this newest addition as an honored part of the family line.

Ann had also gone to the big house and found Harkin wandering the rooms. She updated him on everything that had happened since she had left him by Nola's cabinet of curiosities and headed off for Larch Street to determine if the Professor was really Henry Tollman. She also told him that Alana and Kepi were coming to Pennsylvania to finalize transfer of ownership of the winery to the teenager, as well as the fact that Ed Kujala had extended to Harkin's son the same offer he had made to Harkin for the business.

"Do you think he'll take it?" she asked.

"He'd be a fool not to," replied Harkin. "When Alana and Kepi get here, can you help me talk with them?"

"Sure."

He smiled—a smile that smoothed out the frown lines around his mouth but didn't hide his underlying restlessness. "Just one more favor for the Lynch clan."

The next day, Ann mediated a conversation between Rowan and Harkin. Rowan asked for and received Harkin's forgiveness for being responsible, however unknowingly, for directing Henry Tollman's murderous attention her brother's way. Harkin asked for and received Rowan's forgiveness for, as he put it, "generally being a jerk to you and Del." Ann was pleased that, afterwards, the conversation shifted to some of the happier memories they shared from their childhoods.

Corey was back in L.A., periodically texting Ann photos of some of the places he'd like to take her if she came out for a visit.

Ann also phoned Marsha Duff.

"I'm sorry I haven't had a chance to get out to Pittsburgh to see what we can do about Carl," said Ann. "It's been crazy here."

"I've been following the news about Henry Tollman and the Cabinet," said Marsha. "I can imagine you have your hands full. There's no rush."

"Maybe next week—"

"Really, no rush," said Marsha. She was silent for a moment, then continued. "When Larry and I ran into each other at the shore, it seemed so exciting: summer love, romantic moonlit walks on the beach. And he's such a good man—so kind, and respectful of the fact that Carl passed away not that long ago. Corey says he really likes him, and I believe he does. And then we got back to Pittsburgh, back to real life, and I thought ..." She sighed. "I thought I needed a little more time. Time to mourn Carl and time to get my head around the idea of living with someone else." She laughed. "After living with Carl for so many years, it's a little scary to think about getting used to someone else. And I found—well, I found that I kind of like having the house to myself, at least for a little while."

Ann smiled. "I can understand that."

"And after all," Marsha continued cheerfully, "I'm not really alone, am I? I have Carl here with me."

"I imagine so. That sounds like a good plan—just let me know if and when you'd like me to come out there. No charge for the engagement."

"The engagement?" asked Marsha, sounding excited.

Ann sighed. "No charge for the *sensing* engagement."

Marsha laughed self-consciously. "Oh, right."

58

Ann stepped out onto the porch of the Curragh, a book tucked under her arm, and surveyed the scene. In the vineyard, workers bustled and machinery buzzed among the vines. The weather leading up to the harvest had been wet, and Rowan, as the vineyard manager, had agonized over the timing. Too early, and the grapes wouldn't be fully mature. Too late, and after too much rain, the fruit's essence would be diluted. She had held off on the harvest and her intuition had paid off: the weather had turned dry, the days of bright sunshine bringing the grapes to their ideal condition.

Ann imagined that the knowledge that this harvest would be the last for Lynch and Son must have made Rowan's triumph bittersweet. Rowan had tried to sound upbeat when she told Ann that she and Del had found some possible positions in California, albeit at different wineries, but she clearly would have preferred to stay in Pennsylvania. At least they had Rose as a distraction.

She descended the steps of the Curragh's front porch and, leaving the bustle of the harvest behind, climbed the drive.

She was almost at the entrance when she saw Nola Lynch

sitting on a bench just outside the front door. Ann hadn't spoken with her since the first, unsuccessful search for Niall.

Nola stood as Ann approached. "Hello, Ann. I was hoping I might have a quick word with you."

Ann stopped in front of her. Was it her imagination that her left arm, no longer in a sling, gave a little throb, a reminder of her altercation with Nola's former fiancé?

Nola took a deep breath, then continued in a rush. "I wanted to say how very sorry I am about what happened to you, not to mention to Mike and Scott ... and to Del, of course. And I'm even sorrier about what happened to Niall and Harkin. I didn't know Henry was responsible for Niall's death, and ..." She looked down the hill, toward where the sun glittered off the surface of the Tarn. "... I tried to convince myself that he wasn't responsible for Harkin's death. I know that's cold consolation, but I felt I owed you—owed all of you—an apology."

"What was Rowan and Del's response to your apology?"

"They've forgiven me ... or at least they're trying to. They're such good people."

"Yes, they are," said Ann. She was quite certain that she'd never completely forgive Nola Lynch for whatever part she had played in the chain of events that had ended with two dead men and the trauma of the events at Larch Street. "Well, if they've forgiven you, I could hardly do less."

"And I also want to thank you for agreeing to talk with Henry," said Nola. "The police tell me that based on the information you got, it's likely he's going to be in prison for a very long time."

"I can't say I'm sorry to hear that."

"Neither am I." Nola glanced at her watch. "I can't stay, I have a client meeting, but I'm glad I saw you. I hope I'll be seeing more of you in the future, under better circumstances."

Nola hurried to her car, climbed in, and disappeared down the drive.

With the winery about to be sold, Ann couldn't imagine under what circumstances she would run into Nola Lynch again.

She stepped inside the house and heard the buzz of conversation coming from the library.

Del and Rowan, with Rose in her arms, were there, along with a woman in her mid-thirties whose curtain of black hair hung almost to her waist and a teenage boy who had the woman's black hair but Harkin Lynch's hazel eyes.

"Ann," said Rowan, smiling, "I'd like to introduce you to Harkin's partner, Alana Kane, and their son, Kepi, the new owner of Lynch winery."

Kepi blushed and looked at his feet.

"Not really ..." he said.

"Yes, really," said Rowan, looking at the teenager fondly. "But Kepi isn't any more interested in wine than his father was—am I right, Kepakiano?"

"No offense," he said, shooting awkward looks at Rowan and Del, "but it isn't really my thing."

"I understand scuba is your thing," said Ann.

"Yeah," he said, enthusiasm transforming his features. "It's the best. Like floating through a world from a sci-fi book—crazy fish, crazy plants, and the peace and quiet to enjoy it all. I'm going to start my own scuba tour operation when I'm out of school." His smile faded, but only a bit. "It's what Mom and Dad and I planned."

His mother laid a hand on his shoulder. "Your father would be so proud of you, Kepi."

"And while Kepi's finishing school," said Del, "Rowan's going to be gradually buying back the winery from him. That will give us a few years to get the money together."

"Eight years," said Alana, "since I'm holding Kepi to our agreement that 'out of school' means out of college."

"I'm going to study marine biology," said Kepi. "Like Mom."

Rowan beamed at her nephew, and Kepi immediately retreated into pleased embarrassment. "It seemed like having Aunt Rowan get the winery would work out good all around," he mumbled.

"That's great news," said Ann.

"Yes, we're so pleased it's going to stay in the family," said Rowan. "And we have big plans. We're going to replant some of the vineyard to Cab Franc. If it works out, in a few years Del might be able to put out another release of the Sapele, except with our own grapes. And if we re-orient the rows to run north to south, they'll get more light, which should increase the harvest."

"Plus," said Del, "we're going to add some Zweigelt grapes, which should do well here, and maybe even some Albariño. That will make a nice, easy-drinking summer wine."

"Tell them what you plan to do with the house," Alana said to Rowan.

"We're going to turn this monstrosity," Rowan said, waving her hand to encompass the entirety of the big house, "into an event venue. Aunt Nola's going to help. And we're putting in two apartments upstairs—one for me, Del, and Rose, and one for Alana and Kepi for when they visit."

"Kepi," Alana asked, "do you think you can tear yourself away from the water long enough for trips back to Pennsylvania?"

Kepi smiled sheepishly. "It would be nice to visit Aunt Rowan and Uncle Del and cousin Rose."

"It looks like the name *Lynch and Son Winery* isn't going to work for much longer," said Ann.

"No," said Rowan. "Kepi picked the new name: Mahalo Vineyard and Winery."

"What does that mean?" Ann asked Kepi.

"All sorts of things," he said. "Thanks, gratefulness, admiration, respect." He smiled. "Us Hawaiians can pack a lot of meaning into one word."

Rowan turned to Ann. "I know you wanted to talk to Alana and Kepi. Do you need me and Del for anything else? We have some things we need to take care of at the Ark. Plus," she nodded toward Rose, who was starting to fuss, "someone's getting hungry."

"I can take it from here. But I'm really glad I ran into you guys—this is all great news."

"You'll be running into us a lot because it looks like there's no need for you to move out of the Curragh. We'd love for you to stay. Plus, the offer of free rent still stands."

"I'm thrilled to stay—and happy to pay rent. But I will take you up on the complimentary wine offer."

Rowan smiled. "Deal."

Rowan and Del left, and Ann turned to the mother and son. "Has anyone explained to you what I do?"

"You ... talk to dead people, right?" Kepi said hesitantly.

"That's right. I spoke with your dad. He asked me to give you this." She handed Alana a tattered copy of James Michener's *Hawaii*. "He was reading this the night he died and marking the pages he thought you two would enjoy."

Alana took the book and opened it to one of the dog-eared pages. She held it so that Kepi could read as well. After a minute, she nodded, wiping a tear from her cheek. "I remember him showing me that passage when we were dating." She handed the book to Kepi. "Let's look through that tonight."

"Harkin also asked me to mediate a conversation between him and the two of you," said Ann.

Alana's hand went to her throat. "Would that be possible?"

"I think so. Would you like to try?"

"I would," said Alana. She turned to Kepi. "What do you think?"

"Sure," he said, his eyes big.

Alana slipped her arm around his shoulders. "What do we do?" she asked Ann.

"Let's go to the kitchen. That's where I run into him most often."

Kepi led the way to the kitchen, and they sat down around the kitchen table.

"What now?" asked Kepi.

"We wait for him to arrive."

They sat in silence for a few moments, then Alana said, "I'm not surprised you run into him here. In this big, dark, drafty house, this is the only homey room. I'm guessing this house is going to look a lot different when Rowan and Del and Nola are done with it."

"I think you're right," said Ann. "You've never been to the winery before?"

"Kepi has, but I haven't. I offered to come along when Harkin flew out for the family business meetings—I thought he might have an easier time if he had a couple of people with him that he knew were in his corner—but he didn't want me to. He said he didn't want me to see how he was around his family."

"Dad was pretty ... different when he was here," said Kepi. "Especially when he was around Grandfather Lynch."

"Yeah," said Ann, "I think the relationship Harkin had with your grandfather was a lot different than the relationship you had with Harkin."

"We were buddies." Kepi dropped his head and wiped his nose with the back of his hand.

Alana pulled a tissue from her purse and passed it to him.

"Kepi is a great name.," said Ann. "Is it Hawaiian?"

"Yeah."

"Does it have a lot of meanings, like *mahalo*?"

He blushed and looked toward Alana, who gave a soft laugh. She covered Kepi's hand with hers.

"When I told Harkin I was pregnant," she said, "he was so worried. Not that I was going to have a baby, but that he was going to be a father." Her smile dimmed. "With Niall being the only model of fatherhood he had, he was so sure he'd make a mess of it." She smiled at Kepi. "But when our baby came along, Harkin's joy overcame his fear. He was so excited to be a father to this beautiful, perfect little boy." She squeezed her son's hand. "Harkin asked that we name him Kepakiano, which means 'a gift from the Gods.'"

Kepi was squirming with embarrassment. Ann glanced away to hide her smile, which she was sure would send the teenager into even deeper paroxysms of embarrassment, and she saw Harkin standing in the doorway. Without taking his eyes off his wife and son, he came to the table and lowered himself into the fourth seat.

Ann looked at Alana and Kepi. "He's here."

THEY TALKED FOR ALMOST AN HOUR, exchanging reminiscences about Alana and Harkin's favorite restaurant, about Kepi and Harkin's favorite diving spot, about the kitten Kepi had recently adopted that was being cared for by a neighbor. They talked about trips they had taken, and about trips they had planned and that Alana and Kepi still needed to take.

As they talked, Harkin's form became dimmer and dimmer, his voice fainter and fainter.

"Harkin, I'm losing you," said Ann.

"That's all right," he said. "I've almost said what I wanted to say. Just two more things. Can you get a paper and pencil out of that drawer?"

When she was back at the table, Harkin said, "I have a message for each of them. It's in Hawaiian. I'll spell it out for you."

Ann nodded, pencil poised over the paper.

"The first one is for Kepi." He spelled out the message, Ann leaning closer to him to catch his words. When he was done, she tore off the piece of paper and gave it to Kepi.

He read and swiped the back of his hand across his eyes. "Thanks, Dad."

"This one is for Alana," said Harkin. He spelled out the second message. When Ann handed her the piece of paper, she blushed even deeper than Kepi had. "Harkin, really," she said, a laugh mixing with her tears.

"Harkin, is there anything else?" Ann asked. "If there is, you need to hurry."

"That's it," he said. "Except a message for you, Ann—"

His presence faded away, but Ann just caught the last two words, like the shush of water on sand.

Thank you.

THE END

ALSO BY MATTY DALRYMPLE

Community, and Income

ABOUT THE AUTHOR

Matty Dalrymple is the author of the Ann Kinnear Suspense Novels *The Sense of Death*, *The Sense of Reckoning*, *The Falcon and the Owl, A Furnace for Your Foe*, and *A Serpent's Tooth*; the Ann Kinnear Suspense Shorts, including *Close These Eyes* and *Sea of Troubles*; and the Lizzy Ballard Thrillers *Rock Paper Scissors, Snakes and Ladders*, and *The Iron Ring*. Matty and her husband, Wade Walton, live in Chester County, Pennsylvania, and enjoy vacationing on Mt. Desert Island, Maine, and in Sedona, Arizona, locations that serve as settings for Matty's stories.

Matty is a member of International Thriller Writers and Sisters in Crime.

Go to www.mattydalrymple.com > About & Contact for more information and to sign up for Matty's occasional email newsletter.

facebook.com/matty.dalrymple

twitter.com/mattydalrymple

instagram.com/matty.dalrymple

ACKNOWLEDGMENTS

Huge thanks to everyone who contributed their expertise and support to this book:

For insights into vineyards and wineries, Lele Galer and Miles Basila of Galer Estate Vineyard and Winery and James McCrone.

For inspiration for the Cabinet of Curiosities, Jesse Sheidlower and N.D. Austin of the (completely legal and much less ominous) Threesome Tollbooth.

For the details of Victorian cocktails, ingredients, and preparation, Ted Haigh, Dr. Cocktail.

For medical expertise, David Fried and David Page.

For information on police and first responders, Rodger Ollis and Ken Fritz.

For insights into Mike Kinnear's previous financial planning career, David Berkeihiser.

For providing a retreat that enabled this book to get written, Margi and Rob Eden.

For inspiration for the setting and interior of 46 Larch Street, Lanny Larcinese.

For plot brainstorming and general moral support, Jane Kelly and Lisa Regan.

For expert editorial insights, Jon McGoran.

Any deviations from strict accuracy—intentional or unintentional—are solely the responsibility of the author.

Cover design: Lindsay Heider Diamond

ISBN-13: 978-1-7344799-7-3 (Paperback edition)

ISBN-13: 978-1-7344799-8-0 (Large print edition)

Made in United States
Troutdale, OR
12/21/2023

16319380R00206